K E OSBORN

EXPLOSIVE

The Houston Defiance MC Series Book 1

K E OSBORN

Disclaimer: The material in this book contains graphic language and sexual content and is intended for mature audiences, ages 18 and older.
This book contains triggers of a violent and sexual nature.
If you, or anyone you know needs help, do not hesitate to seek it. There is information at the end of the book for your information.

ISBN: 9798673381663

Editing by Swish Design & Editing
Formatting by Swish Design & Editing
Proofreading by Swish Design & Editing
Cover model by Kevin Creekman
Cover design by Designs by Dana
Cover image Copyright 2020

First Edition

Cindy,

Thank you so much for everything you have done toward Texafying (is that a word?) me and my story. Without your input, these books/series wouldn't be as genuine. The locations and events in Explosive are inspired by my time in Houston spent with you and your gorgeous family. This was, in all honesty, one of the best times in my life, and nothing can *ever* convey the fondness of my time in Texas, and the memories I have of Houston.

Thank you, Cindy.

I am so **tremendously** grateful.

NOTE FOR THE READER

For your convenience, below is a list of terms used in this book.
Any questions, please do not hesitate to contact the author.

Chapel—The room where the Defiance club members congregate to have their 'church' meetings.
Church—The name of important club business meetings where only patched members can attend.
Cut—Vest with club colors
Duck Walk—Navigating into parking space using your feet.
Hammer Down—Accelerate quickly.
Hangaround—The hangaround period is a relatively informal time for someone who is interested in the club to spend some time with club members, go on some club rides, etc.
The Heat—Police.
Road Captain—The name for a rider who coordinates a multiple bike ride. Also refers to the leader who makes sure the riders are safe.
Road Name— Nickname.
Snow White — Code name for cocaine.
Wise One— The Wise One, also known as 'Chaplain' in clubs who often looks after the spiritual needs of club members, helps out when someone goes to jail, conducts marriages, funerals, and helps with

general counseling for the members.

1% Badge—Some outlaw motorcycle clubs can be distinguished by a "1%" patch worn on the colors. This is said to refer to a comment by the American Motorcyclist Association (AMA) that 99% of motorcyclists were law-abiding citizens, implying the last one percent were outlaws.

EXPLOSIVE

CHAPTER 1

ZERO

Houston Defiance—this MC means something to me.

It always has.

I grew up in this club, so have my younger siblings.

As I glance around the clubroom, the stale smell of tobacco lingers in the air while my brothers sit at the long wooden-top bar. The corrugated iron flashing around the bottom edge is showing signs of rust from all the beer that's been spilled over the many years it's been there. Tennessee, our head club girl, mans the bar. Her long, chocolate brown hair flowing down over her shoulders as she wipes over the counter. The wooden stools are all filled with my brothers drinking and eating the Texas barbecue Fox cooked up for us earlier. The smell of the brisket lingers in the air, a sweet mix of tang and spice. There's nothing like a hunk of slowly smoked beef to get your taste buds watering.

I slump my ass at one of the four-seater tables, my belly overfull as I people-watch.

Wraith sits by himself with his bulldog, Mack, drinking the night away at a table by one of the four beams holding up the second story, while Ax and Neon play a rowdy game of pool, keeping us all aware that Ax is winning—by a fucking lot.

It's a calm evening, everyone having a good time just getting by and doing what comes naturally. Houston Defiance is a family affair, there's no doubting that, so when you become a member of this club, you're a part of our family. Houston Defiance may be overrun by men with the Walker surname, but the legacy belongs to us all. We're a tight-knit group, and though we've had our differences, we've got each other's backs—no matter what.

But now, our war with the Bayou Militia is at a pivotal crossroad. We can either brokerage a peace between us, or it's going to end up bloody. I just don't know which way it's going to go.

For tonight, though, we're taking the time to be together as a brotherhood before shit gets real. Before we need to make up our minds on whether to fight or stand for a truce.

A jolt of the table has my head turning when Prinie and Koda slide in beside me. My chest squeezes with warmth. My sister, Kharlie—we all call her Prinie because she's the princess of the club—is a free spirit. Strong-willed, sassy, every older brothers' nightmare because the guys at this club adore her. Then there's my youngest sibling, Koda, he's not like either of us—quiet, reserved, not really cut out for this life, but it's the hand he's been dealt. Poor kid, being fifteen is hard, but I'll toughen him. We're a close family, tight as you can get.

"I ate so much," Koda whines, his voice cracking a little.

"Me, too, dude. I need to lay off the mac and cheese. Fox makes it too freaking good," Prinie boasts.

I chuckle. "You'd think by now we'd learn not to overeat at his cookouts."

"It's damn good to see you kids eating, you all need a little more meat on your bones if you ask me," Dad calls out as he strides up, sliding onto the last remaining seat. My father, Frenzy, is the club president. Tough as old boot leather, loyal to a fault, but a true family man at heart.

"I'm perfect the way I am, Dad," Prinie replies sarcastically, casually throwing her dark hair over her shoulder.

Dad's eyes light up, the way they always do when he looks at his only daughter. "Yeah... yeah, you are, Kharlie."

Dad always calls her by her actual name. No idea why.

Prinie smiles so damn wide it's like she can't contain it. She loves

Dad more than anything, a true daddy's girl. We all love our father. It's hard not to. Then again, we love our mother equally as much.

Wherever she is.

As the VP of this club, and with my family so entrenched in the Houston Defiance MC, we need to be a tight-knit unit. Us Walkers need to stick together.

"Where's Mom?" I ask what I was thinking.

Dad turns around toward the kitchen, then lets out a loud whistle. "Hey, Moonshine, your kid wants you."

I shake my head. "Jesus, Dad, I could have done that."

He turns back to face me. "Then why didn't you, asshole?"

I shove him in the shoulder. "'Cause I respect her. And hollerin' at my mama ain't what nice boys do."

Dad turns back toward the kitchen. "Moonshine! Lady… get your sweet little ass out here."

Prinie giggles. "And you wonder why we want peace with the Militia, Dad? This… this is why. So, we can keep having days like today."

Well, that brought the mood down.

Dad's beard jostles with the movement of his mouth downward while he takes a centering breath, then turns to face Prinie reaching out for her hands. "Kharlie, I know you want peace. I know you want this war to end, but sometimes, baby, it's not as simple as that."

Mom steps over, her long blonde hair with flecks of gray sweeping through it is tied back in a low, messy bun. "Well, this seems like a serious conversation."

Dad pats his lap. Mom instantly slides down on it like she always does. It's not weird for us, we've grown up seeing Mom sitting on Dad's lap. It's just how it is. The love they have for each other is something I thought I had once and don't think I'll ever have again.

"Kharlie wants us to aim for peace."

Mom raises her brow, turning to Prinie. "You know we're trying, don't you, Prinie?"

"I hope so."

"You know how much your father and I love you, Prinie…" She

turns. "All of you, right?"

I reach out for her hand. "Of course, she does. We do, too. Don't we, Koda?"

Koda's head pops up like he wasn't even listening, then he nods. "Yep."

"Ahh, look at us… all us Walkers here together. My whole family part of the Houston Defiance. I couldn't be prouder," Dad boasts, making my damn chest warm.

Without warning, a loud explosion rocks the side of the clubhouse. Screams and gasps echo from the club girls as dust sprays down on us from above. The walls tremble, shaking in a violent reaction to the blast. It takes us all a second to register what's happened, but once it does, we stand and move into action.

"Neon, status on the gates?" Dad yells out as we draw our guns.

Our resident tech guy, Neon, pulls out his tablet checking the outside surveillance footage. "Gate's gone, pres. We got company."

"Shit! How many?"

"A fucking lot. And they're at the door." Neon quickly drops his device, then pulls out his gun, loading it.

My heart slams against my chest as I turn to Prinie. "Get under the table. Now! Don't come out, not for anything. You damn-well hear me?" I yell at her, probably too forcefully.

The sheer terror in her eyes tells me everything. I fucking hate that this is happening to her again. Prinie's seen enough biker battles to last her a lifetime. She's only eighteen, she doesn't need this shit.

She grabs Koda, pulling him with her under the table as my parents and I head for cover behind the bar. Bullets crash through the front door as we duck for cover, waiting for the onslaught to halt.

Then suddenly, the doors slam open to the Bayou Militia storming inside our clubhouse.

Peace is definitely off the table.

Their Captain, Igor Collins, leads the way.

Damn asshole didn't even give us the time to come up with the peace agreement.

His recruits swarm in wearing their camo greens with guns at the ready. And the bastards don't hesitate in shooting at every-fucking-thing. Bullets fly as my muscles clench.

But I'm ready for this fight.

Hell, I was born for this fight.

I aim my gun preparing to unleash fury.

These fuckers don't come into my family's clubhouse and start this shit.

Oh, hell, no!

Prepare to meet Zero.

Prepare to meet your end.

"Three... two.... one... *zero.*" I stand abruptly, launching over the bar.

Mom screams out for me to stop, but I don't hesitate as I unload a couple of rounds into a nearby recruit. Blood spurts from his head splattering in the eyes of the guy next to him. He starts running toward me, blinded by blood as it oozes down his face. If he's incapacitated, I need not waste bullets, so I pull out my hunting knife, thrusting it straight into his gut. The push and pull of the sinew is a glorious feeling against my blade. I twist, he gurgles out a moan. His hands grip on my shoulders for support, but I'm not here to support this bastard, I'm here to bring him to the reaper. With a swift pull, I yank the blade out, then thrust it back in with an extra grunt. Blood oozes over my fingers as his hands drop from my shoulders. I slide the blade from him, with a shove, then he falls backward to the concrete floor with a thud.

A bullet whizzes past my ear nicking it. The burn ignites me instantly as I turn to see Igor's butt- ugly smirking face. Either his aim was off, or he purposely missed to gain my attention. Despite his intentions, I have my next target in view.

I race forward with one thought in mind—his demise.

We bolt toward each other, guns drawn, but not firing, all the while my brothers are in the fight of their lives around me. Bullets flying, knives wielding, punches thrown, it's all-round chaos in the Defiance clubhouse.

Igor stops in front of me, the scar running through his left eye appearing more prominent today—the scar my father gave him from his switchblade. Their hatred for each other runs deep.

Igor's lip curls. "Zero, you're looking more like your father every day."

"And you're growing uglier every damn second I have to witness your face. Why are you delaying me killing you, Igor?"

His smirk turns up a notch as his eyes leave mine, shooting behind me. I don't want to turn my back on him, but I know if his attention is behind me, it's for a reason.

I peer over my shoulder. Two of his recruits are holding my parents captive, one's holding Mom by her hair while she kneels, the other has Dad's arms behind his back and a knife to his throat—their eyes both wide in fear.

I let out an exacerbated exhale as I turn back to Igor. "What the fuck do you want?" I yell over the gunfire still raging through the clubhouse.

It's like an ominous black cloud descends over the clubroom. A thunderstorm erupts, hailing down the anticipation of dread.

Darkness is coming.

I sense it looming like the hovering of an angel of death waiting for her prey.

"I want to watch you suffer." Igor's words send a chill through me as he signals to his men.

My muscles almost seize on the spot as I spin, the recruits run their knives mercilessly along the throats of my parents. My mother, my father—both of their necks burst wide open, blood pooling and running down their bodies.

"Nooo," I scream out in undeniable gut-wrenching agony.

"And now it's your turn," Igor grumbles from behind me.

I spin back to face him, the cold metal of his pistol presses directly against my temple. My lip curls as I glare at him, pure hatred running through me.

"Any last words?" he mocks like he's king fucking dick.

My lips slowly creep up my face. "*Zero.*" I don't have time for the rest of my countdown right now, the asshole has a gun pressed to my head. *Straight to zero it will have to be.*

He raises his brow as if he doesn't understand. I have him off-guard. Bringing my hand up, I wrap my palm around his wrist, twisting it away from my head. The gun fires, the noise sends a ringing through my ears as I twist his arm back around toward him. He yelps out in pain, his knees buckling under the pressure of his arm being twisted as I aim his own gun at his ugly-ass face. It shakes and rattles with him trying to fight me. His eyes bug out of his head as some of his recruits make their way over.

I don't have much time.

Igor fights me with everything he has, so with my free hand, I pull out my gun aiming it at his head.

He stops struggling.

The fear in his eyes tells me everything.

He's a dead man.

"For my parents." I don't hesitate, aiming the gun right in the middle of his greasy fucking forehead. He closes his eyes, and I pull the trigger. Blood splatters all over my jeans as the sounds of bullets immediately start. One whizzes past my face making me duck, another slamming straight into my bicep. I groan out loud, the burn intense as I drop Igor's lifeless body, and race back toward the bar, my chest squeezing at the sight of both of my parents dead on the floor.

I jump over the woodgrain, unloading more rounds into the recruits trying to head my way.

Wraith, our Sergeant-at-Arms, comes in from behind. He jumps on the back of one of the men, snapping his neck with the grace of a gazelle. The other turns to face him, pulling his gun on Wraith. I aim at the recruit and fire, the blood splatter spraying all over Wraith's cut. He peers down, shrugs, then takes off in the other direction.

My eyes search frantically through the clubhouse.

I have to find Prinie and Koda.

My eyes fall back to the table they ducked under when this all started. Prinie's sheltering Koda, her hands over her ears, tears streaming from her eyes as they focus on Mom and Dad's dead bodies.

They've seen the whole damn thing.

Fuck.

I need this to be over, now. This whole fucking thing. As I stand back up to shoot recruits, they turn scurrying toward the exit.

What the fuck?

I look over near the Chapel, Texas storms out with a machine gun aiming it at the retreating assholes. Ax throws his fist in the air in celebration as Texas lets rip. The hammering of the machine gun ripples through the clubhouse as Texas' big body jolts with the force. The Militia recruits are mowed down like rabbits. Blood and innards bursting out all over the damn place.

If I had the will in me to smile, I would.

But I can't.

Even seeing the Militia scum falling like the dogs they are isn't bringing me any kind of joy.

Not when I've lost so much tonight.

The roar of the gunfire slows to a halt. The cheering of my brothers soon takes its place as I check around at the great big fucking mess. Militia have been massacred here tonight. Their captain is out, which will only make way for a new scumbag leader to rise.

With the fall of my father–our president–it means the next man, the VP, automatically steps in to be president.

That man is me.

I wasn't supposed to fill the position for years. I'm not ready for the role. Hell, I'm not fucking ready to be without my damn father.

He was supposed to groom me for this.

Teach me how to do shit properly.

I don't know if I can lead this club without him.

The cheering dies down as I walk out from behind the bar. My hero, my president, my dad is dead on the concrete. My mom lying next to him, both in a pool of their own blood.

They deserved better than this.

A hand slaps my back comfortingly, and I turn. Wraith's broody sad expression he always sports is even more pronounced. "Fuck, brother. Frenzy was a damn good president. An even better man. He'd want you to fill his shoes, though. He wouldn't want *anyone* but you, Zero."

My jaw racks from side to side as I turn away from their bodies running my hand over my hair. "How did we get to the point where peace was an option, only for both sides to lose their leaders?"

Wraith cracks his neck in the way he does, the crunch popping through the air. "No fucking idea. What I *do* know is this war has just started afresh, and it can go one of two ways."

"How's that?" I raise a brow.

"You're the man in charge, whether you wanna be or not. They'll have a new captain, too. We don't know what he's gonna be like, but if he's reasonable, peace may *not* be off the table. You killed the man responsible for your parents' deaths, you don't want any more blood on your hands if you don't have to." His eyes turn to Prinie and Koda who are slowly making their way out from under the table.

I get what he's saying. If we retaliate, what's to stop the new guy from going after all I have left? I need to try and settle this if I can for the sake of Prinie and Koda.

I need them safe.

"You know, Wraith, sometimes you can be a smart bastard."

I almost think he's going to crack a smile. He doesn't. Just dips his head, then walks off, his dog, Mack, running to his side as he goes.

I need to check on Prinie and Koda, make sure they're not injured. Storming over to them, Prinie's milk chocolate orbs glisten with unshed tears as she watches me approaching. The protruding whites of her eyes show me exactly how frightened she really is. Her long dark hair a tangled web. I hate seeing my baby sister like this. All I've ever wanted is to protect her, to watch over her and Koda like a big brother should. Her bottom lip trembles as she clings to Koda, it's as if he's having trouble even standing.

"How many times are we gonna have to go through this, Krew?" she yells loud enough for everyone in the clubhouse to turn around and focus their attention on us.

I exhale, rubbing the back of my neck. Prinie knows not to call me by my name in front of my brothers. It's a sign of disrespect, but she's hurting right now, so I let it slide. "Prinie, Dad…" I pause, saying his name causes my chest to ache, "… Dad and me were working on—"

"Peace? If you say peace, I swear to God, dude, I'm gonna take your gun and shove it right up your fucking ass!"

"Prinie!"

"No! Mom and Dad are dead! I saw their throats slit right in front of my very eyes. *Koda saw it.* You said this place was going to get better. You said we were going to be safe here as a fam—"

"We will be—"

"We're *not* even a family anymore. Can't you see that? They're d-dead," her voice cracks on the last word as she bursts into a river of tears.

I step forward, moving to pull her and Koda to me, but Prinie slaps at my chest trying to push me away through her sobs.

But I don't let her.

I won't let her push me away.

I grab them both, yanking them to me, all the while Prinie continues to beat into my chest until I hold Prinie too tight for her to keep fighting me. She sobs into my bloodstained chest as Koda wraps his arms around me tightly. I lean my head against the top of Prinie's, embracing the only family I have left.

"I love you. I don't say it enough," I say quietly.

Prinie sniffles, pulling her head back from my chest to peer up at me. "Then let's go. Let's leave. The three of us. Make a new life away from this place. It's too dangerous here. We could go tonight. Leave all this shit behind."

My stomach flips at the desperation in Prinie's eyes but more so in her voice.

Koda peeks up slowly bobbing his head. "Yeah, I'm with Prinie. I don't wanna be here anymore, Zero."

Rolling my shoulders, I pull back with guilt settling over me. "I can't leave. With what… happened, I have to step up. I have to take Dad's place—"

"As *president?*" Prinie's high-pitched voice echoes through the clubroom. I nod. "That's even more reason for us to go. The target on our backs will be even larger. You *have* to see that!"

I glance over my shoulder at Dad. I want to make him proud. I *need* to make him proud. Prinie and Koda will understand in time. I know they will. "It *has* to be this way."

Prinie scoffs, grabbing Koda's hand and starts walking off.

"Where are you going?" I yell.

Her head snaps back my way. "Away from *you!*" She heads under the second level and makes her way for the stairs taking Koda with her. Those two are like an inseparable pair. It's good they have each other at the moment because my first action as president is going to be a fucking clean-up. Then to work on the handovers for Mom and Dad. I have no time to grieve.

I walk into the middle of the clubroom, and all eyes turn to me. I stand taller puffing out my chest to show authority. If I'm being honest, I'm shitting myself, but I can't show my brothers. If I'm going to do this, I need to think like a damn president.

Three... two... one... zero.

"Brothers, we weren't expecting this. For the Militia to come here on our fucking turf and take out our president and our first lady, this shit doesn't sit right with me..." The boys all stomp their feet in agreement, hollering as I continue, "I killed Igor. I shot him square in his beady fucking eyes. Y'all know he deserved it." My brothers cheer. "Now I don't know who's gonna take up the head of the Bayou Militia, but I'm not gonna put the rest of my family, or my brothers, in jeopardy without finding out all I can about the motherfucker first."

My brothers quiet down, their heads nodding like they're onboard.

"Neon, get on your systems, hack in, tell me their chatter, get me info on them..." I spin my eyes around to Kevlar. "Rally the prospects and get these fucking Militia scum out of here. Slick..." I pause taking a moment, "... prepare Frenzy and Moonshine for the handover."

Everyone turns their eyes to the floor in a show of respect for their fallen president, but I need to continue, so I straighten my shoulders. "And Wraith..." His eyes shoot to mine. "You're my VP. After the handover, we'll talk everyone's ranks, but for now, you have your new pres and VP. Anyone object?" Silence fills the room. "Good... now, get to work."

I turn, letting out a heavy breath. The weight of this situation is getting on top of me, but I can't let it. I need to keep my shit together. When I head to my room later, then I can grab a bottle of Jack and fall apart.

For now, I need to lead.

I have to be the president Frenzy would want me to be.

Stepping over to the bar as brothers frantically get to work, Kevlar orders the prospects, Blake and Cannon, around as the club girls slowly filter back out from the kitchen. I pick up the tipped-over barstool with blood smeared all over it. I curl my lip, then sit on it anyway.

Tennessee moves into position behind the bar. Her red crop top appears shorter today than normal, and her tiny denim shorts aren't having the same effect they usually do. She grabs a short glass, fills it with Jack, then slides it over. "You look like you need one of these."

I snort out a laugh. "I need the whole fucking bottle, Nessie."

She reaches out patting my blood-soaked forearm. "If it's any consolation, Zero, you're going to make a great president."

Hearing it said out loud hits me like a sucker punch straight to my gut. I dip my head at Nessie, pick up the glass, then throw back the contents, the amber nectar burning all the way down like a glorious fire from the depths of hell. Nessie goes to pour me another, but I wave my hand to stop her, then wiggle my fingers at her to hand me the damn bottle. She grimaces but slides it over. I yank off the pouring nozzle bringing the open neck to my lips, then spin on the stool to take in the state of the club.

My club.

Fucking hell.

Fox rushes over, his lengthy gray beard now smothered in red.

"What the hell happened to you?" I ask as he catches his breath.

He holds a piece of paper in his hand. "They must have come down the stairs when you were giving out your instructions, and gone out the back door while no one was looking."

I scrunch up my face. "What? Who? What are you talking about, old man?"

He shoves the note in my chest. "I found the note on the pool table, pres. If we leave now, they can't have gotten far."

I jerk back a little. That's the first time someone's actually called me pres, and I'm surprised at how good it felt.

Opening the note, it's Prinie's handwriting.

My heart rapid fires.

My eyes shooting back up to Fox, he bows his head confirming my thoughts.

So, I read the note.

Krew,
We can't be a part of this anymore. We wanted you to come with us, but we know you're far too in this now to leave. You want to be a president more than you want to be with your family. You have a thirst for this MC life, it's in your blood. The need to see this through with the Militia.
All I know is Koda and I can't be a part of this world anymore.
We love you. Never doubt that. We just don't love the club or what it represents.
It took something from us today. It stole our family. We can never get that back.
Don't look for us.
We're safer far away from the Houston Defiance MC.
Prinie and Koda xo

My entire body shakes with undeniable dread. Fear that Prinie is out there, not only trying to do this on her own, but trying to do it taking care of a fifteen-year-old boy. She's young herself, barely even a woman. Anger flares inside of me.

Of all the times for her to pull a stunt like this, she has to do it fucking now.

"Do you want me to rally the guys?" Fox asks.

Wraith approaches, his brows knotted together. "Something going down?"

Handing him the note. He skims the message, and as he does, his breathing is short and sharp, then scrunches the piece of paper tightly in his grip. "What the fuck game is she playing at?" His anger seems unwarranted. It's not *his* damn sister.

My mind ticks over.

Maybe if they're not here, then they won't be in danger.

Maybe she is doing the right thing?

"What if I let them leave?"

"What?" Fox and Wraith both yell at the same time.

"Hear me out… if they're not here, they're not in danger… not constantly under threat."

"If they're not here, they're also out in the open unprotected," Wraith argues.

I rub the back of my neck. "Then we find them, put eyes on them. Watch them. Make sure they're okay but keep our distance. We let them have a chance at a *normal* life."

Wraith throws his hands in the air. "They belong to the club. They should be here!" He storms away from us not adding anything else.

What the fuck was that about?

Fox reaches out placing his hand on my forearm. "I think you're doing the right thing. Let them have a chance at a life outside of the club but put a prospect on their tails. Have Cannon watch them."

I drop my chin to my chest once in agreement, even though the thought of not having any of my family here absolutely guts me. My father, my mother, my sister, and my brother. Gone! No one will be here to support me through my presidency.

Not the way I wanted to start this process.

An ominous cloud washes over this entire new beginning. I hope it's not a sign of things to come. I turn back to the bar, grab the bottle of Jack, bringing it to my lips. I take a long sip walking toward the stairs to head to my bedroom.

I went from having my entire family to having no one—happy fucking presidency to me.

CHAPTER 2

RAYNE

Four Months Later

My knees scrape along the asphalt as I fall. The strike of his palm to my face sends a shudder through me that I should have seen coming. With panting heavy breaths, my fingers dig into the loose pebbles on the sidewalk as I try to remain calm. But his heavy boot slams into my ribs, causing my body to jerk and fall sideways onto the path with a thud.

I don't fight back.

I know better than that.

"Why, Rayne? Why do you make me do this?" Chuck yells at me down the back alley.

My bottom lip trembles, but I won't let tears fall from my eyes.

Not for him.

He squats, my body shakes, his dark eyes meet mine. An intense, fevered stare shines back at me, letting me know how angry he is at this very moment. "Answer. Me," he grits out, a small amount of spittle flying from his mouth.

Licking my lip, I taste the blood pooling from the deep split. I clear my throat to speak, but he shakes his head while pulling back and then thumps the back of his hand across my face with so much force my body catapults across the ground. My head slams into the pavement with a harsh thud. My eyes roll around the back of my head as I lie on the ground dazing in and out of consciousness.

"Fuck, Rayne, you've really gone and made a mess of yourself this time," Chuck murmurs.

His boots are the last thing I see walking away from me before everything turns black.

I'm not sure how long I've been lying in the alley for, but I can tell by the lack of sun, it's late. My body aches so fucking much I can barely move. Chuck beating me up again was my own fault. I provoked him like I somehow always manage to do. You'd think I'd learn by now to play the perfect little housewife. The problem is it's just not me. I can't sit back and not tell him when he's being a dick. My mouth gets me in trouble every damn time.

Tonight, we were waiting for our dessert at an upscale Chicago restaurant, and he was telling the waitress that the chef was too slow with our orders.

I told him to be patient—the restaurant was packed.

Chuck didn't like me disrespecting him in front of another woman. *I should have known better.* So, he took me out the side of the restaurant and taught me 'his' lesson. It seems like I'm getting one of 'his' lessons daily at this point. Though, he's never been quite as public about it—never outside of our home. I guess he couldn't hold his anger in this time, but this alley is deserted enough.

No one saw.

No one has come to check on me.

He's gotten away with it as always.

Slowly pulling myself together, I sit on the pavement for a second before attempting to stand. My ribs ache with such intense pain that a surge of nausea rolls over me like a tidal wave. A cold sweat invades my body as my skin prickles, but not in a good way. I feel hot and cold at the same time. *Is that even possible?*

Trying to keep my dinner down, I move my hand to my head to feel a wet patch. Pulling my hand away, I see a small amount of blood from where I hit the pavement.

"Great," I murmur to myself as I grab my purse and attempt to get up.

Moaning, I stand and then gingerly hobble and wobble as I manage to find my straightened form. Intense nausea takes over while I lean against the brick wall and just breathe.

In slowly.

Out slowly.

You've got this, Rayne.

Chuck's done worse in the past.

He knew I'd have to find a way home when he left me here.

I'm not sure what his end game is right now.

My footsteps are uneven. I swear I look drunk as I finally make it to the end of the alley. I quickly realize there's no fucking way I can make the trip home. I don't even think I can make it to the end of the street. So, I sit my ass down on the curb and pull out my cell. I'm sure Chuck thought I would walk home, and it would teach me a lesson.

Well, he can go to hell.

Bringing up my Uber app, I place the request for a driver. There's three in the area, but I say yes to the female. At this point, it makes me feel safer.

As I wait, I attempt to assess the damage. I know my ribs have probably been dealt a harsh blow from Chuck's boot. They're hurting so bad. If I wasn't wearing a dress, I'd lift it and have a look. I'm aware my lip's split not only from the pain but the amount of blood. I wouldn't be surprised if I have a concussion because my head's spinning, the waves of nausea keep rolling through me, and my stomach's churning so bad.

I could use some painkillers right now. But most of all I want to go to sleep, and I know that's not a good sign. I hunch over, putting my head between my knees to try and calm the queasiness, but nothing's helping.

I don't even care when I see the flash of headlights illuminate my side vision. I'm sure it's my Uber driver, but I honestly don't have the ability to stand.

Light footsteps sound next to me as I slowly lift my head. A grungy looking female stands before me, she's all black leather with a purple streak in her hair. Her eyeliner's so dark she could be mistaken for a panda.

But beneath all that makeup and costume she's so obviously hiding behind, she's pretty.

Really pretty.

"Hey! Looks like you've had a rough night," she soothes. She's not mocking nor making a joke. Her voice is sympathetic as she moves in, sitting beside me on the curb.

I wince a little from the pain in my head as I look up. "I'm sorry. I tried to walk home, but—"

"Don't be sorry. Whatever happened tonight is not your fault."

Taking in a deep breath, I clear my throat. "I shouldn't be wasting your time. I'll try and make it to the car."

Her hand comes out across my chest, stopping me. "Hey, it's fine. I have all the time in the world..." She smiles and introduces herself, "I'm Prinie."

"Rayne."

Prinie exhales. "I have to ask, Rayne. Did the muggers... assault you? Sexually?"

I jerk my head back, which only causes excruciating pain. I groan as I bring my hand up to my forehead to ease the ache. "I wasn't mugged. No sexual assault, just physical. It's always only physical."

Prinie looks at my hand on my head and zeros in on my ring finger.

I drop my hand and twirl my ring.

She cranes her neck to the side. "Your husband?" she asks, incredulously.

"He doesn't mean to go off—"

"Bullshit! Rayne, don't protect the asshole. If he hits you, it's his issue, and you shouldn't protect him. It's never ever *your* fault."

Letting out a small laugh, I sigh. "You're right. I don't know why I said that. It's never my fault. I'm quite simply scared of him. Scared of what he represents."

Prinie places her hand on my knee. "I know I'm just your Uber driver. I know we've only just met, but how about I take you to the hospital. I'll stay and help you however you need."

I wave my hand through the air. "Honestly, I'm fine." I go to stand but sway.

Prinie moves into my side, wrapping her arm around me. "I got you. Okay, let's get into the car, and we can figure it out as we go. Okay, hon?"

I weakly smile at her caring tone. "Thank you, Prinie."

She grabs my purse and helps me into the passenger side of the blue Honda Civic. Then Prinie jumps into the driver's side quickly. I had put in my address for the destination of this trip, but honestly, I don't want to go home right now. *I don't want to go back to him.*

Prinie starts the car, glancing over to me. "You sure you don't want to go to the hospital?"

"I'm sure. But I don't want to go home either."

Prinie scrunches up her face, her eyes shifting to her cell with Uber information coming in hot and fast. She switches it off, then turns to me again. "Then, where do you wanna go?"

"I'm sorry. I'm stopping you from doing your job—"

"You're more important right now."

Gnawing on my split lip, I sink into the seat, the nausea beginning to settle. "Somewhere where we can just sit."

Prinie smiles. It's warm and genuine.

I don't know what it is about this woman who I hardly know. She's swept in like some version of Wonder Woman to save the day. I owe her so much, and she doesn't even know it.

"I know this great park. Well lit. Super cute. Very calming. And the bonus is it's close by."

She takes off, the car falling into a comfortable silence. She probably has so many questions she would like to ask me, but right now, she's letting me rest. I need it. She's more than likely right that I need to go to the hospital, but Chuck would hate that, and ultimately, I would pay for it in one way or another. So, for now, I'll try to spend as much time as I can away from Chuck before the cycle starts all over again.

We pull up at this gorgeous little park, and Prinie helps me out of the car. We walk over to a bench and sit looking out over a large water fountain. We don't talk, just watch as she lets me gather my thoughts. I don't know if Prinie is a psych major, but she's doing a great job of letting me process this in the best way possible for me.

I turn to face her, now ready to open up. "Chuck... my husband... his family is from big money. So are mine. Together we're supposed to be this power couple. So, he thinks it gives him the right to beat the living shit out of me when I don't do what's 'expected.'" I use air quotes around the word.

"His name is Chuck?" I nod, and she snorts. "More like Up-Chuck."

My eyes widen in shock, but I can't help but let out a laugh. I don't remember the last time I laughed. Like truly found something funny. Prinie smiles as I giggle. "You and Chuck would *not* get along."

She grins. "Good! Sounds like a fuckwit to me, Rayne."

I tilt my head. "Yes, he is."

Prinie scrunches up her face. "Then why stay?"

Why am I staying? I have no answer to that question.

"It's complicated. He has power, privilege. He would find me, no matter where I went. I can't escape him. So why even try?"

"Because life can always be better, Rayne. Trust me. I know firsthand."

I raise my brow. "God, look at me taking all the spotlight. I'm sorry. What's your story?"

Prinie's eye twitches like she remembers something she simply doesn't want to. "My past is something we need vodka and cake for. Bottles of vodka and so much chocolate cake..." she trails off and pauses then continues, "Let me give you my number, and we can pencil in an afternoon where I can tell you my side of things."

"You'd like to catch up again?"

Prinie smirks. "I think we're bonded now. Plus, I need to meet this Up-Chuck in person."

"I don't think that's such a good idea."

She waves her hand through the air. "Pfft. He won't bite me. Those types of men are too weak. And if he does, I'll bite back just as hard. My older brother…" She hesitates like she's remembering something again, but the memory is painful. "My older brother taught me how to fight. If Up-Chuck starts with me, or with you while I'm around, I'll kick him in the nads. I got your back now, girlfriend."

Gripping her hand, I give it a little squeeze. "Thank you. No one has ever put themselves out for me before."

Prinie wraps her arm around my shoulders carefully. The feeling of a new friendship forming is comforting, but for some reason, it's like I've known her for longer than I could imagine. I feel an ease with her. She calms my nerves and understands me, and I've only known her for barely half an hour.

"You know, Rayne… when I saw your request, I thought… what the hell is this girl doing on that street at this time of night? It was all a little freaking weird, and I nearly didn't take the job. But now I know it was kismet. I was meant to meet you tonight. I want to help you. To be your support. And I'm going to be if you'll let me."

Tears threaten to fall, but I won't let them. I never do. But this woman, this remarkable woman, who makes herself up to look like a punk, who hides herself under a mask of make-up, I see it's all just a camouflage.

There's more to her story.

Just like I have a story with Chuck, she has a back story, and I want to find out everything there is to know about Prinie. So, I'm going to take her up on her offer. I haven't had a friend, a true friend, in as long as I can remember. Chuck's seen to that. I just hope he doesn't push her away too.

"You know what, Prinie? I think I will let you take me to the hospital. Fuck what Chuck thinks."

"Yeah, girl," she exclaims while throwing her hands in the air. "I got your back, Rayne. Whenever you need me, I'm gonna be right by your side."

Warmth swirls inside me because I believe her.

I don't know what I've done to deserve meeting Prinie like this tonight, but I won't look a gift horse in the mouth. If she's been sent to me, I'm going to take this blessing and run with it.

I lean over and wrap my arms around her, taking her into an embrace. Prinie hugs me back with a squeeze, and I wince with a slight moan as my ribs pinch, sending a shockwave right through my center.

Prinie pulls back, assessing me then shakes her head. "Okay, let's get you to the hospital."

"Yes, let's do this." I weakly smile.

Six Months Later

The last six months have been a crazy ride, mainly because shit with Chuck hasn't changed, even though Prinie is adamant I should leave him. She doesn't understand why I stay, but she's my constant support and rock.

No matter what.

No matter what she thinks.

She's always there to pick up the pieces of Chuck's mess. I honestly don't know what I'd do without her.

I just wish I could help her more. She moved to Chicago from Houston to escape a bad family drama. She mentioned something about bikers, but she doesn't like to open up much about that part of her life. I've had nothing more than they stole her parents from her. It's why she took her baby brother, Koda, and up and left.

He's a sweet kid. Would do anything for her. All I want for them is to have a roof over their heads and somewhere safe to call home. Prinie's working nonstop to bring in money for them, but it doesn't help. Koda's getting himself into trouble with the local gangs. I tried to give them some of my money—I don't need it. But when Chuck realized money was missing from my account, well, Prinie was there to clean up that bloody mess.

After, she felt horrible and wouldn't accept another single cent from me from then on.

Prinie's just called me and said she's met someone and has news for me. So, while Chuck is out at work, she's coming around. The purple streak is now gone from her hair, but that grunge look she has going on is still present and accounted for. She's hiding—from her past trying to put on a fake persona to conceal her true feelings—that she's just as lost as I am.

As I grimace, stretching my sore arm out to try and release the strained wrist, I walk to the window upon hearing her car drive in.

A genuine smile lights my face as I pull back the door. "Good morning!" I chime with vigorous pep.

Prinie's sour expression, however, does *not* match my own. "I'm not so sure it is."

My smile falls from my face as I usher her inside and to the sofa. "Bad night?"

She exhales, slumping onto the soft white cushions. "I met someone really interesting."

"And that's a bad thing?" I ask while sitting next to her.

"He offered me a waiting job at his club."

"Prinie, that's amazing. Think of all those freaking tips you can make."

She groans, pinching the bridge of her nose. "It's at Club Modesty."

"Wait! What? You mean that biker bar?"

She exhales. "It's not really a biker bar as such. Just owned by them. But yeah, working in there. He said I could keep driving Uber, too. But that's not all."

I sit taller, not liking the pain written across her face. "Prinie, talk to me."

She turns to face me. "When I left Houston, I said I'd never be put back in a situation where I felt vulnerable again. Where Koda and I would be in danger."

Where the hell is she going with this?

"Prinie?"

"The man I talked to was the President of the Chicago Defiance MC. He saw that Koda and I were living out of my car, and he wouldn't have it."

"I-I don't know what you're saying." Tension rolls over me as I stare at her.

"He offered for Koda and me to stay at the clubhouse... you know, till we can find our feet. Until I make enough money from my tips to get us a real apartment. Somewhere decent for us to live."

I exhale. "Okay. And this clubhouse? Are they in danger constantly?"

She shrugs. "I don't think so. But honestly, Rayne, I can't let Koda continually live in the car. I'm at my wit's end. You know I wouldn't do this unless it was my last resort."

I can't help Prinie.

Chuck won't let me.

But worse than that, Prinie won't let me because of Chuck.

It's a catch-22.

All I want is for them to have a roof over their heads. If this Chicago Defiance MC is going to give her and Koda that opportunity and keep them safe, then I guess I have to go with it. "I only have one question."

Prinie nods. "Okay?"

"Will they stop us from seeing each other?"

She slides closer, grabbing both my hands in hers. "Nothing, and no one, is ever going to stop me from being your friend, Rayne. Anywhere you go, I go, right? We're in this fucked-up mess of a life together."

I chuckle, pulling her into an embrace. "This could be the start of something big for you, Prinie. It's going to open up new doors. Just you wait and see."

Prinie pulls back with an evil smirk. "Now that I'm in good with the pres, want me to get the boys to deal with Chuck?"

I gasp, playfully slapping her arm. "Prinie! No... *yes,*" I whisper. "No. You're bad!"

She bursts out laughing, pulling me back in for another embrace. Prinie might be heading for a new home in a biker clubhouse, but she will always hold a home in my heart. I have no idea what my life would be like without her, and I wouldn't want to even imagine it.

Though, I can only imagine what living with a bunch of bikers is going to be like. I'd feel anxious for her, but honestly, I think the Chicago Defiance needs to be ready for Prinie because she's one hell of a woman, a whole lot of attitude, and she fights for anything and everything she believes in.

I'd say good luck to Prinie, but I think it's more appropriate that I say good luck to them.

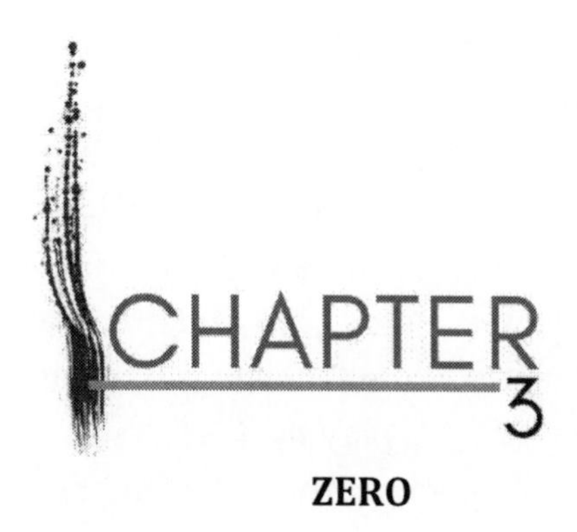

ZERO

Two Months Later

The one-year anniversary of my presidency is coming up in a few weeks, which also means I'll be mourning the loss of my parents and my siblings from my life. I've been a good president this past year. Hell, I think I've been a fucking *great* president.

I did what I said I would do.

I made Frenzy proud of me.

At least I think he'd be proud of me.

The new captain of the Militia, Hawke Hernandez, is a reasonable guy. He's not straight up and down, we still have trouble occasionally, but for the most part, the Militia and Defiance are at peace.

We have an understanding—we don't go near their side of the Bayou borders, they don't cross into our side of town. It works.

But with the looming deadline of the anniversary coming, I thought it was time for the club to go for a long-haul ride. It's been a year—it's time for Prinie and Koda to come home. Cannon's been watching over them, following them for the entire year. He's well and truly earned his patch. When we get back, I'll see to it.

When he reported to me that Prinie was in contact with Torque, the President of Chicago Defiance, needless to say I was shocked. Prinie was so dead set against being part of MC club life. So, when I heard she was not only working for Chicago in their local bar, she was also living at their clubhouse, yeah, I was fucking angry.

If Prinie can live with the Chicago Defiance MC, she can fucking live in Houston with her family where she belongs.

I'm damn well bringing them home.

Torque doesn't know we're on our way. Hell, he doesn't know we've been watching his club. Trouble with the Irish is brewing, and I don't want my siblings in the way of *their* damn war. They've seen enough. Our club is at peace while Chicago is batting up for combat. I don't know what game Prinie's playing. Maybe she's on to Cannon's tail. Maybe she knows I'm watching them. Maybe this is her trying to gain my attention. Either way, I need to get to her before shit starts in Chicago.

My ass is chafing from two days of riding. The guys are worn out as we pull into a gas station. The roar of my engine draws to silence as I flex out my aching hands. Cracking my stiff neck from side to side, I yawn. This riding long distances shit is hard work. I hope Prinie realizes the effort I'm putting in for her. I hope this shows how much I want her and Koda back in my life. I need them at the club with me. They've been gone long enough.

The van pulls in, delayed a little behind us. Lexi, the one club girl we brought along, is sitting in the front with Fox. As I slowly edge off my ride, my knees feel like they are crunching with the movement. Fucking hell, what am I, like eighty? I definitely don't feel twenty-six right now. I need to head to the gym more and eat a lot less of Fox's brisket.

Who am I kidding, that's never going to happen.

Moving to the pump, I place the nozzle in my tank and begin to fill. My eyes wander over my guys, they're all as wrecked as I feel. I hope Torque's going to put us up for the night. If not, we'll have to find a hotel close by. Brother clubs are usually pretty damn accommodating when another chapter rolls in.

Finishing up, I place the nozzle on the pump, pay, then figure I need a quick pick-me-up before we take off again. We're not far away. Cannon said everything appears to be fine at Chicago Defiance MC, so he's gone for a break. Kid needs to sleep. He was up all night keeping guard on the Chicago clubhouse. With us heading there in just under an hour or so, we can take over patrol while he gets some much-needed rest before the start of our journey home tomorrow.

I bring my fingers to my lips letting out a loud whistle grabbing everyone's attention. Even the busybodies who are sticking in their fat noses give the dirty bikers from Houston the evil eye from the other side of the parking lot.

"Listen up, y'all. Move your rides to a parking space, then grab yourself some grub. Let's get ourselves refreshed, then we'll head off."

They all dip their heads and start wheeling their rides into the spaces by the front door. I do the same, kicking back my stand, then start rolling my ride to the front door, parking it right by the entrance, so if I need to get to my bike fast, I can.

I sweep my hand through the air, signaling for my men to enter the store. We all stride in, heavy boots thumping on the floor. The entire place falls to silence as parents grab their kids, yanking them toward their legs for protection. A lone child's eyes, who's licking his ice cream, slowly drift up as I walk past him. His ice cream falls to the floor in fright.

I know I look scary. I realize what this 1% cut represents to the outside world. I don't deny we're not good people. I've done shit—bad fucking shit.

But I love fiercely, protecting those I care about.

I protect those who need protection. I'm not fucking heartless.

The boy's father reaches out grabbing him, quickly pulling him away from me as I let out a small chuckle. Wraith shakes his head as he strides past me. The man has an air about him too. His dark features feel like there's an ominous cloud constantly surrounding him. His mood has worsened since the attack last year. His hollowness grows deeper. His judgment isn't impaired, never has been, just his mood, or should I say lack thereof.

Something changed in the club when Frenzy died. We're all a little more on edge, even if we are at some version of peace. We know at any time something could fracture the treaty. If that happens, this war could start up again and people we love could be hurt. None of us want that—our family blood or otherwise mean everything to us.

We make our way over to the food counter, the smell of fried chicken smacks me square in the face. My stomach growls instantly.

The short, stumpy woman wearing too much hooker-style makeup behind the counter eyes me up and down with an I-don't-give-a-shit-who-you-are expression.

I like her.

"Welcome to Flavor Hit, where every piece of chicken is a flavor hit," she drones like she's said the fucking line a million times before.

"Hey…" I take in her name badge, "… Rhonda." I smirk.

"Yeah," she replies monotone.

"Me and my brothers here would like all the chicken you have in your fryers…" I turn looking at my guys trying to quickly do the math. "Say, ten large fries, extra salt. Same number of sodas. Some of those little popcorn things you do. Wraith loves them, don't you, Wraith?"

He glares at me, blinks, but says nothing.

My brothers laugh as I continue, "Anyone want anything else?"

Kevlar steps forward. "I'll have a one of those side salads."

"Of course, you will." Kevlar likes to keep fit.

Rhonda raises her brow at me like she doesn't give two shits. "Mm-hmm… will that be all?"

I roll my shoulders. "And an ice cream in a cone."

"All that fat, you're gonna lose those abs, Zero." Fox nudges me in the ribs as Rhonda tallies the total.

"Shut up, old man. I'll burn it off later, whooping your damn ass."

"I'd like to see you try." He rushes off. Guy's fit as a fucking ox. When I call him old man, it's only teasing because, in all honestly, he's anything but. He may have gray hair, wrinkles, and sun-weathered skin, but in personality and stamina, Fox's age is probably still in his teens. Guy's a fucking machine.

"That'll be two fifty-six ninety-nine," Rhonda monotones.

She really hates her job.

I yank out my wallet, grabbing three hundred-dollar bills and slide them across the counter. "Keep the change, Rhonda. Merry Christmas."

Her eyes widen, her lips turning up for the first time since we walked in here. The way her pink lips meet the middle of her dimpled cheeks makes her quite beautiful. "Thanks. You don't know how much this means to me… but, ahh… you know it's April, right?"

I shrug. "Is it? Then buy your kids something nice when Christmas rolls around."

Her eyes glisten. "I will. This will help. I… I'll get your order right away."

I give her my signature wink, then turn toward my guys. The damn bastards are all staring at me, with their eyebrows raised. "What?"

"You've been shut off this past year. I mean you get shit done, there's no denying that. You're a fucking great president. But emotionally, pres, you've been…" Texas shrugs, "… checked out."

Everyone bobs their heads agreeing with the New Jersey-born native.

I groan, rubbing the back of my neck. "Knowing we're so close to my family and getting them back makes me feel, well… fuck, I don't know."

"Hopeful," Ax answers for me.

"Yeah."

"We all want them back, pres. Not having your sassy sister around has made the clubhouse a lot quieter. And Koda, he's a good kid, has a lot to learn, but even more to give," Neon suggests as silence falls over us.

I give him a nod. Shit might still be strained between us since all that crap went down a while ago, but he always has my back.

"That's why we must get them both back," Wraith breaks the tension.

"And straight after we eat, we're gonna get them. We just gotta make it look like we're here on a ride and dropped in for a catch-up.

If Prinie realizes I've come for them, she won't come willingly. Hell, she still probably won't, but I need her back with me at the club. Fucking hell, if she can stay with Chicago, then she can damn well come home."

They all voice their approval.

"Your ice cream, sir," Rhonda calls from behind me.

"Thanks, Rhonda."

I take the small cone from her, my brothers all attempting to keep their laughter at bay at the tiny thing in my oversized man hands. Even I have to admit it looks ridiculous. "Boys, grab the food when it's ready and y'all go sit and take a load off. I got something I need to do."

They head for the counter as I duck back toward the entry in search of the person I need. My eyes wander the aisles hoping they haven't left yet as customers' eyes follow my every move. I'm sure they're scared I'm going to shoot them if they look at me the wrong way.

I just might.

I spot the little boy with his parents heading for their car outside. My stride's extra-long as I head for their four-door red sedan. His father's in the driver's side fumbling with the keys in the ignition, but I step up to the kid's window, tapping on it. The little boy's eyes light up seeing the replacement ice cream for the one he dropped. His hand moves to the window, but it doesn't open. Instead, the front passenger opens, the mother peeps out.

"H-Hi... can I help you, s-sir?"

I slide to my right, standing in front of the mother's door, her short red hair sitting perfectly on her head, styled to perfection. I don't miss the silver cross teamed with a naked Jesus nailed to it hanging around her neck.

"Ma'am, your son dropped his ice cream earlier. I bought him a replacement."

Her eyes widen. "Oh, that's not necessary."

"Mommy, ice cweam," the kid calls out.

"Think of it as a charitable donation. I'm in the mood for giving, and your son lost something important to him. I just want to give back to him what he lost. Help a brother out, will ya?"

His mom peeks back at her son who's bouncing up and down in his car seat. "Pwease, Mommy."

She turns back to me. "Jesus thanks you."

"I'd prefer it if *you* thanked me, but I'll take it. Have a good day, y'all."

"Fank yooo," the kid calls out, then shoves the ice cream in his mouth like it's the best thing in the fucking world.

Seems the thought of getting my family back is making me soft.

I dip my head, turn, and hightail it back inside, heading to the booths where my guys are currently chowing down all the fast food they can eat—except for Kevlar who's eating his damn salad. I slide in next to Wraith, pick up my soda and slam it down. Glancing at the fried chicken—I'm gonna enjoy this.

We eat, make far too much noise and make a hell of a mess but most of all we're relaxing, having a good time before the real action starts. The long ride into Chicago to try and convince my siblings to come back with us may not be so easy.

My cell beeps. I grab a napkin, wipe my hands, and yank it from my pocket. It's the Chicago Defiance president, and I'm instantly on high alert. This particular chat line is only used when one of the clubs is in trouble.

I slide open the message from Torque, and every inch of me goes on high alert.

> **Torque:** *Zero, I know you're riding into Chicago, no idea why. I've seen your prospect Cannon watching the club. We have the Irish Mob coming in half an hour. I fear the fallout will be bloody. WE NEED ASSISTANCE, NOW.*

My eyes go wide as I read the text.

My body turns icy cold.

Prinie and Koda are at Chicago, and we're over half an hour away.

"Fuck," I murmur to myself.

"Problem?" Wraith asks.

I don't answer him, instead I send a message back to Torque.

> **Zero:** *We're at least 45 mins away. Can try to make it in 35/40. Leaving the gas station now. Will be there soon. Houston is coming.*

"Zero, talk to me, brother. I don't like the look on your face," Wraith states beside me.

I stand from the booth shoving my cell in my pocket. "Brothers, mount up. We're leaving, right now."

"What? Why?" Wraith asks.

"Because the Irish are gonna attack the Chicago clubhouse in thirty. We're not gonna make it in time to get Prinie and Koda out."

CHAPTER 4

ZERO

I haven't seen Prinie and Koda for so long—almost a full fucking year to be exact—and that's on me. I'm fucking annoyed, thinking my brother and sister could get caught up in a biker war I'm not there to protect them against.

My heart hammers so hard I can hardly think straight. My hand pulls back on the throttle with such intensity, pins and needles shoot through my hand while I weave in and out of traffic to reach my destination. The vibration of my engine purrs like a kitten, and normally the sound would soothe me, but right now, it's sending waves of anxiety through my body.

We're close.

Not close enough.

My brothers keep pace with my manic speed as we pick up speed faster than the legal limit, making our way down the long access road toward the Chicago clubhouse. There are black vans out the front with more Irish in gray suits running in. The unmistakable popping sound of gunfire echoes through the air as we pull up to the open gates. Gatekeeper salutes me as we pull in. My stomach's twisting on itself as my brothers jump off their rides rapidly drawing their weapons. The thirst for a good fight now in the air.

"Don't get yourselves killed, boys."

They aim their weapons as the roaring of gunfire blasts around us, a bullet piercing through the metal of the wall, flying straight past me into the fence beside my head. I follow the line, then turn back to the clubhouse leading the way inside.

Anger fueling my blood, I burst through the door. These Irish bastards didn't just come into a Defiance clubhouse tearing shit up, they came to the place my siblings call their home. That shit doesn't fly with me. You Irish assholes wanted a fight with Chicago, you just got one hell of a war with Houston.

"Zero," I yell, without the rest of my countdown. Pulling up a gun in each hand, I fire at anything wearing a gray suit.

The pushback from each weapon after it's fired sends a surge of adrenaline through me as I watch the Irishmen's bodies flailing about, bursting open like a cacophony of beautiful art. Blood splashes against the walls of the clubhouse as my brothers fall in, spreading out over the room.

Chicago was outnumbered.

There's some fucking Italian crew here too. They seem to be helping, so I'm avoiding shooting them as I continue walking and shooting pretty much anything that moves.

My thirst for blood is high.

The need to kill, unwavering.

Someone pokes their head out from behind the pool table. I aim at him but don't pull the trigger when I realize it's Chains, Chicago's Sergeant-at-Arms. Spinning around, I rush toward an Irish, stashing one of my guns down my jeans and reach for my knife. I move in behind him, stabbing in the side of his ribs. He screams out as the gunfire begins to settle. Blood spills down my hand, dripping to the floor below. Out the corner of my eye, Chains throws his hands into the air in celebration as I dump the dead Irishman to the floor.

Another blast echoes through the room. A warm spray of blood catches the side of my face as the Irishman falls to the floor beside me.

"Shit, my bad, pres."

I turn slowly glaring at Texas. He grimaces backing away slowly, then turns, heading for the other side of the room. Houston's overrun this joint.

The second wave of Irish who arrived are now all dead thanks to us. Torque was right. It is a blood bath. If he hadn't have called for help, it would have been Chicago's blood staining these floors. Plus, Prinie and Koda's, wherever they are.

I'm glad we got here in time. Through all of this, I need to keep up the pretense that we're not in fact here for Prinie, or she'll only fight me harder.

Play your role, Zero.

Checking my guys, I make sure none of them are hurt in the gunfight. They all tip their heads at me—everyone's accounted for. *Good.* I turn back as I put my knife away spotting Chains helping a fumbling Torque up from behind the pool table.

He's hit.

Fuck.

Chains assists Torque toward me as I wipe the fucking blood spatter off my cheek and nose with the back of my hand. Wraith's by my side taking everything in, saying nothing but always on guard.

Watching Torque holding his bloodied side makes me angry we didn't arrive earlier. If we hadn't have stopped for fucking fried chicken, we could have been here sooner.

"Better late than never, hey Torque?" I call out as another Irish jumps up from behind a barricade running for the door. I waste no time bringing up my gun, firing off three rounds into his back, his body pushing forward before crashing to the floor, his blood oozing out to a pool from his dead body. I wipe a sheen of sweat from my forehead, my gun still firmly in my grip.

"Could've come a little sooner," Torque jabs, the corner of his lips turns up.

"Where's the gratitude, old pal?"

He staggers up to me, clutching his bleeding side. "Five minutes sooner and one less bullet in my side, that's all I'm saying, Zero."

I can't help but smirk. "Sorry, bro, there was road works. We couldn't break the speed limit, y'all know how Kevlar gets." My eyes shift to Kevlar with a smirk. He scrunches his brows at me in disapproval.

"Seriously? You were late 'cause you were obeying the fuckin' speed limit? We're at war, and you were fuckin' dawdlin'!"

I lean out resting my hand on Torque's shoulder, trying my hardest not to lose my shit at him. He doesn't know we're here for Prinie. He doesn't know I'm beating myself up for not getting here sooner. He doesn't know I want to punch him in his fucking face to shut him up, so I can go find my siblings.

No.

I have to play a part for this to all work out. So, a part I will play. "Nah, brother. It's just a long-ass ride. We pushed like shit to get here as quick as we could. Believe me. Sorry y'all took some lead."

Next thing I know, a couple more Irish make themselves known, and I do what I have got to do. I take them out without a second thought, then walk over to my guys standing with them.

"Have you seen them? Prinie and Koda?" I whisper the last part.

Everyone shakes their heads as I overhear Torque chatting with a woman dressed in a pinstriped suit. "I look forward to working with the new Andretti Order."

I turn back. Andrettis are mafia. *What kind of deal is Torque playing with here?*

She dips her head. "I'm going to take better care of things from now on. I'm going to make sure Enzo's ideals and views live on."

Right, so Queen Bee here is the leader of the Andrettis. Good to know.

A few stragglers slowly filter from down the hall. Then I see it. In with the stragglers is Prinie, she has her arms wrapped around Koda, who's terrified. My heart thuds frantically.

They're okay.

Relief washes over me for the briefest of seconds before the wave of anger smacks into me again full force. She's thin. They both are. Prinie's got this punk goth vibe going on now which I don't care for, and Koda's in need of some new clothes.

This isn't fucking good enough, princess!

Plus, the fact she ran away from Houston because of the anarchy and madness living with bikers entails, to find her living here in the midst of a war. *Hell fucking no.* There better be a damn good excuse for her being here and not at home where she belongs.

I scrunch up my face, folding my arms over my chest. "*What the actual fuck!*" I yell not being able to keep my cool.

Prinie turns, the whites of her eyes showing in fear. Koda, on the other hand, smiles so fucking wide he can hardly contain his excitement. *I missed you too, kid.* Koda goes to move toward me. My chest squeezes, but then he stops, hesitating between me and Prinie. *What the fuck?*

Shit, I need to play the role.

"Prinie?" I whisper as if I'm seeing a ghost.

She folds her arms over her chest. "What the hell are *you* doing here?" she grunts with more anger than I was hoping for. But really, what did I expect. Her to throw out the welcoming parade?

Koda's happiness falls as he takes a step back toward Prinie away from me. I get it. He feels like because he's spent the last year by her side, he needs to stick by her.

This isn't about choosing sides, kid.

It's about being a fucking family. Prinie's the one stopping us from being that family. Anger ignites in me again, causing me to surge forward toward them. I'm fuming, and I am about to let Prinie know it. "What am I doing here? *What am I doing here?* Jesus Christ Kharlie, that's a bit rich coming from you," I grunt out going for the low blow. I need to remind her about home. About where she really comes from. About Dad.

Prinie turns up her head. "Don't call me that! And anyway, I can go wherever I want to. I'm old enough."

Glaring at her, my fists ball together as I lean closer. "You left because you didn't want anything to do with the club life. You *took* Koda because you didn't want anything to do with the club. Now you're here, in Chicago, at an MC club? What the fuck, princess?"

She stomps her foot in frustration. "You don't know what it's like out there. I had no choice but to come here."

Rage ignites inside me hotter than it ever has before. It burns like the fury of a thousand suns scorching my skin so hot, a bead of sweat runs down my temple. I puff out my chest, towering over her. She's not intimidated, not one little bit. "You always had a choice. You could've come home. I know what happened affected us differently, but Prinie, we're family. We should have stuck together."

Koda glances from Prinie to me. "I agree, Prinie… we *should* go home."

My anger softens slightly, my temper simmering at my brother's understanding of this situation. *He gets it. Why can't Prinie?*

Prinie juts out her hip. "How do I know if we come back we're going to be safe? How do I know shit like what happened here isn't going to happen back home?"

I let out a booming laugh at her ridiculous comment but reach forward placing both hands on her shoulders. "Prinie, I'm your big brother. I'm never going to ever let anyone hurt you. Is shit like this…" I wave my hand around, "… going to happen in Houston? Fuck yeah. But I will lay everything on the line to protect you both. I thought I made it perfectly clear already before you up and left."

"If we moved back, then what? We're just a happy little family all over again?"

I groan dropping my hands from her shoulders. "Fuck! I don't know, Prinie. I'm not a fucking psychic. All I know is if y'all can live here in the Chicago Defiance clubhouse, then you're more than capable of living at my club. I *demand* you come back with us."

Fuck, why the hell did I say that?

Prinie folds her arms over her chest narrowing her eyes on me. *Shit, she's gonna fight me.* "You *demand* it? Always fucking bossing me around, and you wonder why I up and left you, Krew."

Wraith steps forward glaring at Prinie. "Show a little respect for your brother, princess. You might know him as Krew, but in public his name is Zero. Treat him with the admiration he deserves."

"How about you go fuck yourself, *Wraith.*" She mocks his name just to add insult to injury.

Wraith steps forward, disdain leeching off him. Prinie doesn't hold back lunging forward to meet his advances. She's not afraid of anyone in Houston, not even Wraith. I step in pushing them apart, exhaling dramatically. "Enough. Prinie, you and Koda are coming with us even if I have to drag y'all by your hair. You've been away from us for too damn long. I've let you have your tantrum, and you're obviously over your phobia of bikers if you're living with the Chicago boys, so now there's no excuse."

I shouldn't be so hard. My plan was to come at this softly, to make it her idea to come home, but she's pissing me off. If she thinks I won't drag her out of here, she has another thing coming.

Prinie sniffs, a steely determination in her eyes when she peers back at Koda. There's a desperation, a pleading in his. He wants to come home. She groans, throwing her hands up in the air. "Okay, fine! Dammit! Looks like we're moving back to Houston." Her tone is sarcastic. I don't even care as elation washes over me. I keep my face neutral, though, as Wraith grunts, turns, and storms off, kicking a dead Irishman as he goes.

The hell was that about?

"Thanks, Prinie," Koda murmurs as he finally walks over to me. I lift my fist. and he bangs it to mine in a fist bump. Man, it's good to do that again. I slowly feel the tide changing—the pieces of my puzzle sliding back into their rightful places. *My family is coming home.*

Prinie groans, turns, storming off toward the bar where the Mafia woman is fixing a drink already for my sister. My family might be coming home, but by no means is it going to be smooth sailing.

Torque glances at Prinie, then to me. "Little sisters, huh?"

I crack my neck to the side. "Yeah, thanks for keeping her safe here, man. Little heads up she was here would've been cool, though." Obviously, I knew she was here, Torque doesn't know, though. I need to keep the charade going.

"Had no fuckin' idea they were your family, brother. Otherwise, I would have been on the line."

I reach out wrapping my arm around my little brother, finally beginning to relax. "Yeah, true. Just glad to see them in one piece."

"Right, well, you've been on the road for a while, I know you have shit to do in town while you're here…" *ahh, yeah, I just did it,* "… but how about we get this place cleaned up, then you stay for a while and have a few brews to celebrate? Really wanna thank you for showing up when you did."

I turn to Wraith for confirmation who's standing out of the way but can hear us.

He dips his head. "Could do with a drink, pres." His eyes wash over Prinie while I narrow mine on him. Whatever their deal is, he needs to get the fuck over it. She's coming home. End of discussion.

Torque's still hunched over from his wound but manages to stand a little taller. "Right, drinks it is. But first, let's get rid of some dead Irishmen."

I can't wait to hear all about Chicago's war with the Irish.

A story I'm sure Torque will fill me in on over drinks.

Lots and lots of fucking drinks.

But for now, I need to go find Prinie. We have some shit we need to discuss.

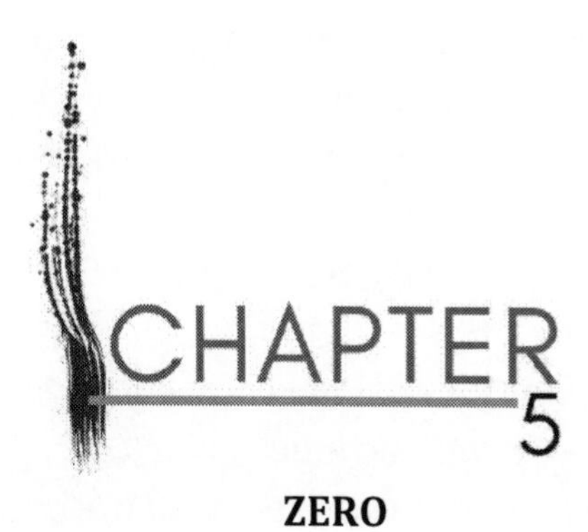

ZERO

One can only assume Prinie has escaped the commotion out here to hide in the room she's been staying in. While sitting out here bonding with my brothers from another chapter is important, mending my family exceeds that tenfold. *I need to find her.*

Glancing over the bar, a brunette club girl, gorgeous as anything, studies me. "You doing all right there, pres?" Her voice is sickly sweet. I'd do anything to hear what she sounds like while I fuck her against a wall—but I'm not here for her.

"What's your name?" I ask curtly.

She tenses a little but continues wiping down the bar. "Ruby, head club girl 'round these parts."

"Hmm, bet they love having you here, Ruby. But never mind that. My sister, Prinie… you know where she's at right now?"

She glances to the hall, throwing the rag over her shoulder. "She's been a good fit here, pres. I'm gonna be sad to see her go. I hope she'll be well taken care of back in Houston."

I raise my brow at her sass. This club girl has balls. Normally, they wouldn't dare talk to a brother this way, not to mention a damn president. *I like her.* "You're full of spirit, Ruby. Why hasn't a brother claimed you?"

Her eyes shift to the other side of the room, landing on a Chicago prospect. She exhales with a shrug. "A work in progress, pres."

"Prospect, hey? Can't claim you 'til he gets his patch." I chuckle. "That old chestnut, hey?"

She tilts her head, a slow, gorgeous smile crossing her plump lips. "Second door on the right. She and Koda were bunking in there. Don't tell her I told you. Girl code and all."

"Thanks, Ruby. As an older brother, I appreciate it."

"Just take good care of them."

"I will." Standing, I wink, turn, then head for the hall.

Second on the right.

My heart hammers furiously. I haven't been alone with Prinie for so damn long. Has she changed so much I won't recognize the woman she's become? Is she still my baby sister in there, or has living by the skin of their teeth, fighting for their survival, turned her harder? Turned her against me? There's only one way to find out.

Halting at the door, I reach for the handle but stop myself. *I need to do this right.* Rolling my shoulders, I take a deep breath, then knock. "Prinie? Prinie, you in there?"

"Fuck off, dude, I'm packing."

Clenching my eyes closed, I lean my head against the door. "Prinie, c'mon, we need to talk."

Her audible groan echoes through the door, then it's suddenly pulled back making me fall toward her. She jerks back as I steady myself. "Geez, get a grip. You been snortin' too much of Houston's product or something?"

I glance around making sure no one heard that bullshit. The coast is clear, so I step through the open doorway, then close it behind me. Prinie storms back toward one of the two beds in the small room. I grimace at the tiny space my siblings have been living in. At Houston they have their own rooms—each room is bigger than this one. Not that I'm ungrateful for Torque putting them up, it's just they deserve the best, and this sure as shit isn't it.

"Prinie, take a seat before you spout off something you'll regret." I gesture for her to sit on the edge of the bed.

She rolls her eyes but does so with an exaggerated flop. I move over to her. For a nineteen-year-old, she sure is acting like a brat.

"Look, I know what happened at home was mess—"

"Messy! *Messy?* Krew, Igor killed our parents in front of us. That's not messy, that's fucked up! How the hell can you stand to even be at that place anymore?"

I face her, grabbing her hands in mine. "Because, Prinie, for the one horrendous memory I have of our parents there at the club... every other memory I have of them is there, too. Every single inch of the clubhouse holds a memory of Mom and Dad. A great one. Like the time when you were ten, and I was trying to teach you how to ride a bike, but Dad didn't want it to be just any bike..."

"He painted it up like his Harley. Even added an exhaust pipe," she adds with a chuckle.

"You were so excited to be a part of the club, we couldn't get you off it for weeks. I had to ride with you for hours around the compound to make sure you wouldn't fall. Dad stood by the back door watching us the entire time. His eyes *never* left us."

She sniffles. "Or the time when it was your twelfth birthday, and Dad made all the brothers dress up as cowboys and Indians..." Prinie closes her eyes and reopens them. "We had shootouts all day long for your party with fake guns and cork bullets." She giggles. "Dad kept crawling on all fours with me on his back pretending to be a horse because I wanted to be an Indian who rode a damn horse."

I grip her hand tighter. "Or the time Mom stayed up all night with Koda because he was so sick, we were worried we'd have to take him to the emergency room. But she comforted him singing his favorite songs. We both got up in the middle of the night, snuggled in tight around her... the three of us being there to support Koda while he recovered from croup."

"Wow! We were so young, I'd almost forgotten about that."

"So, you see, there are so many memories at the clubhouse I want to remember. One horrific one doesn't define the club. Our parents live on in the Defiance clubhouse every single damn day. At *every* turn, everywhere I look, all around me I see another memory of them, Prinie. I don't see their deaths... I see their lives. I see *our* lives with them. *That's* what keeps me there."

"It makes sense... I just hope *I* can see that, too."

"When you're having trouble remembering, don't hold it in, Prinie. I'm your brother, you can come to me. I want you, me, and Koda to be able to talk about Mom and Dad."

Her dark shadowed eyes glisten as she gnaws on her bottom lip. "I miss them... so much it never stops hurting."

It really fucking hurts.

"I know." I reach up wiping a falling tear from her cheek with my thumb. "But we need to come together, get through this pain as a family. We can't do this apart. Not anymore."

"This change isn't good for Koda."

"All the more reason to get him settled back at home and enrolled in his old school. With his friends. Around good people."

She cocks her brow. "It's almost like you know what's been happening around here."

"What does that mean? What's been happening?"

"Koda kinda got involved with some street thugs. It didn't amount to anything. He got out in time—"

"Jesus, Prinie." I swipe my hand through my hair, standing from the bed. "All the more reason to get him far away from Chicago. He's too young to be involved in this kind of shit."

"It's why we're staying at Chicago Defiance. For their protection. But also because I knew Torque would take care of us."

I let out a long exhale. "Why Chicago, Prinie? It's so far from home."

"*Because* it's so far from home. From the Militia. From the memories. Once we started running north, I just kept going. I didn't plan to end up in Chicago, it's just where my wheels took us."

"Why did you settle here?"

She stands from the bed striding over to me. "That's actually something I want to talk to you about."

"Okay?"

"I started driving for Uber, to get some cash flow for me and Koda while we've been traveling."

"Right."

"Well, one night, I was working late and got an Uber job for a chick on some random street. I thought the location was weird, but at the time, I thought, hey… money's money, you know?"

"I'm not going to like where this leads, am I?"

"Just listen… anyway, I pulled up to the meeting place and see the lady hunched over in the curb, grabbing at her ribs. My alarm bells were ringing, but I got out to check if she was okay."

"She'd been beaten." I let out a grunt.

"Yeah, *real* fucking bad. She was dressed so damn posh like she came from money, so I assumed she was mugged. I saw her purse sitting next to her, picked it up and helped her into the car. She was quiet for a while, I asked if she needed the hospital. She was adamant she didn't, she wanted to go somewhere and sit for a while." I tense, my muscles burning with tightness. "That wasn't in my job description. I knew I would lose out on the night's rides if I helped her, but she needed me." *My caring sister is still in there.* "I took her to a park where we sat talking for ages."

"Under all your bravado and hardassery you're a good person, Prinie."

The corner of her lip slips up, just a fraction. "Rayne's married to a guy named Chuck. His family's from big money. So is hers. Together they're a power couple. So, he thinks this gives him the right to beat the fucking shit out of her when she doesn't do what's expected."

"Chuck sounds like a fuckhead."

"I call him Up-Chuck…" Prinie shrugs, "… not to his face, of course."

"So, what happened?"

"I took Rayne to the hospital. Two broken ribs. Concussion. Split lip. He did all this on a back street in Chicago. Imagine what he does in the privacy of their own home."

"Fucker," I mumble under my breath.

Prinie gnaws on her bottom lip. "I gave Rayne my number. Told her when she needed me again to call. She did a few days later, and I went straight to her. Took her to the hospital. It kind of became a ritual for us. Then, I started calling her. When I was feeling lost or sad, she would help me out of the black hole I was heading down. We were there for each other…" She sighs heavily. "I'm worried if I leave without saying goodbye—"

"She'll wonder what happened to you and do something stupid?"

Prinie grimaces. "Maybe not something stupid, but without me there to depend on, I worry who's going to take care of her?"

My mind swarms with uncertainty. Hearing about Rayne irks me. There's nothing I hate more than domestic violence. Striking or hurting a woman is *never* okay. I might be an asshole. I might be a murderer. I might traffic drugs and wear this 1% badge with pride, but the one thing I will *never* do, is hit a woman. "You wanna see her before we head off tomorrow?" I ask.

Prinie's eyes light up. "Can I? You don't mind?"

"No, you misunderstand me. You're not going on your own, princess. *I'm* coming with you."

Prinie's eyes widen. "Wait! What? No! You'll terrify her."

"I'm one of the good guys compared to Up-Chuck, Prinie. I want Rayne to know she's going to be fine. I'll make sure of it."

Prinie groans. "Oh, geez. What the hell are you gonna do?"

"Not sure yet. I'll figure it out tomorrow. For now, though, there's a party happening soon. Plus, you and Koda need to pack. Get ready, we leave in the morning."

Her eyes linger on me. She exhales, stepping up. "I'm sorry I took Koda and bailed. It must have been hard for you to let us go, but thank you for not coming after us until now. I needed this time, I needed it to heal. And although I'm not yet fully back to my old self, I'm definitely on the way."

My chest warms at her honesty. I never thought I'd hear her say that to me. "I've missed you, Kharlie."

She sniffles, her eyes glistening with unshed tears. Prinie's arms open, then loop around my neck. I wrap my arms around her tightly, the hug unexpected, but I will take every minute of it.

"I missed you, too, Krew. I missed you, too."

As I embrace my sister, her words ring in my ears. '*Thank you for not coming after us.*' I simply have to hope she never finds out I've done just that because the last thing I need is for Prinie to turn her back on her family again. I can't have her take Koda and leave again because if she did it a second time, it would be my fault for not telling her the real reason for us being here.

It's just a risk I'm going to have to take—for the sake of *my* family.

ZERO

The party's in full swing. Chicago sure knows how to turn it on. But hell, so does Houston when the time calls for it. Over the past year, we haven't felt the need to party. There's been nothing to celebrate. So, we're all letting our hair down, so to speak.

I'm sitting at a giant table with Wraith, Texas, and Kevlar from my side of town. Then Torque and his Old Lady, Foxy, Chains, Trax, and the prospect, Luc, from Chicago take up the rest of the seats at the table. Torque's medics patched up his wound, and although he probably shouldn't be drinking, he is. He's doing exactly what I would be after a win like they had. They're in celebration mode—when's a bullet ever stopped a biker from partying with his brothers?

"So, you're really not from Texas?" Trax, Chicago's VP, directs his question to Texas, my Sergeant-at-Arms.

The Houston guys chuckle, but Texas replies, "Nah, bruh, New Jersey-born and raised."

"Then why *that* road name?" Foxy narrows her eyes at Texas.

"You know what they say about Texas?" He smirks cheekily at Foxy.

The Chicago boys fall silent trying to figure out what the hell he's talking about while Houston all snicker.

"Oh, fuck... everything's *bigger* in Texas," Foxy mumbles as Torque rolls his eyes.

I let out a chuckle along with my brothers as Texas raises his drink, then takes a long sip.

"Of course, you know guys who normally brag about it means it's the complete opposite," Foxy mocks.

A loud belly laugh erupts from me as Texas chokes on his beer, coughing and spluttering.

I wink at Foxy.

I like her. Torque's done well for himself.

"You know, y'all should come down and have a cookout at the club. Old man Fox does the best Texas barbecue," I offer.

Chains lifts his head like he's unsure of whether to talk or not. "Zero, you got spare rooms at your clubhouse? For occasional visitors, I mean?"

Where is Chains going with this?

"Yeah, brother, we got plenty of space. The clubhouse's huge. If any of you wanna head on over anytime, y'all are welcome. Just let us know when and we can have rooms ready."

Chains rubs his chin, his focus on Torque then back on me. "What about kids... babies? Are your guys cool with kids?"

We all turn to Kevlar who lifts his chin in answer. "They're used to kids. I have one who comes by the clubhouse from my past marriage. Kids aren't an issue."

"Where's this coming from, Chains?" Torque asks his Sergeant-at-Arms.

Chains' eyes shift from me to Torque and he exhales. "Kobe's been offered an opportunity to have his last surgery at the Children's Hospital in Houston with a specialist doctor down there. So he'd need to be there for aftercare. The travel for us will be an issue. We'd need to be there for a while if we were to take up the offer."

Kobe is Chains' very young son. I knew he was sick, I just didn't realize it was surgery sick.

"Why didn't you come to me with this?" Torque questions Chains.

"Didn't think it was an option until now. Didn't want to leave the club."

"If you head to Houston you'll still be in Defiance, just a different chapter," I state.

Chains face softens slightly. "Exactly."

Torque rolls his shoulders. A sense of unease washes over his face. "Have you spoken to Chills about this?"

Chains cracks his neck to the side. "Not yet. I only just thought about it when we were talking. And I want to gauge where you all sat with the idea?"

I glance across at my brothers, they all shrug like they don't mind taking in new family. "We're fine with poaching a brother as long as Torque is down with it. I know y'all wouldn't just be losing your Sergeant-at-Arms, you'd be losing your doctor, too."

Chills is Chicago's head doctor. Foxy's in training, but Chills is their main go-to.

Torque's eyes shift to a civilian seated at another table, his eyes brighten in intensity. "Ben," Torque calls out.

His head pops up reminding me of a damn meerkat, then he stands and walks over. "Pres?"

"How'd you feel about being the club doctor? Being on call when we need you?"

Ben narrows his eyes looking right at Chains. "What about Bex?"

Chills' actual name is Rebecca, Bex for short. She was named Chills once Chains claimed her.

"We might be heading to Houston, but she doesn't know it yet," Chains replies.

Ben sits taller. "For Kobe's surgery? Oh, fuck! She's gonna go crazy. If it means Kobe gets his surgery by the best, then yes. I'll still have to work at the hospital, though. But I can work around it like Bex does. I'll chat with her about the best workarounds before you guys leave. I got this, and I'm in… I'm all-in, Torque. I wanted to stay on at the club, just didn't think it was a possibility. So… thanks."

All this bullshit talk is boring the hell out of me. Can we get on with it?

"Well then, brother..." Torque takes in a deep breath. "That settles it."

"It doesn't settle everything," the prospect, Luc, pipes up.

We all shoot our eyes to Luc. His face is long and worn. Luc turns to me, fear etched in his features. "I have no right to ask this, but Chains and I have been through so much. I'm a prospect. I'm owed nothing, I know. But if Chains is heading to Houston, would you consider taking me, too?"

Torque's shoulders sink a little, losing two of his men is a hit. I don't know how I feel about this. It's all kinds of wrong.

Ruby, the hot club girl from earlier, places some beers down for us all. She gasps, her eyes falling on Luc in horror. He sits taller puffing out his shoulders. "And Ruby, too."

Torque flares his nostrils with a grunt. "Luc, you can go, but Ruby stays."

Ruby's head snaps toward Torque as her eyes flood with tears.

The prospect really means something to her.

Ruby made an impression on me as well. Normally taking on another prospect wouldn't do me any damn favors, but seeing as Cannon's going to be patched in, we're going to be a prospect short anyway. So, why the hell not. If it means Ruby's coming with, then hell yeah, I'm all for it. I want her sassy ass at my clubhouse too.

Foxy's hand splays out over Torque's forearm. "Okay, a lot's happening right now, and it's a bunch to digest, Torque. We all know Luc has to go with Chains, that's a no-brainer." *There's obviously some sort of story there?* "Ruby and Luc are an item, they have been for a while, and we all know Luc doesn't have his patch so he can't claim Ruby. So, while technically she can't go with him as his property, him leaving without her, Torque... it's simply not right."

Torque rubs his chin focusing his attention on Ruby, the club girl who seems to be a hot commodity around these parts. Everyone can see her potential. "Zero, you okay taking on Chains, Chills, baby Kobe, Luc, and Ruby?" Torque asks.

I turn to my brothers who all drop their chins in approval. "Yeah, if they wanna come over... for a month, for a year, or for good, we're good with it. Don't want it to start any animosity between us, though."

"The only time it will start shit between us is if you treat any of them like fuckin' crap. If I hear word they're not being shown the respect they deserve—"

"Torque, the second they cross over, they're one of us. We treat our members like nothing but the family they deserve." *I mean every damn word.*

Torque rolls his shoulders. "Okay. As long as Chills agrees, we'll get the transfer paperwork underway so you guys can get settled before Kobe's operation." Torque lifts his glass clinking it with Chains'. "It's been an honor, brother."

Chains dips his head. "A fucking privilege, pres."

This might be the start of something. A new bond, forging a stronger relationship between Chicago and Houston. The two clubs combining together. I see this as a good thing.

My eyes meet Ruby's, her joy is weak, but it's there. I can only imagine leaving her home is going to be hard on her, but she's leaving with the man she loves. We won't make life for her in Houston hard. She has nothing to worry herself with. I want her to feel as at home in Houston as she does here. Chicago runs smoothly because of Ruby. With her at the helm of Houston, things will only go upward, even if it might ruffle a few of the club girls' feathers.

Houston is evolving with new blood—it means change, it means growth. Maybe we can all move forward. A baby will be living in the clubhouse permanently. That, in itself, is something we will all need to get used to. Sure, when Kevlar's kids first started coming to the club, we got used to the noise, now only his daughter, Sadie, visits. His son, Lucas, doesn't drop by often, hardly at all.

His Uncle Ethan, who's a policeman, doesn't bring him. Says he doesn't want the club to influence his upbringing. I get it. With what happened to the kids' mother, they don't need negative shit in their lives. The club doesn't exactly exude positivity for the upstanding lieutenant.

Plus, Ethan's still jaded his brother, Kevlar, left the force for the club. Ethan and his wife may take care of Sadie and Lucas while Kevlar's at the club, but it doesn't make them the kids' parents. Kevlar loves them both. Maybe having Kobe at the club will give Kevlar the edge he needs to fight a little harder to bring Lucas back into the club fold.

It's not my fight, but I fucking hate seeing one of my brothers torn up about shit like this. If bringing in another family can help one we already have, then hell, I'm all for it. Even though the sound of a screaming baby will probably do my fucking head in.

But for now, I'm going to drink, spend what little time I have left in Chicago partying with my brothers, and get my ass drunk.

It's time to really get this party started.

"Ruby, grab me another beer, will ya?"

Her lips turn up, showing me her perfect, dazzling white teeth. The woman seems so genuinely sweet it sends a rush of warmth right through me.

"Sure thing, pres."

My head throbs like a motherfucking bitch. I definitely drank too much last night. My neck hurts like hell as I turn it hearing the unmistakable rustling of beanbag pebbles jostling. I groan as I open my eyes. Snoring echoes through the clubhouse, and it vibrates against the metal walls sending a damn agony through my brain. I blink a few times trying to get shit under control. Sitting up, the pebbles shift beneath me which only makes me sink lower. One boot is missing from my foot—it's under the pool table in front of me. *How the fuck did it get there?*

I rub the back of my neck as I let out a yawn, trying to sit forward on the bean bag which is a damn impossibility. When I look down, a bra falls from my lap. I raise my brow, glancing around, but no one's near me apart from Texas sprawled out on the concrete, face down, snoring his head off.

Fucking hell, is he wearing bunny ears?

I rub my face as I fling the fluorescent pink bra off me, then reach for my boot. I yank it on, then somehow—with much fucking difficulty—I stand from the children's beanbag. My muscles ache in ways I haven't felt for years. After riding for so long yesterday, then sleeping in a beanbag, I swear I'm getting too old for this shit, and I am not even fucking old.

My eyes shift around the clubroom.

Torque's sitting at the bar with Ruby as they chat casually. My happiness radiates through me as I walk on over to her.

"Mornin'," I mumble, my voice is raspy and thick. My happiness fades. *Did I sing fucking karaoke?*

"Morning, pres. You let your hair down last night." Torque smirks, then sips on a steaming hot mug of coffee.

My eyes linger on the mug, probably longer than necessary.

"You want a cup?" Ruby asks, already picking up a black mug from under the bar and begins to pour.

"I think I'm gonna like having you around, Ruby."

"I've gotten good at reading the brothers. The way you were ogling Torque's mug like you wanted to fuck it, yeah, I get it… you need coffee. Stat."

I burst out laughing. "Beautiful, sassy, and funny. No wonder the prospect snapped you up."

"Nice singing voice, Zero. Your rendition of 'Want a Whole Lotta Love' was… something else." Torque raises his eyebrow.

I grimace. "There was karaoke, wasn't there?"

Torque slaps my back as Ruby slides over the mug. "On a side note, you and Prinie seem to be doing okay. Do you remember singing with her?"

My head snaps toward Torque. "I did?"

He pulls out his cell, pressing play. It shows me with my arm around Prinie and Koda, standing watching as I sing with my sister. Prinie's obviously drunk off her damn face—the fact she's underage doesn't slip past me, but I let it go because we were bonding.

I just can't remember the bonding part.

The chorus to 'Lean on Me' by Bill Withers blasts out of both of our mouths as we sway to and fro, holding onto each other tightly. Koda's observing us with the brightest smile. A sense of calm washes over me even though the singing is fucking terrible. Prinie and I announced that we're here for each other. No matter what. I just hope she can remember the conversation and isn't too hungover like I am this morning.

"Can you send this to me?" I ask.

Torque fiddles with his cell, then a few moments later, mine buzzes. "It was messy, but you guys made a breakthrough last night. Whether Prinie remembers today… I don't know. But now you have the evidence to back it up." Torque laughs.

I tilt my head. "That's why you recorded us? Not to mock me, but so I had a memory of the moment."

"Always a step ahead, our Torque," Ruby offers filling his empty coffee mug.

"You're new at this, Zero," Torque exhales. "You're still finding your feet. Thing is, I've learned the only way is to stay ahead of the game. Always think two steps ahead of the play. If you see a situation unfolding, think of all the possible outcomes and plan ahead for all of them. Make contingencies…" He taps me on the shoulder. "Fuck, brother, it's damn hard work. There's a lot of sneaking around, but it's the only way to keep ahead of everyone else."

I appreciate his input more than he realizes. "Thanks, brother. Y'all's support means a lot to me."

"You ever need to run a play by me, pick up the line."

"I'll be taking you up on that."

A giant yawning sound echoes behind me. I turn seeing Prinie walk out, stretching her arms wide as she enters the clubroom.

"Morning, brat… your head hurting as much as mine?" I call her the nickname I used to tease her with when we were kids.

"Probably more, ogre…" she mumbles back her nickname for me. I got to say it gives me all the feels. She may not realize it, but I'm glad she remembers.

"Coffee?" Ruby asks.

Prinie nods emphatically. "What time are we leaving today?"

"I'm thinking breakfast, gather your stuff, then hightail it over to Rayne's before coming back to get the guys. Thoughts?"

"Yeah, perfect. Breakfast, then I will say goodbye to a dear friend."

"I know you're reluctant to leave her behind. I spoke to Torque a little about Rayne last night."

"We're gonna keep an eye out. Zero's gonna talk to her about it when you head over there," Torque states.

"Okay, yeah. That'll be great. If you could have Foxy check on her once in a while that would make me happy. Make sure she's not too badly injured from.... well, you know."

"Of course."

The thought of leaving this Rayne woman here to fend for herself is eating the fuck at me. But if I know Torque like I think I do, then he's going to do everything in his power to watch out for Rayne. I just need to get Prinie over there to say her goodbyes, then we'll be on our way back to Houston.

Back home.

Back to being a real family.

RAYNE

"Clean up this fucking mess!"

The slam of the door makes my aching body jolt. I'm trembling as I cower on the floor with blood pooling from my nose. My eye's swelling, and as I blink it, the pain radiates through to my brain. I try my hardest to stop it from watering.

I will not cry.

I won't give him my tears.

Chuck's car engine roars to life which helps to wash a calmness over me. I will finally be able to relax knowing he'll be gone for the next twelve hours of his shift. During this absence, I'll have time to recover. I should call Prinie, but I know I shouldn't put so much on her. She's been a godsend—I don't know what I'd do without her. I don't know how I did all this before she miraculously entered my life.

I peer at my shaking hands—they're bloodied and cut. The shattered glass from the coffee table Chuck threw me into is splintered all around me.

Was the asshole hoping the glass would stab me?

Or did he know it would shatter and cut me everywhere like it has?

Either way, he's got me good this time. Plus, the couple of punches he managed to land into my head before I so graciously landed on the table doesn't help with the pain I'm feeling.

Now I have the task of cleaning up the living room before Chuck gets home. At least I have hours before that happens. I know I can't do this job quickly. I'm going to have to pace myself, a few things at a time, breaking it up so the pain doesn't make me pass out. Chuck's long shift gives me time to recoup before the next beating comes. No matter how sparkling I make this living room, it won't be good enough for the bastard.

My bottom lip trembles, but I sit taller, blinking a few times.

I will not cry.

Taking a deep centering breath, I move to stand when the low hum of an engine rattling pulls into my drive. My heart leaps with fright. *He can't be back already.* Fuck, I haven't even had time to stand, let alone clean. He's going to fucking kill me.

Panic washes over me like a torrential downpour. With each wave of terror, the pressure builds and hits me feeling as bad a Chuck's fists. I frantically try to get up from the floor, my bare feet crunching on the broken glass. Pain shoots through the soles of my feet as I yelp out in agony from the shards of glass that are now embedded in the skin.

I will not cry.

I stumble, staggering, leaving bloodstains on the pristine cream carpet which I will have to clean.

Shit, that's only going to make him worse.

I move toward the door to greet him, my feet hurting like a bitch. I have to pull the glass out, but first I need to apologize for not cleaning quicker.

Of course, I'm not sorry, not at all.

But if I don't, the asshole will rain chaos down on me again, and I don't know how much more of this I can take.

I didn't even cause the damn argument. Hell, it's not my fault the postman delivered the neighbor's letters to us. Because the postman got it wrong, I got the mother of all beatings. Chuck assumed the postman did it as an excuse to see me, but to be honest, if it wasn't that, Chuck would have found some other stupid reason.

He always does.

I'm so used to my daily beatings, I can't tell where my old bruises have faded and my new ones begin.

Dread flows through me as I stumble to the door hearing the engine shut off, but I try so hard to put a smile on my face to greet him.

Footsteps.

Multiple footsteps.

Maybe Chuck's hired people to take me out?

Calm washes over me.

If it gets me away from this hell, I welcome death with open arms.

Grabbing the handle, I yank the door open with the little energy I have. My hand slips off the knob from the blood. As I open the door with a smile, always with a smile, a tall man steps onto the porch. His dusky blond hair is pulled back into a man bun. A beard lines his gorgeous face, but his eyes, his ice-blue eyes are so haunted as they take me in.

I don't miss the biker's cut he's wearing.

Or the black and gray tattoos covering his body.

Even all the way up his neck.

He's definitely here to kill me.

I stand taller, even though my bloodied feet are screaming at me. "At least the last thing I see will be good to look at."

The sexy-as-sin biker narrows his eyes at me. "What the fuck happened to you, Rayne?"

He knows my name? How?

Chuck wouldn't give specifics. But the way this guy said my name—shit, his voice is drool-worthy. But then again, maybe I'm concussed and have no idea who's standing in front of me right now.

"I'm sure you don't need details. My feet are killing me, so can we just go inside and get this over with."

The biker hesitates like he's unsure of himself. "Did Prinie call ahead?"

My ears pick up. "Prinie?"

Shit! Maybe this is one of her guys from the Chicago Clubhouse. I should have been paying more attention to who they are. But if he's been sent here to kill me, then maybe Chuck had him deal with Prinie first. "What did you do to Prinie? I swear if you hurt her, I will—"

"Calm down, cherry bomb. I don't think you're in the position to be making threats. Prinie's fine. I'd never hurt her. She's standing back. Told her to wait at the van 'til I saw what was happening, and if Up-Chuck was here."

Up-Chuck? That's what Prinie calls him.

Maybe she *is* okay.

"Wait… who are you?" I ask.

His lips slowly turn up. That look spreads warmth through me like a summer's day. I haven't seen a smile in so long, not from Chuck and certainly not from my own reflection. It's nice to see, especially one as glorious as his.

"I'm Prinie's older brother, Zero. Prinie wants to say goodbye. She's heading back to Houston."

My eyes widen as anxiety damn near cripples me. I stumble on the spot taking a step back. He reaches out holding my arm to steady me. A sudden blast of electricity shoots up my arm like a wave of energy. *Well, that's what it feels like, but maybe it's just pain from my asshole husband pushing me into the table.* But then both our eyes lock onto each other, and my breath catches in my throat. *Again, it's probably from when Chuck choked me.* My heart rapid fires like a drumline, so hard my chest hurts. My entire body's tingling, electro-charged by his touch. *These feelings defy explanation.*

His breathing is short and sharp like he's affected by the moment as well. I'm under the impression he's feeling everything I am, and it has *nothing* to do with Chuck. I've never felt anything like this before.

Certainly not with my bastard of a husband.

Not with anyone.

"Rayne…" His soothing voice brings me back into the now as his ice-blue eyes stare into mine sending an arctic wave shuddering through me. I don't know anything about Zero, all I know is right in this second, in this very moment, he has the power to destroy me and everything I've built here.

I slowly pull back from him, my body warming again as my arm leaves his touch. "Y-You're n-not here to k-kill me?"

He lets out a small laugh. "No. Like I said, Prinie's come to say goodbye."

"You can't take Prinie. I... I... need her."

His brows draw together as his eyes linger over my beaten body. Zero takes in every bruise, every cut, every drop of blood. "Chuck do this shit?"

I exhale, turn, and limp back into the living room. My body jolting with the painful movements. "It doesn't matter."

"It does matter!" his voice booms, making me clench my eyes shut while waiting for a slap that never comes.

I snap my head around, glaring at him. "Nothing can be done about it, is what I mean."

Zero scoffs. "You haven't met the right people then, have you, cherry bomb?"

"Ha! So, what? You're gonna take me on as your pet project? Take out the big bad cop?"

He stills. "Chuck's a cop?"

"Prinie didn't tell you?"

He rolls his shoulders. "Conveniently forgot." His eyes narrow on me. "You're looking a little pale, I think you should sit down."

"Oh, so now you care? Whatever! Can you get Prinie in here?"

"Sit the fuck down. I'll get Prinie."

"We're compromising now?"

"Sit. Down." His tone is strong, harsh but sexy as fuck and for some reason, I'm not afraid of him.

I do as he demands, sitting on the edge of the sofa, the relief hits my feet instantly. I let out an audible moan sinking into the plush cushions as I bend over and pull out a few of the pieces of glass I can see.

"Now, stay there."

"Like a good little dog," I murmur under my breath.

Zero glares at me, and I sink into myself a little.

He wasn't meant to hear that.

Spinning on his heels, his heavy boots thump as he exits. As he leaves, it's like all the air is sucked from the room. I take a second to decompress. The man's sexy as hell. I can't even comprehend he's Prinie's older brother.

How the hell is he not here to kill me?

More importantly, how on earth am I going to cope with Prinie leaving?

She's the only good thing I have in my life right now. Sure, I have work, but everyone knows I'm only working there because it's my dad's store. I want to own my own pharmacy. I want to do things my way. I want to live the life I want, not trapped in a loveless, violent marriage forever because our parents think it's what's best. I can hear my father's voice, 'After all, it's mutually beneficial for our families.'

Closing my eyes, I rest. I need it. I know it.

Any second, Prinie's going to run in, taking over the situation like she always does. But right now, I just need a second to try and relax.

From Chuck.

From the intense moment with Zero.

From life.

"Rayne? Fucking hell, he did it again?" Prinie's shrill voice rings from the doorway.

My sore eyes shoot open even though it's hard. Her grungy appearance runs toward me as I relax back into the sofa.

My saving grace.

"You're really surprised?" I mock as she takes in the broken table, me in my nightgown, bare feet, and bloodstained body.

"He got you good this time, hon." Prinie's tone is somber. She moves onto the sofa beside me pulling my hands up, taking a look at my bloodied palms. "How much glass is in them?"

I shrug taking in Zero from the corner of my eye.

He's standing back observing us, his strong arms folded over his broad chest. "How often does Up-Chuck do this, Rayne?" Zero's voice is gruff and has a take-no-prisoners air to it.

While Prinie fusses about in her handbag, I glimpse over at him.

"When doesn't he do this is more the answer these days."

A low growl rumbles from his chest all the way up as he turns away from me pacing the hall.

I grimace facing Prinie as she pulls some tweezers from her bag.

"Let me know if this hurts, okay?"

"You're good. I've felt worse… much, much worse."

A loud bang blasts from behind us making me jump. I turn as Zero's pulling his fist from the drywall, where he's left a gaping hole by the front door.

My eyes widen as I let out a gasp.

Chuck's going to go to town on my face for that hole in the wall.

Thanks, biker, you've just landed me a night in the hospital.

Zero storms back inside the living room with his nostrils flaring, the vein in his neck pulses so much I'm worried it might burst. His face turns redder by the second. "Why have you let him get away with this, Rayne?" His booming voice is so loud, it's a wonder the pictures on the wall don't shake with the vibration.

I don't react.

Prinie doesn't react.

We both know he's right, but it's not as simple as that. I peep at Prinie as she continues to take the shards of glass from my palms. I wince but keep my eyes on the short-tempered Zero. "You think if I could leave, I wouldn't?" I let out a small laugh. "I'd be gone in a heartbeat, but it's not that easy, Zero."

"Like fuck, it isn't. Pack your damn bags and leave the asshole."

This is what angers me about these kinds of situations. People are so quick to judge me and the situation.

"You don't know, Chuck. He's a cop, remember? He'll find me. His family is from big-time money. They will pay people to hunt me the fuck down. If I leave, his anger will be so intense, the next beating…" I shake my head, "… well, I won't wake up from it. I'm sure."

Zero turns, running his hands over his gorgeous threads of hair in frustration. He lets out a huff as he begins to pace. "No! This is bullshit. You're not staying here."

Prinie's eyes widen taking in what her brother's saying. Though,

I'm not entirely sure what he's telling me.

"I have nowhere else to go."

"Yes, you do," Prinie answers, her eyes focused on her brother.

I turn back to Zero.

He narrows his eyes on me. "You're coming with us. No arguments."

"Wait… what? Where?" My eyes widen.

"To Houston. It's far enough away that by the time he figures out where you are, we'll be prepared for him."

I hold my hands up. "Whoa, whoa, whoa… I can't ask you guys to risk your lives for me."

"You're not asking, I'm telling. Now pack a bag. Bring only essentials. We might be able to come back for more at another time but consider this a goodbye to your home. Bring only what you can. Take what you hold dear. What you need. Keep it light, cherry bomb. We only have so much room in the van."

"This a joke?" I scoff.

He looks at me deadpan. "This is about as serious as it gets. Now, c'mon, we don't have much time. I need to get you back to Chicago Defiance so I can have Chills look you over. Make sure you're okay to travel today."

"Chills?" I murmur. My head's spinning with all this information and the thought of finally leaving my nightmare on repeat.

"She's our club doctor. Prinie, help her pack. I gotta make a call."

Prinie wraps her arm around me. "Yeah… sure, of course, I will."

Zero's eyes lock on me again, and for a brief moment, emotion of some kind envelops his features. I can't tell which. Then as quickly as it comes, it's gone, and he spins, hightailing it for the door.

Prinie pulls me to her, her hand sliding over my hair in a comforting gesture. "Hey, I know this is a lot to take in, but my brother, he and the Houston guys will do everything to protect you. I've seen that look from Zero before. He's taking you under his protection. Zero will do everything to guard you from Up-Chuck. Don't worry."

I glance at her. I love Prinie so much. She's been such great support to me over this past eight months. I can't believe she and her family are providing me a way out. I just hope when, and I honestly mean *when* Chuck finds me, it isn't the downfall of them all.

"It isn't me I'm worried about," I reply.

ZERO

Storming outside, my emotions are all over the fucking place. Seeing Rayne in her salmon-colored silk nightgown, the way it clings to her body, showing me the perfect curves of her hips. She's sexy as fuck even with all the bruises and blood.

I'm a twisted fuck.

I need to calm my shit down, especially with the semi-hard state my cock is fighting. My hot head has to cool down. Why does this woman have such an effect on me? I need to rein this shit in.

For one—she's damaged.

And two—she's Prinie's friend.

But most of all three—she's married to a damn cop!

That shit complicates things.

My attraction to her is something I cannot act on.

No way.

No how.

Storming over to the van, I sit in the open doorway, yanking out my cell. I dial Wraith trying to get my head back in the game.

Focus, Zero, focus.

"Yeah?" Wraith answers with his usual greeting.

"Well, hello to you, too," I mock.

"I'm in the middle of something with Lexi, so if you don't have shit that's important to tell me, you can fuck right off."

Rolling my shoulders, I envy Wraith, he's about to get his dick wet.

When I look at Rayne, I want to pin her against a wall and fuck her until she screams my name. I'd give anything to be doing that right now, rather than talking to my fucking VP, but here we are–me still battling with my semi and Wraith about to deal with his.

"Look… need you to do something for me before you and Lexi get down to business."

He groans. "She's practically sucking my cock, so this better be good."

"Can you find Chills and tell her to get ready for her first Houston incoming?"

Shuffling echoes down the line, then he exhales. "Everyone okay?" His tone's more serious now.

"I have a beaten woman with me. Fragments of glass in her body. She's pretty bad—"

"What the fuck did you do, Zero?"

"You honestly think I would do anything like that? You know me better, brother." Anger flares inside of me.

Wraith exhales clearing his throat. "Yeah… I do know you better than that. I'll go find Chills. See you when you get in."

"Thanks, brother. Sorry about Lexi, I know she sucks like a hoover."

"Yeah, fucker… you damn well owe me." He ends the call as I roll my eyes.

I place my cell in my pocket, then run my hands over my face, scrubbing it to relieve some of the tension. I don't know this Rayne from a bar of soap. I don't know her story, other than the obvious. All I do know is there's a spark about her which ignites something inside of me. Something that's been dead for years. Something that maybe wasn't even there to begin with. Maybe it's the protector in me, my savior complex kicking in.

How she's put up with Up-Chuck for so long, I'll never understand. Well, no more. I won't stand for this shit. If having to put my attraction for her aside, so I can protect her is what's needed, then that's what I'm gonna do.

I head back inside, my stomach twisting at the thought of seeing those bruises lining her skin again. But the rest of her makes up for those blemishes on her flawless body. As I walk into the chaos of her living room, my heart leaps into my throat.

Prinie and Rayne are nowhere to be seen.

I spin on my heels, racing down the hall to go in search of my sister and her friend. I didn't see anyone come in while I was out the front, but the back door is always a possibility. "Prinie, where the fuck are you?" I yell not caring about my tone.

Prinie groans audibly from down the hall, and I follow the sound. "In the bedroom, you overprotective asshole."

I let out a relieved exhale. Her groan was one of frustration, not because they're being held captive by Up-Chuck. *Thank fuck.* I let out a grumble and storm down the hall, slamming open each door, peering inside until I find them. I can't help but take in the expensive, upscale appearance of Rayne's home. She's obviously dripping in coin.

With force, I yank the last door open. Rayne and Prinie both turn dramatically, eyes narrowed and the sight almost knocks me over. I'm lucky I'm holding onto the doorframe, otherwise I'm sure I would have fallen to my knees.

Rayne has changed into a slim-fit yellow dress. Damn! She looks sexy as sin, even in the state she's in. A suitcase sits on top of her bed as she stares at me. My eyes linger up and down her long, toned legs. Her eyes wander along the length of my body at the same time. I know that expression—she's attracted to me as well.

Shit, this is going to be harder than I thought.

Prinie's eyes dance from Rayne to me and back to Rayne. "We should get this packed quickly, Rayne. Don't want anyone knowing what we're doing before we can get out of here."

"Prinie's right. We need to leave as fast as we can."

Rayne continues to pack. I walk into the room checking it out. It's not very feminine in here. You'd think after being married, she'd have some personal touches which are hers, but everything is masculine. Up-Chuck controls everything, even the bedroom décor.

Damn dickhead.

I watch Rayne and Prinie work together packing essentials as I stand out of the way. Their relationship is effortless. I'm glad my sister's found friendship in someone while she was here. It's good to know she wasn't completely on her own.

I left her to fend for herself for too long, and I have to deal with that guilt for as long as I live.

Letting Prinie and Koda live their lives as they wanted was okay for a couple of months, but I let it go on for way too long. Though, I guess, if we didn't come down here at this specific moment in time, Torque and Chicago would have been in a world of hurt. So maybe it was for the best. All I know is, I'm getting my family back, plus some extra tagalongs.

Rayne finishes packing her bag and takes a long look around her room. "I hope I never have to come back."

I dip my chin, then swipe my hand to lead the way out. "Well, then, cherry bomb... let's get you the hell outta here."

"With pleasure." She starts walking, but she's limping. The glass in her feet making it harder for her to walk. Her face grimaces with the pain rocking through her.

The protector in me shudders at watching her jerk with every step. Letting out a groan, I storm toward Rayne. "Prinie, grab her bag."

Prinie takes it from Rayne swiftly as I swoop in and scoop Rayne up in my arms. She doesn't squeal, she doesn't fight, she simply loops her arms around my neck, her fingers threading into the loose tendrils of hair. Her eyes meet with mine—they're soft, warm, inviting. It's like she's thanking me without saying anything at all.

I start moving toward the exit. My chest heats so fucking much it's like I'm on fire. I don't know what the hell's happening right now, but having Rayne in my arms, knowing while I'm holding her, and no fucking person in the world can touch her, it has my body flaming in adrenaline.

This woman is bad news.

Real bad fucking news.

Her eyes linger on me as I walk with her from the bedroom, down the hall, and outside to the waiting van. Having her right up against me like this is not doing my cock any favors. She smells like peaches and fucking sunsets.

How the fuck can someone smell like a sunset? It's like I'm going out of my damn mind right now.

She's invading my senses as I help her inside the van, placing her in the rear seat.

"I don't understand why you're helping me?" Her eyes lock onto mine.

My protector mode rears its head yet again as I lean over her grabbing at the seat belt to pull over her. Our faces come in line with each other.

Rayne scrunches up her face, reaching for the seat belt. "I can put on my own seat belt."

I jerk my head back as she removes it from my grip while trying to gain control of the situation. I pull it back from her and click it into position. "I'm sure you can, but I need to ensure you're taken care of. Can't get you out of this situation and have you injured on the way into the club because you're not buckled in properly."

Her eyes widen. "There are so many things wrong with what you just said. One, you think I'm incapable of something as simple as doing up a seat belt. And two, you believe your driving is so bad I'm going to be injured on the way to wherever it is you're taking me?"

"That's not what I meant—"

"Then you need to think about how you word shit, 'cause you're coming across as an arrogant ass."

I glare at her smug, insolent, beautiful face. "You have an attitude problem, cherry bomb."

She snorts. "And you think you can control me because I get beaten up by my husband? He might walk all over me, but you…" she tilts her head smugly, "… not so much."

Hmm. She has a feisty side.

I lean in closer. Her eyes widen, and her breathing hitches. *She's affected.* "I like your fighting spirit, Rayne. You *are* a wild one."

She leans in closer, we're only an inch apart, the smell of peach surrounds me. It takes every ounce of strength I have not to rush forward pressing my lips to hers. My eyes stare into her incandescent emerald green eyes, they're so alive, so alight with fire. She has so much fight in her. As she licks her bottom lip, my cock twitches when she whispers, "You ain't seen nothing yet."

A low hum vibrates from my chest as I exhale, backing away from Rayne slowly.

She's trouble with a capital 'I'm screwed.'

I slowly exit the van, slamming the back door shut.

Prinie's standing, arms folded across her chest glaring at me like she isn't amused by what she's just witnessed.

"Get in the van, princess."

She huffs dramatically dropping her arms to her sides as she jumps in the front passenger side, and I storm to the driver's side. Rayne's a fighter. She has a way about her. What I don't understand is why doesn't she fight against Up-Chuck? I slide into the van starting the ignition.

Maybe Rayne *does* fight back. Maybe that's why he hurts her so viciously because of that sassy mouth of hers. *That sassy mouth I'd like wrapped around my cock.*

Fuck, she's married—to a cop.

I need to remember that.

My eyes shift to the rearview mirror.

Rayne's watching her home as I pull away. Sternness falls over her eyes. There are no tears, no grief, just a hard demeanor. She's not going to take off in the middle of the night and find her way back here in a loveless marriage to a guy who manhandles her, so I know I have done the right thing.

Rayne is done—and with it, Chuck's possession of her.

This is my time.

Stop it, Zero.

She is *not* yours.

She can't be.

"Keep your damn hands to yourself," Prinie whispers, leaning across to hide her tone from Rayne.

I shrug, turning my eyes back on the road ahead. "I don't know what the fuck you're talking about."

Prinie snorts, folding her arms across her chest in defiance. "Like fuck you don't, asshole."

I chuckle, continuing to drive, ignoring my bratty sister.

How the hell am I going to keep my hands to myself?

All I know is I'm damn well going to try.

The rest of the drive back to the clubhouse has been rife with tension. Prinie glares at me every time my eyes shift to the rearview, while Rayne's effectively ignoring everyone. It's tense. So, when we pull up to the gates of the Chicago Defiance clubhouse, it fills me with fucking relief.

Getting Rayne out of this van and into a place that's safe is definitely what's needed.

Gatekeeper pulls open the giant gate, and I drive in without hesitation. My eyes want to lift to the mirror, but instead, they focus on Chills, Wraith, and Torque who are outside in the compound waiting for us.

Prinie turns around in her seat to face Rayne. "Don't worry, they're all good people. No one will hurt you here."

Rayne scoffs. "I'm not scared of being hurt. There's nothing they could do to me that hasn't already been done, other than kill me. Hell, I've even been close to that a couple times, too."

Grunting, I jump out of the van and slide open the door to help her out. I pull her into my arms again to stop her from walking on her cut feet.

A crinkle appears on Wraith's forehead as he watches the scene unfold in front of him. "I thought you went to say goodbye, not bring her back looking like a run-over raccoon."

"Shut it, Wraith," I warn.

Chills and Torque step over to us, their brows both pulled in tight on their faces as they assess the situation.

"Rayne, welcome to Chicago Defiance. I'm Torque, this here is Chills. You okay for her to check you over?"

Rayne nods, but for some reason, she clings tighter to me. "I'll take her wherever you need her, Chills. She's got glass in her feet. Can't walk."

"Okay. Come inside, we'll fix you up."

"Thanks. Thank you all for helping me," Rayne offers, her tone different from the sass she was showing me earlier.

I glance at Prinie, then at Rayne's luggage. Prinie huffs, grabbing it as I walk off with Rayne in my arms following Chills inside the clubhouse.

"So, Rayne, I know this has happened before. Have you sustained any permanent injuries from previous—" Chills stops her line of questioning as she continues walking.

We enter the clubhouse, and all eyes fall to us—brothers, old ladies, club girls—all watching as I carry Rayne through.

She tenses in my arms. I doubt she likes the attention as she hesitates to answer. We reach the hall, and her body relaxes when the weight of the staring eyes is off us again, and it's then she finds her voice. "Sorry, umm… I don't think so. I have a crooked left pinky finger from when Chuck snapped it. It's never fully healed back in the right position, but I'm always bruised and broken somewhere, so honestly, I'm not sure."

Chills hums under her breath. "Well, I'm glad you're out of there. The body can only handle so much." She points. "In here, Zero." Chills leads me through to a bedroom with a giant bed and a baby's crib in the corner.

It must be their bedroom. There are boxes stacked with shelves now empty. Chains and Chills have obviously started packing for their impending move.

"Place Rayne on the bed, I'll grab my kit."

I walk Rayne over, her eyes shifting up to gaze at me. "Thank you for taking care of me. I'm sorry about in the van. I just—"

"Want to be in control again?"

She nods as I softly lower her down. As I place her on the mattress, our faces inch closer together. Her breath on my face hits me like a warm breeze, sending a tingle straight to my cock. My eyes lock with hers. Even with the swollen eye, she's stunningly gorgeous. I'm held captive in her gaze, my heart rapid firing, my breathing quickening as the room spins around me. We stare at each other, held captive by our gaze. Rayne's pulling me in like a moth to a flame. She's burning bright, so fucking luminescent, her glow is scorching my senses, but it's like I can't avert my eyes. I know she's going to burn me. She's going to set me on fire turning me to ash, yet, I can't look away.

What the fuck?

"I might have to do some sutures depending on how deep those lacerations are," Chills calls out walking back in.

I'm shocked away from Rayne's eyes. She blinks a few times as I stand up straight, taking a step back to put some much-needed distance between us. Chills is oblivious that she's just walked in on something, some kind of fucking moment.

I'm glad she did.

I try to gain control of my breathing again.

Rayne looks away from me to Chills who grabs the desk chair, wheels it over and sits in front of her. "Feet up, Rayne," Chills instructs. Rayne complies, lifting one of her gorgeous legs onto Chills' lap. Chills pulls out some tweezers while shaking her head. "Damn, girl, you did a good job."

A low rumble escapes my throat. I didn't even know it was going to.

Rayne and Chills both turn their eyes up at me in question. Fuck! I need to pull my shit together. I'm working myself up. I hardly know Rayne, yet every time I hear about her injuries or the pain she's suffering, it's like my inner protector wants to go on a murderous fucking rampage.

I need to leave.

"I have to go make sure everyone's ready to move out. You gonna be okay in here?"

"I got this, pres. I'll take good care of her."

"Make sure you do."

"Zero?" Rayne's sickly-sweet voice calls out as I walk to the door.

I clench my eyes, take a deep breath in, then turn back to her. "Yeah?"

"Thank you."

I let out another grumble as I turn back toward the door. She shouldn't be thanking me. I'm not sure if me taking her into my protection is going to be better or worse for her. All I know is she has some kind of profound damn effect on me. I need to rein myself in around her, which means I need to limit our contact. Because getting involved with a married woman is not something I'm up for, especially when the husband's a cop. Yeah, that shit's fucked and doesn't sit well with me. As it is, if he finds out I took her, he's probably going to come after the club.

I need to make sure we're squeaky clean while she's with us—everything we do is untraceable.

Rayne is a problem, a sexy, feisty, broken problem. She could be the downfall of not only me, but my club. So, I need to keep a close eye on everything that happens around her.

I step out into the clubroom where Wraith is waiting for me with Torque. I march up to them, unease flowing through me like never before. Rayne uneases me at the same time she ignites something inside of me. I can't explain it, nor do I like it.

Wraith throws his hands to the side. "So? What the fuck do you call this, then?"

I rub the back of my neck. "Just get off your high fucking horse for two damn seconds… I had no choice."

"Well, whoever the fuck beat the shit out of her will probably come looking. Am I right?"

"Yeah, that's why she's coming with us. To get as far away from the prick as possible."

"You're taking her with you? Does she know this?" Torque's eyes widen as he speaks.

"Yeah, she packed a suitcase. She's tight with Prinie, so at least she'll have her in Houston."

"Yeah, and your cock to ride," Wraith grumbles under his breath.

"Shut the fuck up, VP. The woman's married."

"Well, there's a reason to fuck her off right no—"

"To a cop."

Torque and Wraith both stop, glaring at me like I've lost my damn mind. *Pretty sure I have.*

"Who beat her?"

"Cop husband."

"Jesus Christ! A fucking crooked cop is all we need on our tails, Zero. What were you thinking?" Wraith grumbles.

"Did you see her? I couldn't leave her there. Prinie wouldn't have let me even if I wanted to."

"Your sister is more trouble than this trip was worth."

I glare at him. "Be careful, Wraith."

"Whatever! Just know this is all going to bite *you* in the ass. The woman is married to the damn heat!"

"This is not up for debate. She needs our protection. She needs to be far away from Chicago. She's coming. End of fucking discussion."

Wraith lets out a low growl then turns, storming off.

Torque folds his arms across his chest letting out a chuckle. "I see he's still as temperamental as ever."

"He's all over the fucking place. One minute he makes more sense than any of us. The next the smallest thing triggers him off. He's a damn good VP, but sometimes he's an asshole of a friend."

"Hmm... it was like that with Trax. Until Sparx came along. She changed him. Mellowed him out. Turned him into a family man. Sparx calmed his demons."

"You saying I need to find Wraith a good woman?"

Torque snorts, gripping my shoulder. "Couldn't hurt, brother."

My eyes shift to Wraith as he watches Prinie drag the luggage in on her own. He doesn't offer to help her but just watches like the sadistic prick he is. "Wraith isn't capable of love. Talk later, gotta go help Prinie."

Torque salutes me as I rush over to Prinie.

She's dragging the suitcase along the floor in front of Wraith all the while he's sipping his whiskey like a damn ass, eyeing her with no concern. *Fucker.*

I grab the heavy bag, lugging it over toward the bar. "I got it, sis."

She lets out an exaggerated huff, throwing her long hair over her shoulder. "At least someone still has their manners," she chides while staring directly at Wraith.

He curls up his lip, swirls on the barstool, turning his back to her.

"Don't worry about snookums, he's got a pole up his ass today."

She laughs. "He's got a pole shoved up his tight ass constantly. I just hope the wood's leaving splinters." She narrows her eyes on his back in a death stare. "He deserves all the pain he can get."

Wraith lets out a snort. I can't tell whether it was a laugh or huff. Either way, he reacted and that's odd.

I roll my shoulders. "Okay, you two, back in your corners. It's a long way home, and we need to get the fuck along."

"Tell that to the deserter," Wraith grunts, then downs the last of his drink. He stands, walking off effectively ending our conversation.

"He's pissed at me because I left?" Prinie scrunches up her face.

"Honestly I don't know what Wraith thinks half the time. He wants you guys to come back, then he's angry when you do. I swear his mood changes quicker than a set of damn traffic lights."

Prinie shrugs. "Whatever! As if I care about Wraith, anyway. He means jack of all shits to me."

"He's your VP. You're going to have to find a way to coexist and get along."

"He's *your* VP. I'm not a member of the club, Zero. Just born into it."

"It's the same thing, princess. Born into… serve under… it's all a part of it."

"Needless to say, he's not *my* VP. I don't take orders from him, nor will I ever."

"If I'm not around—"

"*Ever,* Zero. I mean it. The man irks me. He's… he's, urgh… I don't know. Frustratingly annoying."

Shaking my head at her petulance, I'll let this go for now. Prinie will have to learn Wraith might be a loose cannon, but when I'm not around, what he says goes. She'll learn it quickly enough. But for now, I have other drama I need to be concerned about. Like getting the rest of my crew ready to ride, not to mention a certain little cherry bomb who's bound to make my world explode.

God help us all.

CHAPTER 9

RAYNE

Today has been a freaking whirlwind. Being beaten by Chuck, the asshole, then rescued—if I can call it that—by Zero and Prinie, kind of has my head spinning. I'm not one hundred percent sure Chuck didn't kill me, and now I'm in some weird kind of purgatory or something with Zero being the angel coming in to save me. From Chuck. From myself. I don't know. Either way, as I sit here with Chills finishing up her check over, I don't even know where to start in thanking her.

She's been super sweet and caring. While looking me over, she told me about her baby boy, Kobe. He's sick with a heart condition. *How much more difficult would this have been if I'd conceived a baby with Chuck?* He didn't know I was secretly taking the pill. I didn't want to bring a baby into this world with a father like him. Problem was every time the test came back negative, Chuck would punch me some more. I figure he thought the reason I didn't conceive is because he was too busy beating me up all the time for a baby to actually survive. If he was a smart man, he would have stopped the beatings, but if there's one thing Chuck isn't, it's smart. It's a blessing really, I didn't want to bring a child into a world with violence like that. If he stopped, I might have had to stop taking the pill and actually start trying.

Chuck said he would change.

That a baby would turn him into a good person.

At least, he acknowledged he's an asshole.

My mind's racing. Zero came in, literally sweeping me off my feet like some kind of fucking superhero, but I can't think of him like that. He's not a white knight, and he's not here to save me. These bikers are just as debauched as Chuck.

I know going with them will probably mean I will have to do things, things I don't want to do. But honestly, anything has to be better than living with that douchebag. Sure, I can take the beatings. I'm kind of numb to them now, but living that life, one where I have to hide who I am all the time, hide what he's done to me—no, I can't do it. No more.

If I can lay low while Zero deals with Chuck for me, whatever! I'm all for it. I'm past caring. I sometimes wonder if I'm actually even still alive inside or if I'm dead and living in hell. It's hard to know. The only reason I can tell I'm not in hell right now is because of Zero. He wasn't the angel I was expecting, but I would take it if it meant getting out of there.

Chills hands me a pair of comfy-looking shoes, breaking me from my raging thoughts. "They have extra padding, so hopefully they should be gentle on your cuts. I have padded the bandages as well."

"You're amazing, thank you."

Movement in the doorway lets me know Zero's back. I feel his deep penetrating stare on me, but I don't return his gaze. I don't want to get lost in him right now.

"Your feet are going to be really sore for a while. It's best if you can keep off them as much as you can for the next couple of days."

Nodding, I can't stop the pull as my eyes shift up.

Zero's eyes are firmly on me as I thought they would be. "How is she, doc?"

Chills turns to Zero with a warm smile. "She's going to be just fine. Some ibuprofen and rest will do the trick. She has a couple of butterfly stitches on her right heel. It's not a huge cut, though. Her eye is puffy and could close off, but I don't believe it's fractured. I'll keep a watch over her in the next few days. Ribs are still mending from a previous…" She pauses with an exhale. "Rayne's quite the tough woman. But I'm glad you got her out when you did, pres." Chills glances back at me squeezing my hand.

I'm going to like having Chills around the clubhouse, she's good at what she does and is nice on top of it.

"Me, too. I want you to keep me updated with any of Rayne's medical issues. I need to know everything, Chills."

Chills folds up her med-kit walking over to Zero. "Of course. I have to go check on Chains and Kobe, but feel free to stay in here for as long as you need. We'll be back shortly to collect the rest of our stuff for the trip. Chain's still has to take the crib apart, so *that* will be fun."

Zero's lip turns up in the corner. "Get Kevlar to help. He's a pro at that shit. Two kids later, he should know what he's doing."

"Thanks, pres, will do." Chills exits the room while I sit here watching their interaction with curiosity. She has the utmost respect for him, though from what I can tell, she doesn't know him all that well. Interesting what the rank of president automatically grants you.

Zero's eyes focus on me as he walks over, sitting in the chair Chills recently vacated. He's so close and yet has just enough distance so we're not touching. He looks me up and down, his eyes devouring my body in my yellow dress, and he exhales, his hand snaking up behind his neck as he rubs his muscles. "You're gonna ride in the van with Fox and Koda. Can't have you on the back of a bike. Not in your state. You're too weak."

I dip my chin in agreement. Though I would give anything right now to be on the back of his ride. "Where will Prinie be?"

"On my bike with me. Need her to remember her place is at the club with her family."

I clear my throat. "You think she doesn't know that?"

He recoils at my question. "I don't… know. Sometimes I don't think she does."

"She does. She knows she belongs there. She's just fighting it because of what happened to your parents. She doesn't want that to happen to you. She loves you too much, Zero. She simply can't bear the thought."

He scoffs. "She'd rather leave me altogether and never see me than spend time with me?"

I shrug. "Sometimes, it's easier not to be with the people you love than to see them hurt, or worse."

"That's being a chicken shit," he berates.

"It's called trauma. You have to remember Prinie and Koda haven't been raised with the blood and gore you were. So, seeing what they did, the way their parents went out like that, it's pure PTSD. Think about it from *their* point of view. They didn't want to watch the only remaining member of their family be killed in front of them again. Neither of them will cope with it."

Recognition clicks in his features. "It's why she didn't want to leave *you*. She didn't want to go with the thought something could happen to you, too," he mumbles more to himself than to me.

"As much as she helps me through everything, I know her seeing me beaten is a trigger for her. Prinie wants to help me so badly, but she never could. The only way she was able to was by being there to help me through. To take me to the doctor, or to help me clean up the mess before the bastard returned home. Honestly, your sister has been through so much, but you don't understand the demons she's fighting within. That grunge get-up she's sporting now, she didn't have that when she left, did she?"

"No. That's new."

"A coping mechanism. The dark eyeshadow is to hide the circles under her eyes from lack of sleep. Thin… she struggles to eat properly. The added sass, a protection method to make up for the insecurities she feels. She's lost, Zero. I think coming home will help find her again. I'm glad I'll be there to support her."

Zero exhales leaning forward, causing his knees to meet mine. I inhale sharply at the contact while he stares right into my eyes. "You're smart, Rayne. You're wasting your talents holed up here in Chicago in a marriage that's slowly killing you."

His words couldn't ring truer.

"My parents own a chain of pharmacies. I'm the head pharmacist in one downtown. I'm going to need to tell my dad I'm taking an extended leave of absence."

"Tell him you quit, cherry bomb. You're not coming back here."

My eyes widen as he leans back in the chair, putting some much-needed distance between us. "My job is here, Zero. My family—"

"Your wife-bashing husband? Yeah, he's the reason you're not coming back, Rayne. If your family loved you, they would have pulled you out of that fucking loveless disaster of a marriage when the bruises started. There's *no* excuse. They're just as guilty in my eyes."

I huff. "I can't sit around the clubhouse in Houston and do nothing all day, Zero. That's not me."

He rolls his shoulders. "So, then... what do you want to do?"

"I don't know... work?"

He lets out a loud laugh. "And let him track you. No."

I slump into the bed. "Give me a false name and let me work. He can't track that, can he?"

"You really wanna work in a pharmacy in Houston?" He groans.

"Yes. I love helping people."

Zero closes his eyes like he's thinking things through. "Then I'll buy you a store, put all the security in place, and you can run it exactly how you want."

"Wait, what?" My stomach falls through the floor.

"Your own pharmacy. A small to medium-sized shop near the clubhouse, so we can keep an eye on you. Obviously, there will be one of us there at all times, plus, security measures in place, but it will be yours to run as you see fit. Hire who you want once Neon runs a check on them, then... off you go."

"Y-You'd do all that... for me?"

A dimple dips in his cheek as the corner of his lip turns up. "Yeah... I would, and I will. One thing you will need to know going into this, Rayne, the pharmacy will be owned by the club. That's how we will get around having anything in your name. I'll talk to Chills, see if she knows some workarounds, so as not to have your name plastered in every facet of it. If not, then you'll have to be a simple employee, so nothing's registered in your name. But *you* will run it, Rayne. However, you want."

My entire body feels like it's floating. This is all I've ever wanted. My own store. My father wouldn't let me run one. I've known Zero all of an hour and he's offering me my dream on a plate.

Jesus, this guy is something else.

"Why? Why are you offering me this? What's the catch?"

"Let's just say with every good deed comes a reward."

I snort out a laugh. "Right. So, this goodwill isn't just a kind gesture, there's something in it for you?"

His face scrunches in what appears to be confusion. It's hard to read—he's hard to read. "I don't know yet, but I'll let you know when I do."

Not sure I like the idea of owing Zero one, but if it means I get to start a new life and have my own pharmacy, then I guess whatever will come out of it can't be too bad, I hope.

"Okay, let's do it."

"Oh, cherry bomb… it was already a done deal."

"You're so sure of yourself."

"I have to be." He pats the word president on his chest. "Comes with the patch."

"The biker, or the president's patch?"

"Both. A thing you'll learn pretty damn fast is… what I want, I damn well get."

"Kinda sounds like you're a spoiled brat to me."

He hesitates for a second. "For a woman who gets herself beat up for a living, you sure have a smart mouth."

"Probably why I get beat up for a living." I shrug.

"You haven't learned pushing people's buttons gets you in trouble?"

I sink into the bed with a sigh. "I figured no matter what I said or did, I was always in trouble with Chuck. So, I may as well be myself around him. No point stopping who I am just to please someone who can't be pleased."

"And you think being a smartass here won't get you into a

different kind of trouble?"

I roll my shoulders. "The way I see it, Zero, the only thing left for me that's worse than what I've been through is death. If that comes at the hands of you or your club, then honestly, I'm ready for it. My life as it was isn't worth living, so if it's my time, then so be it. But, if what you're offering means I get to start something new and different, without my asshole husband, then maybe it's worth taking the risk."

The whites of his eyes show he's shocked by my admission. I don't have a death wish, far from it. I've just thought about this for months. What it would be like to end it all and be free from Chuck.

Prinie was the only one keeping me here.

I'm not sure even *she* knows that.

"Do I need to get Chills to do a psych evaluation on you?"

"Pfft, nope, I'm fine. I just didn't want to be in a world with Chuck forever. Death doesn't scare me anymore. I've resigned myself to the fact that it's simply the next step."

Zero leans forward, pressing our knees together. His hands move out grabbing mine. A blast of electricity shoots up my arms slamming straight into my heart. It beats so fucking fast I can hardly breathe. His ice blues stare at me sternly as he shakes his head. "You're not dying, Rayne. You're just starting to live. I'm going to show you how good life can be without Up-Chuck."

For the first time in as long as I can remember, a slow smile crosses my face. I let out a small giggle. "I have to admit, hearing you call him Up-Chuck really does something to my insides."

Zero's hand slowly moves up, sliding a stray piece of hair behind my ear, his thumb ever so gently caressing my tender bruised cheek. "He didn't deserve you. You're far too beautiful for him."

A lump catches in my throat. My eyes leave his, dropping to my lap. His fingers move to my chin lifting my face to look at him again. "Don't. Don't do that. Don't let whatever bullshit he's made you think, made you believe, made you feel get inside your head. You're gorgeous, Rayne... even swollen, bruised, and bloody."

"So, you're a phobophile, then?" I quip.

"I don't consider myself someone who loves all things disturbing and horrifying. No. You, Rayne, are neither of those things." He laughs.

I lean forward feeling slightly cheeky. "I'm actually surprised you knew what that meant."

Zero leans a little closer, the space between us becoming smaller and smaller. "I might seem like your typical tattooed, wrong-side-of-the-tracks-bad-boy, but I assure you I went to school. I did everything I was meant to."

"You saying you look dumb but you're actually smart?" I tease.

A low growl rumbles from his chest. "You better be careful with that mouth of yours, cherry bomb."

I exhale, his eyes harden, a warning behind the tension in his brow. I don't think he'd hurt me. I'm not getting that vibe. Not at all. I'm getting something much, much different. The atmosphere in the room charges like there's a continual buzz filtering between us. It tingles against my skin, causing the hairs on my arm and neck to stand at attention. I've never felt this kind of energy between myself and another person before.

It's exhilarating.

It's exhausting.

It's confusing.

Footsteps thunder as I snap my head up. There are two burly bikers standing in the doorway watching us. Huge-ass grins on their faces. "Sorry, pres, need us to come back?" the one with the beard asks.

"No, Chains, we're good. I'll get out of your hair so you can finish packing. Think you'll be done in thirty?" Zero asks.

Chains views the surroundings of the room, his eyes heavy with obvious memories flowing through him. "Yeah, Kevlar's here to help."

"I know this is a big deal, brother, but you're doing this for Kobe. Plus, anytime you and Chills wanna come back to Chicago, it's a no brainer. No questions asked," Zero advises.

Chains' shoulders relax, his lips slowly spreading into a smile across his bearded face. "Thanks, pres, I needed to hear that."

Zero dips his chin, then turns back to me. "C'mon, miss, let's go get you some food."

Nodding, I move to get up, but Zero stands, then hoists me up into his arms again.

I giggle, rolling my eyes. "I can walk, you know?"

He groans. "Did you not hear the doctor's damn orders? Less time on your feet, the quicker you heal."

"So what? You're gonna carry me everywhere?"

"Not everywhere. But when I can, I will."

He walks us past Chains and Kevlar. They dip their heads as they get to work on the room. Zero strides with me in his arms down the hall. Led Zeppelin sounds over the speakers in the clubroom as we enter, the room alive and buzzing.

Children are playing in the corner by the pool table. Brothers are at the bar drinking, others at the tables eating. Women mingling and chatting in a group.

Prinie's standing with a few of the women when she spots us walking in. She hurries over as Zero places me on a stool at the bar. "Hey, girlfriend, how are you feeling?" She pushes Zero out of the way.

He leans over the bar to some brunette woman with a lot of cleavage and says something to her, but I'm too far away to hear.

Fingers click in front of my face, and I'm forced back into reality. "Sorry, what?"

"Did Chills give you some pain meds or something? You zoned out."

I let out a small laugh. "Sorry, Prin, it's been a hell of a day."

She slides into the stool next to me reaching for my hand. "How are you? Are you okay… mentally, I mean?"

Exhaling, I think on that for a moment. *Am I okay?* I've basically fled from my home with limited supplies, and I'm going to be taken across the other side of the country while running for my life.

Am I okay? Yeah, I think I am and that thought makes me happy.

"Running from Chuck is messy. I know this won't be the end of it, but I feel safe with your brother. I don't know why, but I'm sure being with the club is going to be a good thing."

"Wait until the club is attacked by the Bayou Militia or raided by the poli—" Her eyes open wide as she stops midsentence. I know why she stopped. Next time they're raided by the police, it will probably be because Chuck's searching for me. "Shit, sorry, Rayne, I didn't think."

"No, it's fine, hon. I know he's going to come for me. I just hope he doesn't do anything stupid."

Zero raises his chin. "An asshole like Up-Chuck will try to fuck us over, Rayne, but we won't let him. Don't worry, cherry bomb, we'll deal with him *if* he comes."

"When," I mumble under my breath.

Zero walks over and swivels my stool so I face him. "I have a burger coming for you. We're leaving in just under half an hour. Eat everything on your plate, so you're full for the ride. Don't fight me on this, Rayne."

I roll my eyes. "Okay, Dad."

He recoils. "Don't… ever… *ever*… call me that again. I'm not your dad, but you *will* do what you're fucking told. Eat. Your. Food. Stay here until it's time to leave, Rayne, then I will take you to the van. I have shit to organize before we leave. Prinie, keep her the fuck here, will you!"

"Yes. Drill. Sergeant." Prinie salutes him, causing a low grumble from his chest as he turns storming off while mumbling to himself. "Geez, he's moodier than normal."

"I guess he has a lot on his plate. He didn't expect to have me tagging along."

Prinie faces me, taking my hands into hers. Her dark-rimmed eyes meet mine glistening somberly. "You are not a burden, Rayne. I know you put up this I-don't-care-about-myself attitude, and you think you're worth nothing… but you are. You're worth so much more. Stop letting Chuck get inside your head. You're worthy of having a life. A great life. You're an amazing woman. You brought me out of my own hell so many times—"

"You did the same for me, Prinie," I cut in.

She slumps, pursing her lips together. "We're just a couple of broken women finding our feet, which will be landing firmly back in Houston."

"Maybe this will be good for us both. A fresh start together. New city. Well, original for you, but you know what I mean. New beginnings from where we were a year ago, but more importantly, we're doing it together."

Prinie squeezes my hands tighter. "Always together, Rayne. You're my best friend, you don't think I'd leave without you, did you?"

I laugh. "If I recall, you were coming to say goodbye."

"Ha! Shows what you know. I thought once Zero saw you... whatever state of disarray you would have been in, his protector side would enact. The minute he said he was coming, I knew this would happen."

"You really thought this through, didn't you?"

"Like I said... leave no BFF behind."

I lean forward, pulling Prinie into a warm hug. My body aches like hell, but I embrace her anyway. She holds me back as the brunette places the burgers on the bar in front of us.

"Here you go, ladies. I hope you enjoy your last meal here at Chicago."

We pull apart, and Prinie smiles at her. "Thanks, Ruby. I'm so glad you're coming with us."

My eyes widen. "You're coming, too? Oh, and thanks." I wrap my hand around the giant burger and take a bite, ketchup sliding down my twisted-up pinky.

Ruby's eyes take in the clubroom, a warm glow emanating from her. "You know, I've spent so long here, it seems strange to leave. But, when you love someone, you have to follow them, right?"

"Right," Prinie answers, but I keep silent.

I thought I knew what love was. And for the briefest of moments with Chuck, I thought we had that life. The perfect engagement. The extravagant wedding. We were going to have it all. *Until we didn't.*

I don't know if love is just a charade or if only the lucky ones are capable of having something so truly extraordinary. All I do know is what my asshole husband and I had wasn't love. It was infatuation. Then it was convenience for the families. My family marrying into his. I don't know how it worked, but the business side of things was what our parents made sure kept us together.

But not anymore.

I have a way out.

A way that can keep me safe, or as safe as I can be before he finds me. I have a chance at making a life again.

Hell, if I'm not going to take it by the horns and ride the bronco, even if it bucks like a damn bitch.

Because if there's one thing I know, I can buck like a bitch just as hard if life wants to throw shit back in my face.

I'm ready for this new phase of my life, and I'm coming for it, full force.

ZERO

It's been a hell of a long time since I've ridden with Prinie on the back of my bike. When she was younger, she used to love it so much. Then, for some reason which I realized later, she started avoiding it. She was distancing herself with every fresh drama Igor and the Militia brought to the club.

I don't blame her. She saw what we all knew was coming, a war to end all wars between Houston Defiance and the Bayou Militia.

We lost our parents.

The Militia lost a lot of men.

Their captain in that battle.

And in the fallout, I lost my siblings.

But a year later, when the dust has settled, a new reign rules over the streets of Houston, and now my sister is back behind me on my bike. Her arms gripping around my waist as she moves with me like she's missed the feel of the open road. The whole reason I wanted her on my bike and not in the van was because I needed her to remember the love of two wheels. What this club is about. Hell, what her family is about.

She might have turned her back on the club.

But we won't turn our back on her.

Ever.

The club is all about family—blood or not.

Surprisingly, though, she didn't fight me as hard as I thought she would. I'd prepared myself for her to kick up a stink and argue her way out of it.

She has fears about the club, and what's more, they're warranted.

But she's safer under our protection than she is on her own. That much I'm sure of.

My ass is going numb. The vibration of the engine doing nothing to help ease the ache in my hands. I'm riding behind our Road Captain, Slick, in a long-ass convoy of the brothers on bikes, Chills and Ruby in their cars with their belongings, and also the van hauling Koda and Rayne.

Needless to say, we're gaining a lot of attention from the drivers around us, but I honestly don't give two shits just as long as I get everyone home safe.

Unfortunately, we're gonna have to stop halfway like on the way over. There's no possible way to do the trip from Chicago to Houston in one trip. So right now, we need to stop for gas and a fucking break. My ass is chafing. So, I speed up to Slick signaling for him to pull in to the nearest gas station.

He veers off to the right. I follow him indicating to everyone behind to follow us.

I pull up at the pump, turn off the engine, the vibration halts as I tap Prinie's leg.

She slides off with an exhale. "I forgot how nice it is on the back of a bike."

Pride swirls through me as the van pulls in.

That's when my thoughts instantly turn to Rayne.

How is she doing?

What the fuck?

I need to keep my distance from her. Having Rayne racing through my mind is not something I need right now.

Everyone pulls in to gas up as I slide off my ride, then wrap my arm around Prinie pulling her to my side. "It's good to have you back, sis. You belong with me and the club."

"Don't get any ideas about this being a regular thing. My arms are tired as hell."

"We're only a quarter of the way home, princess. You're out of the game."

"Maybe I should ride in the truck for the next part of the journey."

"Not on my life." I scoff. "You didn't earn your princess badge for nothing, Prinie. You're the *only* daughter of a president. You need to cope with long hauls."

She groans. "Sometimes being a princess is a royal pain in my ass. Fucking literally."

I rub my butt in understanding. We still have hours of riding ahead of us. "I know what you mean, but it's who we are. We just gotta deal with it, Prinie. Show the others we're deserving of the Walker name."

She rolls her eyes. "Yeah, yeah… I got ya. Want me to pump your gas while you go check on everything?"

I furrow my brows.

Is she being serious?

"Yes, I'm actually being nice to you. You have presidential shit to attend to, and I know how to pump gas into a bike, Zero. So, go. Do what you gotta do. Plus, Cannon's watching me, so I'm sure he'll offer to help if I need it."

I glance over at Cannon, our prospect, who was tasked with guarding Prinie this last year. His skills haven't lapsed since being dismissed from the duty.

Cannon's eyes meet mine, and I signal for him to come over. He does so without question. He doesn't look at Prinie, but directly at me. "Yeah, pres?"

"Can you help Prinie fill up my tank while I go deal with some shit? Make sure she's taken care of while we're here."

Joy lights his face.

Prinie bites her bottom lip fighting back something.

Oh, hell no.

She's into him!

Great! Just another thing I'm going to have to keep my eye on.

"Yeah, of course."

Prinie's eyes are firmly on my prospect as he swipes his card to pay, then picks up the gas pump. *Fuck my life.* I turn heading straight for Wraith in the next bay. He's pumping gas and pulls out his pack of cigarettes.

I glare at him. "Don't be a damn dickhead."

"Wasn't gonna light it 'til I'd finished pumping."

"You shouldn't be smoking anywhere near a gas station, fuckhead. Not when there's too much precious cargo with us."

His eyes shift to Prinie. "Your sister… Koda?"

"And Kobe in Chills' car. Not to mention Rayne in the van… you know, a cop's wife."

He grunts, shoving the packet back inside his vest. "I don't get why we're bringing her with us. Seems like we're asking for the heat to come break our door down. And Zero, there's a shit load of stuff at the clubhouse right now that could get us all in a hell of a lotta shit. We'll do jail time."

I nod. "I know. We're gonna have to be extra vigilant."

"Vigilant, that's your grand fucking plan?"

"It's going to be fine, Wraith. We have our safety protocols in place for a reason."

His finishes and detaches the nozzle placing it back on the pump. "You really think bringing this Rayne chick with us was the right move… for the club?"

I grit my teeth. "For the club… probably not. But for her, for Prinie, and for Koda… yeah."

Wraith faces me, his hands moving up gripping either side of his cut in an authoritative stance. "So, you're telling me you made this dick move because you want to get in the good graces with your bratty sister?"

"What's your problem with Prinie?" I ask him straight.

His line of sight moves past me over to where Cannon and Prinie are making damn googly eyes at each other.

Mental note—I need to deal with that shit.

He huffs, turning up his lip. "She's spoiled. Has a superiority complex. Treats people like they mean nothing to her."

"If you hate her this much, why do *you* care if she treats *me* like I mean nothing to her?"

Wraith's eyes meet mine, an intensity blaring in them. His anger toward Prinie is something deeper. It's something I don't know about. "Forget it! She's not worth even talking about." He spins, hightailing it away from me so fast I don't even have a second to answer before he's gone.

I huff, glancing back at Prinie and Cannon. *She could probably do worse.* He's observed her, kept her safe for the last year. Cannon's had her best interests at heart.

Spinning on my heels, I head toward the front of the convenience store. There's a small food stop inside, so I let out a whistle gaining everyone's attention. "Y'all wanna stop for some grub?"

A general sound of "fuck yeah" rings out through the station as a couple paying for their gas watch the commotion.

I walk inside to see a Subway, not my first choice, but hey, I'll eat anything at this point. At least Kevlar will be happy—he'll get to have his damn salad.

I stroll in noticing a group of men sitting at a table. They're dressed like hicks, flannel shirts, torn jeans, long hair, beards. One's even wearing an American flag bandana.

The heat of their eyes burns into the back of my cut as I stride up to the Subway server. The whites of her eyes widen as she takes in my tall stature. "Hi, w-welcome to Subway."

"I'm gonna have one hell of a party coming in here shortly, so if y'all have extra staff out the back, you might wanna bring 'em on out here."

"Charlie, Annika… might need a hand out here, please."

I glance at her name badge. "Thanks, Lana."

The thunderous stomping of my brothers' boots echo as they all storm inside.

I stand back gesturing for them to order as I make sure everyone comes inside.

I watch. Wait. Check.

Chains and Chills walk in with baby Kobe, and I can't help the smile crossing my face. I dip my chin at the happy family as they walk in taking a seat with Luc and Ruby. It will take time, but eventually, the Chicago brothers will sit with the Houston boys. For now, they will stick together. I get it.

I wait impatiently, tapping my foot as I catch a glimpse of Fox helping Rayne. She's slow. Taking delicate steps. Damn! I want to carry her but doing that here will draw added unwanted attention to her. She doesn't need that shit. With her face the way it is, she's already going to have people staring.

Fox helps her inside, and her eyes meet mine. I smile trying to give her the confidence she needs right now.

She's doing well, just a few more steps and she makes it inside.

I can't hold myself back anymore as I take long, purposeful strides over to her, then reach out for her hand. "Here… take a seat, Rayne. I'll get one of the guys to grab you whatever you want."

Relief floods her eyes as she peers at me. 'Thank you,' she mouths as she falls dramatically into the seat.

"Tell Fox what you want, cherry bomb."

Her sweet face softens from the pain she was so obviously suffering. "You're a godsend, Fox. Honestly, I'm happy with anything. Chicken, beef, bacon, I don't mind, as long as it has pickles."

Fox and I both snort out a laugh. "You sound like Zero. He's a lover of pickles, too."

"It's the only essential to have on a po' boy, which I wish we were having instead."

"I know, right? Who doesn't love those Louisiana sandwiches?" Her face lights up, so beautiful and harmonious, it makes me warm inside just staring at the happiness oozing from her. We've found common ground—pickles and po' boys. *Who would have thought?*

Fox clears his throat. "So, ah, you want your usual, Zero?"

I snap my head to him breaking eye contact with Rayne. "Ah… yeah. Thanks, brother."

Fox tries to hide his smirk but fails miserably as I slide into the bench seat next to Rayne. The line is long as everyone orders.

I don't miss the hicks eyeing Rayne and me suspiciously.

Dickheads.

"How was the van? Are you comfortable in there?"

She shrugs. "It's not the Ritz, but it's better than being on the back of a bike."

I clutch at my chest. "You wound me, woman."

Rayne's lips turn up, her face glowing like the sun on a warm summer's day.

Fuck, she's gorgeous.

"I can, in all honesty say… that I've never been on the back of a bike."

I grin. "I'm going to change that when you're healed."

Her eyes light up. "You're going to take me for a ride?"

"Yes. You're going to think the Ritz is like a dungeon in comparison to the freedom and open spaces of being one with the road."

"You talk a big game, Zero. What if I don't like it?"

"You will."

She grins as Fox heads over with our food.

We all sit and eat. Food's a welcomed treat. I didn't realize how hungry I was until I started eating.

I can't help but watch Rayne. The way her mouth wraps around the sandwich so delicately. My cock jerks in my jeans at that thought, but I can't keep my eyes off her delectable, supple lips. *She's so fucking gorgeous.*

Fox is watching me watching her with a smirk on his face. Out the corner of my eye, I notice those same hicks focused completely on Rayne and me. I don't like the way they're staring at her whispering among themselves.

That looks like trouble to me with a capital fucking T.

As soon as we finish our food, I give the signal for us to leave. I don't want shit to start up between the hicks and us, so it's best we get back on the road. Everyone gathers heading for the exit, brothers leaving before us chatting among themselves as Wraith moves into my side next to Rayne. He must sense the tension on my face as we walk past the hicks.

"Stupid biker bitch, letting herself get beat up by the club. Nothing but a worthless whore." The hick with the flag bandana mutters under his breath as we pass.

I don't think he meant for me to hear, but I sure as hell did. Anger sweeps over my entire body like a raging inferno from my toes all the way to the top of my head. How dare he think we did this to Rayne.

She grips my bicep—she must have heard them too.

I step forward. "Wanna say that to her face?" I spit.

The asshole glares at me while shifting in his seat. "Wasn't talking to *you*."

Everyone stops, turning, to take in the situation I've found myself in. My guys have my back, this much I know. The hick knows it too, and he's retreating back into his seat, a little less confident now my boys are surrounding me.

"I said… tell. Her. To. Her. Face!"

He stands holding his hands out as if to placate me. "Look, man, didn't mean anything by it."

"But you did. You made an assumption. So, tell her what you called her."

The ass focuses on Rayne, his eyes heavy with regret. He turns looking down at his friends, who nod their heads as if to tell him to just do whatever I say. "I-I said you were a biker bitch. I was wrong, okay? I'm sorry."

I glance at Rayne who raises her brow at me seemingly unsatisfied.

A girl after my own heart.

So, I take a step closer. "I don't think that's *all* you said. There was something else at the end of your sentence… worthless… something…" The ass exhales, his face crinkling like he's scared as hell to say it again. *He damn well should be.* "You better tell the lady."

"You're a worthless whore!" he yells frantically trying to placate me, but all it does is rile me up.

My hand balls into a fist, pulls back, and I let it fly straight into the guy's face. He doesn't even see it coming. I hit him square in the jaw, he falls into the table, spitting out a tooth mixed with a line of blood. My knuckles sting as I move in to punch him again, but Wraith pulls me back. I struggle in his grip to get back to the asshole, but then a glimmer of something shiny catches my attention. I still as the other hicks stand with their switchblades drawn.

Texas and Neon stride in beside us pulling out their Glock's aiming it at the other hicks while bandana guy bleeds all over the table.

I try to calm my shit down as tension reaches critical level while we all standoff. My guys with guns aimed at the hicks who are staring back at us with their knives pointed at me.

"I've called the cops," someone yells out from behind the counter.

We turn as Lana, the Subway server, ducks behind the desk with a phone in her hand.

Shit.

Fuck! Can't have the heat on us.

"Time to go," I call out as I signal to my men. "It's been fun but we're out." I turn toward Rayne, who's attempting to fight back a smile. I lean down hoisting her up into my arms, then take off leading the way. We all rush to get out of here before the cops show. Last thing we need is the heat, especially considering they could give news to Chuck on Rayne's whereabouts.

Yeah, we need to *get the fuck outta Dodge.*

The hicks rush off. I hope I've taught them a lesson or two in being judgmental, but I highly doubt it. Prinie's by my side in a flash, she pulls open the van door as I move to place Rayne inside. I'm pretty sure she's shaking. I hope it's from adrenaline and not fear.

I buckle her in staring right in her eyes. "It's going to be okay. I'll always protect you."

Rayne grips my forearm. "Thanks. No one's ever done anything like that for me before."

Warmth floods me, I want to jump in the van and travel with her all the way back to Houston, but I can't. I need to get my guys back, and to do that, I need to lead them.

I move out of the van, sliding the door closed, then turn to Prinie.

"Well, that was intense," Prinie chimes.

Clenching my eyes shut, I know what needs to be done. The sacrifice that needs to be made. Prinie was getting reacquainted with riding, with the club, and our family, but right now Rayne needs her more. That cunt said some pretty fucking shitty things, and Rayne needs a friend more than I need my sister.

"Get in the van."

Prinie's head jerks back in confusion. "But you said—"

"I know what I said, Prinie, but I need you to support Rayne. Okay?"

She grips my bicep in a gesture of thanks, then slides open the door and hops inside. I shut it with a rush and head back to my bike. Throwing my leg over, I start the engine. The vibration rolls over me like it always does. I love this life. I love riding. I wish more than anything right now after that bullshit, after what Rayne just went through, she could be on the back of this bike with me.

It would help clear her mind.

Help ease her stress.

Slick accelerates, and I take off after him starting the convoy. We're back on the road at a quick pace before the cops arrive.

We have to keep our heads down.

I can't have Chuck finding Rayne, not now, not before we've even made it back to the safety of the clubhouse.

ZERO

It's late, we've pulled into Memphis to stop overnight at a motel. Needless to say, everyone's restless and tired from the long ride and the damn bullshit at lunchtime. Luckily, we had no trouble from the cops.

Fox is allocating room keys to everyone, but I know exactly who I want to be paired with. I walk up to Fox as he hands Cannon his key to share with Blake.

I reach out and grab a key. "I'm sharing with Rayne," I announce loudly enough for everyone to hear, including Rayne.

"Whoa, what? Why aren't you sharing with Prinie or Koda?" Rayne queries.

Key in hand, I storm over to Rayne as she sits in the van. "No. You need someone on guard to protect you. Right now, *I* want that person to be me."

Prinie turns up her lip but doesn't argue.

Rayne scrunches up her face. "Fine. I guess having you in the room with me won't be so bad. You did knock a guy's tooth out for my honor."

I chuckle. "Also, for the club's honor, cherry bomb. We don't hit women. I didn't want anyone in that shithole believing we did."

"So, not for my virtue then?"

"No." I smirk.

"Mm-hmm..." She pulls her lips in tight.

Rayne doesn't believe me. Rightly so. But both reasons are true. I don't want the public thinking we beat our women, that's not us, but I was trying to defend Rayne.

I don't know a lot about her, but I do know she isn't a worthless whore.

"C'mon, let's get you settled in," I tell her.

After I grab her suitcase, we walk together toward our allotted room on the ground floor.

As we edge past Chills, she takes in how Rayne's walking. "How's your feet, Rayne?"

"Okay. Little tender." She grimaces.

"Let me get Kobe down then I'll come see you."

Rayne nods as we reach our door, and I work the lock. She steps in first as my brothers all mingle outside. They will probably party for a little while, but I want to get Rayne resting. The woman's had a huge day. As we walk further inside the room, I can't help but notice there's only one large queen bed. Searching around, I look for a sofa, but there's nothing.

Great. Looks like I'm spending the night on the floor.

"Only one bed," Rayne voices exactly what I was thinking.

"It's fine. I'll sleep on the floor."

She spins around, her eyes firm. "Don't be ridiculous. You rode all day, you'll be sore as hell. I'm not letting you sleep on the floor."

"Well, I'm not letting *you* sleep on the floor."

"Then we'll have to share the bed."

My cock instantly wakes up as I stare at her.

Is she serious?

I kick the door closed, so the fuckers outside don't get any ideas from overhearing. "You okay with that?"

"Jesus, you look like a teenage boy. A *virgin* teenage boy..." She snorts out a laugh. "I'm not going to steal your virtue, Zero."

Fuck! This woman.

"I just thought with you being married—"

"I don't consider myself married. Didn't when we were, and certainly not the second I left that house. I've left that asshole and life behind. He just doesn't know it yet. Though, by now, he'll know I'm missing. So, he might get an idea with a suitcase gone. Fingers crossed."

"Right. Same bed it is."

"We can put up a pillow wall if you're scared."

I narrow my eyes on her. "Hardy-fucking-har. No wall, I'm good. Didn't wanna make shit awkward."

She tilts her head. "Well, you're doing a fine-ass job of doing just that."

I throw my hands in the air. "Okay, fine. Topic closed. Now get changed and into bed. You need rest."

Rayne's dimples pop in. "Yes, sir." She gestures to the suitcase in my hand, so I lift it onto the bed. She slides the zipper open and pulls out an aqua-colored nightgown, then twirls her finger. "Go on, turn around."

I chuckle while spinning to face the wall. Instantly, I spot a mirror and her reflection. I should avert my eyes, but as she pulls her yellow sundress up, my eyes don't focus on the natural curves of her body, but the bruising and the damage that Up-Chuck has inflicted on her beautiful skin.

She has bruises fucking *everywhere.*

My stomach rolls as I try to keep my shit together. My top lip curls in anger as she takes off her bra. Under her breasts a dull purple color fans out shadowing her pale skin in the shape of a dusky cloud. It must be from where her ribs were previously broken and are still recovering. My eyes wander down to her thighs where it appears like something long and hard has been smacked straight into both of her legs. Maybe a bat? My hands ball together as she pulls her nightgown over her damaged body.

"All done, you can look now." Rayne's innocent voice makes me angry at myself for watching her, but at least now I understand the extent of what I'm dealing with. I need to be careful with Rayne. The outside persona she's putting on is tough, but she has to be broken on the inside. No one can be unscathed by what she's been through.

I turn around slowly, unclenching my hands so I don't give myself away. With a passive face, I shrug out of my cut placing it on the television cabinet opposite the bed. Bending down, I start to unlace my boots as there's a knock on the door. I wait until I slide my boots off before walking to the entry to peek through an opening in the blind on the side window to see who it is.

"Hey, doc, how's Kobe?"

She enters with her medkit in hand. "Actually, he seems to like the car. He was quiet the whole drive, now he's out like a light. Think I've found something to calm him... driving. Who would have thought he'd like the open road like his daddy?"

I tilt my head. "It does have a certain appeal."

"Well, there's nothing like the wind blowing through your hair. You'd know, pres, you have enough of it," Chills teases.

"Not a fan of the man bun, Chills?"

She grins at me. "Actually, quite the opposite. I think it suits you. Rugged and manly, pres."

"I agree," Rayne adds from the edge of the bed.

My eyes meet hers. I can't help but feel a sense of accomplishment as she's just given me a compliment. I shouldn't be searching for them. I shouldn't want them, but fuck if it doesn't make my cock want her even more.

"How about I check you over, Rayne, you've had a big day," Chills offers, breaking the staring between Rayne and me.

I lean back against the wall and cross one leg over the other while Chills checks Rayne over from top to bottom. I like how thorough Chills is being, she's damn good at her job. She's going to be a great asset to our club. As they chat, my mind wanders to what I just saw in the mirror—all the marks marring Rayne's body.

How long must this have been going on?

How bad must that shit have been for her to sustain so many bruises?

How much pain she must have suffered.

It only fuels my hatred for Chuck even more.

"Okay, you're good. Get some rest. I'll see you in the morning," Chills adds as she heads toward me.

I lead her out then lock the door behind her. Moving to the side of the bed, I yank off my shirt. The heat of Rayne's eyes on me burns into my chest, but I ignore it and continue to undress. I throw my shirt on the floor, then move to my jeans unbuckling them and slide them off leaving me in just my boxer briefs.

I shift under the covers. "C'mon, in you get."

She follows suit, and we both lay on our backs staring at the ceiling with the table lamp on. She's so close, but she feels like she's a lifetime away from me. I want to touch her, but that's not my place. The tension's rife as an awkward silence fills the room. Neither of us knows what to say.

Should I just turn off the light?

"Does it hurt?" she asks out of nowhere.

My head turns to the side, looking at her in confusion. "Does what hurt?"

She turns to face me. We're now staring at each other. *Fuck her eyes are stunning.*

"Riding for this long, I mean. I'm in the comfort of a van. You, though… you have to hang onto those handlebars and ride for those long hours. I can't imagine that's enjoyable."

"Hanging on and riding can be enjoyable."

A blush creeps over her face which makes me laugh as I turn glancing back up to the ceiling. "The thing about riding is your muscles might get tired, but it's your soul that connects to it. It's hard to explain unless you've been on a bike."

"It's absolute freedom," she answers for me.

She gets it.

"Exactly. It's just you and your beast, the wind against your face, that power vibrating through your body. It's a natural high, cherry bomb."

"I can't wait to experience it with you."

With me?

"You will, just gotta get you better first."

She rolls on her side facing me, her balled hands coming up under her chin. She's cute as hell, and I know I'm fucked. "Zero?"

I narrow my eyes on her. "Mmm?"

"Your family chose this life for you. But if you had the choice not to be in the club…" she pauses then continues, "… would you take it? Take Koda and Prinie and go?"

I inhale deeply. There's no one around to hear my answer. Not Prinie, not my brothers. It's just Rayne and me. I have a feeling what I say won't go any further, so I can be honest. I take a second to deeply think about the question, though my answer doesn't take long to come. I turn on my side facing her, my arm propped up under me as I rest on my hand. "Could I not be a part of Defiance?" I shake my head. "No. This is my life. I grew up there. It's all I know. My life without Defiance is not a life at all."

I'm not sure how she will take my answer, but her lips slowly turn up in the corners of her mouth.

"I see that. Prinie has a hard time with it, but you, you were born for this club. You lead it well. Everyone worships you."

"I don't know about worship, but respect… is earned. What about you? Did you always want to be a pharmacist?"

"God no, I wanted to be a vet. But because my father was a pharmacist, he chose my path for me. I'm not mad, though because turns out I love it, and I'm damn good at it. So, there's that."

"Well, you can use your love of animals at the clubhouse then because Wraith has a bulldog called Mack. Got him for Wraith as a patching-in present. He needed something to keep him grounded. Mack's the only living thing Wraith shows any compassion for."

"Sounds like Wraith has an unhealthy attachment to a dog and not enough healthy attachments to people."

"You can say that again."

A comfortable silence falls over us as we stare at each other. Despite her injuries, she's so fucking gorgeous.

"Did you grow up in Chicago?" I ask her.

"Born and raised. I can tell by your twang you're a Texan through and through."

"Gimmie barbecue, longhorns, and sweet tea any time, y'all."

She snickers. "You drink sweet tea?"

"Man, on those real scorchers when the heat makes the sweat drip from the tip of your nose, Nessie makes the best refreshing sweet tea you have ever tasted. But yeah, not a lot. Mainly when the sweltering heat gets to us."

"I forgot I'm changing climates. I'll have to get used to the heat."

I waggle my brows. "Just means wearing less."

Rayne rolls her eyes as I chuckle.

I'm comfortable with her as we continue chatting, getting to know each other, talking about meaningless things and about deeper issues. Politics. Religion. About all the things you aren't supposed to talk about when you first meet someone, but somehow the conversation flows. We laugh. We get along. Ease washes over the both of us.

The night drifts on. It's getting late as her eyes blink, starting to close, and we let the quiet wash over us. She's exhausted, and I need to get some rest as well. We have another big ride tomorrow.

Heavy breaths fall from her slightly open mouth—she's fallen asleep. She looks so peaceful. Like she's finally calm. I can't help myself as I lay watching her. I get that it's fucking creepy, but she's so untouched by anything right now. She's relaxed, and I like seeing her this way.

Slowly, I move my hand over to her face to slide a stray strand of hair back behind her ear. She doesn't even move. I pull the covers up and over her completely.

Rolling over on my back carefully, I reach for the lamp and switch it off sending the room into a blanket of darkness. There's a slight glow from behind the curtain giving the room a dull hue.

While staring at the ceiling, I am unsure where my head is at right now.

Rayne's so fucking amazing. She doesn't deserve the life she was thrown into.

I'm drawn to her.

But is it because I want to protect her?

Or do I actually have a crazy attraction to her.
I simply don’t know.

ZERO

The Next Morning

I'm coming to after a fucking great night's sleep, but something feels different. There's a weight on my chest which is not the normal occurrence. My eyes burst open, ready to attack as the smell of peach invades my senses. When I peer down, Rayne's snuggled into me. Her head on my chest, her arm draped across my torso. She's made herself at home all over me. And to my surprise, I fucking like it.

A lump catches in my throat as the silk fabric of her nightgown rubs against my rough skin—her soft against my hard. I clench my eyes shut trying to calm myself. I don't want to move. Scared to wake her. Worried I'll never get to wake up to this feeling again.

I'm troubled because I like how good this feels.

Too fucking good.

But the fact remains she's married to a cop. No matter which way I spin that shit, it's trouble.

I'm trying to compose myself and my dick, but my nose has other ideas as it nuzzles into her peach perfumed hair. Inhaling deeply, she smells like heaven, and my cock grows rock hard. My eyes clench. I'm in one hell of a situation right now. Instead of composing myself, my hand moves up tracing the small opening at the back of her nightgown, running my fingers along her spine. Her warm skin against my fingers makes it difficult for me not to roll her over and take total control of her right here and now.

I need to keep away from Rayne—she's off-limits.

But right here, in this moment, with her up against me, I couldn't feel more at peace.

Suddenly, she murmurs. My heart gallops at lightning speed. My hand falls from her back, my nose pulls away from her hair. I lay back stock still not touching her in any way, just letting her lay all over me. I try to keep my breathing even not to let her know how affected I am.

Rayne's hand slides up my chest stopping above my racing heart. Her head suddenly snaps up as her glassy eyes stare down at me. She pulls back dramatically, my body instantly turning icy cold from her absence. She scurries across the other side of the bed, pulling the sheets to cover her breasts. I have no idea why she's done that, she's wearing a nightgown.

"Jesus."

I let out a laugh. "Not Jesus, but women have called me god before, or more like... *oh god.*"

She scrunches up her face as she shakes her head. "I was... *on* you."

I tilt my head. "I noticed that, too."

"Like... cuddling you."

"Got the memo, cherry bomb."

Rayne turns her head away from me after I notice a flush crossing her pale cheeks. "I don't..." she pauses, pulling the sheets higher like they're a security blanket. "I haven't done that for so long."

My eyes widen. "You haven't cuddled?"

She peeks back at me. "Chuck... he put pillows between us so I won't touch him. He likes his space."

Well, damn! I thought she was making a joke about the pillow wall, and that cunt actually does it. If I had her hot piece of ass next to me each night, I'd have her naked and all over me.

What in the fucking hell is wrong with Up-Chuck?

I can't focus on him right now. I need her to feel like she isn't crazy.

"I haven't had someone cuddle me for a long time either, so it's something new for both of us."

She bites on her swollen bottom lip, it's sexy as fuck.

"I'm sorry… I don't know what came over me. I didn't even realize I was doing it."

I want to comfort her, but the tiniest amount of sheet is covering my junk. If it moves a fraction, she's gonna see my raging hard-on. So, I stay where I am. "Ain't even a thing. Don't stress over it."

She finally lowers the sheet from around her supple tits and exhales. "Are you this protective of everyone?"

Well, that question came out of nowhere.

"It's gotten worse over the years."

"Why?"

"Started with my dad always telling me to take care of my siblings when we were growing up. I always felt like I needed to be the protective older brother."

She shifts a little closer. "But that can't be all of it?"

My mind wanders back to high school, back to a time I'd rather forget.

It was getting toward the end of the day. I had my action plan in place. I knew what was going to happen. Anna Creed and I were going to meet under the bleachers. Her brother and I had talked a few times. He was a good kid, a bit of a tech nerd, but he was great to hang around. His sister though, Anna, she was who I really wanted to spend my time with.

The bell rang announcing the end of the school term. Excitement pummeled through me.

Summer was here. If things panned out the way I thought they would, Anna would be mine for the break, maybe even longer. I packed away my stuff in record time, grabbed my bag and ran out to the field. My heart was racing faster than I thought possible.

This was it.

But as I ran toward the bleachers, boys were surrounding the stairs in a circle. Confusion rattled through me as I lunged forward.

Anna was on the ground with Tommy Miller sitting on top of her trying to rip her shirt open.

Anger flared through me like nothing before. I raced forward throwing my bag on the dirt. Being a biker brat meant I knew how to fight. It didn't matter to me that there were four of them and only one of me. My father taught me to protect what was important to me.

Anna was important.

My fist connected with Dylan who was standing guard, he went down like a lead weight, then I went in straight for Tommy. I grabbed the back of his shirt yanking him backward off Anna. Her screams piercing my ears as I kneeled over Tommy and landed blow after painful blow into his face.

A slam into the side of my head had me falling into the dirt. My eyes filling with grit as I tried to steady myself, but a kick landed in my stomach.

"Asher, help!" Anna's voice screamed out her brother's name.

A punch landed on my face, but then all of a sudden, it was gone. The body on top of me catapulted to the side managing to allow me to gather my bearings. I sat up seeing her brother Asher laying into Greg.

Somehow, I found the strength to stand and help Asher. I landed another blow into Tommy for good measure as the other three ran off leaving Tommy there on his own.

Asher wiped blood from his nose as I stood over Tommy landing a final kick to his balls. "Don't you ever, ever, lay a hand on Anna or any other girl again, you piece of shit," I yelled at him.

Asher spat at his feet as I turned, holding out my hand to Anna. Her top folded down showing her white lacy bra. But I wasn't turned on at all. At that moment I was more concerned about how she was feeling.

Anna folded her arms over her chest as she walked right into my arms. "My very own protector."

"Zero?" Rayne's concerned voice snaps me out of my reverie. I blink a couple of times. "Where did you go just now?"

I move to sit up in the bed, my erection rendered useless. Rubbing the back of my neck, I exhale. "Let's just say, I helped someone out of a bad situation once when I was younger. It pushed me to help if I can."

"Your first love?"

It's like she sees right through me.

"Something like that. Was Chuck your first love?"

She blanches at my question. "I… I don't know. I would have said yes earlier when we were first married, but now I question… did I ever truly love him? The answer is… I'm not sure."

"So, in honesty, you haven't had a first love yet?"

She exhales. "Maybe not."

I hum under my breath as I glance at my watch. "We better get up. We need to grab some breakfast then get on the road."

She slides out of bed slowly making her way to the bathroom. "Hey, Zero?"

My eyes shift up as she turns back to face me. "Yeah?"

"Thanks for the cuddles."

I snort out a laugh while sliding out of bed to get dressed straight into my jeans.

Pulling into the compound after the long-as-hell ride, it's been a big couple of days. I'm glad to be back in Houston and back at the clubhouse. Albeit with a few new people in tow to add to our chapter, but new blood is always good.

As I park my ride, I'm fucking tired, even though I slept like a baby last night. Over eight hours riding today, the same yesterday will do strange things to the body. No matter how many times you've done long haul you never adjust to it.

I slide off my bike, my muscles twitching. I'm in need of a good drink, but I have shit to do, people to take care of first. We have five new guests, plus a baby, and my brother and sister coming back from an extended vacation. I need to make sure everyone settles in. Not just Rayne.

Mack waddles over to Wraith, his rotund body wobbling to and fro as he rushes to his owner. Wraith bends down scrunching his fat rolls in his hands then he pulls the dog's face to his own. I leave them to their bonding session as I head inside. I want to get to Nessie to give her some instructions before everything gets out of fucking control.

She's already walking toward me like she knew I'd be in search of her. That's why she's our head club girl because she knows what to do and when to do it. "Good ride, pres?"

Rolling my shoulders, I crack my neck to the side, my spine adjusting all the way down. "Long… eventful."

"I see we have some newbies? Fox called ahead. I've already prepared three rooms. Two couple rooms and one single. The single close to yours as requested. Also, one of the couple rooms has been soundproofed on the inside."

"Good work, Nessie, you've been busy."

She stands taller. "We have our part to play here, pres. Gotta keep our end up while you're doing your thing."

"Appreciate it, Ness..." I reach out placing my hand on her shoulder. "Right, the run down. Chills and Chains, they're the couple with the baby, they're going in the soundproofed room."

"Ahh, now I get it. So, the rest of us can't hear the crying baby. After what we went through with Kevlar's kids, I totally get it."

"Exactly. The new prospect, Luc, and the new club girl, Ruby, are going in the other couple's room—"

"Club girl and a prospect? Together?"

"They're very much a couple. Once he earns his patch, he'll claim her."

She flashes me her pearly whites. "That's so cool."

"The single room is for Rayne. She'll be staying with us indefinitely. Not as a club girl, as a guest."

"Got it! We made sure Prinie and Koda's rooms are sparkling for them to go straight back into."

"Great work, Nessie. Thank you."

Ruby and Luc walk in taking in the size of the place. The clubhouse is much bigger than Chicago, so I'm sure they're a little shocked. I gesture for them to come over.

"Thanks again, pres, for taking us both in," Luc offers, his arm firmly around Ruby's waist.

"Yes, thanks. I couldn't imagine not coming with Luc," Ruby adds.

"We're pleased to have another girl here, Ruby!" Nessie beams wide at Ruby.

"Rubes, I know you were the head club girl at Chicago, but you won't be here. It's a change but don't worry. You're sharing a room with Luc. All the brothers know that while you might be a club girl and your duties are the same, you are off-limits."

Ruby's eyes light up, so do Luc's. I guess neither of them was sure how this would work and how Ruby being a club girl here would impact their relationship.

"Thanks, Zero, you don't know what this means to us," Ruby gushes.

"Yeah, pres, this means a lot. I know I'm only a prospect, so showing us this kind of courtesy is..." He pauses glancing at Ruby lovingly. "Thanks, pres."

I reach out gripping his shoulder. I get it. Last thing I'd want is for a bunch of my new brothers to be hitting the ass of the woman I'm in love with. That's why I'm doing it for him. Normally, a prospect and a club girl wouldn't get any special treatment, but when it's something like this, special circumstances take precedence. "If a brother is with a woman here, we take that seriously. You won't be touched, Ruby. Now Nessie, show everyone to their rooms, I have other shit to deal with."

"Sure thing, pres."

I dip my head, then make my way over to my siblings. Prinie's eyes are wandering all over the clubhouse like a million memories are flooding back to her all at once. Only pride is filling me. They're back where they finally belong. I step up to Prinie, gripping her arm. She turns to face me, her darkened eyes are flooding with unshed tears.

The sight pounds me hard right in the chest. I pull her to me, wrapping my arms around her tight. I should have been with her when she walked in, not tending to other people.

I'm an asshole.

I need to make this shit right.

Taking in a deep breath, I smooth my hand over her hair. "I'm glad you've come home. I know it's hard but think of all the good times we had here."

She slowly glances up at me. "Do I still have my old room?"

"It hasn't been touched. Only kept clean."

Her lips slowly spread into a smile across her face. "Thank you."

"Prinie, if you feel like this life is getting on top of you again, talk to me before making any rash decisions. Okay? Promise me?"

"I promise." A single tear slides down her cheek. I wipe it away with my finger. I hate coming back has brought up so many emotions for her. She leans up on her toes pressing a kiss to my cheek, then takes Koda, and they walk off to their rooms. Heaviness washes over me. I hope Prinie's going to be okay here. The memories of what happened are still raw for her. I hope new good ones will outweigh the bad.

Glancing over, Lexi is talking to Rayne. There are so many things I've overlooked since we arrived back here tonight.

I let Prinie walk in here on her own—mistake.

I let Rayne walk in here on her own—mistake.

But I can't be fucking everywhere at once.

I have to be where I am needed, but I'm needed in multiple places at once.

I've let important people to me down.

I let Prinie down.

I just hope Rayne isn't too badly affected from walking in here by herself without my support.

Time to find out.

Striding over to Lexi and Rayne, they're fucking chuckling. Well, damn! Sounds like Rayne's enjoying herself. I step up.

Lexi smiles at me. "Hey, pres, Rayne's gonna fit in here just fine."

I cock my chin. "And why's that?"

"Because Rayne prefers whiskey over vodka."

"Didn't picture you as a whiskey girl," I direct to Rayne.

She shrugs. "I'm sure there's many things about me you can't picture."

"I'm sure there's many things I can and have," I insinuate.

Rayne's eyes stare into mine. The world stops revolving, and we're stationary, locked in a trance. The energy around us magnetizing, intensifying, causing the hairs on the back of my neck to stand from the adrenaline of the moment.

I need to stop this shit.

Flirting with Rayne is pointless.

I take in a deep breath breaking our intense eye contact. "I'll get Nessie to show you to your room. It's close to mine, so I can keep an eye on you."

"Mm-hmm," she mumbles.

"Rayne."

"Yeah?"

"Don't leave the clubhouse unless you're told to."

Her eyes narrow in on me. "What! Like some kind of prisoner?"

"Don't be dramatic. Just until I clear some shit up. I don't need Chuck finding you before I've had a chance to properly hide you."

She gnaws on her bottom lip. "Okay. I'll be good."

"Yeah… sure you will," I mock.

Rayne tries to hide her smirk as I take a deep breath.

Leaving her is the right choice. She's in a good mood and not affected by being here. She's fine. There's no need to take care of her. The woman can take care of herself, so I go in search of the guy I need to talk to. Though, after having a flashback earlier, I'm unsettled, and seeing him isn't going to make talking to him any easier.

ZERO

Marching over to Neon's den, I punch in the code to enter. I crack the seal and walk in, closing the door behind me with a thud. Neon's been back all of a half an hour, and he's already working on something. His set up's like something you'd see in a Sci-Fi movie—*The Matrix* springs to mind.

Many screens plaster one wall with code running up and down them, filing cabinets on the opposite wall. There's a long desk in front of the screens. It's a hacker's paradise. The door to the room has a combination key code, and only those with the six-digit passcode can enter.

Neon glances up at me briefly, annoyance on his face. "Long ride," he offers.

"Yeah, my ass still has pins and needles."

He stops typing, turning to give me his full attention. "She called as I got in. She knew we were out on a long haul."

I clench my eyes tight. A sudden wave of panic washes over me, but I let it roll right off as I open my eyes letting out a small grunt. "What did Anna want?"

Neon relaxes in his high-backed chair as he studies me. "To ask how you're doing. You know I can't be the go-between for you two forever."

"Fuck off, Asher, I'm not asking you to. Your sister's the one doing that... I let her go when she did what she did. Remember? And you trying to continuously make me and Anna happen is what's making..." I wave my hand between the two of us, "... you and me so fucking awkward with each other."

He scrubs his hands over his jaw, then pulls his baseball cap off. "Fuck, brother, I know. It's just... it was us three against the world..." I flare my nostrils, "... now you hardly talk to me unless it's club business. Wraith's your best friend. I get it. He's there for you without all *our* baggage. I miss our damn friendship, Krew. We grew up together, man. I joined this fucking club because of you..." He runs his hand over his short, buzzed scalp. "Hell, I thought you were gonna be my brother-in-law—"

"You think I didn't want that? You think that's why it doesn't hurt so much to see you all the time, Neon? Your sister fucked with my head. She fucked up *our* friendship, too. You want someone to blame? Direct that shit toward Anna."

Neon turns back to his computers, letting out a long exhale. "She still loves you."

"I don't need to hear that, man. Look, I came in here for something. If you're gonna try and guilt me into something that's not going to happen, I'll find someone else to help me."

He turns back to face me. "What do you need, pres?"

"The woman we've brought with us, Rayne—"

"Yeah, the cop's wife."

"I need her untraceable. I don't know what you're going to have to do, new name or what not, but we need her to not be found."

"Got it! Any name in particular?"

I sturdy my shoulders. "Not Anna."

Neon swallows hard, but turns to his computers getting to work.

"Let me know when you're done. We will need to add the name to her pharmacist license. Change some stuff around so she can work."

Neon nods. "Too easy."

"Thanks, brother."

He dips his head while he's busy tapping away. Neon's already in the zone, so I walk out of his den in search of the next person I need to see. I have the technical side of this shit dealt with, now I have to get the physical side managed. I have only one person in mind who can help me with this. I walk over to the stairs taking them two at a time. My body is screaming at me from the long ride, but I need to get this settled. I have to make sure everything's taken care of for Rayne. I have to know she has a place here and it's safe as it can be. So, as I reach the hall, the door opens to Chains' and Chills' bedroom, and I walk straight for it.

As I enter, Kevlar and Chains are busy setting up Kobe's crib, while Chills is rocking the seven-month-old to sleep. I grin at Kevlar, on his knees, working with the wood. It's been three years since Kevlar was last doing this with Lucas, and it's got to be bringing up some memories for him.

My eyes shift to Chills as she cuddles her sick son. You wouldn't even know there's anything wrong with him, but a heart condition is always hidden from view. Kobe's surgery will happen when he's around two years old, but he needs to be here for all his checkups and pre-op procedures. Plus, getting him settled in now is a good idea.

"Chills, can we have a chat?" My voice is lowered so I don't wake Kobe.

"Come on in," she whispers, all the while Chains and Kevlar grunt and groan trying to fuck about with the crib. "What's on your mind, pres?"

Straight to the point.

I heard Chills is a straight shooter.

I walk in taking a seat on the bed. "I need to ask some medical favors of you."

"You not feeling well?"

"No nothing like that. I need to open a pharmacy. I'll fund it, but it will belong to the club."

"A pharmacy?"

Kevlar stops building, turning to face me momentarily. The wheels turning in his mind.

"Yeah, it's for Rayne. Once Neon has a new name setup for her, one she can hide under, he's going to doctor her license and degree."

"Why am I not surprised by any of this?"

"Thing is, doc, I don't know the first thing about opening a pharmacy, and I think opening it in her new name might be a bad idea."

Chills drops her head assessing me. "You want me to open it?" Her tone is accusatory.

"Can you do that?"

Her eyes move to Chains, who exhales. "I'm happy for you to do whatever you wanna do, woman."

She rolls her eyes. "Pfft, you're no help. Okay, the only thing that might work is if I open a not-for-profit walk-in clinic with an attached pharmacy. That way it's kind of like an urgent care and one-stop-shop. I'll work there when I'm not on shift at the hospital. We'll hire a GP to staff it the other times. Then Rayne will head up the pharmacy department, but it will all be under my name. The thing is, though, you'll need to buy an already established pharmacy and take over the licenses, otherwise it will take too long to get all the approvals in place."

My smile is wide as I reach out placing my hand on her shoulder. "You know what, Chills? I think I'm gonna like having y'all 'round here."

She stifles a laugh. "You're welcome, Zero."

"You tell Neon whatever you need to get started, and we will get it underway."

Her eyes light up. "What, tonight?"

"Yes. I need to get this thing happening, so Rayne feels like she has something to do. A place to belong."

Chains and Kevlar both snort out some kind of muffled reaction as I turn to them. "Got something to say, fuckheads?"

Chains raises his brow and continues working while Kevlar places the Allen wrench down and assesses me. "You trying to make Rayne comfortable here, or comfortable enough so she doesn't leave?"

I let out a grunt. "The fuck would you know, asshole."

"I've seen the way you eye fuck her, pres. I can read that expression. It's how I looked at Em."

"You were madly in love with Em, Kevlar. What kind of shit are you trying to pull here?"

"I'm *still* madly in love with Em, pres. It never stops. That's how I remember it. The feeling you get when you connect with someone."

"I've seen it, too," Chains adds. "The way you want to take possession of her."

"True," Chills puts her nose in just to add salt to the gaping fucking wound. "When she's in pain, the fight in your eyes is how Chains looks at me. You want to protect her. You want her to be safe—"

"Fuck off. I come in here for some help with a problem, not a damn counseling session."

They all laugh as Chills grips my arm. "She's pretty."

I stand from the bed. "That's e-fucking-nough. Chills... see Neon about the clinic. I'm your fucking president, show me some respect." I storm for the door, anger seeping off me in waves, but not because they were harassing me, but because they're damn well right.

Rayne is getting to me.

I have to put some distance between us, and I need to do it today.

RAYNE

I thought I'd be overwhelmed. I've basically uprooted my life without telling anyone. Not my deadbeat husband. Not my family. Not the people I worked with. Not a damn soul except for Prinie knows I'm here, but that's okay because Prinie's here too, experiencing this move with me. If she wasn't here, I don't think I'd be handling it as well as I am. But, to be honest, as I sit at this bar, my hand running over the smooth stained woodgrain, I can't help but feel like I'm free. Like I'm a bird who's flying high in the sky after being in a rusted cage for so long. I can finally grace the bright blue sky and see what it's like from the outside looking in.

I was trapped with Chuck.

Life was tedious and dangerous.

Zero gave me an out.

I had to take it.

Sure, it was a rush.

It was a whirlwind.

I didn't have time to catch my breath or much less think about my actions.

But as the night falls on another day, I'm beginning to see my new life here, at this club, might just be the best version of my life so far.

I swivel on the stool glancing around the vast open space. The clubhouse is a converted warehouse. The main room is a giant open expanse with high ceilings. Large rusted metal bars line the ceiling giving it the complete industrial warehouse feel.

Then, the second story kicks in, but underneath is an all-metal staircase leading to the rooms above. The pool table sits in the opening beneath the second story. And just before the stairs in the corner is a unisex bathroom.

Where the second level stops and the open expanse starts, giant poles hold the second story up, obviously for structural reasons. There's a room under the second level with large double black wooden doors which open outward. On the doors, I assume is the club logo—two bike engines with skulls coming out the sides and a pair of wings with Houston Defiance MC written underneath.

To my right is the kitchen which has no doors, just a giant entry. It has state-of-the-art supplies with a massive stainless-steel fridge and appliances of all types on the counters. I can't help but notice the massive coffee machine.

Next to the kitchen there's another room but that door's shut. It has the appearance of a giant safe. It's gray, made of concrete, and next to it is a keypad. I'm guessing whatever's in there is supposed to be well-protected.

Sporadically around the main room there are tables and chairs strategically placed, obviously so the brothers can mingle and eat in a common room.

The place is a lot cleaner, and actually more family friendly than I was expecting. I'm not sure what I was thinking it was going to be like when I got here, but stripper poles certainly crossed my mind on more than one occasion with semi-clothed women running around.

The people are also nothing like what I thought they would be. So far, they're completely welcoming. The club girls are super friendly. My impression of this place was completely wrong.

I can see myself becoming a part of this club and loving it.

My upbringing was proper and strait-laced. My father ran a chain of pharmacies in Chicago. My mother a free bird, flapping about as a socialite, so I've never had a chance to sow my wild oats.

I feel like I could do that here.

There's a couple of girls who should be able to teach me the ropes. Prinie, she's lived here most of her life—she understands the rules. Chills, she knows club business but, like me, is also new to Houston. We have a commonality and with them both on my side, I *can* get through this.

The one thing I didn't count on is my attraction to Zero.

He's strong, tall, gorgeous as hell, and as he storms through the clubroom, his stance demands attention. He's the perfect match of bad boy but with wit, charm, and arrogance. You wouldn't think all those things work together, but somehow, they do.

I focus on my left hand where my wedding ring sits gracefully on my finger. I take in the gold band. *I don't even like gold.* I prefer white gold, but I remember Chuck saying it had to be gold to represent wealth.

I spin the rings on my finger.

Maybe I should take them off?

"Penny for your thoughts?" Prinie asks, sliding in beside me.

My head snaps up, and I exhale. "My rings."

"You hate those things."

I chuckle. "How did you know?"

"Because they're hideous. I mean shit, girlfriend, if you liked them, I'd have to question our friendship."

I place my hands on the bar. "Maybe I should take them off."

She wraps her arm around my shoulders, pulling me to her. "That's a huge step. Just because you're here doesn't mean you have to jump into this life full steam ahead... you do it when you're ready, babe. Not before. It might cause that hard shell of yours to crack."

She knows me so well.

Prinie's never seen me cry, not in the entire time she's been my savior. Through all the beatings, through all the untold hours of agony, I've never shed a tear. Chuck's not worth my distress. She knows as well as I do, if doing anything is going to jeopardize that dam wall breaking, then it's not worth that either.

"You're right... not yet. When I'm ready."

She cuddles into me further. "Good plan. There's no rush."

"I can't believe I'm here with you. You talked about this place like you'd never come back… now we're *both* here."

Prinie snorts, letting me go. "I honestly can't believe it either. I guess sometimes home is in your blood."

"I think this place is going to be good for us, Prinie. For *both* of us."

"I like your optimism, but I'll wait and see what you say after the Militia come around shooting up the clubhouse to high hell. *Then* tell me how you *really* feel about being here."

"You've talked about this Militia only in pieces. Do they really come here attacking that brutally?"

Prinie's eyes darken as she focuses on the end of the bar. Her eyes glisten with unshed tears. She exhales. "Yeah. Yeah, they do." She clears her throat, shaking her head as if trying to remove a distant memory. Her eyes slowly move back to mine. "Apparently, a new captain is in place at the Militia now, though. Him and Zero are at some version of peace, but I'll believe that when I see it."

"You think we're not safe here?"

"Any clubhouse is going to be rife with danger. I figure if we're here, at least we'll have people looking out for us. Chicago had other people who were higher up the totem pole of protection before Koda and me. Here, well here, I'm royalty so…" She shrugs.

"You and Koda come first."

"Yeah… being out on our own was hard, so much harder than I thought it would be. At least here, Koda will have everything he needs. That's the main reason for coming back."

"So, Koda's taken care of?"

"Yeah, he was missing too much school… getting involved with the wrong people. He needs stability. Me taking him away from here wasn't giving him that. I was scared, running scared of this place and what happened here, but that's not fair on Koda."

"He left willingly, though."

"He did, but he's young, and he doesn't really know what he wants. Koda didn't truly grasp what it meant to leave. He just wanted to be away from the place that took our mom and dad. Just like I needed to be at that time. We did that, now we're back. I guess I just need to find a way to deal with seeing their dead bodies over by the bar every time I look that way."

"Oh, Prinie." I sink in on myself.

Her eyes water again as she holds up her hand. "I'm fine, really. At least, I will be. Just gotta keep myself busy."

"Well, I'm here, and plan on occupying *all* your time."

"Sounds good to me."

My eyes drift to Zero who's standing with his brothers talking to them about who knows what. Waking up with my arms wrapped around him this morning was something I wasn't planning on, but a feeling I know I could get used to.

Though, being a married woman, should I be having those thoughts? My answer is simple—in my mind I knew my marriage was over the first time Chuck landed his fist in my face.

I have no understanding about why I stayed.

Out of a debt to my father? Maybe.

Out of fear of what would happen if I left? Definitely.

Zero gave me the protection I needed to make a clean escape. I hope I can make a fresh start here without my past coming to haunt my present.

Zero walks past gaining my attention. *God, he's so good-looking.* My heart skips a beat as I take in his strong arms and broad shoulders. Seeing him practically naked and lying next to him in bed was hard work on my libido. Then waking up on top of him, all his hard muscles clenched beneath me, shit, my clit's throbbing just thinking about him again. My eyes blink rapidly waking from my memory as he walks right past me. Butterflies swarm in my stomach as I sit taller. "Thanks for bringing me here, Zero."

He turns his head to me, dips his chin, then keeps walking basically ignoring me. Those butterflies shrivel up and die as my heart thuds hard.

What the hell? I'm confused.

We were on really good speaking terms, and I thought we had a good thing going.

I sit back against the bar letting out a huff. "What the fuck?"

Prinie grips my shoulder with a sympathetic frown. "Don't worry, it's not you. He's a temperamental asshole most of the time."

It still doesn't make sense to me. Something's shifted between us, the only problem is, I'm not privy as to what. If he needs some space, I'll give it to him as much as I don't want to.

"C'mon, hon, let me show you to your room," Prinie suggests.

I weakly smile as we stand then move toward the stairs. We take them slowly, my feet hurting like a bitch. It's going to take me a little while to get used to walking up and down these each day with my feet still cut up, but Prinie helps me. Once we get to the top of the stairs, Prinie leads me to the second door on the right. "This is your room. You're right next door to Wraith. Opposite of you, over there, is Zero. So you're going to be so protected up here."

I glimpse over at Zero's room as a wave of sadness washes over me. I hate he's avoiding me if that's what it was.

Prinie opens my door, leading me inside. The room's lovely. It's not huge, but it's big enough. It has a queen-size bed with a beautiful white silk cover, desk space with a laptop, a giant window with black curtains that overlook the main room of the clubhouse, and a separate room which contains a small bathroom.

I inhale, taking in the smell of the room. "What's that smell?"

Prinie sniffs the air dragging my suitcase that was already in here up onto my bed. "It smells like peach to me."

I glance to the bookshelf on the side wall where there's a candle burning. I love all the little touches. It might be a fluke that a peach-smelling candle's burning in my room when my hair shampoo is peach scented, or did Zero call ahead because he's taken extra notice?

Either way, I'm impressed.

"Nice touch," I say.

Prinie opens my luggage. "Want me to help you unpack?"

I take in my new room, my new life, and I know I need to get acquainted with it all. "I think I can manage. Thanks, though, Prin. I don't know how I'd cope if you weren't here with me."

She leans in giving me the tightest of hugs, then pulls back looking in my eyes. "The feeling is definitely mutual. I'm at the end of the hall if you need me, okay?"

"Got it."

Prinie exits my room, and I start to pull out the life I brought with me. The closet space isn't huge, but it comes with hangers, so I move about placing what little clothes I brought inside. The three pairs of shoes in the bottom of the closet. My makeup in the bathroom along with my straightener. A picture of my parents and me on the desk. I don't have much, and it makes me sad. I also didn't tell my family I left, nor did I bring my cell with me.

I have no way of telling them where I am.

My body slumps.

I know I can't tell them where I am because they'll tell Chuck.

Suddenly, the weight of this situation weighs down on me full force. I've been coping well until now, right when I'm here setting up my new life with the barest of minimums.

I will not cry.

Sitting down on the softness of the bed, I gnaw on my bottom lip when there's a knock at my door. My head snaps up hoping it's Zero, but Chills stands there and extends a warm greeting. "How are you feeling?"

"A little overwhelmed," I answer honestly.

Chills walks inside my room and shuts the door with a click. Then she sits next to me on the bed, the mattress dipping with the movement. "This is a huge thing that's happening to you, but I want you to know Zero has put something in motion to help you adjust to life here."

My eyes narrow on her. "He has?"

"He's going to purchase a business property in my name. From that place of business is going to be a walk-in clinic and a pharmacy."

My eyes widen as I let out a gasp. "He's making a pharmacy and a clinic for us?"

"For *you*. The clinic will be a side note, only open sporadically. The pharmacy is *your* baby for you to run as you see fit."

I let out a bemused scoff—this can't be real. "But how? Won't Chuck find me?"

She pats me knee. "Neon's updating your records as we speak. He's effectively changing your name. Here you'll be Rayne, and outside of the club, you'll be called something else. You'll have to work on knowing what your new backstory is."

"I was always good at drama in school." I grin.

"Good, because this will be it for the rest of your life, Rayne. Once that name change takes place, that's it. We don't want Chuck to know it's you."

I can't believe this is happening. With Zero's attitude before, I can't understand why he's doing this while being an asshole toward me. "Zero was weird just a little while ago. He walked right by me, ignoring me when I talked to him. I can't understand why he would be doing all this for me, then on the other hand treating me like I don't matter."

Chills exhales. "He's a man, which means he's an idiot to begin with, but he's also a president *and* an older brother. He has a lot of people to take care of... to keep an eye on. He has a ton of shit going on, so don't take it to heart too much if he's all over the place."

That makes sense. I shouldn't read into it.

"Okay, thanks, Chills. And thanks for helping with the pharmacy. It's going to be amazing, I love my work. When do you think it will all start happening?"

"I just talked with Neon. He's already doctored your records and made you disappear. We should be able to start the paperwork tomorrow. Then we'll go in search of a location. But I can assure you, it *will* be close to the clubhouse."

I chuckle. "I'm sure it will be. They'll wanna keep an eye on us. Thanks again, Chills, from the bottom of my heart. I really didn't think something like this would even be possible."

"It's amazing what you can do when you know the right people."

"The right people?"

"Yeah, apparently Neon was telling me there's this oil tycoon, who's known as the Baron, and he practically owns Texas. The guys are tight with him. He helps them when they need people to move paperwork along quickly. I'm sure he gets some sort of kickback from the club, I just don't know what."

A crooked oil baron, who would have guessed?

I figure if I'm going to be living here, I better get used to seeing things from a new perspective. I was used to living with a cop where everything was clean-cut and straight down the line. Everything had a place. Things were done by the book. Well, now I need to let go of everything and just go with the flow. Because everything I've been taught, everything that's been drilled into me, is about to go out the window.

"Guess I need to thank this oil baron when I see him."

"Me, too… I'll leave you to it. I'm down the hall, near Prinie. Just let me know if you need anything."

"Will do. Have a good night."

Chills turns, walking out of my room, I follow behind closing my door to finally have some alone time since this all began.

I spin around taking in my new room.

My safe haven.

Even though this place is new and nothing like my old home with Chuck, maybe I can make this my new home.

Maybe I'm going to fit in here just fine.

ZERO

The Next Day

I opened my balcony window before sunrise this morning, the curtains now waving with the slight breeze. It isn't a massively hot April morning, just a little humidity in the air. After moving back to bed and falling back to sleep, my eyes eventually flicker open bringing in the dawn of a new day. In the light of the morning, though, waking up in my bed alone has left me cold. My thoughts linger on the previous morning with Rayne sprawled all over me.

Fuck, I'd love to feel that again.

But I can't.

Things are far too fucking complicated.

Just thinking of her has my cock hard. Groaning, I throw my covers off, making my way to my bathroom. I need to get her out of my head. Rayne isn't going anywhere. So if I'm going to get her out of my system, I need to stop thinking about her in any kind of sexual way.

Walking into the bathroom, I turn to look at myself in the mirror. My raging hard-on proudly bouncing high in the air as I head for the shower. I need to calm the fuck down. Turning on the faucet, I adjust the temperature, then slide under the spray. The water pummels my tired and weary flesh. It's a welcomed pleasure as I press my hands on the wall letting the water run along my back. It careens back over my chest and slides against my throbbing cock. I close my eyes trying to shift my mind to anything I can to calm this boner I am sporting.

I don't want to think about Rayne.

Not her supple lips.

Not the way her ass curves in such a fine fucking way.

Not the way she smells like peaches.

My hand slides instinctively to my cock. The thick, hard length pulses between my fingers.

Her stunning doe eyes, the way they stare at me. *Pump.*

Her full and pert tits sitting perfectly waiting for me to squeeze them. *Pump.*

The way she fires back her sassy tone at me. *Pump.*

I can't help myself as an image of her in the shower flashes behind my tightly closed eyelids. It's enough to set me off. My hand pumps harder on my aching cock, the pleasurable sensation rolling through me instantly. I've needed this since the first moment I laid eyes on Rayne. My body prickles in goosebumps even though I'm burning up from the heat of the shower. Having the image of Rayne running through my mind and the pleasure wrapping around my cock, it's so fucking intense I let out a deep guttural groan.

Fuck, I need her.

I pump harder, faster, the pressure builds from the base of my spine, pulsing all the way to the top of my head. My balls tighten, squeezing hard. I gasp at the intense spasm shooting through me. My muscles tense, my eyes clench tighter, my skin sheens in a fine mist of sweat as I pump so fast forcing out every inch of pleasure from Rayne's images flashing in my mind. My balls squeeze as the tingles shoot from my toes straight to my balls. My cock throbs, and with a throaty groan, I explode all over the shower wall. The climax hitting me like I haven't had for a long fucking time.

My body sags as I lean against the wall trying to catch my breath.

"Fuck," I murmur.

Hopefully, allowing that shit to happen means Rayne's now out of my system.

I find the strength to open my eyes and wash myself off, not forgetting to clean the fucking mess I made of the wall. I do feel better letting off some of the tension I've built up in my shoulders.

Turning off the shower, I hop out, dry myself off, and move around getting dressed.

I need to get ready for the day. We have new people in the club, so there will be teething issues I need to address.

I open the door to my room, and as I walk out into the hall, Rayne steps out opposite me. A flash of the pleasure I had while jerking off to her image rolls over me, and I flush red hot. Her eyes wander my face strangely like she can tell what I'm thinking, or maybe I'm just fucking paranoid.

"Good morning," her angelic voice offers through the silence.

I dip my head in response as we both head for the stairs at the same time blocking each other's paths. Our bodies connect, and we turn, face to face. My eyes lock onto hers, those same eyes I'd fantasized about in the shower. *Fuck.*

My breathing quickens as does hers. I grip her biceps, so she doesn't fall down the stairs. Rayne's gaze on me is intense like she can't figure me out.

Join the fucking club because hell, I can't figure me out either.

She licks her supple lips, the movement enough to have my cock hardening again almost instantly.

This wasn't supposed to happen.

She was supposed to be out of my system.

This is bad. Real bad.

The energy surrounding us draws me closer to her. She doesn't pull away like I need her to, her breasts heave with her breathing as her eyes focus on my lips.

Fuck, I want to taste her mouth.

See if she tastes like she smells—fucking heavenly.

My cock presses against the seam of my jeans, making me all too aware we're heading into dangerous damn territory. I snap out of it taking a step back, putting some much-needed space between us. I don't miss the downturn in her hopeful eyes as I swipe my hand toward the stairs. "Ladies first."

She clears her throat, then turns slowly hobbling down the stairs. I hate she's in pain, so I avert my eyes, but they land on her ass instead as I follow her down. My cock grows harder. *Fucking hell, this woman will be the death of me.* I rearrange my cock in my jeans as I avert my eyes away from her body and continue to follow her down the stairs.

"Do you want to join me for breakfast?"

I want to eat you for breakfast.

"I have some work I need to do. Enjoy your day," I tell her as we reach the bottom.

Her lips turn up making her eyes shine like the stars in the darkened night sky. For a moment, my heart leaps into my throat as I admire her—she's fucking stunning as she saunters off toward the kitchen. I groan while rubbing the back of my neck, trying to ease the tension that has now come back.

I make my way to Neon's den, enter the six-digit code, then walk through. Neon's head is down on his desk, fast asleep. I smirk, feeling some of the tension from moments before washing away. I walk over, ball my fist, then slam it down hard on the wood, sending a loud reverberating noise through the small room.

Neon jolts awake, drawing his gun from his waist and aims it in my direction without even looking. I let out a bellowing laugh as he blinks a few times trying to gain his bearings.

"Fucking asshole," Neon mutters as he rubs his face, gun still in hand.

"Sorry, brother, couldn't resist. You been in here all night?"

He holsters his gun back in his jeans with a nod. "Yeah, been working on Rayne's paperwork."

My chest squeezes. Even with all the shit between us, he still goes above and beyond. "What do you have for me?"

Neon turns around, grabbing a file and slides it over. "The paperwork's done. Rayne Rosenberg is now known as Harper Johnson. PharmD, Doctor of Medicine... it's all in there. She can now practice in Houston. I also found an existing location, it's literally down the other end of Clinton Street. Next to the McDonald's, so we could get there fast if we need to."

"So, the public goes to McDonald's, then to the pharmacy to get their diabetes medication. Couldn't be more perfect."

Neon chuckles. "Exactly. We can also purchase the place next door and knock down the joining wall to make that into the consulting area."

"When can we tee it all up?"

"I put the call into the Baron last night."

I dip my head at him. "Thanks, Neon… appreciate you staying up all night taking care of this for me. You did me a solid."

He rolls his shoulders, I assume they ache from sleeping on his desk. "It's what I'm here for, pres."

"Tell me when you get word from the Baron. I wanna try and get this place set up for them as soon as I can."

"Will do."

I grip his shoulder in a gesture of thanks, then turn to leave. "Neon…" I peer over my shoulder, "… get some actual sleep today. Yeah?" I turn walking out of his den to go in search of Chills. I can't help but notice Rayne on my way out. It's like I'm attuned to her. But then again maybe she's attuned to me too. She's watching my every move as I go in search of Chills.

Why does Rayne unnerve me so much? The whole fucking thing's beginning to bug me.

I head for the stairs and make my way to Chills' room then gently rap on the door. I don't want to wake Kobe if he's sleeping. It opens soon after to a shirtless Chains rocking a grumbling Kobe. "Hey pres, had a rough night. Think Kobe doesn't like being in an unfamiliar setting."

"Take all the time you need to get him settled, Chains. Then when you guys are on your feet, we'll talk about your position here at the club."

"Appreciate it, pres."

"Chills around?"

Chains smirks. "I'm beginning to think you like my woman more than you like me, pres. I'm getting a damn complex."

"Then you're an insecure pussy. How may I be of be of assistance, Zero?" Chills teases her old man stepping into view. She's wearing a robe and her hair's disheveled like she's had no sleep either.

"I'll let you guys sleep. I just wanted to let y'all know we've secured a building down the road. This should all happen rather fast. We might need you to sign some paperwork and other shit when the time comes."

"Whatever you need."

"You guys sleep. We'll come get you if we need you."

"Thanks, Zero," Chains answers as I turn walking back down the hall.

RAYNE

Two Days Later

I've been at the Houston Defiance clubhouse for a couple of days now. While everyone else is settled into their normal rhythm, I'm wandering around with nothing to do. I spend my time with Prinie when she's not occupied with other things, but I'm feeling a little redundant at the moment. I guess I thought life here would be a little more, well, exciting.

It's the middle of the day, and Zero's been avoiding me since our brief, but energized encounter at the top of the stairs. I sense the tension between us, but I have no idea what it means. All I know is waking up in his arms was the most relaxed I've felt in as long as I can remember.

I want to feel like that again.

Sitting at a table, picking at my lunch, I try to think about how I can waste away the rest of the afternoon when pounding feet take my attention. I glance up as Zero and Chills rush toward me. I sit taller, the sight of Zero appearing so excited sends a wave of something through me. My tummy swirls in delight at his gorgeous face as he and Chills pull up a chair in front of me, sitting down like they mean business.

"I have a surprise for you," Zero states as he slides a folder across the table toward me.

Chills grins like she's in on this secret. I grab the folder, opening it to a sheet of information with my photograph, but the details are of another person—Harper Johnson.

"Harper Johnson?" *I'm confused.*

Zero sits forward more. "She's your Houston identity. You need to be her when you're not at the club, to keep your identity a secret."

My stomach flips in excitement. "You mean I can go out and do things now?"

"Not only can you go out, you can work," Zero tells me.

I gasp, almost falling off my seat. "No fucking way."

Chills slides a picture of a building to me, and I take it in. "It's a little run down, but with some TLC, it could be great. It's yours. Your pharmacy. Also, a walk-in clinic two days a week, but it's yours to run as you see fit. You will hire the staff and do everything Zero promised."

My heart races so fast I know I'm overwhelmed. I never thought this day would come, that I would have my own pharmacy. Now Zero's bent over backward to make this happen for me. I stand and race around the table taking Zero into a giant embrace. His hands loop around me, sliding up my back, pulling me onto his lap. His hands on me again is what I've been missing these past two days. This contact, this closeness. I pull back. Our eyes connect as I stare at him, my breath catches as his intense eyes study mine. That same pull, the energy I feel whenever I look at him has me drawing closer to him. It's like we're magnets. I can't pull away. Instead, we're being drawn together. My stomach flutters with those same butterflies while his hand caresses my bicep, his thumb grazing up and down my skin in a tender moment.

A simple touch, but it's setting me on fire.

I want him to touch me everywhere.

Zero's free hand shifts up, swiping a strand of hair behind my ear, my cheek instantly leaning into his palm. We lean closer. Our eyes connect so intensely it's like there are fireworks exploding around us. Zero leans in further. He's intoxicating.

A movement to our left catches both our attention. Chills tries to make a stealthy exit, and she fumbles as her top gets caught on the table making it groan against the concrete floor, and just like that, our chemistry is gone.

"Fuck! Sorry, I was trying to leave you guys to it."

Zero quickly hoists me off his knee, clearing his throat. "It's fine! We're done here... I'll take you to your store tomorrow."

"Tomorrow," I reply trying to fight back my smile.

He stands, then walks off as Chills grimaces. "I'm *so* sorry. I was trying to make a stealthy getaway to leave you two to... whatever *that* was."

I let out an exhale. "I have no idea what that was. He's all over the place with me. One minute he's about to kiss me, the next he's running away like you just saw. I can't keep up with him. He gives me whiplash."

Chills sits and exhales. "Hmm... maybe underneath the tattoos and all that bravado, he's actually got a moral compass. I bet those rings on your finger mean something to him."

I peek down at them. They're a reminder of everything that's wrong in my life right now.

So why can't I take them off?

Chills reaches out grabbing my hand. "Hey, it's okay if you can't do it yet. It's only been a couple of days. Hell, you haven't even had the chance to tell your husband it's over. That's probably half your problem... and you may not get the chance to see him again. I suggest you write him a letter, not necessarily to send, just as a cathartic way to let go. Tell him you're through. That it's over. It might help."

She's making sense. "I'm gonna do that. Thanks, Chills."

"You're welcome. Now go and start planning everything you want in your pharmacy because every decision is yours, hon."

Excitement bubbles inside of me as Chills rushes off. I turn back to the documents on the table, grabbing them to head for my room. I need to study them, learn who I am, then make all the plans I can.

But first maybe I need to have a cold shower.

ZERO

A Week Later

Rayne rushing about her pharmacy like this is setting me on fire. I'm standing back while the prospects help her place everything where she needs it. The store isn't huge, medium in size, but she knows exactly where she wants everything, and what Rayne wants, she gets. I've told the boys if she asks for something, they make it happen. We owe the Baron for this. The pharmacy wasn't set to go on the market for another month, but he forced the old owners out, so we could purchase the place and the one next door. They're ours outright which is helpful. The club owns them. Well, technically, Chills owns them, but they're bought with club money, more specifically, *my* money.

Who knew accepting Chains and Chills into the fold would have come in handy so damn early.

Rayne's in her element. She even has on her little white lab coat making her look so fucking nerdy, but it has my insides wreaking havoc. The back area of the pharmacy is all set up with the dispensing stations and the locked cabinets to keep the medications.

The middle section is where all the over-the-counter medications will go. The cashier counters are at the front. To the right where the wall has been knocked out into the other shop is the walk-in clinic. It's the perfect size, and it is all taking shape. When you know the right people, things can happen real damn quick. We owe the Baron an extra shipment for this.

I move to the rear of the pharmacy to stack some of the medications. I figure I better make myself useful rather than standing around staring at Rayne all afternoon. I'm out the back in between the shelves and out of the view of everyone. As I reach up to put some pills in the cabinets, light footsteps approach. I turn and watch Rayne walking in. She hesitates, her eyes going wide when she sees me. She turns back the way she came like she's unsure of whether to come back here or not.

"I'm not gonna bite you, Harper."

She recoils like she's confused, but then recognition crosses her face. "Harper, right." Then she takes a deep breath, slowly moving down next to me and starts stocking the shelves.

Her peach scent wafts over to me while I try to keep myself in check as her arm brushes mine.

She recoils back. "Sorry."

"Nothing to be sorry for."

She continues to stock as the energy surrounding us makes me uncomfortable. I don't know what the fuck I'm feeling, but we're back here, alone, where no one can see or hear us, and I have no idea what the hell she's thinking.

My eyes glance at her sideways, locking onto hers. She's observing me too, and she gasps suddenly dropping a box to the floor. "Shit," she blurts out as we both squat down to pick it up the contents, our eyes connecting again as we face each other. My breathing becomes heavy. Her eyes sparkling as she stares at me with such intensity I can hardly keep my thoughts contained. Her plump, supple lips look so inviting right now. Too fucking good as her bottom lip darts followed by her teeth grazing her lip. My cock jerks against the seam of my jeans as my chest constricts with warmth.

Rayne is bad for me.

I know that.

This is all kinds of wrong.

But hell, if sometimes wrong can't feel so damn right.

"Fuck it." I reach forward, my hand thrusting into the back of her hair, gripping onto her tightly.

I yank her face to mine. Our lips connect at the same time I topple backward, and she lands on top of me. My hand in her hair grips tightly, holding her to me, taking possession, my other hand sliding to her ass, pulling her on me further. She rubs against my cock as our tongues collide with each other. It's intense, it is passionate. Kissing Rayne is like nothing I've experienced before. She tastes exactly as I imagined, fucking perfect.

My cock grows hard against her as I kiss her like I damn well mean it. Like I've been needing to, wanting to, for so long now. The energy surging through me only causes my blood to pump harder.

The world dissolves around us. It's just Rayne and me on the floor kissing with nothing but blackness surrounding us. A spotlight, a fucking glow shines down on us, and it's like this is the best moment on earth.

My fingers clench in her hair, pulling it. She moans in my mouth sending a shockwave straight to my cock. I bite her bottom lip between my teeth letting out an animalistic growl as she pants for heady breaths. My cock is so fucking hard right now that I want to take her on the damn floor.

"Harper?" a voice calls out, but it feels like it's way away in the distance.

My foggy head becomes clear as my lips leave Rayne's while panting for breath. She stares down at me as we pull apart. Our eyes widen, lips swollen and puffy from our frantic kissing.

"Harper?"

I move to sit, taking Rayne with me, placing her on the floor beside me as Chills walks in. My eyes don't leave Rayne's. I'm lost for damn words. That was the most intense, sensual, frenzied, perfect fucking kiss I've ever had in my life. I am trying to catch my breath, but it's hard when Rayne's taken it away. She's having trouble catching hers too.

Chills stops dead staring at us both. "Oh… um… sorry, there's another delivery."

Rayne clears her throat, her eyes not leaving mine. "Okay, I'll be there in a minute."

Chills pulls her lips into a tight thin line. "Yep." Her voice is high-pitched as she leaves without saying another word.

This is too much.

That went too far.

The fact is Rayne's married.

To a cop.

I don't meddle with married women.

My muscles clench as a wave of anxiety almost cripples me. "Go."

Her eyes droop, the sadness taking over sends a stab right into my chest. "Don't you think we need to talk abou—"

"Just go."

She hesitates but stands, dusts herself off, then walks out leaving me fucking reeling.

What the fuck was I thinking?

I groan, falling back to the floor on my back staring at the ceiling.

I let myself go.

I let myself taste her, now I'm never going to have enough.

Dodge—evade her at all costs.

Complete and utter avoidance.

I can't risk it.

Standing from the floor, I head straight for the door.

"Zero, do you wanna—"

I slam the back door on Chills as I exit to get on my bike and head back to the clubhouse.

What a fucking mess!

A Week Later

It's been nearly three weeks since bringing Prinie and Koda home. They're both settling back into their routines. Koda's been enrolled in school which goes back after spring break. Prinie's prancing around the clubhouse like she owns it—it's as if she never left—while I try to keep everything in motion.

Chains and Chills are settling in. Baby Kobe's pretty damn cute when he's not crying.

Ruby's found her rhythm as a club girl, and Luc's a damn good prospect. So, with that in mind, we're promoting Cannon from prospect to full patch.

Dipshit just doesn't know it yet.

"Everything's in position," Wraith tells me on the down-low.

I turn around bringing my fingers to my lips, sending a loud whistle reverberating through the main room. "Everyone, gather 'round."

My brothers, club girls, and everyone else turn to look at me, then they head to the middle of the main room. The hairs on the back of my neck stand to attention—I know Rayne's near. I glance to my left, and she's making her way in with the others. Fuck, she's even more stunning than when she first came here. The bruises on her face are slowly fading making her beauty even more noticeable. I've been steering clear of her this past week.

I'm sure she's detected the distance between us, but I had to do it, though the draw to her, that pull, that energy I feel for her is getting stronger.

A scraping chair along the middle of the concrete floor pulls my attention back to the matter at hand. I focus on what I need to do right now.

"Cannon, get over here."

"Sure thing, pres," Cannon fires back, racing over as Wraith places the chair in the center of the room.

I grab Cannon by the scruff, forcing him to sit on the chair. His eyes scrunch in confusion as everyone observes the scene playing out. "I've been monitoring you, Cannon. Your eyes are always so attuned, so fixated. You're constantly watching. Always focused on the bigger picture." Cannon's eyes fall to Prinie. Everyone knows Cannon was tasked to protect her and Koda this last year—everyone except

Prinie and Koda. "Loyalty and trust are big issues in Defiance. If we can't trust those brothers around us, then they don't belong in the brotherhood at all."

"Here, here," my brothers all call out making Cannon swallow a nervous lump down his throat.

A bead of sweat rolls down his temple as I circle him.

"The thing we've been trying to figure out, Cannon, is… can we trust you?"

He flashes his eyes around the room like he's trying to find a way out.

"Can we, Cannon? Can we trust you?" I goad.

Kid's scared out of his brain. Just one more taunt, and I'll put him out of his misery. "Is there anything you wanna tell me, Cannon? Now's the time to confess."

His eyes widen as he sits taller like he has no idea what I'm talking about. His eyes shoot to Prinie.

Whatever he's going to blurt out in his fear might be about her.

"Okay, I did it!"

I jerk my head back in shock.

Wraith stands taller too.

This took a turn.

I'm only hazing him, so I continue. "I need you to spell it out for me, Cannon. What. Did. You. Do?"

He slumps in the chair, his head hanging low. "My first week here as a prospect, you got me to help with the packaging, and, well, I sampled some. Just one time, only one line, I wanted to know if it was good shit or not."

Wraith rolls his eyes, and I smile. As if we haven't all sampled the Snow White from time to time while packaging it. If that's his biggest confession, I have no reason not to move forward with this. I grip his shoulder letting out a heavy exhale. "Well, shit, Cannon, now you've told me the truth, there's only one course of action I can take."

His eyes shoot up to mine, fear creeps over his face as his nostrils flare. "Fuck, pres, I'm sorry. I'll do anything. Please, this club means everything to me."

I raise my brow. "Anything?" I question while he nods frantically. "Then quit apologizing and stand up to accept your cut. Phantom."

Cannon lets out a nervous snort, then his eyes widen in delight at his new road name.

Wraith walks over handing me Phantom's new cut. I kick his foot, and he stands abruptly, then I ease his cut onto his back. He loops his arms through his new vest beaming with nothing but pride as the other guys cheer.

I slap him on the back as he grips onto his new vest like it's his lifeline. "A phantom is like a shadow, always there in the background keeping an eye on things, stepping in if the need calls for it. He's always observing, keeping things in control... the comic book *Phantom* relies on his strength and intelligence to get him out of situations. Your strength is there, your intelligence however..." I mock.

Everyone laughs as Phantom rolls his eyes. "Thanks for this, pres. I won't let you down."

"I know. You've already proven yourself." I subtly peek at Prinie, her forehead crinkling like she's utterly confused. She has no idea why Cannon's known as the guy who watches, and I need to keep it that way.

"Right, let's celebrate! Nessie, beer for everyone," I call out, and she spins, hightailing it for the bar. "Fox, fire up the grill, let's make a night of this."

"Sure thing, pres. I'll get Bub to make that queso you like."

"Fuck, yeah, your Old Lady rocks that shit. Let's do this cookout right seeing as it's such nice weather outside."

Beer, brisket, and Tex-Mex. What else could a guy want?

I turn seeing Rayne walking up behind me. I've been avoiding her all week. Now, that she's right here, cornering me, I have nowhere to go.

I have to talk to her.

Fox dips his head, spins on his heels, and walks off leaving me alone with Rayne.

Fucking traitor.

Rayne stops in front of me, her gorgeous emerald eyes assessing me cautiously. I exhale, I can't avoid her forever, so small talk it is. "How are you healing?"

She shrugs, the awkwardness between us is palpable. All I can think about is that fucking electric kiss we shared on the pharmacy floor—Rayne's body on top of mine, her grinding against my cock. *Fuck.*

"I'm feeling better, my feet hardly hurt at all now."

More small talk. Yeah, 'cause we're so great at that.

"Good, I'm glad... well, I better get back to—"

"Have I done something wrong? Was our kiss *that* bad?"

Well, doesn't that make me feel like shit. She's done absolutely nothing wrong. The kiss was amazing. The only thing she's done wrong was marry a damn cop.

I exhale. "No, nothing."

"Are you purposely avoiding me?"

Shit.

"Rayne... you're married."

She shrugs. "Only legally."

A small laugh escapes me as her soft lips stretch cheekily. "Funny... what does that even mean?"

She exhales, stepping into my space, so close I smell her peach shampoo. It's intoxicating. "It means I don't want to be. It's only paperwork. I hate him."

I take those words in.

She doesn't love Chuck.

I suppose that was clear.

The fact of the matter is, he's still a cop—bikers and cops don't mix. "Paperwork or not, cherry bomb. The man's a cop."

She tilts her head. "I didn't take you to be afraid of anything."

Fucking minx. Playing on just the right thing to say.

I step closer, her big doe eyes peep up at me, blinking like she's having trouble focusing as I tower over her. "Listen and listen good, Rayne. I'm not scared of the heat, I just don't need to delve into anything that's gonna bring trouble to the club."

"And you think *I'm* trouble?"

"Cherry bomb, unless we keep you hidden, Chuck *will* come for you. I need to keep my head focused for *if* that happens."

Rayne's eyes are clear as she steps closer, our bodies aligned in every way. Fuck, if the tension isn't catapulting through me like a tornado. She's a typhoon, a swirling cacophony of chaos swarming my mind.

"Zero…" Her hand snakes up to rest on my chest. I let her, needing to feel her against me. "What if I want you to focus on me?"

A deep groan echoes from low in my chest. *She's good.* I don't know why she's chosen now to turn this on. All I do know is we have an audience, and I'm not about to give in to her. I grip her wrist against my chest, hope lights in her eyes as I lean closer. Her breathing hitches as I breath against her ear. "Don't make a scene in front of my brothers, Rayne, you won't like how the story ends." I drop her hand from my chest and turn, storming away from her. The thought of leaving her, of hurting her with my words and actions stings, but I can't lead her on. I can't have her believe there's something here.

I won't get involved with her.

I'm the President of the Houston Defiance MC. I need to keep my head in the damn game, not lost in the thoughts of a woman who I have no right to want.

I storm off feeling the eyes of everyone in the room on me, but I ignore it, moving outside to Fox to check on the grill for the celebrations.

Fox glances me up and down, a concerned frown on his face. "You look stressed. Everything all right?"

I check around, it's just us. Everyone else is inside, so I decide to talk to him—man to fucking man. Fox has been my sounding board for many things. He's been at this club since before I was even born, so his advice means everything to me. He usually catches on pretty quick when something isn't right with me.

"Look, Zero, it's just us. Everyone's inside right now. You know there's no judgment from me."

I lean against the wall next to the grill where he's cooking, letting out a long breath. "Right… Rayne… I'm avoiding her."

His head flinches back slightly. "But you went out of your way to help her."

I roll my shoulders. "I did. I still am… with the pharmacy and shit. But being near her, Fox, it's dangerous territory. Her husband's a cop, that's bad for the club."

He chuckles. "You knew he was a cop when you kidnapped her. You're not making sense."

"She came willingly, old man."

"I'm teasing. But honestly, is this avoidance because of who she's attached to or because she brings out feelings you don't want to feel again…" he pauses, "… because of what happened last time you felt something in here?" He taps over my heart.

Tightness forms in my chest. "You think I don't want Rayne because of Anna?"

"I've seen the chemistry between the two of you. You didn't even look at Anna the way your eyes devour Rayne."

"She's fucking married."

"Is she? Way I see it… she's been separated from her husband mentally for a hell of a long time."

"Mentally and *legally* are two different things. You know what commitment to someone means to me, Fox. Honestly, if Rayne is the type of woman who seeks comfort in another man while married, then there's not much hope there."

Fox reaches out slapping me with his tongs. Hard. "You're an ass judging her like that. Her husband abused her, *relentlessly*. She doesn't love him, she was forced to stay married to him by her family. She doesn't want to be in that marriage, Zero. So why should she fight the urge to want something better, to fight for *someone* better when *you* came along."

I rub the back of my neck. "When *I* came along?"

"Yes. Her something better. Think about that. She might have those rings on her finger, the paperwork might say she's taken, but in her mind, Zero, she's one hundred percent single. I see it when she looks at you. Her damn husband's not even on her radar."

I run my hand through my hair. "Fuck, man, Anna's messing with my head, and she isn't even here. Every time I see Rayne's left hand... those rings on her finger... I think of Anna. The pain I felt when she told me what she did."

Fox turns, clasping my shoulder. "Zero, I know Anna hurt you like hell."

Pain ripples through me like it was yesterday, though, in reality, it was four years ago. You think I'd be over it by now. That my balls would have grown back. Letting Anna's betrayal get to me like this continually is not doing me any favors. "I need to get Anna the fuck out of my head, Fox."

"Then what better way than by putting someone else in there?"

"Someone like Rayne?"

He shrugs. "I can't tell you who to move on with, kid. All I can tell you to do is to live your life. Stop dwelling on the past and move forward. Anna's a cunt, we all know that. You're letting her and what she did define the rest of your life. *Don't let it.* You have enough shit to deal with. Let Anna go. Accept someone else in."

"Right. Thanks, old man, you always bring things into perspective."

He turns back to the grill. "That's what I'm here for. Now go tell Bub the food will be ready in about thirty. She's gotta get the rest of the shit together."

"Will do."

I walk back inside where Chills and Rayne are sitting quietly in the corner. Rayne appears a little reserved and distant. I know I've done that to her.

I make my way to the kitchen, the club girls and Bub are making all the side dishes and prepping the rest of the food for the celebratory feast. "Bub, grubs up in thirty."

"Thanks, pres."

I turn back, Rayne and Chills are still deep in conversation. I want to go over to see if she's okay. I laid it on thick before, and I feel damn awful about it.

Prinie strides up to my side. "If you stare any harder at Rayne, you're gonna shoot laser beams out your eyes."

I laugh. "Your imagination is so vivid."

"Don't hurt her, okay? I know you like her. It's just... she's fragile. She might put up this tough façade, but she's a broken woman. I don't want you to be the final piece that breaks her."

My mind ticks over. Rayne's just as broken as I am. And that makes me wonder whether us exploring this chemistry together will end up hurting us both even more, or maybe it will be the glue that binds us together. It's so fucking hard to know the right call on this one.

"I don't want to hurt her, Prinie. I was talking to Fox before about me being cautious of her."

Prinie's eyes narrow. "Come again?"

"This isn't something I need to talk to my sister about."

"When it comes to a woman I consider one of my closest friends, yeah, I fucking think it does."

"Anna," I grumble.

Prinie understands immediately. "You like Rayne? You actually like her?" The shock in her voice is evident.

My eyes shift over to Chills and Rayne deep in conversation, and I harrumph. "Doesn't matter... she's married."

Prinie snorts. "Seriously? You and Anna are totally different to Rayne and Up-Chuck. You and Anna were in love. Anna made a drunken mistake costing you your marriage. You were both hurt after it ended. Rayne, on the other hand... yes, she might be married legally, and starting something up with you while still married is technically cheating on Up-Chuck, but... is it really, when she doesn't love him? When she has no intention of going back to the bastard? Is it when he beats her relentlessly every day without fail for breathing the wrong fucking way? That's not a marriage, Zero, that's a dictatorship. You're not breaking up a relationship by going after Rayne, you're helping her escape a damn death sentence. She may never have had the strength to do it without you. You saved her, assisted her in getting away from a damn abuser."

"She did have it rough, didn't she?"

Prinie shifts her gaze to Rayne. "You don't even know the half of it, big brother."

Wraith strolls up, butting in, "And if you keep staring at her like that, you're going to give yourself away, brother."

I scoff. "And what am I giving away?"

"How badly you want to fucking own her."

I snort. "That's a little over the top, don't you think?"

Wraith curls up his lip. "Zero, you either have to hold on for the ride or get rid of her. 'Cause there's one thing I know for sure…"

I narrow my eyes at Wraith. "What's that?"

"The way you're headed, she's gonna fuck with your head, and you'll lose focus at a crucial time. So, deal with your blue balls or kick her the fuck out. Either way… fucking deal with it."

"You don't know what the hell you're talking about, Wraith!" Prinie blasts him, and he glares at her, turning around, then walks off leaving me with my thoughts.

He's right.

I know it.

Maybe trying to fight this attraction to Rayne is only going to make this harder for us both. Maybe I need to see how this pans out, put no pressure on anything, just see where the wind takes us. One thing is for certain, though, I need to keep my mind clear for when Chuck comes searching for her. I don't know when or how long it's going to take, but I know it *will* happen, and when it does, the club will suffer if I'm not ready.

I have to be prepared for that day.

But first, I need to figure out which path I'm going to choose.

CHAPTER 17

RAYNE

Zero's eyes have been on me all night. In fact, I have felt his eyes on me for the past week ever since he's been avoiding me, but tonight they're extra intense. I've been left feeling bereft since our intense-as-hell kiss. All I'm craving is the taste of his lips once more, but he's so closed off from me I don't know where his head's at. But he's a biker—he shouldn't be easy to read.

I'm sitting with Chills and Prinie, laughing, enjoying our time, though my laughs are shallow. Zero's sitting by the fire pit, and the way the reflection of the flames dance along his face makes him even more intense, more gorgeous.

"I need a refill," I blurt out wanting to get away, even if just for a moment. I want his eyes off me because if I don't and I keep drinking, I don't know if I'm going to be able to control myself. I head inside to the bar.

Nessie's standing behind it wiping down the stained woodgrain. Her brilliant smile dazzles me as I approach her. "What can I get ya?"

I lean against the bar letting out a long exhale. "A shot… something strong."

She raises her brow but reaches behind her for the tequila.

My skin prickles in goosebumps, my senses come alive.

I know that feeling.

Zero is near.

I turn as he slides in next to me at the bar. He's all dark and broody, smelling of bonfire and booze, but I like it. It suits him. His eyes wander up and down my body like they've been doing for weeks.

I can't help myself as I quip cockily, "Enjoying the show?"

He smirks. "You having a good night?"

Avoidance. Didn't answer my question. Interesting.

"I'm perplexed."

"How so?"

"See, I come to this clubhouse for protection. The president goes out of his way to be hospitable. Gives me a new identity so I can work. Basically, gives me my own business, kisses me in the most *amazing* way, then poof, he vanishes from my life. It's like he's a ghost haunting me because I sense him in the shadows, watching me from afar… always there, but never game to talk to me."

"Hmm… sounds like a creeper."

I let out a snicker at his self-deprecating humor. "So, what would be your suggestion to handle said creeper?"

He rubs his chin. "I think the best course of action is to let the creeper know who's boss. I have a feeling he likes it when you get all assertive on him."

"So, you want me to what? Tell you to stop being a jackass and talk to me?"

"We're not talking in third person anymore?"

I flare my nostrils at his mocking tone, folding my arms over my chest. "Zero, I'm serious. Why have you been avoiding me?"

He takes a long sip of his beer, then faces me dead on. "Rayne, I know I've been acting standoffish—"

"No shit—"

"Shut it! I'm trying here. Listen, or I'm walking off." I look and wait for him to continue, "Okay… there's reasons for my behavior. It's not just because you're married, though that's a big reason because the sanctity of marriage means something to me. So, to see you quite freely breaking your vows is unsettling."

Who knew Zero had a moral compass this strong?

I certainly didn't.

I guess there's a lot about Zero I don't know, but I want to find out.

"The thing is, Zero, I don't consider myself married. Not really. To do that I'd have to love Chuck. I'd have to want to stay with him. I really, really don't. Not in any way, shape, or form. I am never going back. Even if I walk away from here, I will never go back to him. You made me see that by breaking the abuse cycle."

"But you still have your rings on your finger."

I peek down to my rings, twisting them on my finger. "I do, but that's not because it ties me to him per se, but to Rayne Version one point zero. The Rayne who was strong but oh so weak at the same time. It's hard to explain."

"So, you're keeping your rings on to remind you of where you came from?"

"Yeah. To keep reminding me that no matter who I become while I'm here, that Rayne version two point zero is going to be nothing like the faulty older version. Am I making any sense?"

"Yeah, you actually are. Your rings ground you. They are *not* a reminder of Chuck."

He does get it.

"Exactly. It's more about me. More about who I was when I wore these rings and before I came here. I don't want to ever be *her* again. I want to keep them on until I'm sure I can be the new me. Till I'm strong enough to stand on my own two feet."

He exhales, now calmer in himself. "You are a constant breath of fresh air, you know that?"

"Me?"

"Yes, you..." He stands shaking his head. "I have to go before I..." he pauses, scrunching his face, then turns heading for the stairs.

Annoyance flows through me that he's leaving mid-conversation. Not only that, but a conversation I thought was quite important. So, I take off after him. His giant strides have him already across the main room and halfway up the stairs by the time I catch up.

He turns hearing me chasing after him. His eyes burn with anger or is it lust, I can't quite place it. He stops mid-step, dropping back down one step to meet me. "I said I had to go."

"And I wasn't finished talking with you!"

A low growl erupts from his chest as he turns to head back up the stairs, so again I take off after him. "Zero, we're *not* done."

"I think we are, cherry bomb."

We make it to the top of the stairs, and I reach out grabbing his bicep. He flicks around, his eyes hard on me as he backs me up against the opposite wall. My heart beats hard in my chest as my eyes meet his ice blues.

"Stop. Pushing. Rayne." The venom in his words should scare me, it should send a shockwave of fear straight to my soul. But I know Zero won't hurt me, not physically anyway. He has a restraint in his eyes that tells me even though I'm pushing all his buttons, he'd never lay a hand on me. So even though he's told me to stop, I push further.

"What has you running scared?" I yell.

He groans, spinning around and moving to walk off.

"Am I too damaged for you?"

His body moves quicker than I thought possible. His fists slamming either side of my head against the wall locking me in place. I don't flinch from his harsh movement. Hell, that's the kind of reaction I was trying to incite. His eyes lock on mine, those intense blues staring straight into the depths of my soul like he's trying to figure me out. Our breathing is rushed, his woodsy aftershave teamed with the leather of his cut is making my senses work overtime. He smells divine, and I'm having trouble composing myself. My tongue darts out licking my bottom lip suggestively as he shakes his head.

"You're trying to make me mad. Why?"

Exhaling, I slide my hands up the sides of his legs to rest on his hips. He doesn't make a move to stop me. "I need to see how you feel."

Zero snorts out a laugh. "How I feel?" He takes a step closer, the buzz in the air instantly electro-charging to a critical level. He's toe-to-toe with me, his eyes locked on mine as his body lines with me completely. "You want to know how I feel?"

My hands on his hips slide around his back holding him closer to me, *needing* him closer. My heart pummels so damn hard it might burst as he leans his lips closer to mine.

"Yes," I whisper.

Zero's hand moves from the wall beside my head and scoops in behind me, fisting in my hair as he slams his entire body forward, pushing me against the wall. His lips assault mine in the most astonishing way as I open my mouth allowing our tongues to dance in unison.

I feel everything.

His hard cock pressing, his body rubbing against mine.

My hands snake up gripping onto his back, pulling him closer as he kisses me like he damn well means it. It's not a gentle kiss, it's hard, it's carnal, the need in me to be close to him is palpable. The energy surging through me ignites my body. A low growl echoes from deep in his chest as his free hand slides down grabbing my leg, hoisting it up. I wrap it around his ass, and he presses his cock against my aching pussy. I moan into his mouth, my need for him is overwhelming. I haven't wanted anyone like this for as long as I can remember, and having Zero ghosting me for the last week has only made this moment even more intoxicating.

His mouth leaves mine, his lips trailing down my neck toward the upper fullness of my breast. I throw my head back against the wall as his tongue darts out sliding across my skin. I pant trying to catch my breath, my hand moving up to the base of his neck, holding him in place.

This is heating up real fast. My clit throbs letting me know where I want this to go. I just hope Zero's on the same page. His mouth makes its way up my neck and back to mine as we kiss frantically while grinding on each other against the wall at the top of the stairs.

His hands snake down, gripping onto my ass, and he hoists me up. My legs instinctively wrap around his waist as we kiss so fucking passionately, I'm light-headed. Zero turns, heading for his room, kicking the door open on our way through. Once inside, he kicks it again closing it, all the while our lips remain locked together, kissing each other as if our lives depend on it. He backs me up against the door.

One of his hands leaves my ass, sliding up my arm and pins my wrist beside my head on the door. His grip is firm, not enough to bruise but enough to mark his dominance. His hips thrust forward, his hard cock pressing against the seam of my denim shorts. The ache against my clit makes me moan into his mouth as I clench my fingers together in tight fists needing some tension relief.

His lips leave mine as he eases my legs to the floor, exhales loudly, his eyes devouring my body as he reaches into my tank top with his fingers, ripping it clean in two.

"Holy heck," I murmur. *That was the sexiest thing I've ever seen.*

My legs are wobbly as he moves in kissing me again, his fingers sliding in behind me and detaching my bra with ease. The material falls to the floor leaving me completely open to him. You'd think I'd feel a little self-conscious, but with Zero, I'm completely safe and secure. He makes me feel like I'm the most attractive woman he's ever seen. The way his eyes linger on me, the way he kisses me, it's all there in his body language.

He takes a step back, leaving me against the door as his hand comes up rubbing his beard. "Sweet Jesus, cherry bomb… take off your shorts."

My eyes widen at his demand, but he isn't fucking around. The strength in his tone tells me he'll make me do this one way or another. I'm a strong, confident woman—if he wants a striptease, I'll give him a hell of a show.

I slowly unclip the first button, my hips begin to sway as a low growl reverbs from his chest. He rearranges his jeans as he stands back watching. I undo the last button then start on the zipper. With one hand, I slide it down while my other hand slides up my stomach to my breast.

"Fuck, Rayne."

I squeeze my nipple, tweaking it as a long breath leaves my mouth. My nipple hardens as I sashay out of my shorts. They fall to the floor, and I kick them in his direction—they shoot up straight into his face.

While he's blinded temporarily by my shorts, I turn, bending over to give him a full view of my ass in my lace panties. I know exactly when his sight is back by the throaty moan that leaves his mouth.

"You tryin' to make me come over there?"

I sway my ass in the air, looping my fingers through the edges of my panties. I slowly slide them over my taut ass as he groans again. Sliding them down to my ankles, I turn around kicking them to him as well. He catches them this time, shoving them straight into his jeans' pocket.

I face him straight on, my hand running up to my breast rubbing my nipple, my other hand slides down toward my pussy.

His eyes widen as he takes two large steps toward me. "No, you don't, that pussy is only for me tonight. Do you understand, cherry bomb?" He grabs my arms, spinning me around to face the door. "I said... do you understand?" A slap stings across my ass. I smile as I peer over my shoulder at him with a nod.

"I need to hear you say it, cherry bomb."

"My pussy is yours tonight."

He places his foot at the edge of mine. "Spread your legs wider."

The anticipation inside of me is building. I'm completely naked, but he's still fully clothed. I have no idea what he has in store, but hell if I'm not excited to find out.

Zero's hand slides down the center of my back. I tense a little—butt play isn't my thing—but he slides around, pressing his front into my back, running his hand straight down to my pussy. "Hands on the door, cherry bomb."

I do as he says, even though everything in me wants to run my fingers through his gorgeous locks of hair. I place my palms on the door just in time for him to circle on my clit. I gasp at the sensation as it hits me. My knees wobble while his other hand wraps around my waist applying pressure to my stomach. I'm not sure what he's doing, but the mixed feeling of him applying pressure to my clit and holding me tight is doing something, something I'm not used to. My body trembles with the pleasure as I pant, my head lolling back against his shoulder, needing to touch him a little more.

"Come for me, Rayne."

I clench my eyes shut as I let the incredible sensations wash over me, his finger working my clit in just the right way. He's bringing me to a new height, and it's exactly what I've been needing for longer than I can possibly even know.

My muscles tense, tightening with the impending orgasm. My body shudders and slickening with a fine sheen of sweat. Lights flash behind my closed eyelids as he presses hard on my clit, the same time his teeth clamp down on my earlobe, and it sends me off. My world shatters. All the walls I had built, all the emotion I'd been holding onto, fracture. Hell, it shatters as I fall apart.

"Fuck, Zero," I moan as his hands leave me as I try to steady myself against the door.

His hands are gone only briefly. I don't even know what he's doing. I'm far too zoned out to care when his hands snake around my waist, and he lifts me from behind.

Suddenly, I'm very awake. "Shit, Zero—"

"See the workout bar hanging from the door. Grip it, then wrap your legs around me. This is going to be wild, cherry bomb."

My eyes widen at the thought of this crazy position, basically riding him backward. He's holding my thighs, supporting them as I grip the workout bar. My clit's still throbbing from my climax. The head of his cock lines up with my pussy as I face the door. I'm still not sure how this is going to work, but hey, I'm down for anything at this point.

"Hold on. Don't let go." With that, his thick, hard length thrusts up inside of me.

I gasp as it slides all the way in, slamming straight to my g-spot. Lights flash behind my eyes giving me a mini-orgasm immediately while I pant, struggling to breathe.

He stills, letting me adapt to the sensation.

"Holy fucking Christ almighty," I murmur more to myself.

He chuckles. "Told you it was going to be wild. You ready?"

No.

"Yes."

He slowly withdraws his long length, then pushes back inside of me, the rhythm painfully incredible. The angle we're in is making this so I'm right on the edge in an instant. My body's alive, tingling and buzzing. My fingers are gripping hard on the workout bar, so hard my knuckles are turning white from the pressure.

He pulls back, thrusting in a little quicker this time.

"Fuck," I murmur as he lets out a deep throaty groan.

"You feel so damn good, Rayne." He moves a little faster now, the energy in the room pops and sizzles as I pant, trying to catch my breath, but it's not coming. I'm feeling lightheaded as pleasure rolls through me.

His thick cock pulses inside of me. I can't help but love every dominant move he makes from his fingers gripping into my thighs tightly to the way his balls sound slapping against his skin. This is quite possibly one of the kinkiest, most insanely pleasurable fucks I've ever had in my life. As he pushes me higher, I let out a loud moan, my head falling back in ecstasy. My skin prickles in goosebumps. My muscles begin to contract and tighten as everything spasms, then it's like the heavens open up, and a wave of euphoria explodes all around me. My body comes alive with endorphins as my orgasm riddles my body.

"Zero!" I scream out his name as my grip on the bars weakens.

His cock jerks inside of me as he stumbles his grip. "Let go," he demands.

I know he won't drop me, so I let go. He's still inside me as he carries me over to the bed, pulls me off him, and throws me on the mattress. I turn my head to him. His cock's in his hand, pumping, his face strained in the most delicious way. He leans over me, pumping hard, then he groans, his body jolting as he unloads his hot cum all over my back. The warmth of his release settles over me, and I relax into his bed. His breath labored as he stands makes me crane my neck in order to take in his full nakedness.

Fucking hell.

His body is covered in black and gray tattoos. Everywhere. From his neck to his feet. The only thing which isn't is his ginormous cock, but that thing doesn't need any artwork—it's a masterpiece in itself.

Zero walks over to the bedside table grabbing some tissues. He sits on the edge of the bed next to me still trying to catch his breath. Pulling out a tissue, he wipes me down. "Sorry, I didn't use a condom. I normally do. I just needed you."

I reach out placing my hand on his thigh. "It's okay, I'm on the pill."

Zero leans down planting a kiss on my cheek. "That's good to hear."

He falls back onto the bed staring up at the ceiling.

I move up to lay with him. "That was..."

"Fucking indescribable," he finishes.

"Yeah, that's exactly what I was going to say."

"I don't think I'm ever not going to want to be fucking you."

He knows exactly the right things to say.

"As much as I love this idea, I have a job to do. And you, sir, have a club to run. I don't really want to be serving customers with your cock inside of me and me screaming out in orgasm every half hour."

He waggles his brows. "Sounds fucking good to me. See nothing wrong with that."

"You're insatiable."

"I like seeing my cum all over your body, and now I've had you. Yes, yes, I am."

"Well, then we'd better have another go at this but in the shower. I need to clean off."

His eyes light up, and he sits dramatically on the bed holding out his hand. "M'lady, your shower awaits."

You can lead a cock to water, but it will always want to fuck.

ZERO

The Next Morning

A soft breeze washes over my skin causing goosebumps to prickle. My eyes slowly open as I take in the weight nestled into the side of my body. A slow grin forms across my face as I glance down. Rayne's asleep on my chest. Her arm's draped across my torso, her face is smothered into the crook of my neck and shoulder. She's dead to the world. I wore her out. Hell, she wore me out.

My hand comes up gently running up and down the smooth skin on her arm. I couldn't be more relaxed if I tried. My eyes take in and trace her breasts underneath the white sheets, my cock instantly grows harder. The idea of her naked body pressed against mine is making me want to start this all over again.

But she's tired, so I need to let her sleep.

My eyes shift to Rayne's face, her beautiful sleeping face. She's a natural beauty. She doesn't need makeup, not that I've ever seen her wear copious amounts, but she's flawless without it. She has an aura about her, something Anna never had. She was always so done up, so over the top with her fashion and accessories.

Anna was plastic.

Rayne is natural.

I was never truly sure I could let go of Anna and the baggage she left behind. She broke a part of me, but with Rayne, it feels like maybe that piece of the puzzle which was broken can maybe not be replaced, but mended, patched over and rebuilt. Rayne may not be the fix for all my demons, but resisting this, whatever this is, was stupid. At least, this way, I will be giving in to temptation and know Rayne is doing it for the right reasons, without any kind of feelings in her heart which may be left over for Chuck.

I'm not breaking up a marriage.

That marriage was finished the second Chuck landed his fist in her face. I simply gave Rayne the ability to leave without getting too badly hurt by Chuck's rage.

As my fingers run up and down her arm tenderly, her eyelashes slowly flutter open.

"Morning." Her voice is raspy, and it's sexy as hell.

I lean in planting a kiss on her lips. "Morning."

She wriggles a little, her arms stretching out. I can't help but see the bruising under her breast which is still a little yellow from that bastard's assault.

Did I hurt her last night?

"How are you feeling? Your body? Is it sore?"

Her sparkling green eyes light up. "In *all* the good ways." Her leg slides over me as her body moves quicker than I can register. Before I have a second to think, she's straddling me, her warm pussy pressing down on my hard cock. Her hands reach out grabbing my wrists as she leans over me, pinning me to the bed.

Fuck, yes!

"Time for me to be in control this time." Rayne's eyes are hooded as she leans down pressing her swollen lips to mine.

I have no way of touching her. She's pinning me completely. I'm strong, of course I could turn this around in an instant, but her taking charge like this, fuck if it isn't turning me the hell on.

Rayne slips her tongue into my mouth, her pussy grinding against my cock. I groan needing the friction harder. My hands ball into fists.

I want to touch her so bad as I kiss her with everything I have. My cock's throbbing with need. If she angled just the right way, it would slip inside her. Fuck, I want that right now, I'm aching for it, almost pleading for it when there's a damn knock at the door.

She lifts her head from mine dramatically, her head snapping around. Her hands let my wrists go as I signal for her to get under the covers. She hops off me, my cock mourning the loss of her.

"What?" I call out to whatever asshole interrupted me getting some more.

The door opens as Rayne covers her breasts.

Wraith opens his eyes wide while Rayne ducks in behind me as I sit up in the bed.

Her embarrassment is endearing.

Wraith's eyes meet mine, then shift behind me. He huffs and averts his eyes. "There's a problem with the shipment."

"Be there in a minute."

Wraith exhales, takes one more look at Rayne, who's trying her hardest to be invisible, and he turns for the door closing it behind him.

"Oh my God," Rayne whispers under her breath as I turn to face her, humor in my mood as I grab her and pin her to the bed beneath me. I lean in planting a long kiss on her lips.

"You're adorable," I murmur against her. "Get dressed. But tonight, I want you in my bed just like this." I run my hand down the center of her body, straight between her folds and inside of her. She's wet for me as she moans with my movements. I circle, pushing deep, then withdraw, to slide up over her clit, causing her to quiver. Bringing my finger up, I place it in my mouth, sucking it clean then release it slowly with a pop. She tastes as sweet as I knew she would be.

"Jesus," she whimpers as she clamps down on her bottom lip with her teeth.

"Not Jesus, cherry bomb, but I promise I'll take you to heaven, multiple times."

She grins as I jump out of bed trying to control my raging hard-on.

I need to cool myself off. Otherwise, I'm never going to leave this room.

Fucking Rayne was everything I thought it would be. I could get addicted to screwing her, but hell if she doesn't make me feel *more.*

As I move about trying to get dressed, she hops out of bed and pulls her clothing on too, but in such a way she's trying to shield herself from me. I chuckle at how uncomfortable she seems to be.

"I've been inside of you, Rayne. You did a striptease for me last night. You don't need to hide yourself from me."

She exhales lowering her top so she's completely bare. Her ample breasts, the fading bruising, she's gorgeous to me.

"You're stunning, Rayne. Don't ever think you're not."

She chews on her bottom lip yanking on her bra. "The… the bruising… it doesn't turn you off?"

I have to play this right.

I storm up to her, grab her hands and stare her dead in the eyes. "I see *you*, Rayne, not the colors on your skin. You. And *you* are flawless just the way you are. Don't let *him* get into your head. Not now. Not after a great night like that."

She stands taller, her shoulders straightening. "Thank you."

I lean in pressing my lips to hers briefly and pull back smiling at her. Then rush my hand around behind her, smacking her on the ass. She smirks, then pulls one of my shirts over her head. I walk back over to my cut, pulling it over my arms as she slides her shoes on, and we're ready to go.

We make it downstairs where the main room is alive and buzzing. We stayed in bed late this morning. Let's face it, we were up half the night.

Everyone's eating their breakfast, and as we walk in I lean into her side giving her a peck on the cheek. "I gotta go deal with whatever Wraith needs me for. You gonna be okay to—"

"Go. Do your president thing. I can find something to amuse myself."

"See you later." I wink.

"Later."

There's a promise in the air, a promise of a repeat of last night's activities, and I'm so down for that. But now, now I have to go deal with my VP.

I make way for the Chapel where I know Wraith will be waiting for me. Any club talk is conducted away from listening ears. I walk through the large double black doors where Wraith and Texas are both sitting at the massive church table, the one that's been in this club since its inception. Making my way to the head of the table, I pull out my seat and sit. Placing my hands on the table and sinking into the seat, I exhale. "Hit me. What shit are we facing?"

Wraith rolls his shoulders. "Nice of you to come up for air."

"Get the fuck on with it."

"A number of boxes in our shipments are going missing in transit," Wraith blurts out.

"The fuck? That's a huge payload of Snow White just to vanish."

Wraith widens his eyes mockingly. "No shit! While you were screwing our new house guest, we were out here trying to track it."

"You got something to say, Wraith?" I narrow my eyes on my VP.

Wraith curls up his lip. "Rayne's gonna be trouble. Just don't want to see you get caught up in her storm."

The tension in my shoulders eases. He's just looking out for me in his roundabout way. "Better to be caught in the storm than swept away by it."

Texas cackles. "Look at you two poetic fucks."

Wraith and I both turn to Texas. "Enough of this shit. Tell me what's happening."

Texas rolls out a map, pinpointing the places the cargo's gone missing. It's right on the border of the turf divider between the Bayou Militia and us.

"So, you sayin' this could be the Militia? Or just someone making it appear that way?"

"That was my thought process, too. Do we want to risk going to war with them again when you've just got Prinie and Koda back?" Wraith asks.

"It's not worth heading into their territory to find out. We have to do this the old way. Ask around... First stop, the Baron. He's got his finger on the pulse. He knows everything that's going on in Houston."

Wraith's eyes light with mischief. "I love visiting him. The people in Mont Belvieu hate it when our bikes roar through their quiet little town."

"Yeah, well, we don't all need to go, just us three and Neon. If there's anything shady going on here, I don't want too many of us riding out bringing attention to the club."

Meeting up with the Baron never has me in a calm state, but at least riding my bike takes the tension down a notch. I always love the way my bike makes any problem somehow seem smaller than it is. With the wind whipping at your face, the feel of the open road at your beck and call, it's like you're the king of the world, or should I say the king of the road.

Pulling past the Mont Belvieu city limits sign, the roar of the Harleys echoes through the quaint town. It's pristine greenery and upscale houses make sure we're out of place. It's why I love coming here, to rock the neighborhood. To rattle the Baron and cause a little chaos.

Call me an asshole, but I love watching the fucker squirm.

We pull into his two-story home. It's not overstated like you'd expect for an oil baron, but in saying that, it's only one of the seventeen properties he owns.

The door flies open as I turn off my engine, and he barrels outside. I chuckle as his short stature waddles down the path toward me. His tan suit ever immaculate with his black and gold bolo tie strung around his neck as always. You've never met a more Texas-loving Texan than the Baron. Even his bolo tie has the Texas state seal embellished on it.

"Damn you to hell, Zero. I told y'all not to ride on out here no more."

Smirking, I hop off my bike as he approaches waving his hands about in a flurry. He holds power, more than the police, more than the government. He's one of America's wealthiest men, so I have to play this shit right. Wraith's eyes shift to me as he and the others step to my side.

"Tilman, it's nice to see you again on this glorious day," I smother it on thick.

"Don't patronize me, son. Get the fuck inside before locals start yammerin'. Sweet Lord, have mercy."

Tilting my head at Wraith, he, Texas, and Neon follow behind as we enter the lavish home. Walking through the double stained-glass doors, the polished wooden floorboards squeak underfoot. I always feel like a little kid when I come here, mainly because everything is so fucking pristine. I want to run through the house touching everything leaving grease marks all over the cream leather furniture.

He closes the door behind us, leading us past the grand staircase made of white carpet and wooden railings to the living room, where the cream sofas and ornate wooden cabinetry is located. It's a cross between upscale *Modern Housewives of Houston* and a hunter's cabin. The mix of sophisticated and old shouldn't work, but somehow, it does. I guess the many wives he's had over the years have all had their input in his houses. I have no idea which one helped him here if not multiple. Honestly, I don't even care.

"Now, I was fixin' to leave for rest of the day to settle a business deal. You're holdin' me up. What the hell's so important y'all had to ride on out here?"

I take a seat, the leather squeaking under my weight. I grimace at the noise as my brothers all do the same thing. The Baron continues to stand like he expects this shit won't take long.

"You not gonna offer us a drink, Tilman?"

He groans throwing his hands in the air. "Fuckin' bikers, always makin' demands. Fine. Whiskey?"

"Yeah, that'll do nicely."

He rolls his eyes, the wrinkles on his face showing he's had too much sun in his life as he pulls off his cowboy hat, placing it carefully on the sofa. He walks to the bar, then pours five short glasses. "I'm assumin' by the avoidance of topic, this drop by isn't a 'hey, Tilman, nice to see ya,' kind of visit." He walks over with two glasses, handing one to me, the other to Wraith.

I grab it from him, take a small sip, the amber nectar burns, but I like the feeling as I swallow it down. Then, I exhale and shrug. "I need some intel."

He scoffs walking the other drinks over to Texas and Neon. "You always need intel, Zero. I'm beginin' to think this relationship is one-sided."

"The shipments we send out for you every month is a testament to the fact it's not. I *know* you benefit from that Snow White, Tilman. I don't know what you do with it, but I'm sure it's not fucking legal."

His eyes brighten with a sense of humor. "All right… what do y'all wanna know?"

I sit forward in my seat, looking him dead in the eyes. "Is there any word on the grapevine about missing shipments? Particularly *our* shipments?"

He scrunches up his face. "Haven't heard anythin' about missin' shipments… but, word on the street is the Militia are makin' moves. Promotin' men in their camp. Growin' their numbers. Whether they're preparin' for somethin'… I don't know. Just thought that might be of interest to y'all. I'd hate to see another slaughter like what happened a year ago. Things in Houston are calm. No need to go rockin' the oil rig."

Texas chuckles at the Baron's lame joke while I glare at him. Texas quickly quiets down as I turn back to Tilman.

"Maybe it's best to stay out of the Militia's way for now. We have our own shit to deal with."

Tilman's eyes open wider. "Oh, yeah? What's that?"

I know better than to tell him. There's a reason we go to the Baron for information because he spills it—everyone else's and ours. So, it's best to remember whatever I tell him will be told to whoever the fuck knows how many others.

"Nothing we can't handle. Thanks for your help, Tilman." I stand, throwing back the last of my whiskey and place the glass on the coffee table. He places his hand out for me to shake. His grip's firm. So, I tighten mine. His eyes stay focused while we shake. It's a standoff, it's always this way, but inevitably, we both know I will be the one to let go first because as much as I hate it, he has the damn power in Houston. Hell, in all of Texas. So, if I want to keep my club running smoothly, I need to keep in Tilman's good graces.

"Till next time, Baron." I let his hand go, and his lips turn up, his wrinkles becoming more pronounced around his mouth just like they always do, knowing he's gotten the upper hand. *Bastard.*

"Next time you plan on comin' into Mont Belvieu, gimmie some warnin', will ya? Or come in a damn car. Y'all are noisy as fuck."

"Bikers not riding bikes? Yeah, right. Good one."

Stepping outside, I slide onto my ride as he grumbles to himself, "I mean it, Zero."

I start my engine letting it roar to life revving it extra loudly. "I can't hear you," I yell out making my brothers laugh as I duck walk my bike out of his drive.

"Zero, you're a damn fool, you sonofabitch, you know that?" He waves his fist in the air as I continue to rev my bike over his yelling. I can only just hear him.

I turn back just before I take off. "Sorry, Baron, bike's too loud. I'll catch ya next time." With that, I hammer down, taking off at breakneck speed down the suburban street. My brothers at my flank and rear as I chuckle to myself.

I might have annoyed the Baron, but not enough to cause any trouble. That much I know. The one thing which does have me worried now is the mention of the Militia.

They're growing in size. They were already a much larger force than us. If they get much bigger and the peace treaty breaks down between us, the ensuing war could be over in an instant.

We're merely a bullet—the Militia could be a nuke.

But I'm not ready to implode just yet.

ZERO

"I don't know what this could mean, in all honesty," I tell my brothers around the church table. Wraith to my left, Texas to my right, the rest of my brothers taking their places at the table.

"So, it's not certain the Militia took the missing shipments?" Slick asks from the other end of the room.

"At this point we have no solid leads. I don't want to be the one to make the call that it's the Militia and start something without irrefutable proof."

"Makes sense. No need to initiate another war if it's not necessary," Ax offers.

"My thoughts exactly. We know the Militia have the numbers, and if they're increasing, then we could be in trouble. Best not to poke the bear unless it truly needs to be poked… agreed?"

A resounding "aye" rings through the chapel, so I bang my gavel making it so.

"Neon, keep digging, see what you can find out. We need to find our shipments. That shit doesn't just disappear. How many boxes have gone astray so far?"

"Three in total."

I rub the back of my neck. "That's a hell of a lot of money. Someone's just come into a payload of cash if they're distributing *our*

Snow White. Search for someone who's suddenly wealthy. It might help pinpoint who we're after."

"Got it."

I sit back into my chair, relaxing a little. "Now, for other business... Chains, you've been here long enough, you're settled in. It's time to discuss your new role here at Houston Defiance."

Chains sits forward in his chair. "Thanks for giving me the time to adjust and have quality time with Chills and Kobe, but I want you to know I'm one hundred percent committed to you guys and Defiance."

I glance at Texas, and he subtly nods. "Texas and I have been talking it over, discussing how this could all work. You were Sergeant-at-Arms in Chicago, and that's quite an achievement. Being demoted to a plain patch doesn't sit right with me, so Texas is willing to share the role with you seeing as he's only a year in it. With your experience and his fresh blood, I believe the two of you will make a great duo. It also means, Chains, that you can take the time when you need to be with Kobe, and Texas can take full rein."

"Fuck. Thanks, pres, I don't know what to say."

"Well, don't say anything yet, it has to be voted in," I tell him. His eyes weaken as he views the brothers in the room. "On the matter of Chains and Texas being joint SAA, those for?"

The room join together in agreement, "Aye."

"Those against?"

Silence.

"Good." I bang my gavel. "Welcome to club officially, Chains."

Everyone cheers as Texas slaps him on the back. Even with the uncertainty surrounding the club right now, we can still take a moment to celebrate the good things.

Fox sits forward. "While we're celebratin', I wanna take a minute to say how great it is I think you and Rayne are in a good place. That you're giving her a chance."

"Here, here," resounds from most of my brothers.

"Not sure this is the place to talk about my love life, but I appreciate y'all are on our side. I can't pretend to know how all this is going to go, but—"

Suddenly, loud yelling resounds in the main room. We all turn toward the door. I can't figure out the words being screamed, but I do know it's Prinie and her tone is distraught.

Some shit's going down.

I stand abruptly pulling my gun from my waistband as I rush for the door. My brothers follow, their guns all drawing at the same time as I take a breath, prepare myself for whatever it is I'm about to face. I yank open the door, gun aimed in front of me and rush out. Brothers flanking my sides as Prinie's screaming her ass off at Phantom.

What the fuck?

"You're nothing but a lying sack of shit!"

My heart rate begins to slow as I place my gun back in my jeans while walking over to the two of them. Prinie's face is bright red. She's fuming and on the brink of tears.

"I can't believe I ever thought you were a decent human being!"

Whatever Phantom's gone and done, he's really pissed her off.

Her eyes catch a glimpse of me walking up. Her head turns almost like slow motion, all her anger, frustration, hell, maybe even hatred, is pouring out of her as she unleashes it now toward me. "I can't believe you, Zero. You, out of everyone. Fucking hell, you're the most un-fucking-trustworthy of them all!"

"What the hell are you on about?"

"Did you come to Chicago, especially to bring me and Koda home?"

My eyes shift to Rayne who's standing back letting this happen.

I was wondering if Prinie would ever find out the truth about our trip to Chicago.

I guess that time is now.

Exhaling, I step closer, but she takes a step back. "Your place is here, princess."

She scoffs. "So, you fucking *lied* to get me home?"

I attempt to hide my grimace, but to her it must be an answer because she picks up a beer bottle from the bar and hurtles it right at my head. I duck, and it smashes into the support beam behind me sending shards of glass all over the floor next to Wraith, but he doesn't flinch.

"You pride yourself on honesty and loyalty, yet, *you... lied,* you flat out lied to me and Koda. How can I trust anything anyone says to me here?"

I step forward reaching out to grab for her, but she pushes me away. I reach to grab her again, but she turns with a clenched fist, and it lands straight in my jaw, stunning me as my head snaps to the side.

She fucking hit me.

It didn't hurt. Maybe a light sting physically, but emotionally having Prinie punch me, hurts more than I want to let on.

As she bolts away from me, she races for the front door. I move to take off after her. Fear creeps over me that she's running away again, but a gentle hand reaches out gripping my forearm stopping me. "Let her cool off," Rayne's calm voice instructs.

Unease washes over me as Rayne pulls me closer to her. Feeling her presence soothes me a little. "Are you okay?" she asks pulling my face into her hands as she assesses my now-bruising jaw. "Look at us getting bruises all the time. We're a mess, aren't we?"

"Don't even joke about this, Rayne."

She winces as I revel in the soothing touch of her hands on my face. "What if she doesn't come back?"

"She will."

"How are you so sure?"

She weakly smiles. "Koda's here. She wouldn't leave him behind. Trust me, she's just taking a moment."

Letting out a long exhale, my eyes shift around the room. My brothers are all watching and waiting to see what I want them to do. I signal for them go about their business. "I need a damn drink."

We head over to the bar and sit, Lexi has already poured out some of Fox's home-brewed whiskey in a short glass. I sip slowly savoring the flavor as Rayne rubs my back.

I hate fighting with Prinie.

But I am glad Koda didn't see any of it.

Neon slowly edges over with his tablet in hand. "I did what you asked me to do the day we came back. You want me to activate it?"

Rayne's confusion is evident on her face, but my curiosity is outweighing everything else. "Yes, activate."

Neon slides a green tab across, and it beeps, then a map lights up on the screen while Rayne peeks over my shoulder at what we're watching. "She's getting very close to Militia territory. Does she know about the truce?"

"She does, but I doubt Prinie knows the boundary lines. If any of the Militia recognize her..." I leave it hanging more because I'm too scared to finish my own sentence.

"What are you saying, Zero? Is Prinie in danger?" The fear in Rayne's eyes is palpable.

"If she drives any further west, she will be."

It's as if Prinie hears me, and to spite me, she continues her course heading straight over the territory lines.

"Fuck," I murmur glancing at Neon.

"If she keeps moving and doesn't stop, she should be fine."

Damn! The stupid girl is driving right in the depths of Militia territory. Peace was signed that no Defiance member crosses into their zone, and no Militia enters ours. If they see her, it could mean all-out damn war.

"Turn around, Prinie," I murmur staring at the screen.

"I'll go get her. They don't know me," Rayne blurts out.

"No."

"Zero, it's your best option."

"If they've spotted Prinie, and you go in, they'll take you both. I won't risk you, Rayne."

"Motherfucker," Neon groans.

"What?"

"Her car stopped."

"Where?"

"Outside a café by the looks of it. Zero, we have to get her the hell outta there."

I pick up my cell, frantically dialing her number. A phone rings on the bar—it's Prinie's. "Fuck!"

Wraith walks over, his brows drawn together. "What's going on?"

"Prinie's driven into Militia territory and stopped at a café."

Wraith's eyes widen. "Fucking impossible, stupid, damn woman…" He runs his hand over his head. "I'll go, pres, she'll run from you. We can't risk you. We lost one president to that scum already. No sense losing another."

"I should be there!"

"Wraith's right. Prinie will just take off if she sees you again. You don't want to drive her deeper into Militia territory, do you?" Rayne questions.

I exhale. "Fuck… fine. But I need an open line of communication, Wraith. The entire time you're with her."

He dips his chin, turning on his heels then races for the door.

Rayne pulls me over to a chair, sitting next to me as I try to calm my shit. Prinie's gone. A-fucking-gain, and I have no clue if she's coming back.

Rayne strokes my arm, somehow it helps. "Why? Why did you wait for a year to come and get Prinie? She needed you sooner, Zero."

I roll my shoulders. "Cannon was watching her. He gave me reports. I knew she was struggling, but things here were being dealt with. I wanted Houston to be in peace with the Militia before I got them back. I wanted to show Prinie that life here could be good… not all death and damn chaos."

"You could have kept in touch—"

"She could have, too. When she left, it hurt like fucking hell. She didn't even give me a damn goodbye." I let out a huff. "I've lost a lot in my life, but losing my *entire* family in one day? Fuck, Rayne, it was the hardest damn day of my life. And trust me, I've had hard days."

"I don't doubt it."

"Family means everything to me. So, when I found the right time, I took it. Now she's taken off again. It makes me think when the going gets tough, she's just gonna take Koda and bolt. I'm gonna lose them all over again."

"Then don't give her a chance to leave, Zero. Make her want to stay. Make her know she's wanted and loved here."

"She is!"

"*I* know that, *you* know that... make *her* feel it."

"For a civilian, you really know a lot about how a club and brotherhood works, you know that?"

She shrugs. "I don't know anything about how this club works. It just comes down to human decency, Zero. If you treat people the way they deserve to be treated, they're going to want to stay. They're going to respect you, love you. Zero, show Prinie the brotherly love you have for her, and I don't mean a president's love."

Neon casually sits opposite us. "I have Wraith on coms," he states, then slides the receiver to the middle of the table.

"I'm coming up to the café now." Wraith's bike roars in the background then slows down to a stop.

The general hum of road noise echoes down the line as we sit, waiting. I wish I had a visual, but coms is better than nothing.

"Approaching now." His voice is low, so he's not heard by passersby. "Princess," Wraith calls out.

"What the?" Prinie pauses for a second, then starts again. "Guess I shouldn't be surprised. You probably put a tracker in my arm while I slept."

Wraith chuckles. "Not in your arm."

"Pfft... figures. 'Spose everyone's losing their shit?"

"Finish your drink and let's go back."

"Like *you* care," she scoffs.

I frown at her accusatory tone toward my VP—she needs to learn damn respect.

"Don't start this shit, Prinie. We're not safe here. You need to get up and let's leave."

"Not safe? *You* want to talk to *me* about not being safe? Why did *you* come for me, Wraith, huh? Why *you* out of everyone?"

"This isn't the time to discuss this, Kharlie—"

"Don't Kharlie me, asshole. You don't deserve the right to call me that."

Neon shrugs, he's just as confused as I am about the hostility between my best friend and my sister.

Something's happened.

Something I don't know about.

"Stop being a brat. Get in your damn car and leave, Prinie. Go back to the club. Stop acting out. You're in Militia territory. If they see you here… fuck, if they see *me* here, do you know what that means?"

She inhales sharply, then a chair scrapes like she's standing up. "Why didn't you lead with that, dickface? You always were crap at following through."

Footsteps pound the pavement as the line muffles. I turn up the volume and listen closer because the coms is muted somehow, but not fully.

"Prinie, stop! You left, *you* did, not me."

"Why did you think I did that, Wraith. Huh? It wasn't only because of Mom and Dad, and you know it. I'm going back to the clubhouse so don't worry. I won't cause any more trouble. Just stay out of my way, and I'll stay out of yours."

Anger flares inside of me. What the fuck's happened between Wraith and Prinie that aided her leaving the clubhouse? I have no fucking idea but I intend to find out.

The coms come back into full volume as a door slams then a car takes off.

"Prinie's just left… I'm assuming back to the clubhouse, pres." Wraith's voice is tight with tension. He knows we've heard it all, even if he did try to muffle some of it.

He has some explaining to do.

"I need to talk to you when you get back," I grunt out.

"Yeah," is all he replies. The roar of his bike blasts down the line, then it goes dead.

I turn to Rayne, she's as shocked as I feel. "You know anything about that?"

"Nothing. Though I have to admit, every time I see Prinie and Wraith in the same vicinity, the tension's thick."

"I swear to God if he's hurt her in some way, I'm gonna kill him."

Neon continues to track Prinie's car. "She's headed back this way. Hopefully, no one saw them."

"When Wraith gets in, tell him I wanna see him."

Neon nods, stands, and walks away.

Rayne wraps herself around me to try and calm my raging thoughts. It works for a moment.

"I can't figure out what the fuck is going on."

"Don't worry about it or try and figure it out until you talk to them. No point in guessing, it will only lead to incorrect assumptions. That *always* ends badly."

"Where have you been all my life. Your level head is a calming influence."

She laughs. "I needed a level and calm head living the life I was subjected to. If I tried too hard to fight back, it only got worse for me. I learned pretty quick to play it smart, not stupid. But I guess I wasn't that smart, or I would have left a long time ago."

I pull her closer, kissing her nose. "Sometimes we all need a little bit of extra help."

She leans in kissing my lips, and a tingle shoots straight to my cock. "I'm glad you helped me out of that place. I wouldn't want to be anywhere but here."

I don't know if I would be keeping my cool if it weren't for Rayne. I'd probably be on some tyrannical tirade right now, fucking screaming at everyone. As much as I was there to be her white knight in her time of need, she's here right now to be my saving grace. We're there for each other in our hour of need. That thought not only terrifies me but electrifies me. She's the calm in my storm, and the storm is raging at gale-force right now.

I need Prinie home.

Because while she's out in Militia territory, the thought of losing her like I lost my parents can't help but flood my mind.

And that thought is crippling to the very core.

CHAPTER 20

ZERO

My mind's racing. Thoughts of a call, and me having to identify Prinie's body are coming in thick and heavy. I'm probably overreacting, but until she's home, I won't feel like she's safe. Rayne's doing all she can to keep my mind from wandering. I've sent Nessie to keep Koda occupied. Last thing I need is for him to know Prinie's out in Militia territory. The boy's clever, though, he'll know something's up when our head club girl comes knocking on his door to hang out with him.

The screech of car tires in the compound has my ears pricking up.

Rayne grabs my arm. "Let her come to you."

Prinie storms inside the clubhouse like she's on a warpath. Emotions flow through me—relief, happiness, overwhelming joy. Then it hits—anger, insatiable, undeniable anger that she left and put herself in danger. I can't control myself as I stand glaring at her. "Well, that was fucking stupid, Prinie. You never damn well think past yourself and your wants. Why would you leave without checking on the treaty lines? You know how important this peace is with the Militia. Why the fuck would you risk that?"

She storms toward me, contempt written all over her face as she throws her hands in the air. "This is bullshit! I'm not even allowed in half the city anymore!"

I stand my ground glaring right back at her. "It is what it is. If we want to keep the peace—" I stop because I don't have to fucking explain myself. "Don't fucking drive off again. Your first reaction can't be to run when shit doesn't go your way. You gotta learn to stick things out and deal with problems. Running solves nothing."

She turns up her lip folding her arms across her chest. "Fine. Whatever. I was angry y'all were watching me that whole damn time, then lied about coming to get me."

"Prinie, I did what I did to keep you safe. I ain't gonna apologize for it. I should have reached out, but I was there with you the whole time. I had daily reports. If I thought for a second you were in trouble, I would've gotten on a plane or contacted Torque. That's why Cannon was there, to be the first point of protection."

"My very own bodyguard." Her sarcasm doesn't allude me.

"Exactly!"

She sighs. "The Phantom thing actually makes sense to me now." Her sour expression softens. "Well, at least you were there in your own fucked-up way. You didn't give up on me, and that's... actually kinda comforting."

Her back and forth bullshit is giving me whiplash.

Prinie leans in planting a quick kiss on my cheek. "Sorry I took off. Won't happen again." Then she turns and is heading for the stairs.

Rayne lets out a long breath. "You handled that well."

I feel like I've just done ten rounds with Mike Tyson. "You're taking this in your stride. It's not like you signed up for family drama."

"Hey, my life's been one constant drama. This? This is nothing."

I grab her hand, leading her over to a table to sit. I need a drink, or seventeen. Got to have something to take the edge off, something to numb my mind from all this bullshit. I need some meaningless dribble and a few deep breaths.

We sit next to Kevlar and Slick as they chat to each other about the Defiance Race Team. Slick's the Crew Chief for Dan Ferguson, a Top Fuel drag racer. Dan's not a member of the club, but he's basically a hangaround. His race team is owned by the club. Among the fastest-accelerating machines in the world, Top Fuel dragsters are known as the 'kings of the sport'. We all know the brothers here like to live fast, so it was only natural we ventured into something like this. It's just another slice of pie for us to put our fingers into, so to speak.

Slick comes and goes from the club because he's off on the NHRA circuit with Dan and the team. We, as a club, go out there from time to time when they're at the Houston Motorsports Park to support Dan. It's a state of the art 1/8 mile drag strip, where we can get into a lot of trouble, but we're good at not getting caught. The club girls often go as the grid girls to help Dan out with promotion.

The thing is, his trailer is often handy to do deals out of, so if we need anything done on the down-low, Slick can conduct business from the back. Dan's cool with it, he knows it's part and parcel of being a Defiance MC team member.

There's a reason Slick has that road name, and it has nothing to do with tire traction. It's because he's the sneakiest sonofabitch there is. You want something done quietly, Slick's your man.

"So, Dan was saying the TrackBite layer on the Las Vegas track wasn't spread properly, he couldn't gain traction, so the rear tires were slipping. Hence the lower-than-usual quarter mile time for the final."

Kevlar lets out a groan. "Damn! Dan would have been annoyed with that. He's a stickler for maintaining his times."

"He's fast at everything he does. I'm sure he still beat the other guy, right?"

"The other guy, Tom Elway, deep staged and ran a red." Slick snickers.

We burst into laughter.

Rayne gnaws on her bottom lip, and I grimace in sympathy. "Sorry… guy talk."

She scoffs. "Well, that's sexist. Women like cars as much as guys do. Just because I have no fucking idea what deep ramming is, doesn't mean I'm not interested in going to the drags and cheering on Dan one day."

My eyes widen as I try to hold in my laughter. "Ahh... it's deep staging, but I am *really* intrigued by this deep ramming. Can we delve further into that together later tonight?"

Kevlar and Slick chuckle while Rayne huffs. "Not funny... I'm serious, though. I wanna go watch Dan with you guys. I am sure it'll be fun."

This adventurous side of her is damn sexy. "Sure. Dan will be here in a few weeks for a race, we'll go when he's in town."

"Promise?"

"Promise. You can even dress up as a grid girl if you want." I waggle my brows, and she punches my arm.

"You're an asshole."

We all chuckle.

I search the room realizing Wraith hasn't returned. Fucker's probably avoiding the chat he knows is coming.

Though he was in Militia territory, on his bike.

Realization hits me.

Oh fuck, the Militia could have him?

I slide out my chair abruptly, making everyone raise their heads as I turn rushing for Neon. Stepping over, I punch in the code in by the den door, bursting my way inside. Neon looks up at me with concern on his face. "Activate the tracker on Wraith's bike."

He jerks his head back and hesitates. "He'll have an issue with you doing that."

"Don't give a fuck. The Militia might have him."

Neon's eyes widen. He turns and types something into his keyboard. A green ping blasts on the screen. He's at a bar called Hoopla's on our side of the zoning.

A wave of relief flows through me as I grip onto Neon's shoulder. "Thank fuck for that." I grab out my cell dialing Wraith's number. It rings, and rings, then goes to voice mail.

My next point of action is to go check on him. I don't know what the fuck he's doing, or if he's okay, but I want to make sure of it. "I'm gonna ride out and check on him."

Neon grimaces as a ping sounds on my cell.

Wraith: *Needed a damn drink. Be back soon.*

I'm not convinced. The Militia could have sent that message. I walk out to the main room in search of a prospect. I spot Blake by the bar, so I stride up to him. His face lights up when he notices my approach. He stands tall facing me ready for whatever task I'm about to throw his way. Always ready to serve his club—he's a good kid.

"Blake… need you to ride over to Hoopla's to check on Wraith. If you catch a whiff of the Militia, you call for backup."

"Got it, pres." Blake spins taking off faster than necessary.

This whole situation makes me nervous.

If Wraith wanted a drink, we have a perfectly good bar here.

He's avoiding the club.

I need to know why.

Something's gone down with him and Prinie. I intend to find out what.

I head back over to Rayne when the lights suddenly flicker on and off in the clubhouse, eventually sending it into darkness. I reach for my gun at the same time as my brothers. "Rayne, get under the table and turn it over," I yell as I rush over to her.

"What! Why? What's happening?" Her frightened voice almost breaks me, but I need to focus.

I have no idea what's going on.

"Just do it!"

She ducks under the table, pushing it over in front of her. The reinforced metal underneath now shielding her, giving me little comfort. I spin around rushing for Neon, who's come out of his den as the backup lighting kicks in around the main room.

"They've short-circuited the gate," Neon warns, loading his gun.

"Everyone take defensive positions," I call out. My brothers and club girls move behind barriers with guns drawn and ready. I slide behind a support beam, so I can view the front door and whatever is about to make an appearance. I know how this works. Lights out is a warning, letting you know something's happening.

I glance over at Rayne, hoping like hell she doesn't get hurt in what's to come. *Please don't let this be a repeat of what happened a year ago.* Koda's in his room. So is Prinie. They know the drill enough to keep their asses up there.

Suddenly, the front door explodes open. I duck as dust and debris fly around the clubhouse. As I cough and peer out around the beam, Hawke and his Militia men stroll in. I keep my finger on the trigger waiting for them to open fire, but they don't.

"Zero... we're here to talk."

What the fuck?

I'm not sure how to play this.

The second I step out, they could open fire—or, he could be telling the truth.

I have to make a choice.

We broke the treaty. If they're here to talk, I need to take a stand. Show them we're willing to cooperate, or this could fall in a heap really quick. With my stomach churning, I step around the beam.

Rayne's eyes are fixated on me, but I can't focus on her right now. I need to do my job. I keep my gun aimed on Hawke. His camo greens seem far too big for him as they bunch around his legs. His black hair, buzzed in a typical short back and sides, makes his square face seem even more pronounced than possible. His tanned skin, etching his wrinkles deeper into his skin than they actually are. He looks dangerous, and while I might be willing to talk, I'm not stupid enough to lower my weapon.

"What do you want, Hawke?"

"I think you know how this works, Zero. You stick to your side of town, we stick to ours."

I scoff. "Looks to me like you're in our side of town right now—"

"Yes, but who crossed the border first?"

"We don't need this to get bloody," I offer.

"I agree. Hence, why my men aren't demolishing your clubhouse right now... we can monopolize on your... indiscretions."

I lower my gun, and the Militia follow suit. "What do you want as recompense?"

"Two of your club members came into our territory. We *didn't* kill them on sight. One of them was your VP, Zero. *He* should know better."

Exhaling, I take a step forward. "It was a misunderstanding. Won't happen again."

"No… it won't. If it does, our triggers won't be so lenient."

"Understood."

"So… what do we want as compensation?" His curt demeanor tells me I'm in for a rude shock. Hawke might be reasonable, but he's still an asshole when push comes to shove. "You push out Snow White to a hell of a lot of buyers, am I right? You have the market sewn up in Houston?"

I tense up thinking about Rayne. I'd be a fool to think she doesn't know we dabble in illegal shit, but right here, right now, she'll know for sure. I can't let my mind wander right now, though. I have to keep focused on Hawke. "I'm going to dismiss how the hell you came to know that, and replace my question with what the fuck does it have to do with anything?"

Hawke steps forward so we're face to face. "Because, Zero, we want in."

"The fuck?"

"You will have a predetermined amount of Snow White shipped to a location of our choosing, but we don't want it in bricks. You need to find another way to store it."

"And why would we store it differently?"

"Because you're shipping it for us to Juárez."

Anger swarms inside of me. *That's the quickest way to get caught.* "The fuck we are!"

"You do this, Zero, or the next time we come in here, it won't be with pleasantries. *You* broke the treaty. *You* have to suffer the consequences. How you ship the Snow White is up to you. But I will send you the quantity amount and an address in the coming days. How you get it there is of no concern to me. As long as it gets there. Understood?"

If I do this, then his men—who outnumber us—won't come in here on some sort of damn killing spree. If there is one thing I know about Hawke, the man stands by his word.

"This is a one-time deal, Hawke. Then we're on even footing again."

"We'll see."

"No! We do this, that's it. We won't be your errand boys."

Hawke steps closer with a sly smirk on his face. Tension fills the air. "You're a brave soul, Zero. I like that about you. One run. Get it done. We're even. But you cross our lines again… it'll be war."

"I hear you… now get the fuck out of my clubhouse."

Hawke snorts, signaling his men to leave. "And Zero…" He turns back glancing at Prinie who's now standing at the bottom of the stairs. Dammit! The stupid girl knows better. "Keep a leash on your sister. She's far too pretty to wander over the fence."

I get the hidden meaning in Hawke's words. Prinie needs to keep clear of the Militia. Girls like her are a meal for guys like him, and she'd probably end up in sex slavery. I want to tell him he owes me for the broken door, but I know better. Let's face it, he could have come in here and raged carnage, instead he came to barter. No blood was spilled. To me, it's a win, and I'll take it. Hawke turns, his men follow him out of the clubhouse.

Prinie gnaws on her bottom lip. "This is on me, I caused all this trouble. I'm so sorry, Zero. I promise I won't do anything like that again."

I dip my chin to her in acknowledgment. I won't appease her by saying what she did was okay. It wasn't. And right now, I can't coddle her to make her feel better, but I won't berate her either.

Not right now.

Everyone comes out from behind their barricades as I tilt my head toward the chapel. "Church, now. And someone get Wraith here in a hot minute or so help me God…"

My eyes shift over as Rayne scoots out from under the table. I thank whoever's listening she wasn't harmed in whatever the fuck this shit-storm was.

She rushes over to my side appearing rattled, but she's not shaking so that's a good sign. "Is that as bad as it gets?"

I stare at her.

Is that a serious question?

Maybe she's more distressed than she's letting on.

"Cherry bomb, that's the best it can get. It was child's play by comparison."

She bites her bottom lip, there's a hesitation in her like I haven't seen before. It's like she wants to ask something but is afraid of the answer. I don't have time to delve into her concerns because Wraith storms in through the broken doors.

I squeeze her hand. "I need to go. Gotta deal with this. Can you go check on Prinie?"

"Sure... I'll talk to you later."

I lean down planting a gentle kiss on her supple lips. She tastes like everything I want right now but can't have. I can't get lost in her, I have shit to deal with first. "Later," I reiterate, then turn walking toward the chapel. "Phantom, get Blake and Luc to help you deal with the damn doors. I don't care what you have to do, but I need them fixed. Now!"

Phantom dips his head and rushes off toward the two prospects.

Marching into the chapel, I move to the head of the table, then take my seat. My brothers fall into their places as Fox closes the door keeping us securely inside. I run my hand over my beard and exhale. "Well, that was fucking interesting. Wasn't the shower of shit I thought would rain down on us, but still a problem nevertheless." I look around at my brothers. "I need ideas. We gotta ship a shitload of Snow White to fucking Mexico without it being stopped along the way or at the border."

I shift my eyes to Wraith, he's worse for wear. His eyes are vacant like he's not paying attention to anything going on around him. It's concerning, but I need to keep my head in the game and not on my VP's downward spiral right now. "Any fucking ideas?"

"I'm guessing a long-haul ride's out of the question?" Ax asks.

I shrug. "I doubt the quantities they'll want we'll be able to carry on our rides. It's too dangerous. We get caught, we go down."

"I can talk to Dan about the trailer. Shifting the cargo inside by hiding it in tires, etcetera. We can say we're going to Juárez for a fan meet. Of course, we'd need to arrange one to keep up the pretense," Slick offers.

"Sounds risky having Dan involved when he's such a high-profile personality. I mean we know he's already involved in club business, but being caught in something like this... a drug run to Juárez? Nah. I won't bring Dan into this. We need something different, a way to produce and ship the product we normally wouldn't."

Neon places his fists on the table sitting forward. "Pres, what about the pharmacy?"

I narrow my eyes on him. "What about it?"

"We produce the Snow White in pill form. They can crush it down and bag them as prescription meds."

It clicks into place. "Then ship them from the pharmacy to Juárez saying they're for aid relief or some shit," I add.

"We'll have to put some actual prescription drugs in there, in case they open the crates. We could even encase the Snow White in a coating of actual medication that on the other end they just dissolve off, like a capsule and inside is the Snow White. That way it appears legit if they scrape test a pill," Neon suggests.

"Then put legit pills on the top, sides and bottom of the shipping crates and the Snow White hidden in the middle," I ponder.

"It could work. We just have to figure out how to make the pills," Neon replies.

"We could ask Chills and Rayne." Chains grimaces. "Though, I don't know how either of them are going to feel stepping into illegal territory."

The thought of asking Rayne to do something like this so soon seems precarious, but she's part of this club now. I need to see where she sits with everything. The pills are going to be leaving from her pharmacy, of that I'm sure. We just have to find a way to produce them, whether by the new doctor and pharmacist, or by some other means. Either way, this is our plan.

"You've given us something to move forward with. We have to talk to the right people and set the wheels in motion. We'll have to do this delicately. For now, Church dismissed." I bang my gavel, the wheeling of the chairs all rolling back grates on my very last nerve.

I spot Wraith walking out. "Wraith!" He stalls, exhales, then turns to face me. His eyes glaze like he's half-wasted. He must have had a fair bit to drink at the bar before Blake got to him. "What the *fuck* is wrong with you? What happened between you and my sister?"

He avoids eye contact. "Nothing happened. We have bad blood."

I narrow my eyes on him. "Why? Why would you have bad blood? What did *you* do?"

Wraith scoffs and turns to walk away, so I reach out grabbing his arm, turning him back around. He immediately pushes me in the chest, and I take a step back.

"What the hell, brother?" I stare at him in disbelief.

Wraith grumbles under his breath, "Leave it the fuck alone."

"She's my sister."

"Exactly!" Wraith turns storming out of the room.

Confusion takes hold as I attempt to wrap my head around whatever's going on. But, I need to find Chills instead and talk this shit through with her.

Heading out into the main room, I spot Chains already talking to his Old Lady. How much he's filled her in on, I have no idea, but I need to get over there and assess her mood, to see if we can actually make this shit happen. Her body posture is tense as I approach. She's on guard, her expression hard as Chains tries to talk calmly to her, but by the sour expression on Chills' face, she's having none of it.

She exhales excessively as I approach. "Do you really have to send them from a store with *my* damn name on it?"

Okay, recovery mode is needed.

I reach out placing my hand on her arm. "We *won't* get caught."

She snorts. "Famous last words."

"We'll make it untraceable. If, and I mean *if* it does come back on you, someone else will take the fall. Not you, Chills."

"It's still *my* business, under *my* damn name. I'll get in the shit for it happening under my roof. It could mean my license to practice medicine."

"The Baron will help. Trust me, he knows everyone… even cops."

"I'll lose the thing I love doing… being a doctor."

I grip onto her hand. "You're overthinking, Chills, we'll have every aspect covered. It won't come back on you."

She exhales, rubbing the bridge of her nose. "I *won't* make the pills for you. I can't risk going to jail, Zero. I have a sick son to think about. I don't have a choice in them being exported from the pharmacy, but you're the one who's going to have to explain this all to Rayne. This is her baby, too."

I get it, Chills has a family to think of.

My next option is to ask Rayne, but she's married to a cop. It's a gamble. Is she too far to the right to be dragged into this kind of life? She wants to live on the edge, but is she ready to jump over the damn cliff?

Rayne's watching me closely. She'll have questions about what Hawke said. I know she will. I need to face this head-on, so I turn to talk with her. I will make my mind up as I go, gage the situation as it takes place. I walk over to her, and she takes me in her arms. "This is all a little crazy, right?"

Inwardly, I laugh. *This? Crazy? She hasn't seen anything yet.*

I pull back gazing into her eyes. "Rayne, I need to talk to you." I pull her down into the nearest seat, and she follows.

"Is this about the Snow White?" I nod. "That's a code, right?"

Exhaling, I reach out grabbing her hand. "The thing is, cherry bomb, you're married to a cop. While I know you have no love for him, I need to know where you stand."

Her eyebrows draw together. "You think I'm going to go to the cops with what I see and hear? Shit, Zero, you don't know me at all." The hurt in her tone sends a sucker punch straight to my gut.

"That's the thing, Rayne… I don't know you. I don't know whether you're here because you want to stick it to Chuck, or whether you actually want to be here… in the club… as a member. Do you know what that entails?"

She sits forward, her eyes meet mine. "Zero, I've lived all my life as the good girl. Followed the rules, but breaking them in secret and finding cheap thrills where I could, but at every turn, I was pushed down, told I had to be a certain way, dress and act like a lady. I don't want that anymore. I want to live. I want to be dangerous. If that means being part of a one-percenter bike club, then hell, yeah, I'm in. Plus, it means being with you, and that alone… that's worth it all."

She talks a big game, but is it just bravado because she wants to stay? "What about when the Militia come back and start shooting up the damn place?"

"Chuck's a cop. He taught me how to shoot. Give me a gun… I'll shoot Hawke for you myself."

I love her enthusiasm.

"Ever shot anyone?"

"Only on a target, but I imagined Chuck's face on it constantly… so does that count?"

I let out a laugh. "We're not the good guys, Rayne. We deal in bad shit."

"Like trafficking coke throughout the USA? Yeah, got that memo." My eyes widen. "Snow White? Not that hard to work out if you're in the drug industry."

"Figures…" I steel my shoulders.

I can ask. She's not going to go to the cops, my gut assures me of that.

"Rayne?"

"Yeah?"

"Do you know how to make pills?"

"Of course. There was a class on it when I worked through my degree, but it was a while ago. Why?"

Here goes nothing.

"How hard would it be to put the Snow White into a capsule, and coat the capsule in a placebo drug?"

Her lips slowly edge up the side of her face in a look which can only be described as devious. "You wanna disguise Snow White in a capsule, then they'll dissolve the outer coating and break open the capsule revealing the powder." She huffs her lips widening in amusement. "Zero, that's fucking genius!"

"Can it be done?"

"I mean, you'd need a decent outer layer and drying method that wouldn't leach into the Snow White, but I'm sure *I* could find something that wouldn't contaminate the purity of it."

Jesus Christ, she knows about purity?

"Wait, *you* will find something?" I question.

"Well, yeah. I'm assuming you want me to do this, right?"

"Would you?"

"You're not going to find another pharmacy or pharmacist in a hurry, are you? I'm all you've got."

"You don't have to do it if you think the risk's too great."

"I just told you, I'm all for living on the edge. I'm in, Zero. Don't treat me with kid gloves, okay?"

"Right. I'll talk to Neon, tell him you're in. You and he will need to talk, so you can tell him everything you need. Where do you want to do the production?"

"Afterhours at the pharmacy. That way, we don't have to transport and risk getting caught. I might need a safe installed at the pharmacy to store everything. A big one to keep it out of the eyes of the workers during the day."

I narrow my eyes on her. "You're really thinking this through."

"I've got a handle on this, Zero. Like I said… I'm part of this club now, and I want to help in any way I can. If this is my contribution, then consider me your personal chemist."

I lean closer. "Is it wrong I'm fucking turned on right now?"

Her cheeks flush. "Is it bad if I say I am too?"

Standing, I bend down, hoisting her up and over my shoulder in one quick movement. She giggles but doesn't fight me. I feel my brothers' eyes as I make way for the stairs.

Rayne's shown me another side to her tonight, and now I'm about to show her all the ways I appreciate that side, so very much.

RAYNE

Zero grips my biceps moving me under his now naked body swiftly. I squeal with the quick movement as he lands on top pushing his weight over me. He rolls his hips into me on the bed, my teeth sinking into my bottom lip as my legs wrap around his waist, pulling my pussy tight against his hardening cock. He rocks against me in a delightful way as his eyes bore deep into mine.

"So as my own personal chemist, can you prescribe me something for this fever you're giving me?"

My hands loop around his neck as my fingers fiddle with the hair at the nape of his neck. "Wow, are you going for lamest dad joke of the year award right now?"

He leans down, his lips barely touching mine. "Careful, cherry bomb, I know how to ignite a fire inside of you, too." His nose runs along the edge of mine as we both pant heavily from the building tension. The chemistry in the air is palpable as my fingers slide up and down his muscular back needing him closer.

Our lips touch softly, but not kissing as we pant for breath, the emotion of the moment knowing we're both in this fully. I can't hold back any longer as I shift pressing my lips to his. He doesn't hesitate, his lips urgent against mine, the need, the hunger as our tongues find refuge in each other. My fingers thread through his long hair, pulling out his hair tie, letting it fall around his face as I hold him to me kissing him fervently.

His hips rock against me, his cock so hard I don't know how he's keeping himself together not thrusting up inside of me, but he obviously has other ideas. His kiss softens from my lips as he breaks our lips apart, trailing his bearded mouth down my neck. His tongue darts out as he glides it along my sensitive skin. I wriggle beneath him as he edges down my body, his tongue gliding over my nipple. He takes it into his mouth with a deep sucking motion.

My back arches off the bed as I let out a small whimper at the feeling. Tingles sliver from my nipple straight down to my clit as his teeth graze against my flesh. His hand slides between my legs as his finger rotates on my swollen nub, my wetness already greeting him as he circles on me effortlessly. The feeling is exciting, sending a wave of adrenaline through me.

He's working me up so damn well, every touch, every kiss, every flick of his finger and tongue is like a new height of pleasure making every single awful thing that's happened to me disappear into the back recesses of my mind.

All I'm thinking of is *him*.

All I want is *him*.

Zero.

With another rotate of his finger, I soar to dizzying heights. My back arches as I moan, my fingers gripping onto the sheets of my bed tightly. Lights begin to dance behind my eyelids as the muscles in my neck tense. My breathing quickens while the adrenaline courses through my veins. He flicks again.

"Come for me, baby."

Hearing those words, then his mouth sucks on my nipple hard, the same time he presses on my clit—it's all I need to send me over the edge.

My back arches as my entire body shudders splintering off into a million pieces. My fingers grab the sheets gripping so hard if they were his skin, he would bleed as my muscles contract, then explode in an excruciating awesome orgasm.

"God, yes," I moan, my head flopping to the side as he lets out a small chuckle, his mouth slowly kissing under my breast.

"You're so fucking beautiful when you come."

Zero sits up abruptly, grabbing my hips, hoisting us over. I scream out in a laugh as he flips us so dramatically I flop down on top of him while he falls to the mattress below with me straddling him. I somehow find the strength to sit back, looking down at him.

"Have something in mind, do we, cowboy?" I ask.

He waggles his eyebrows. "I want you to feel like you're in control, but I still want to have a little fun while I'm at it," he instructs.

Cocking my brow, my hands move to his chest, but he shakes his head. "Nuh-uh." His legs bend, his knees coming up behind me. I giggle as he tilts his head. I think I see where this is going. His hands slide down my torso seductively, instantly turning the mood back on. My body tingles, his strong hands grab at my waist hoisting me up. My pussy slides to the tip of his hard cock. I stop, looking into his eyes as I pause, and we connect on every level as I slowly slide down onto him. Our eyes never leave each other as we rock together joining completely.

Both our mouths open wide as we pant from the overwhelming feeling of fullness. Him inside me is a feeling I'll never get used to, but one I fucking love the hell out of. His hand slides from my hip up the center of me. We stay still, not moving as he slides his hand to the middle of my chest. Zero pushes me back, my body falling with his instruction as my back rests on his inclined knees. The angle of my body is making his cock take on an amazing direction, and we haven't even started moving yet.

He thrusts up. I gasp as he hits the perfect fucking spot for me to almost come instantly as I try so hard to keep myself together. My hands fall back on the bed to support myself as my head arches in pleasure.

"Shit, Zero," I gasp.

"I know, hold on," he instructs, my hands move to grip his ankles as he starts to move me on top of him at the same time moving himself. He's right. I do have control in this, but so does he. So, I move my body up and down on him as his hand presses me down onto his thighs. It's sexy as fuck as we rock together. The pressure building as he pushes inside of me, and I slam down on him. His face contorting in that delicious way. Seeing him affected by me is empowering as I ride him for all he's worth.

The pressure.

The power.

The pleasure.

Everything feels so incredibly amazing as his free hand slides up my thigh. It feels so damn good, I don't even register what he's doing until it hits. His finger presses on my clit, the wave of ecstasy flows through me instantly as he thrusts upward at the same time.

It's a rush, an undeniable surge of euphoria as I pant, riding him. His cock's so hard inside of me as he thrusts up, the same time his finger rotates on my clit so strongly, so forcefully, it's like all the pleasure in the world is crashing down around me at the same time. My nails rip into his ankles as I ride through the storm. It hits, wave after wave like a typhoon as he presses firmly on my clit. He thrusts up rocking his hips in just the right way to have me seeing goddamn stars.

"Zero, fuck!" I gasp as my eyes roll back in utter contented bliss. My muscles tense around his cock, my body shudders as my breath catches, then everything releases in giant waves.

Relaxing as he groans like he's felt my pleasure rushing through him too, my head's a fog while my body almost stops moving on him in relief because everything's so damn sensitive.

"Shit, Rayne, your pussy feels incredible when you come," Zero murmurs, bringing me back to the now. My eyes open, my head moves forward as I glance down at him. I forgot to keep moving in my climax coma, and he still needs to get there. So, I move, grinding my hips with all I have, putting every scrap of effort I have left in me into it. Even though I thought nothing could possibly waken me back up, I'm starting to feel aroused again as I ride him.

"Fuck, Rayne," he groans as my hands move up into my hair. I gnaw on my bottom lip trying like hell to be sexy for him, to turn him on as he watches my every move with a hard glint in his eyes—a hooded look. One which says he definitely likes what he sees.

Our eyes lock as I feel the pressure building inside of me again, but this isn't about me this time, so I try to ignore it as I focus in on his eyes. They're glassy, unfocused, he's close—so fucking close.

I grind down on him just a little bit deeper. He jerks, his eyes closing as his hands move to my hips, his fingers digging into my skin, tight. He groans as I feel his cock throbbing inside of me. My hands move to his chest as I roll on him to give him as much pleasure as possible.

"Fuuuck," he groans, his head flopping to the side as he thrusts up inside of me, stopping and unloading everything he has.

I bite my bottom lip.

Our sex is amazing.

As he opens his eyes, I know he thinks so too.

His hands loop out yanking me to him. I let out a small squeal as I fall to him. He chuckles as I look into his eyes while his hand strokes through my hair holding me just in front of his face.

"You're fucking perfect."

I snort out a laugh. "Hardly."

Zero shakes his head. "Fucking perfect, Rayne. In every goddamn way."

I push my head into the nook of his neck and shoulder as we lay here, still joined, trying to catch our breath. "You saved me, Zero."

His hands are sliding up and down my back comfortingly. "You saved yourself, Rayne. I'm just here to help you along."

I look back up at him with a warm smile. "Well, I'm glad you're along for this ride. I wouldn't want anyone else on this journey with me."

His hand comes up caressing my cheek. "Cherry bomb, our journey is only just beginning."

One Week Later

The pharmacy has been up and running for a little while now, and everything is finding its groove. The staff I've hired know their shit, I'm glad Zero let me vet them. I was able to employ the best people suited not only to the job, but our situation. People who wouldn't ask questions about bikers coming and going.

I'm out the back working, Neon's with me as we run through some things together. He's on his device while I fill some customer orders.

"So, you think that should be enough for what we need?" I ask.

He closes the lid on his laptop. "Yeah, you nailed it. You know for an ex-wife of a cop, you sure know how to play this shit right, Harper."

"I guess hearing Chuck talk about his work and watching a lot of crime shows will do that for you."

Neon's dimples creep in on the left side. He's crazy good-looking. Hell, I'd be stupid if I didn't notice most of the brothers at the Houston Defiance MC were. I swear it's like criteria for joining or something.

Neon clicks his fingers in front of my face. "Hey, you, where'd you go?"

"Sorry, was off daydreaming."

Neon snorts out his laugh. "About a certain president and his lustrous flowing hair?"

"He does have great hair, doesn't he?"

Neon grins as he moves around pulling a pill press out of its box just as his phone jingles with an incoming call. He slides it from his pocket without checking, pressing speakerphone. "Yo?" Neon answers, then lets out a grunt as he wrangles the heavy pill press on the table awkwardly.

"Asher, you sound weird. What are you doing?"

My eyes widen at the informal way this woman is talking to him. To be honest, I didn't even know Neon's name was Asher. It suits him. His hands are completely full, but his panicked eyes fall on me.

"Anna, you're on speaker."

Anna. Who the hell is Anna?

Anna lets out a heavy exhale like she's slumping into a chair. "Ash, how's Zero?"

I widen my eyes but avert them, continuing to pack the medication for patients as if I'm not listening while Neon tries to frantically finish what he's doing with the machine. "Now's not the time to talk about him, Anna."

"Well, I need him to know—"

"Anna, stop!"

"Ash, I can't stop thinking about him."

My head bobs up, the medication bottle dropping from my hand and clunking on the desk. Neon slams the machine into place, then grabs his cell turning off speaker. "Anna, now's not the time. I'm at the pharmacy. I'll call you later, okay? No. Later. I gotta go, bye."

Anxiety sweeps through me as I fuss about not really doing anything but pretending to be busy, which I am failing at.

Neon exhales rubbing his hand over his head. "Shit, Rayne, I'm sorry. I didn't see it was her."

I gnaw on my bottom lip. "Anna... haven't heard her name before."

"My sister." I drop my chin to my chest. "Zero hasn't told you about them?"

My chest squeezes as I clench my muscles. "About... them?"

Neon winces. "Shit."

"Is this a *now* thing?"

"Oh, fuck no! Years ago but they didn't end on the best of terms."

I wrap my arms around myself more for my own comfort. "She... she still loves him?"

Neon grimaces. "Not my story to tell, Rayne."

My head falls back to my work. My stomach churning in uncertainty. Zero knows all about my past, but I know nothing of his. Maybe I should ask him? Or should I wait for him to open up to me about her?

Fuck, now my head's spinning.

"Don't let it get to you. Anna's the one who fucked up. Zero's a good guy. If he's into you, you should hang onto him. He'll treat you well."

"I think he's into me. I know I'm into him."

Neon's smile is faint, but it's there. "You're a good match for him, Rayne. He deserves someone who'll make him happy. Just… treat him right."

I move my hand out to rest on his forearm. "You really care about him."

"We grew up together. I've known him for what seems like forever. This Anna shit put some space between us. I hate it, but it is what it is. He's my president. She's my sister. You know?"

Jealousy flares inside me for the briefest of moments, but it soon passes as I lean forward taking Neon into a hug. He's stiff like he's unsure of what the hell I'm doing.

I can't help but snicker. "You can hug me back. I'm not going to tell, Zero."

Neon slowly wraps his arms around me holding me tight. The sadness rolls off him as he embraces me. I feel for the guy. Having lost his best friend to keep in his sister's good graces can't be easy. Having to constantly vet phone calls from her about him, that can't be easy either.

I pull back holding him at arm's length. "You're a good man, Neon. And a great brother. To listen to her pine for Zero all the time must be draining. Then to see Zero spending his time with Wraith must be a hit to the system. I'm sorry."

Neon inhales but brightens like he's amazed someone actually understands him. "I simply don't want to have to pick a side."

"You shouldn't have to."

"Anyway, this is not for you to worry about. You certainly weren't supposed to hear about Anna from me. So please don't say anything to Zero."

"Secret's safe."

As if on cue, Zero walks out the back. "What are you up to?"

I lean on my toes kissing his lips briefly before pulling back assessing Neon's handy work. "Neon's setting up the pill press. If we get enough of us in here, we can knock these bad boys out in a few nights."

Zero lights up appearing more than a little impressed. "Good work. I already have the shipment date from Hawke. We have a week to get it on the truck. Is that enough time?"

"We'll get it done. Just might be all hands on deck."

Zero pulls me to him, wrapping his arms around me. "I can't believe my luck finding you. You're perfect for the club and me."

I smile up at him, but I can't help feeling a little awkward around Neon after the phone call I was privy to. If Neon's sister had a thing with Zero, and she still wants him, it does make things a little tense. I reach for Zero's hand, yanking him out into the main area of the pharmacy away from Neon, and pull him into a tight embrace. Maybe I'm feeling a little insecure. Maybe I just need to assert my hold over him. I don't fucking know. I just want to wrap myself around him right now.

He holds on to me for a while, but then as he holds me back he exhales. "You were weird around Neon. Did he do something?"

I gasp. "No. Fuck, no. He's awesome. I really like him. I think you two need to spend more time together."

Zero's body slumps with a groan. "He told you?"

"Anna called while I was in the room, kinda figured it out. Then made him fill in the spaces."

"On *all* of it?"

He's nervous.

"No. He said it wasn't his story to tell. Just that you and Anna were a thing, that it put distance between you and Neon..." I smile. "You shouldn't let it. He's a good guy. Honestly, he just wants what's best for you. You know that, right?"

"I do. It's hard when she's calling all the damn time."

I wrap my arms around him, cuddling him for as much his comfort as mine. "You wanna talk about it?"

He exhales. "Nope."

"Got it!" Have to admit it stings that he doesn't want to open up to me. We haven't known each other a hell of a long time, but I thought we were in a good place.

He senses my apprehension and pulls me back to him. "Just because I don't want to talk about Anna with you doesn't mean shit. We're good. Better than good. Don't let fucking Anna, of all people, get in your head. Don't let her ruin shit between us. That's what she's good at, ruining relationships."

"Yours and hers. Yours and Neon's," I specify.

"Exactly. Don't give her another thought. I try not to as much as fucking possible."

That makes me feel better. The last thing I want is his ex making some sort of an appearance when mine is already a contentious issue in our—whatever this is we have. It's obviously not a relationship. He hasn't said anything to clear that up, but I am not in a hurry because whatever we are, I like where we're heading.

We move back around to check on Neon's progress.

He peers up with a cock of his chin. "The press is ready to go."

Now all we have to do is get the Snow White and off we go.

Tomorrow night we begin.

Zero tasked Texas and Ax to help. We'll make a test batch, then break it down to see if it works. Then we go from there.

"The last of the supplies are coming during the day tomorrow. It should all work out fine."

This is going to work!

The Next Day

The pharmacy isn't busy, but it's slowly ticking along enough to keep me occupied. It was previously an antiquated pharmacy and we have refurbished it with modern sleek lines and new products, so the customers are getting used to how this pharmacy is being run. I'm out the back with Renee, one of the pharmacy assistants, going over Thelma Collins' medication. She has become a regular after this short amount of time. The staff here call her Grandma Thelma. Dear old thing, she's frail as hell but quicker witted than Eddie Murphy on crack.

"So, we need to make sure this all goes into the blister pack for her. Can't have Grandma Thelma missing out on her heart medication," I instruct Renee.

"I'll get right on adding it into her allotments."

"Thanks, Renee."

José pops his head around the corner, his boyish face shining brightly. "Boss, there's a delivery for you. They require a signature."

My initial instinct is to go sign for it, but I know exactly what's in this delivery. If I sign for it, I'm not only implicating myself but Chills and the club.

Shit. I hate myself right now.

"I'm a little tied up here, José. Can you sign for it, and get them to bring it 'round back?"

He nods, the poor unknowing fool. Then he turns heading off to sign for products that are going to be turned into illegal substances in this very place of business. This shit's so freaking risky, but if we can get away with it, the reward will be sweet. I have to admit, being on the other side of this tightrope, walking the fine line without a net, is so much more exhilarating than being on the ground gazing up.

A delivery driver wheels a large box on a trolley around the back. "Where can I put this, miss?"

"Oh, right, yes, just back here if you can?" I lead him toward the safe.

He plants it on the floor, then turns rushing away like he doesn't give two shits about anything. I run my hand over the medium-size box, knowing what's inside, then quickly slide it in under the bench out of everyone's way until tonight when I open it and have a little fun.

I have to admit, doing something illegal right under my employees' noses is strange. There's something about being a bad girl that has me worked-up under the collar, but in a good way.

And they don't suspect a damn thing.

They're all so polite, such do-gooders.

There's no way they would ever expect this pharmacy is a front.

By day—the people's pharmacy.

By night—a drug lab.

I smirk to myself knowing the pharmacy is closing in just a matter of a few minutes, and the brothers will be coming by. So, I walk back out to my station, get back to work and prepare to shut down the store for the evening.

Business as usual.

After we finish our final scripts, everyone is doing their last checks.

I'm getting impatient, my night's just about to begin, and I want it to get underway. So, I clap my hands together gaining everyone's attention. "You all did great work today, everyone, but I got this from here. I only have to count the till and lock up. You guys deserve an early minute. Head on home, and I'll see you tomorrow."

Renee and José thank me as they grab their gear, along with the checkout clerks and head out leaving me alone in the pharmacy.

But I'm not alone.

I already feel that he's here.

As I close the door behind everyone, then switch the roller shutters down to block the view to the city street, I hear the opening of the rear entry door. I know who it is. They were waiting for their moment. I turn as the guys walk in, and a feeling of excitement flows through me.

Neon walks straight through the back and to the safe, pulling out the equipment as I head back to greet Zero. I lean in pressing a kiss to his cheek, his lips turn up as I keep walking to grab the delivery box full of capsules and slide it out next to the table where Neon's setting up for us to work.

"So, how's this going to work, Rayne. What's the process?"

I take in a long breath as I slide on some latex gloves, then dive into the technical stuff, explaining in detail each step of the process. Everyone's following as best they can, and I give them each one task. We're all in this, and everyone has a crucial role to play. If one of us goes down, I guess we all do.

I run through the process of how we will fill the capsules with the cocaine, which will then be covered in a placebo layer, dried in the drier, and then the final coating will be added. Once all this is done, we can test the final pill to see if when pulled apart, it still works. If not, we're screwed.

We get to work.

It's eight o'clock when we start.

Now it's almost five in the morning when the first pill is set to be tested.

We don't have much time, and physically, we're all spent. But Zero gives Neon the seamlessly sized capsule which looks freakishly perfect, just like any normal pill.

Neon examines it under a microscope. "Looks flawless. We now need to test the deconstruction."

Ax comes over with a switchblade to scratch away at the placebo layer. It still appears normal, which is what we want. Then Ax cracks his neck to the side, slices the pill in half, it splits, then he slides the broken capsule ends of each side. The white power cascades all over the bench. A collective exhale resounds around the room.

The product is intact.

Neon grabs a sample, placing it on a slide to test the purity of it. It was ninety percent pure before we started, it will be interesting to see where it's at now. I reach out looping my fingers with Zero's. This is a big moment for us. If the purity of the Snow White is too damaged, all of this was for nothing, and the looming deadline of the shipment for the Militia draws closer. If this fails, Zero could be screwed.

The test lights up revealing eighty-six-point-seven percent purity.

We all cheer, the guys patting each other on the back as Zero turns to me hoisting me up in the air and spins me around. I let out a joyful laugh at his playful side as he slides me back down his body. Our eyes lock, the excitement on his face glows like the midmorning sun. He's beaming. I love seeing him like this.

He's always so focused. His mind always thinking of how things are going to pan out two steps ahead, but with this, he's had no control. So to see him as elated as I feel, it makes him even more fucking sexy if that's possible.

Zero leans in slamming his lips to mine. The pulse, that surge, the way my heart stops then slams back into rhythm when he kisses me takes my breath away as my hands run up into his man bun and I tangle my fingers through his locks. I don't even care about the other guys in the room right now.

This is a win, and I want to show Zero just how fucking happy I am.

My tongue dances with his as he presses his hardening cock against me. I whimper into his mouth as he chuckles against my lips pulling back, slowing this down before we end up fucking in front of his brothers.

"We couldn't have done this without you," he pants breathlessly against my lips.

"It was fun, actually. I like putting my chemistry knowledge into use."

A low growl grumbles from his chest. "I like it when you nerd out on me."

"Save that for later. We need to clean this mess up. Now we know what we're doing, we can begin production later tonight. For now, though, this place opens in four hours. I need to bleach everything. Can't have any traces of Snow White slipping into Grandma Thelma's medication."

Everyone laughs as Neon moves about putting everything away. Zero moves in kissing behind my ear. "You're good at giving orders, you know?"

"Am I? I didn't realize I was even doing it?"

He spins me around to face him. "You're good for this club, Rayne... you're good for me."

I'm smiling at him. He moves in to kiss me as Texas clears his throat walking past. "A little help would be nice."

We both grin but get to work because I have a pharmacy to run in a few hours before we turn this place into a drug production line later tonight.

And that? That's what I'm most excited about.

CHAPTER 22

ZERO

One Week Later

Rayne's been amazing. Working her shifts at the pharmacy by day, then being a chemist by night. There's no way we could have done this without her. We've worked so damn hard over the last week to get the shipment right—to get the pills right.

Fox made the crates to go in the truck with hidden compartments for the Snow White capsules to hide in. Rayne ordered some placebo drugs to place over the top of the crates to act as a deterrent. If the truck is pulled over, and they test the pills on top, and then by some miracle they find the ones below, well, hopefully, they will get the same outcome we did if a scratch test is carried out. If, however, they break our pills apart, well, we're screwed.

The truck is at the rear of the pharmacy. No one's around except for my brothers, and everyone's helping to load the crates. There's six in total. The truck's leaving from the pharmacy and docking for a couple hours, then taking off at ten tonight. According to his schedule, he should be reporting in anywhere from eight to nine am in the morning.

Whether he will report directly to me or straight to Hawke, I'm not sure. The driver isn't saying much. So, we load the truck then send him on his merry way.

I hope like hell we've pulled this off because if we don't, we're all about to be in a shitload of hell. But there's nothing we can do about it now. It's time to get my men back to the clubhouse. I need to see Rayne and tell her the shipment left the pharmacy with ease.

I didn't want her there in case the cops turned up. She doesn't need to be here for that kind of heat. I also don't want to risk Chuck catching wind of where she is if the cops do figure out what we're shipping.

I simply can't risk losing her.

As we all stride back into the clubhouse, Rayne runs like the wind to me. She jumps straight into my arms making me take a step back with the force as she plants one hell of a welcome-home kiss on my lips. I chuckle against her as I kiss her back, my hands clenching onto her ass as her legs wrap around my waist.

Fuck me, my cock's needy for her.

We may have just pulled off something fucking crazy, but right now I want to spend what could possibly be my last night of freedom with her. Part of this night includes inside of her, don't get me wrong, but I want my last night to mean something.

I want a memory to cling to.

So, I pull my lips from hers as she rests her forehead on mine. "I was so fucking scared."

I smirk. "Really? Hadn't noticed."

She scoffs.

"Is there anything you wanna do tonight? This could be our last night of freedom if we're caught. I wanna spend it doing something memorable with you."

Her eyes mist but don't overflow. "Zero, you getting all sweet on me?"

"I can spend it with Wraith if you want?"

She giggles. "Okay… take me anywhere *you* wanna go. Somewhere I wouldn't expect."

My chest fills with warmth. *Fuck, this woman is my everything.* "Challenge accepted. We're going for a ride, cherry bomb."

Her eyes widen in awe. "I'm going on the back of your bike?"

"Hell, yeah, you are!"

She slams her lips to mine again before I have a second to even register. Her pussy pressing against my cock makes me moan in her mouth. The friction in my pants is almost unbearable as chuckling erupts from my brothers around us. I need to break this up, otherwise we won't be going anywhere. I pull back from her fucking insatiable kiss, panting for breath. "Jesus, cherry bomb, you're gonna be the death of me."

"Well, then, I plan to make sure you die a very, very happy man."

Fucking hell.

"Okay, let's go before I can't." I slide her down my body taking her hand in mine.

Fox smirks at me from beside the bar as Bub winks at Rayne. We race outside toward my ride, excitement flowing through us. Besides Prinie, I haven't had another woman on my bike since Anna. So, this is kind of a big deal for me, but I won't let Rayne know that. No need to add pressure on her shoulders. What she doesn't know won't hurt her.

I hand her a helmet. She slides it on then I lean in doing up the strap under her chin. Her eyes don't leave mine, not for one second.

She's fucking adorable.

I move to hop on the bike, and Rayne furrows her brows. "Where's your helmet?"

I point to her. "On your head, cherry bomb."

"But—"

"No buts. Just slide that sweet ass on behind me. C'mon, we've already missed the start."

"The start of what?

"Get on, Rayne," I groan out.

She huffs. "Bossy pants." Sliding on behind me, my body stills as her arms wrap around my waist. I clench my eyes tight trying like hell not to imagine Anna behind me, but Rayne's peach scent wafts over me, and I relax instantly sinking into the leather. Rayne's arms link around my torso—this is where Rayne's meant to belong.

I start my bike, then turn back to face her. "Hold on, cherry bomb."

She squeezes harder around my body. I face the front as Neon electronically opens the gate. He's updated the encryption software since the Militia attack let them short-circuit the gate so easily and gained them entry. Now, no one can get in or out without Neon giving the go ahead.

I hammer down, taking off at record speed. She screams in my ear, but it's filled with laughter, so I know she's enjoying herself as I take the corner as fast as is safe. She moves with me, a complete natural. Riding with Rayne behind me feels effortless. Natural. Like this is how it was meant to be. How it should always be. I never knew having her on the back of my bike would be such an adrenaline rush as I make my way through the Houston streets to Minute Maid Park. Slowing the bike down as we get closer, the traffic gridlocks, so I weave in and out moving toward the parking area and stop my ride. The engine shuts down, the vibration coming to a halt, and we let out a collective exhale.

"That. Was. Epic," Rayne gushes.

I tap her leg for her to hop off, she does so without needing any further instruction. I slide off and move in to undo her helmet. Her eyes meet mine. There's nothing but excitement flashing through her emerald green orbs. She's on a high, and I love that my bike did that for her.

Rayne takes in where we are as the noise from the stadium erupts in a loud roar. "You like baseball?"

"The Astros are our home team. Me and Neon got into it when we were younger. I haven't been for years. C'mon, let's go."

I grab her hand, leading her toward the large stadium.

"The roar of the crowd sounds like it's not natural, like it's not even real from out here," she mentions.

"But once you get inside, once it hits your ears, it vibrates through your body. Your ears rattle with the decibels. It's pure excitement, Rayne."

She's bouncing on her toes with energy. "Look at how enthusiastic about this you are, Zero. I love seeing you so passionate about something. Chuck never took me to anything like this. He was too prim and proper to go to a baseball game. He'd rather go to fancy dinners and upscale events. Yeah, what a pompous asshole."

I can't help but let out a small chuckle at her last comment. "Well, you're here with me, and we're gonna have some fun. C'mon, let's grab the tickets."

I lead us up to the entry and manage to grab the last couple of tickets. If I'd known we were coming sooner, I would have splurged and gotten better seats, but the nosebleed section will have to do. I make sure to keep a good grip on her hand as we walk through the turn styles into the security checkpoint. We're searched, then sent through to the stadium.

I smirk. *If only they knew.*

I lean in next to her ear. "First thing's first, we have to get you a foam finger, a beer, and a hot dog."

We walk around to grab our food and supplies, then take our stuff and walk up the stairs to find our seats. We have to slide in past spectators who are already seated as they duck around us trying to watch. One of them yells out, "The umpire needs new glasses," while we pass. Rayne laughs as we take our seats, and she marvels at the field.

I send off a quick text to Wraith letting him know where we are. Don't need him calling every five minutes interrupting us. I glance up to see the Yankees are pitching and the Astros batting as Altuve bashes the ball so hard it almost smacks into the homerun train they have up near the scoreboard. The crowd erupts in a frenzy, the noise smacking me right in the chest as I admire Rayne's face. Her eyes wide, her mouth open in an O-shape as she takes it all in. That look of awe is fucking adorable on her.

Rayne's enamored by the energy coming from the crowd as we

get comfortable, she's cheering like she's already having the time of her life.

The Astros baseball cap she's wearing looks crazy good on her as she relaxes back in the plastic chairs, drinking her beer. She couldn't be more fucking perfect right now if she tried.

George Springer slams the ball hard making the players on second and third base both run home as he slides into third. The crowd goes ballistic. Rayne jumps up throwing her hands into the air, spilling her beer on me.

I had no idea she'd get so into this.

She sits down, nothing but pure joy on her face as she gushes. "Did you see that? Oh my God, Zero, this is the best! Thanks for bringing me." Rayne leans in kissing me briefly. She tastes like beer and hotdog, but it only turns me on. I slide my hand onto her thigh, sitting back watching the game as she continues to get right into it.

"You're blind, ump!" she yells. Soon after she chants, "Yankees are lightweights," in a long drawn- out song along with the rest of the crowd, not to mention she's screaming when the Astros are running for bases.

She really is a cherry bomb.

This is exactly perfect. Not just for Rayne but for me. This is helping us both relax after what's been going on. I sure as shit hope it's not our last night together, but if it is, it's been fucking perfect. And exactly why I wanted something like this for us—a memory to keep while I am doing time.

The game ends. The Astros won, and Rayne's crazy happy with the outcome.

We make our way back to the bike, and the entire way she's gushing about how amazing the game was. The whole time I'm reflecting on how amazing *she* is.

"I'm boring you with my excitement, aren't I?"

"Just the opposite, cherry bomb. I'm so fucking happy you enjoyed yourself tonight. I'm going to make sure if I am still free in the morning, we'll be doing a lot more of this."

She waves the foam finger high in the air. "Fantastic. Zero for the win!"

I shake my head as she loops her arm with mine as we walk back to the bike. When we reach it, I grab her baseball cap and the foam finger she's grown so attached to, placing them in my saddlebag.

"I want to keep them as mementos of our first date," she blurts out.

I stun back at those words—why I'm shocked to hear them?

This was a date?

I suppose it was, and the weirdest thing is, I'm totally okay with it.

Grabbing the helmet, I plop it on her head, do up the strap, then hop on. She slides in behind me like it's the most natural place for her to be. Rayne fits perfectly to my body. It's like she was made to ride behind me. I start the bike loving how everything feels.

Now, that I know what having her feels like, I can't imagine anything being able to top it.

No one can top her.

Rayne pulls her baseball cap back in position on her head as we walk inside the main room. She's bursting with energy.

Prinie spots us. "Nice cap. It suits you."

Neon, who's behind the bar, lifts his eyes as we walk past. A pang of regret swarms through me as his eyes drop to Rayne's cap. I haven't been to a game with him in four years since all this shit with Anna started, since our friendship turned sour. Fuck! I should have thought about his feelings rather than rubbing shit in his face.

"You went to a game?" Neon's tone is somber.

Rayne steps forward. "Next time you and Zero should go together." We both stare at her like she's lost her damn mind. "You guys would love it. You know... bonding and all that shit."

Neon shrugs. "Yeah."

Rayne nudges me. "Yeah, sure, we'll go to the next home game."

"See, you guys are already on your way."

"On our way to what?" I ask.

"Being friends again."

Anger flares inside of me as I grip Rayne's bicep pulling her to one side. "Stop trying to fix something that's clearly broken."

Her happy expression falls, then she sighs. "It's not broken. You're both adding to the rift. Not Anna."

I don't want to discuss this with Rayne. "We had a good night, let's try and keep it that way."

The corner of her lips turns up ever so slightly. "Okay." She pushes up on her toes, pressing a strong kiss to my lips. That spark, the motherfucking tingle shoots straight to my cock. I want to take care of the urge, but there's a couple of things I need to do before I take Rayne to bed.

I pull back glancing across at Neon. There's so much I should say to him, but I can't find the fucking words, so I say nothing. Rayne smiles at Neon before I spin on my heels, and step over to where Texas and Chains are sitting with Ax and Wraith. They're the men I need right now. "C'mon, let's sit."

I slide in beside Texas with Rayne next to me. "Any word?"

Wraith shakes his head. "Nothing yet."

Prinie's hovering at the end of the table. It's like she's anxious to sit but won't do it because Wraith's there. I want to know what the fuck that's about. But I figure if I ask them now, in front of everyone, they'll both clam up.

Rayne follows my eyesight as hers focuses in on Prinie. Then she winks at me and stands. "Excuse me for a moment." She grabs Prinie, then they walk off together.

It's unsettling that shit's going down with Prinie I have no fucking clue about, but if Rayne can help her through it, then at least Prinie has someone I trust at her side to guide her.

Right now, though, I need to keep my focus on the shipment because it's well on its way to Juárez, and I want to know how it's traveling.

CHAPTER 23

RAYNE

I can tell by the strained expression on Prinie's face something's wrong. As she stands by the end of the table, there's something stopping her. She needs me. As much as I want to stay and hear the updates on how the shipment is going, my friend comes first, always. So, with my arm wrapped around her shoulders, we walk away from the guys, and I pull her closer to me. "You okay, hon? You look a little off?"

Prinie exhales. "I want to know what's happening, but I don't want to be near Wraith."

I halt our walk, turning her to face me. "What is it with you two?"

Prinie's eyes fall to the floor. "It's nothing of any importance. He's just so aggravating, it makes me want to reach over and *strangle* him."

"If I didn't know better I'd say that's sexual frustration talking."

Prinie's eyes widen. "As if. He's disgusting!"

"Mm-hmm... that chiseled body, his gorgeous face, those tattoos," I giggle. "Yeah... he's *really* disgusting."

"You screw him then!"

I jerk back. "Wait! Prinie, have you and Wraith—"

"No. Stop it, Rayne! Stop trying to analyze my situation."

Raising my hands in defeat, I surrender. "Okay, sorry."

"So, you and my brother are getting along all right?"

I glance over at Zero. My hand instinctively sliding to the rings on my left hand, twirling them. "Yeah, we had the best night." I peer back at Prinie. "I know this must be weird for you."

Prinie smiles, but it's genuine. "No, actually, I think you're perfect for him."

"I think *he's* perfect for *me*." I sigh.

Prinie's eyes shift to my nervous habit. Her hand reaches out stopping my fingers from twirling my rings. "Rayne, you've grown since you've been here. I've seen you blossom into this woman who takes control. One who stands up for herself. How long are you going to keep living in the past?"

I glance down at my rings, then over at Zero.

She's right.

It's time.

Taking a deep breath, I slowly slide my rings off, one by one.

An overwhelming feeling of accomplishment rolls through me as they leave my finger. I look at my bare skin and smile the biggest smile I have in years.

I'm finally free.

Free to be who I want to be.

Free to live the life *I* choose.

Free to be with Zero.

Prinie reaches forward, grabbing me in a giant bear hug. "Congratulations, Rayne."

"Damn, that felt good," I say as we pull apart.

I glance over at her brother—something shifts inside me.

Maybe I wasn't giving myself to Zero fully.

Maybe I was holding back, but now I can give myself to him completely.

I just have to wait and see if he wants me like I want him.

ZERO

"Any word?"

"Nothing, pres. We know the shipment got off okay. I'm assuming we'll have to wait to hear when it's landed safely in Juárez. Either that, or we'll get a knock on the clubhouse door during the night," Chains relays.

The mood is tense as we all wait for some kind of indication from the truck driver. Any fucking thing. But so far, nada.

Prinie and Rayne step back into the main room. Prinie's demeanor is calmer, more relaxed than before. Whatever Rayne did, obviously helped. Though, I don't fucking know what the deal is between her and Wraith. Neither of them will spill the beans, but I *will* find out.

Tonight's not that time.

"Okay, everyone, it's fucking late. Staying up all night is only going to make us antsy. Go to bed. It's not supposed to land till the morning, anyway. Keep your phones on you in case. Good work, everyone," I call out.

My brothers slowly stand and move about getting ready for the night. There's no point waiting around for news. We'll all go damn crazy. I glance at Rayne as she says something to Prinie, then saunters over to me taking my hand.

"Ready for bed?" I ask.

"Yeah, it's been a huge twenty-four hours."

Dodging the rotund bulldog, Mack, on our way, we make our way upstairs to my room. Closing the door behind me, Rayne's pulling her clothes off before I have a second to even gather my thoughts. Seeing her gorgeous body is clouding my mind, but I blink a few times to focus while shrugging out of my cut which I place on my desk, kick off my boots, and get completely naked, just like her.

She strides to me, and I reach out grabbing her, pulling her sexy-as-sin body to mine. We collide skin on skin, and I stare down at her. "You unravel me, Rayne."

She runs her fingers into my hair, pulling out the tie letting my hair flow freely. Her fingers then run through the loose tendrils—the feeling thrilling.

"And you've put me back together."

My hands slide up the smooth skin of her back as my lips find hers. Our tongues collide as I step her toward the bed. She falls backward landing on the mattress with a bounce. I tower over her, looking down on her gorgeous body and taking in her curves. Crawling onto the bed and over her, we kiss, the heat is not frenzied, more calm, passionate, almost emotional. We've taken a huge step in this relationship if that's what you call it. I've put a lot of trust in her. Even though whatever this is, is so new, I like where we're heading.

Slowly, I pull back looking into her deep emerald eyes, my hand caressing her cheek. Her skin is slightly flushed, her lips swollen from our deep kiss. Rayne's so fucking perfect.

She lets out a long exhale, her fingers playing with my hair. "I'm sorry if I overstepped the mark with Neon... I'm only trying to help."

Clenching my eyes, I let out a groan. "I know. I know you want to help. It's just—"

"Hard."

I open my eyes again, and her expression is soft. "Exactly."

Her bright luminous eyes are sparkling. "Sometimes the best things in life are the hardest to fight for."

Taking that in, it sends a shockwave straight through me. I roll off her, and she instantly cuddles into my side as I stare at the ceiling pondering that exact thought. After watching her in all her glory at the stadium, it's like I'm seeing her in a way I've never seen any other woman.

I can picture myself with her long term.

Like spending our lives together, and that's starting to scare me.

Last time I thought like that, look where that shit got me.

A broken heart. Embarrassment like I've never felt before on my fucking wedding day, and a fractured relationship with my best friend.

We lay in silence for a while until I notice Rayne's fast asleep on my chest. She's been awake more often than not over the past week, working during the day and making the pills for me at night. She deserves rest. So, I slowly reach over turning off the light, then edge the covers over us.

The ceiling could do with a fresh coat of paint. Even in the dim light, I can see that. I'm spending too much time staring at the damn ceiling. Don't get me wrong, I love the feeling of having Rayne surrounding me, of having my body wrapped up by hers. Having her around is awesome, but is this the right thing for me?

Now, I'm not so sure.

Night shifts to dawn as I watch the ceiling, all the while Rayne sleeps effortlessly on my chest. After staring at the ceiling all night, my mood's all over the place. I reflected a lot over whether the truck is going to make it or not. Is Rayne the right choice in my life right now? What about Prinie and Wraith? Not to mention the tension between Neon and me. And as always, the ever-present threat of the Militia. Plus, the damn ceiling needs painting!

So much is going through my head right now it's fucking me up.

I need a damn breather, something to ease up.

My cell beeps with an alert, breaking my mind from its rapid cycling.

Rayne jolts awake as I lean over reaching for it.

> **Hawke:** *The shipment is late. If it's not there in an hour, we're not coming into the club to take our payment, we're going after everyone you love.*

What the fuck! It hits me like a sledgehammer to the head. I stand, jumping out of bed, rushing around getting dressed.

"What? What's going on?" Rayne's sleepy voice asks with concern.

"Get dressed. Club's going into lockdown." I don't elaborate as she sits in my bed, hair disheveled, sheet covering her breasts and so damn stunning. No, I can't think of that right now as I yank on my cut, then walk out the door.

I rush down the hall, bashing on everyone's doors to wake my brothers. One by one the doors open, my brothers stepping out as I get to the very end and turn back seeing everyone standing in wait.

My eyes fall on Neon as I prepare to relay my message. "Bring your families in. Now. Everyone you hold dear, club's on full lockdown. Tell them to drop everything and get here now. There's no time to fuck about."

Everyone nods.

Neon flares his nostrils. I dip my head at him as I turn back, Rayne's standing at my door with a worried expression.

She knows what this means.

Anna's coming to the clubhouse.

I haven't seen her for over a year.

This is going to be fucking awkward.

CHAPTER 24

RAYNE

Anna's coming to the clubhouse. *How do I feel about that?* What Zero and I have is new, but we're solid, right? Why am I suddenly questioning us? Maybe because I know nothing about Anna or diddly squat about their relationship.

How long were they together?

How did it end?

When did it end?

I have no right to be insecure, but I really am.

Zero's like my white fucking knight. I guess I'm scared Anna's going to swoop in and take him right back from under me. We're going to be locked in here together, in this compound. I have no idea how I'm going to handle that. I'm lost in my running thoughts when Zero walks off downstairs. I follow behind as he rushes about frantically trying to get things in order. I'm like a puppy chasing its master, and it doesn't feel good.

"Zero, can I talk to you for a second?" I ask as he continues to walk anywhere I'm not.

He eyes me sideways, huffs, and finally stops. "I'm busy. I have to get this place in lockdown. I'll come find you later."

The brush off.

The club's just gone into lockdown, so I have to cut him some slack. He's busy. Am I being paranoid?

As I look around, the club's a flurry with brothers on their cells all talking at the same time. Everyone is madly running around as I try to keep out of the way. I'm being a hindrance. I make my way over to the bar and sit, so I don't interfere with anything happening around me.

Nessie wipes down the woodgrain as the corner of her lips turn up into a broad smile.

"Is it always like this? Lockdown, I mean?"

"Yeah, pretty much. You want a coffee or something?"

"Got something a little stiffer?"

Nessie smirks. "It's nine in the morning, hon. You're growing into this club life waaay too quickly."

"No, I'm joking... kinda. Coffee will suffice... thanks."

Nessie exhales. "Lockdown isn't necessarily a bad thing, more a precaution. Don't worry, we'll be okay."

Her kind gesture of trying to make sure I'm not anxious is nice, but it's not my safety I'm concerned about. It's my newfound relationship with Zero.

Nessie slides a mug of piping hot joe across the bar to me. As I sit back, everyone's fussing about.

Prinie walks over shifting onto a stool beside me letting out a long drawn-out groan. "This is the beginning."

My eyebrows squish together. "Of what?"

"Of how shit goes down. This is how war begins. Of how blood gets spilled. It starts with a delayed shipment, then a lockdown, and then while everyone is here, the Militia will attack. It's how it works."

My eyes widen. "You think they're doing it to get everyone here so they can attack us all together?"

"It's what I'd do."

"And you're an evil mastermind?"

She shrugs. "Sometimes."

I bump into her side playfully as I watch Zero.

Prinie's eyes follow my line of sight. "He's not dealing," Prinie declares.

"With what?"

"With Anna coming to the clubhouse. He's distancing himself from you."

I narrow my eyes on her. "Why?"

"For one… he's a damn fool. Two… fear."

"Fear?"

"Of getting hurt again. Anna…" She exhales. "What she did… that bitch messed him up. It's why he's been single ever since."

I hesitate.

Do I want to know? The answer is simple. Yes. Yes, I do.

"What did Anna do?"

Prinie glances at Zero again. "I better let him tell you. If he knew I told you before he was ready to share, he'd kill me. Just don't let Anna mess with your head." Prinie grips my shoulder in some sort of comfort move then starts to walk off as people begin entering the clubhouse.

I sit back people watching as club brothers hug their families and loved ones. I quietly sip on my coffee feeling more like an outsider than ever before as the clubhouse starts to buzz and come alive. I study everyone, waiting anxiously to see who this Anna is.

Then a tall woman walks through the door, her short, dead-straight, jet black hair frames her beautiful tanned face. She's like some kind of goddess. Her eyebrows are perfectly manicured, her lips plump and full, her eyelashes must have extensions because if they don't, I have serious lash envy. Even the way she dresses is gorgeous. A tight-fitting black silk shirt with cutouts along the shoulders making her sexy as hell with ripped skinny jeans. If I were a guy, I'd have a serious hard-on just from looking at her. My heart pounds so hard as she saunters into the clubhouse like she's been here a million times before. Her face showing her growing happiness of being here. She's like a spring flower blossoming in the height of a sunny day. She's shining bright for all to see. Her energy expanding from every part of her, lighting her eyes, spreading across every one of her perfect features as she searches the sea of people.

Please don't be Anna.

Please don't be Anna.

Neon rushes over and pulls her into a tight hug.

My stomach falls through the floor.

Every part of me feels inferior.

How the hell am I ever meant to compete with that?

Turning my head away simply because I can't stand to look at her any longer, I spin on the stool, my eyes fall on Zero.

His are firmly on Anna.

He's unreadable.

I'm watching him watching her.

I'm not even a blip on his radar even though I'm right in front of him.

Prinie's observing this weird fucking staring triangle. The sympathy in her eyes makes me feel even worse. So, I stand, walking right in front of Zero's line of sight and head for the stairs. I need to decompress for a moment. I don't stop to see if he sees me because honestly, right now, I don't fucking care.

I need a second.

I took off my rings.

That's a huge step for me, and Zero didn't even notice.

But in a sea full of people, he noticed *her.*

That says *everything.*

Am I in too deep?

Did I let myself feel things too quickly?

I don't fucking know. All I do know is I'm heading to *my* room.

Who knows if he will need *his* room later for *someone* else?

I'm surprised at how much that thought hurts me to my very core.

I let my walls down.

Maybe it's time to get the bricks out and start building that fortress back up.

ZERO

I was so fucking focused on Anna, I didn't see Rayne sitting right in front of me. Seeing her walking off like that with the amount of hurt in her eyes, I know I'm an asshole. I've never claimed not to be. But this shit's messing with my head.

I know I'm the cause for Rayne's emotions being all over the place like they are. This can't be easy on her. Problem is I don't fucking know if I can do this shit again. Put myself out there. I shouldn't ghost her like this, I know that. I should talk to her, tell her what's going through my mind, but so much shit's happening right now, I don't have a spare minute to have a decent discussion with her, to give her the time she deserves.

Rayne probably thinks I didn't realize she took her rings off last night. *I noticed.* That fact sent a shockwave through me. I'm not sure what it means to Rayne, but it's a pretty fucking huge step in my eyes, which only makes everything clearer. *We're moving too damn fast.* With Anna here, things are bound to get crazy, and I don't want to fuck shit up with Rayne.

So, I may as well quit while I'm ahead.

As I turn back, Anna's walking toward me, and my entire body tenses. I'm not sure I'm ready for this, but I knew the second I called for lockdown, she'd be coming in.

Hawke gave me no damn choice.

Anna saunters up. Neon's eyes staring like lasers into my back make this even harder.

Anna's exactly the same. Gorgeous as ever, but she's too done up. Then there's Rayne. Seeing her in the Astros baseball cap, mad hair from the wind, wild and carefree, she's exactly what beauty is, not this doll-like appearance. I'm starting to wonder what I ever saw in Anna, all before she's even said anything.

"You haven't changed at all." Her voice is exactly the same, deep, sensual, perfect for phone sex. She looks and sounds sexy as hell.

It's no surprise I fell for her charade.

"Actually, I've changed a lot. You know where everything is, make yourself at home. You always do. Try not to cause any trouble. Excuse me."

She gasps. "Krew—"

"Call me, Zero, Anna," I snap back at her, then spin around, heading for the stairs.

I need to find Rayne.

I head to my room. As I open the door and look around, I know she's not in here or the bathroom.

I'm confused, I saw her come up. *Maybe she came back down while I was talking with Anna? I* go to head back down the stairs when it clicks in my mind. I step over to her room, gently knocking on the door.

"Come in." Her tone is somber, and my stomach lurches through the floor.

Rayne went to *her* room, not the room we've been sharing together for weeks.

This is bad.

I've done this.

I enter, she's lying on her bed curled up in a ball. She hasn't been crying, but the somber expression on her face says she's close to it. I exhale closing the door behind me and walk over to her.

Her eyes don't even shift to me as I sit next to her.

"She's pretty," Rayne mutters.

"She's plastic. You're pretty."

Her eyes finally meet mine, and she blinks a few times. Confusion is written across her features. "You couldn't see me. You only saw her."

I exhale, feeling like an asshole. "It was a shock to see her. I knew she was coming and yet seeing her was still... hard." I reach out grabbing Rayne's left hand, running my finger over her vacant ring finger. "Don't think I didn't notice, Rayne."

Her head snaps up, her bottom lip trembling. My hand comes up to caress her cheek. "Then why have you been avoiding me?"

"It's hard to explain—"

"Prinie says it's fear."

I smirk at how Prinie's trying to interfere. I know it's only out of love for both of us. "Prinie needs to mind her own business... but, yeah, maybe."

Rayne slides closer, her peach scent intoxicating. *She's too fucking tempting.* "You're scared of me? As a person, or what my life brings to the club?"

Shit. How the hell do I discuss this? I'm not good at this deep and meaningful crap, but if I like Rayne as much as I feel like I do, then maybe I need to suck this shit up and talk to her. I need to tell her what's going through my head. "Anna was my fiancée." Her eyes widen as she sits back a little from me in shock. "The night before our wedding, she cheated on me with her best friend's brother."

She gasps. "What? The night before?"

My nostrils flare in anger of the memory. "She told me the morning of the wedding."

Rayne's eyes glisten as if she wants to cry but can't. Come to think of it, I've never seen her cry. "That. Vapid. Whore."

The venom in her tone is so adorable, I can't help myself as I let out a small laugh. "You're so fucking cute when you're angry."

Rayne glares. "She's an asshole, Zero. How can you stand to be in the same room as her?"

I shrug. "Have to be. Lockdown. She's a part of this club, so I have no choice. She's under our protection."

Rayne folds her arms over her chest and growls, she actually growls. "Let the Militia have the cheating bitch, I say."

I pull her to me wrapping my arm around her shoulder. "You know, your anger toward her is kind of a turn-on."

She pushes my chest. "Zero, this is serious. She hurt you, and for some reason, you tried to push me away because Anna was coming here, or for some other fucking reason I'm yet to understand. Stop avoiding the issue and talk to me."

I clench my eyes shut, rubbing them with the palms of my hand. "Fuck, okay… kinda thought if I pushed you away, you won't end up hurting me like Anna did."

"You think I'd cheat on you?"

"No… I don't know… fuuuck. This is why I don't talk about this shit."

She narrows her eyes on me. "You don't trust me. That's what it comes down to."

"What? Yes, I do."

"I put my career, *my* career on the line for you and your club, and you *still* don't trust me. I mean, what else do I have to do to prove to you that I'm *in* this, Zero?"

"Rayne, I—"

"Look, I need a second to process this. If you can't trust me, then maybe we shouldn't do this. Maybe I should stay in my room from now on."

What the fuck?

She stands and starts to walk to her door leaving me reeling. My headspace is all over the place, but I don't want this to end. I just needed a second. A moment to gather myself. Now she's made the choice for us. She walks out of her room, exiting as I sit on her bed.

What the hell just happened?

Great! Just fucking great.

ZERO

Rayne is sitting over with Prinie and Chills, their death glares are like laser beams shooting right at me obviously plotting my demise. I'm trying to ignore them as I sit with Wraith waiting to hear more news about the missing shipment. Neon's at the table opposite me with Anna, she's casually staring at me too. All this attention is giving me some sort of fucking complex. I want to get on with the day and not feel like half the women in this club are either lusting after me or plotting my death at midnight.

My cell beeps with a text, so I yank it out.

> **Unknown:** *The shipment made its delivery safe and sound. There was a delay with roadworks into Juárez. But it wasn't stopped or checked at any point in transit. All packages have been transferred with approval. The truck is on return route now.*

I open my mouth to make an announcement, but my cell beeps again.

> **Hawke:** *Congratulations. Everyone is safe, for now. Your debt is paid in full. Until next time, pres.*

We pulled this off. We actually pulled this fucking thing off! I stand up and let out a loud whistle which reverberates through the room. "Everyone, lockdown's lifted. Family, friends, you're safe and free to leave. But we're about to have one hell of a party, so you're more than welcome to stay and celebrate with us."

A round of cheering goes through the clubhouse as Wraith stands. "Wanna tell me what that's all about?"

"Delivery was held up by road works. It got there, without interference. Package is delivered and the truck is on its way back. We actually fucking did it!"

Wraith doesn't smile even though this situation warrants it. Wraith never shows his happiness, but his hand comes out gripping my shoulder. "Good job, pres. You saved our asses."

The heat of Rayne's stare makes me turn. Her eyes are firmly on me.

"It wasn't all me."

Wraith follows my line of sight to Rayne who turns up her nose while talking to Prinie. "You in the doghouse?"

I roll my shoulders. "This shit's fucking hard work. Having Anna here doesn't help. I don't know what the hell I'm doing."

Wraith glances at Neon. "Just remember, if you do anything with Anna, you'll have Neon to deal with, too."

"With Anna? What the hell makes you think I'm going to do anything with her?"

Wraith shrugs. "You and Rayne are having issues. It's fucking obvious. Anna's here, and she's an old habit. Old habits are hard to break."

"Not gonna happen."

"Mm-hmm," Wraith murmurs slapping my back, then he walks off.

I need a damn drink.

As most of our friends and family leave, only a few of them stay behind. Anna, of course, being one of them as the afternoon shifts into evening. Fox has the grill sizzling, and I sit back drinking to try and numb my mind from all the shit going on in my life right now. Even though, technically, we're celebrating this win, we won it only because of Rayne. I should be celebrating with her, but we're at a stalemate, caused by our stubbornness.

I'm chilling out in front of the fire pit, the music aptly blasting Luke Comb's 'Beer Never Broke My Heart' as I down another glass of Fox's moonshine. I'm drowning deeper and deeper in my own misery. But the thing about drowning in moonshine is, it makes you need to piss. So begrudgingly, I stand, wobble slightly as I right myself, then walk inside, through the partying bodies to make way for the unisex bathroom. As I approach, Rayne's talking to Blake's brother, Brodie. I stand studying their body language. They're laughing, having a good time in the shadows of the hall as anger rages inside of me. Brodie leans forward, his hand skirting out like he's playing with her hair, maybe placing it behind her ear.

Is that fucker flirting with her?

I'm probably too drunk for this. I should be calm in this situation, but all I can see is his hand on her, so I storm up to them. I reach Brodie, shoving him so hard he flies back into the wall with such force, his ass leaves a dent in the drywall. Rayne gasps, her eyes going wide with shock as her hand moves to her chest in reaction.

"Stay the hell away from her, Brodie. Or so help me God..."

Rayne narrows her eyes on me as she folds her arms across her chest about to yell back at me, but I cut in first.

"I said I couldn't trust you, and my instincts were right!" I turn to Brodie again. "You better get the fuck out of my clubhouse or I will fuck you up quicker than you blend your fru-fru juices in the morning, you little piece of shit."

Brodie pulls his ass out of the drywall, then scurries away as Rayne rushes forward shoving me hard in the chest. I don't even budge as I glare at her, towering over her. I slam my hands either side of her face onto the drywall. She doesn't flinch, she's not scared of me.

"Fuck you, Zero. You think you can intimidate me? You don't even know what you're fucking talking about, you drunken idiot."

I glare at her, my anger seeping off me in waves. "The hell I don't. I know what I saw, Rayne. You were lapping it up."

Rayne's face scrunches, but her eyes don't leave mine for a second, she's not backing down. "You saw what you wanted to see. Brodie was walking past, saw a leaf in my hair and was joking about it, then he fucking pulled it out. Not that I need to explain myself to you, you arrogant, selfish, pigheaded—"

Anger ignites inside of me as I slam my fist into the drywall beside her head, leaving a hole in my frustration. "Fuck you, Rayne. Why would you let him touch you?"

"It's was a fucking leaf, not his cock in my mouth!"

I turn grabbing at my hair in frustration. "Fuuck! You're so infuriating."

She rushes forward into my space, pushing me back against the wall, this time she's trapping me in. "Me? I'm infuriating? You! You're an asshole, Zero. You're all over the place. I can't *stand* to be near you right now!"

"Feeling's fucking mutual, cherry bomb."

She reaches out, her open palm connecting with my cheek, sending a loud slap through the room. The sting isn't just physical, it's mental as well. But I'm too enraged to care. A low growl rumbles from deep inside my chest as I turn grabbing her wrists and push her back against the wall just as Prinie and Wraith both rush in.

Wraith grabs me, yanking me off Rayne as Prinie runs to Rayne's side wrapping her arms around her in a tight embrace.

I let out a heavy growl as I shove Wraith off me, then pace trying to calm my breathing. "This is fucking bullshit," I murmur as I turn to walk off seeing Anna watching the whole damn thing play out. Groaning, I storm back out to the bar to grab another drink.

I don't care what Rayne does.

I just need to get fucking wasted.

RAYNE

After my altercation with Zero, I'm left feeling deflated. He's outside around the fire pit drowning himself in moonshine, and I simply don't want to be around him. But for some reason, I can't bring myself to be too far away from him either. So, I'm inside sitting at the bar wallowing. I don't want to witness him obliterate himself because of me. I know what can happen when men get drunk, they turn violent. While I don't think Zero would ever hurt me, he got pretty angry before.

Let's face it, I never thought Chuck would get violent with me until he was.

I'm sipping on one of Nessie's famous coffees munching on some Tex-Mex nachos, and as much as I don't want to go to bed, I'm physically and mentally drained. But before I head off, I want to slip my head around the door and check on Zero. While I'm furious with him, I don't want anything to happen to him.

Standing from my seat, I walk to the door peering out to the left and over to the fire pit area. The party's in full swing. Bikers drinking and having a good time. Women everywhere. The fire pit lighting up the night sky and embers racing up into the air. Sitting around it is Zero, slumped back in his low riding chair, still drinking. But that's not what has my heart instantly rapid firing, it's Anna leaning down in front of him. I barely hear her over the chatter of everyone else, but lip reading helps.

"I miss you. I wish things were different."

I clench my eyes tight wishing she had said anything but that. I will myself to open my eyes again, and as I do, Zero's reaching up, pulling Anna down onto his lap. She wraps her arms around his neck, their eyes locking, staring at each other.

Shit.

Fuck.

Holy heck.

Anna slowly leans in toward him.

Oh God, they're going to kiss.

The noise escapes me that I can't even comprehend.

I wasn't expecting this.

When Zero said he couldn't trust me, I never thought for one minute I couldn't trust him. I spin, bumping into Prinie as I stumble back inside heading for the stairs. "Rayne!" Prinie calls out, but I'm too far gone to stop.

Too far gone to care.

My feet carry me quicker than I thought possible as I run like hell before anyone sees me.

I am strong.

I am brave.

I am in control.

I will not cry.

I slam open my bedroom door, then throw it closed. Rushing over to my bed, I flop down onto it curling into a ball, clinging to the foam finger from the baseball game.

I will not cry.

My eyes well as I scrunch them shut.

I will not cry.

"He's not worth your tears, Rayne," I say aloud, but I don't believe myself.

A whimper escapes me, my bottom lip trembles as I pull my knees up to my chest, rocking back and forth.

I will not cry.

He's kissing her right now.

I will not cry.

His heart belongs to her.

I will not cry.

He will never want me the way he wants her.

I can't hold it back as I let out a gut-wrenching sob. Tears stream down my face as the dam wall finally breaks. The tears I've been holding in for years all erupt in one torrential downpour. There's nothing I can do to stem the flow.

I thought Zero was going to be my savior.

But in the end, he's my undoing.

My white knight?

No, my black despair.

ZERO

After our altercation, I had to just carry on with my night. I got so worked up, I let my rage get the better of me. Rayne has known such horrendous violence, and I acted like an asshole toward her tonight. But we're in a weird place right now. I don't know how this is going to play out, all I know is this booze is helping. The party's in full swing, and people are getting rowdier. The fire flickers in front of me keeping my mind focused on the orange dancing embers as they frolic with the slight breeze.

Anna appears in my line of sight, halting my view of the flames. I slowly peer up at her in disdain. "You're blocking my view."

She giggles. "Of the fire? You always did love this fire pit."

"Do you need something, Anna?"

"I am curious about this Rayne girl who's staying here."

My ears pick up and I sit a little taller. "What about her?"

"She's pretty."

I let out a grunt. "She's trouble is what she is."

Anna exhales, then leans forward toward me a little more. I narrow my eyes on the movement. *What the fuck she's up to?*

"I miss you. I wish things were different."

Without warning, Texas and Lexi lose their balance as they joke around, knocking Anna. She falls forward right toward the fire. My instincts kick in, and I reach out grabbing her, pulling her onto my lap. She reaches out wrapping her arms around my neck as she stares into my eyes, but I see nothing but the woman who left me hurt and broken. So many thoughts run through my mind as I stare at her. If things were different, we'd be married now, might even have a kid. I can't even imagine that life now. A life without Rayne. My thoughts are rambling, I haven't even noticed while my mind is off, my eyes have remained focused on Anna's. She reads it all wrong as she leans in to kiss me, misreading my staring as something else. "Jesus, fuck no." I dramatically pull back, standing from the seat, letting her fall to the ground next to the fire pit.

"Ouch. Shit, Zero!"

Everyone looks over to see Anna dusting herself off as I take off inside to get away from her. I should have known she'd take any fucking opportunity she could if given half a chance.

How could I be so stupid?

Anger flares inside of me.

Can this night get any worse?

Prinie's standing by the entry as I fly through it, a pissed-off expression all over her face. "Just FYI… Rayne saw that little display, but she took off before you dumped Anna on her ass. One would assume she thinks you guys kissed by the way Rayne ran off."

"Oh, for fuck's sake… thanks, Prinie."

She reaches out grabbing my arm. "Look, what you two do is none of my business. But she's my friend, and she's been through as much bad shit as you… she's broken as well. You'd do well to remember that, okay?"

My chest feels like it's crushed, but I grit my teeth and take off to the stairs. I need to set Rayne straight, so I take the stairs three at a time. After falsely accusing Rayne of cheating, then her thinking I was going to kiss Anna, this shit's getting out of fucking hand.

We need to settle this.

Now.

I get to her room and don't bother to knock. I slam her door open ready to have it out with her, but the sight I see before me knocks my breath from my lungs. Rayne's curled up on the bed, tissues sprawled out all over the mattress, cuddling into the baseball foam finger we got at the game. *She's a hot mess.* My strong cherry bomb is broken, and *I'm* the damn reason. She didn't even hear me come in over her loud sobs. I slowly close the door behind me and move over to her bed. Sitting on the edge, I lean down and pull her into my arms. The shock on her face is evident as she tries to resist, but I'm too strong for her as I hold her to me. "Shh, I'm here." I run my hand down the back of her hair while she clings to me like I'm her lifeline. All that pent-up emotion she's been holding onto has finally broken through that hard exterior, and it's my fault.

"I'm sorry, Rayne. Don't cry."

She nuzzles into me like she can't get close enough.

Hell, I need her closer too as I hold her as tight as I can.

"Why'd you have to kiss her?"

I lean back assessing in her swollen, red eyes. "I promise, on everything we are, I didn't kiss Anna."

Rayne wipes her eyes, they're full of so much hope. I never want to see her this broken again. I know what it's like to feel this way. To feel betrayed. I don't want her to hurt like this. "Anna leaned in, but I backed away. Actually, I stood up, dropping her on her ass. Everyone saw it."

Her lips turn up, infinitesimally, but it's there. The hint of a smile, then it falls. "You pulled her onto your lap."

My head flinches back slightly. "I pulled her because Texas and Lexi were being dickheads and nearly pushed her into the fire. As much as I'd like to see her burn, Neon wouldn't forgive me."

Her eyes leave mine. I place my fingers under her chin raising her head back up to me. "Hey… I know what you believe you saw, but the whole time all I could think about was how Anna means nothing to me. Not once did I consider anything that would incite me to kiss her. She read the situation wrong. So did you. I'd never kiss Anna again in my life, not even if it was to save it. You hear what I'm saying, cherry bomb?"

She gnaws down on her bottom lip. "I jumped to conclusions. I left before I saw what really happened."

I grab the foam finger, moving it to the edge of the bed and pull her closer. "Just like I jumped to conclusions about Brodie in the hall. Seems like as much as I want to be cautious around you, I'm just too fucking wrapped up in you, Rayne."

She sniffles. "Me, too. Honestly, I didn't know life could ever be good again, but since being here, with you, I've felt more alive than I've felt my entire life. Even tonight. I've been hurting, more than anything, but it's only because I care about you so much."

I lean in pressing my lips to hers. She tastes like coffee. On a night where everyone's been drinking alcohol, that tells me everything. She's been so wrapped up in our drama, she hasn't even let herself unwind. I'm going to help her unwind right now.

I kiss her strongly, letting her know how deeply my feelings run for her. She's like a vine, creeping her way into my soul, wrapping her way around my heart, strangling my lungs making it hard to breathe. She's intoxicating. Infuriating. Breathtaking. But from here on out, most importantly of all, she's mine.

I pull back swiping the tissues off the bed and lay her back down. She moves with me, she's giving in, she's letting me claim her.

I pull back, gazing into her eyes. "I can't fight this anymore, Rayne."

"Then don't."

My lips smash to hers needing a connection with her. Rayne's fingers slide under my shirt against my abs, they pull tight with her delicate touch. My hands move to the buttons on her dress, but my stumpy fingers are having trouble undoing the small plastic domes of hell, so I lean back, bring my hands to the edges of her dress and rip it open, all the little buttons popping off and flying through the air.

Rayne gasps, her eyes widening as she peers down at her gorgeous body. "I liked that dress."

"I'll buy you a new one." I lean down planting a kiss on her stomach.

She squirms at my touch as I run my tongue across her perfect flesh. "It was vintage."

"Don't care." I run my teeth along her hip bone.

Her squirming is only turning me on further as I grab the seam of her underwear, tearing them apart as well.

"Jesus, Zero, I'm going to have nothing left to wear."

"That's the idea, cherry bomb. I want you in my room naked all the time." I run my nose along the apex of her thighs, and she lets out a whimper.

"And what about when I'm not in your room?" Her voice is raspy, laced with lust.

I love it.

"Then you'll walk around naked, but I'd prefer it if you stayed in my room. So, I can do this." My tongue glides out, reaching her clit, circling her nub as her back arches off the bed. She's so reactive.

I lick up the length of her folds. She's sweet as I move a finger to her opening and push in at the same time my tongue flicks her clit. My other hand splays out on her lower abdomen keeping her flush to the mattress. Soft whimpers of ecstasy leave her mouth as her hands ball into fists in the bedsheets.

My cock grows hard against the seam of my jeans. More than anything right now, I want to set him free, but I need to make Rayne feel good. "Zero, fuck."

"I know, baby. Just come for me," I demand, then flick her clit, pushing in higher, rotating my finger to hit her g-spot, just the way she likes it. Her pussy tightens around my finger. She's close. Her body trembles as her frantic breaths are rushed. She's so fucking sexy like this, laid out for me to admire. My eyes shift up, she's squeezing her own breast, and fuck if that doesn't have my cock angry in my pants.

I need her. Now.

So, I put more pressure on her clit working her faster, harder. Bringing her right to the brink. Her body tenses, her eyes clench tight. "Zero!"

Her climax rocks through her body as she trembles and shakes. It only makes me needier for her.

I stand from the edge of the bed, unbuckling my jeans, and they fall, then I step out of my boots, kicking them off with my jeans. My cock springs free desperate for her as she lays on the bed in the afterglow of her orgasm. I'm usually not a massive missionary man, but she's spread open, ready for me. *Fucking hell, I need her right now.*

I climb over the top of her still dressed in my shirt and cut. Rayne in her bra. We're both naked from the waist down, but there's a certain something about fucking Rayne with my cut on. Like she's part of this club if I do it this way. I lean in, kissing her. Her hands slide up into my hair. She pulls out the tie letting my hair fall freely down around us. She always has a thing about my damn hair.

I rock against her as I slide my hand down to her thigh, lifting her leg up, pulling it over my shoulder. Her eyes meet mine as one hand slides around my back, her other grips onto the front of my cut. Fuck, that single move almost has me coming before I'm even inside of her.

I stare in her eyes—so bright, so alert, so full of emotion. She's in this with me, after everything, she's in this.

I am too. So, I push forward, thrusting up inside of her, our eyes remaining locked. We both moan as we stare at each other. Her eyes glass over with lust as I fill her to the brim, pushing her leg back further to get in deeper, thrusting higher, getting just the right spot. She's so fucking tight and warm like the best place on earth.

Heaven on earth.

A place I never want to leave.

Her tight pussy envelops my cock like the best warm fucking hug you've ever had. Her hips rock up to meet mine, and we move together. I pull back, then thrust up into her. All the while our eyes haven't left each other's.

The energy surging through us is building the pleasure rolling through me. My cock has never been as hard as it is right now, and I feel like part of that is because I'm staring at Rayne while fucking her. I never do that. Generally, I always have a woman facing away from me like most other times we've fucked. It's a mechanism I use so I don't get too close. I don't want to get attached, but with Rayne, I know it's happening. Every time I'm around her, the air changes. My skin pebbles in goosebumps, my heart feels like it's squeezing.

Looking at her now, I know why. She means something to me. More than I care to admit. I know because I'm fucking her and thinking about soft-as-fuck sappy shit. My cock feels so damn good inside of her. I never want to lose this feeling. *I don't ever want to go through a day where she isn't in it with me.* That thought scares the hell out of me.

A low growl erupts from my chest as I lean down, slamming my lips to hers. I need to stop thinking and start feeling. My cock's so fucking ready to ramp this up, so I thrust faster, both of us moving in perfect synchronization. Her other leg wraps around my ass pulling me closer.

Fuck, she's perfect.

I pull back, thrust, rotate, and push in harder trying to get her there. The way she clings to my cut holding my body close to hers is turning me the fuck on. My tongue collides with hers, and I kiss her with every ounce of strength I have. I'm close, the pins and needles running down my spine are telling me what's coming. My fingers on the bedsheets ball into a fist with the pleasure rolling through me.

"Fuck, Rayne," I growl while I pump harder into her.

She whimpers, it's sexy as hell as she works with me toward our mutual climaxes.

Her body shakes. Her chest rises and falls with her frantic breaths. She's right on the edge, and I plan to take her over.

I thrust up higher. My balls tightening when her pussy clamps around my cock.

"Harder," she screams, making my cock jolt inside of her. I move quicker, fucking her like she wants.

Whatever *my girl* wants, she gets.

My girl.

Mine.

A low growl vibrates from my chest as the realization hits me, I'm never letting this woman go. Not for anything. She's mine whether she wants to be or not. The thought sends a shockwave straight to my cock. I moan out in satisfaction as I ram in deeper, hitting her at just the right angle.

She screams out my name, her muscles clenching as her entire body erupts in a huge wave of euphoria as it rocks through her. My cock vibrates with her ecstasy making my balls pull up in pleasure. I moan, dropping my head to hers. Her eyes open as we stare at each other, her coming down, me reaching the pinnacle.

She tightens her pussy, which is all I need while keeping my eyes on her. My balls pull tighter than I ever thought possible, the tingle starts all the way from the tips of my toes shooting straight up into my cock. My body jerks as I stare into her eyes. I want to be looking in her eyes when I unload inside of her.

She squeezes her pussy again—I'm done for.

My balls tighten, the pressure builds, my cock throbs with so much heat I can't stand it, then with one last thrust up deep inside of her, my cock erupts filling her with my warm cum. I let out a long drawn-out moan while my hooded eyes stay focused on hers. Nothing but unadulterated lust shines back from hers, but there's something else behind those sparkling emerald eyes—the promise of more, the promise of tomorrow.

It should scare me.

It should terrify me.

But all it does is make me want to bathe in her eyes and know we're going to be in this place forever. I need her. I want her with me always, and if I need to keep her in my life and by my side to have this, to keep what I'm feeling right now, then fuck, I might just do that.

Her hand from my cut reaches up swiping some hair out of my face, coming to rest on my cheek. Our breathing is still frantic and rushed as I let her leg fall back to the bed. I lay on top of her staring in her eyes. We're not saying anything, but the silence says so much.

We're in this.

We're in deep.

I lean in pressing my lips to hers tenderly, a sweeter move I'm not so accustomed to. Her hand slides into the back of my hair, and hell if I don't love this just as much as our carnal fucking. The chemistry is in the air—it's one thing we've never lacked in. She draws me to her like a damn magnet. That pull, that attraction to her is so astonishing, I don't know how any other woman in the world could ever compete.

But I guess this is what it comes down to.

No other woman has to compete now.

I only have eyes for Rayne.

"You're mine," I grunt out running my nose along hers.

Her lips creep up in a sleepy gesture. "Normally, an alpha thing like that would annoy me. But coming from you, Zero, I'll take it as your way of asking me to be your… girl?"

I inhale, then relax. "I'm not asking, cherry bomb. You are, whether you want to be or not."

"All right there, cowboy, I make my own decisions on whether I want to be somebody's girl or not."

"You can't. But, do you… want to be, I mean?" I hesitate a little on the last part.

She presses her lips to mine softly, then runs her tongue across my bottom lip to tease me. "Yes, Krew… I'm your girl."

That's the first time she's called me by my name.

I smirk rocking my freshly-formed erection into her again.

She moans as I thrust inside of her.

"Like I said from the start, cherry bomb… you're *all* mine."

My heart feels full as I lean in kissing her. It's just my head telling me I need to be cautious.

Rayne has baggage, unclaimed baggage, and while we're in a happy little bubble right now, bubbles sooner or later burst.

ZERO

The Next Morning

My connection to Rayne could seriously damage me. It's why I've been so all over the place, but she's worth the risk. We're lying in her bed naked. She's running her fingers up and down my tattooed stomach tracing the lines.

"Why have you got so many tattoos? What do they represent?"

I exhale thinking on that. "Initially, it was an outlet to release the pain I was feeling. To numb myself. And it just didn't stop."

"So, they began with Anna?"

"Before then, out of high school. Neon and I got picked on a lot for being part of the local club. We used to look out for each other. I guess if I appeared to be more part of the lifestyle… you know tats… then maybe I would be scarier to them. Perhaps they wouldn't focus on us so much. We started working out, getting fit, getting ink, riding bikes, and the bullies became less and less. But with that came a sense of the more ink I got, the more protected I would be, and I could protect Neon and Anna."

Her eyes alight, sparkling with intensity. "You really are a white knight."

"No, but I'll always be here to protect you."

She gives me a squeeze, then sits up in the bed. "I'm hungry. Worked up an appetite. Can we get some breakfast?"

"You can have anything you want." My eyes wander over her in delight.

"Ooh... a puppy?"

I snort out a laugh. "Think Wraith and Mack might have something to say about that."

"True, Mack is cute enough, he'll do." Her stomach growls, so I throw back the bedsheets and stand to get dressed. My body wobbles as I hold onto my spinning head.

She grins. "Little dusty there, cowboy?"

I groan. "I'll be fine once I have some coffee and grease."

"Then, let's go get your hangover dealt with."

We dress, then head downstairs, holding hands. My hangover is definitely making itself known, but I won't let it stifle my good mood. Rayne is sprightly as we step into the main room. It's a freaking mess. People lie all over the place.

Rayne snickers. "You guys sure know how to have a good time."

"You don't even know the half of it."

We make our way to the kitchen where Nessie's cooking up some bacon and eggs, the smell's amazing.

"Is there anything I can do to help?" Rayne asks.

"No way. You're a guest of the club. Go. Sit, and I'll bring your breakfast out," Nessie demands.

I wink at our head club girl as I take Rayne, and we go sit.

Prinie and Koda make their way over, laughing at everyone's state of disarray. "Man, I'll never get tired of how this place reminds me of a frat party. Glad you two have dealt with your shit, though."

"Thanks for always being there for me, Prinie," Rayne offers.

"Yeah, thanks, princess. Glad you stepped in last night," I add.

"All part of the service. I'll send my bill."

Slowly, my brothers regain consciousness, everyone waking when the smell of bacon breaks their comatose states.

Now we're all sitting and downing the fatty food we all need to help heal our bodies as Rayne chats with my brothers. I'm finally at ease. Like everything is right where it's meant to be. I know where my life is heading and the path I'm meant to be on, but more importantly who's going to be traveling that road with me.

I stand to send a whistle through the room, gaining everyone's attention. "I have an announcement."

Rayne listens with curiosity as I reach down for her hand, taking it in mine.

"Those who know me probably thought I would never find another woman I could trust. Who I could let in. Who I could be myself around. Rayne, our road hasn't been easy, and yeah, there's still hurdles we'll need to jump to get to our finish line, but baby, I'm going to do everything I can to make sure we cross them together." Her glistening eyes stare up at me. "I'm letting everyone know right here, right now, I'm claiming Rayne."

An audible gasp comes from the direction Anna's standing in, but I don't pay her any mind. She doesn't deserve it. This moment is for Rayne.

"Cherry bomb, I've called you that since I first met you. Maybe even then I knew we would get to this stage. At first sight, I knew there was something about you that drew me in. You were feisty and had a fight in you, even with all the shit you were going through. Yet you're still able to find a calm in the storm when you need to. You balance me out, cherry bomb. I don't want to go another day without making us official." I take a breath. "So, you're mine. I want everyone to know it. From now on you will be known as Cherry Bomb, or Cherry for short."

She jumps up, throwing her arms around my neck and locks her lips with mine. My arms instinctively loop around her waist, pulling her body against me as I kiss her strongly. My tongue collides with hers while my lips tingle with the same sensation I always get when I kiss her. Everyone cheers around us, but it's all white noise as I'm lost in the sensations of my Old Lady. I never thought I would have this again, but fuck, does it feel good.

It feels right.

Cherry slowly pulls back from me, her eyes glistening on the verge of tears, though I'm sure these ones are happy. "I've never felt more liberated, so supported in all my life, Zero. You're the protector and the partner who will always keep me safe, but to be there beside me, not in front of me, or trying to keep me down. That's all I could ever want."

My hand moves out to caress her cheek. "You're my equal, Cherry, and now you're the queen of this place. Your name might now be Cherry, though you'll still reign, it's just spelled differently."

She leans in to kiss me again, but Wraith steps in beside us clearing his throat. I turn my head to him. "Small problem, pres... she's still legally married. The minute she files for divorce, that prick's gonna know exactly where she is."

I glance at Cherry and exhale, then shrug. "Details we will figure out. But for now, we get on with life."

Wraith hesitates like he's unsure but continues on his way.

Cherry presses her lips to me again, then speaks, "This stuff with Chuck—"

"We'll find a way to figure it out, somehow."

She exhales, peeking at her watch. "Crap! I have to leave for work."

"I'll drive you."

She grabs for her handbag.

I finally shift my eyes to Anna as she sits sulking in the corner. Maybe now she'll stop trying shit on with me. I walk over to Wraith. "I'm taking Cherry to work, be back in a few."

He sniffs the air. "Don't get pulled over, you smell like a damn brewery."

I pick up Fox's coffee, taking a giant sip. He chuckles as I place it back on the table.

"Thanks, old man."

Fox shakes his head as Cherry meets up with me, and we walk out to my ride.

As the pharmacy is literally down the road, the ride is quick.

Honestly, we could walk it in ten minutes, but to have her on the back of my bike is something I want to feel as often as possible.

We hop off, and she makes her way to the rear of the store. She makes short work of opening and we move inside. I stand back as she pulls on her lab coat. Fuck, she's hot in that thing as she fucks about doing some shit I don't even know.

She stalls, her eyes shifting toward the safe, her mind ticking over. "Zero, that 'thing' we did for the Militia."

I observe the store, any of the staff could walk in at any moment, so we need to be careful what we say. "Yeah?"

"Could you make a profit from it if we did it again?"

My eyes light up. "Are we talking a one-time thing here, Cherry, or a constant stream like a side business?"

Her lips turn up showing me her gorgeous beaming face. "Side business."

"Shit, Rayne, you're a bad girl."

She moves in wrapping her arms around me. "What do you think? We could make some extra cash for the club?"

"If you're willing, then hell yeah, let's do it. We could do it like a once-a-month thing."

"All right then, you got yourself a partner."

I groan, grinding myself into her. "Fuck, you're making me so hot for you right now."

She laughs, slapping my shoulder, then turns to open the store.

RAYNE

Opening the front shutters to the store, a man wearing a cowboy hat is waiting at the entry. I'm shocked, I wasn't expecting to see anyone. My staff isn't even here yet.

"Zero," I call out.

He walks toward me as I open the door to the cowboy.

"Hello, how can I help you?"

"Well, hello sugar, people call me the Baron. It sure is nice to meet ya." He sticks out his hand for me to shake. I shake it dipping my head at his pleasantries. *The Baron*. I'm sure Zero has talked about him. "I wanted to come see the new business the boys have opened up in town. It's in my best interest to know everythin' that's happenin' in Houston, seein' as it's *my* city."

Zero steps up seeming at ease, but there's something about the Baron that has me on edge. Something I don't find as welcoming.

"Well, then, Baron, welcome to the pharmacy. Cherry here runs it perfectly. She's got the knack and a keen business sense," Zero adds.

It's like he's trying to sell me to the Baron, to make sure I'm up to scratch.

"She *is* an exquisite beauty, Zero. You *are* a lucky man to have caught her eye."

Huh?

"How could you tell?"

The Baron narrows his eyes. "Oh, come now, I'm very attuned to these things. I can read body language."

Zero wraps his arm around me, pulling me to him. "Cherry is my Old Lady... claimed her this morning."

The Baron's eyes widen like he's shocked. "Well, I'll be! Good to know y'all are settlin' down again. Welcome to the family, Rayne."

My face scrunches. Zero only called me Cherry throughout this whole strange interaction. *How did he know my name was Rayne?*

The Baron takes a grip on my hand again, shaking it with one and grabbing and holding it securely with the other. He leans in closer to make sure I'm paying attention to him. "I'll be seein' you again... very, very soon."

I clear my throat. "N-Nice meeting you."

He smiles wider than I thought could be possible as he turns throwing his hand in the air. "Y'all have a good day now," the Baron calls out as he walks off back to his Cadillac.

My heart races frantically. I'm unnerved by the whole exchange, but Zero's unaffected as he turns toward the back of the store.

"He basically runs the city..." I tune out as Zero continues to dribble on about him as I close the door, locking it. I turn around, walking back toward the rear of the store where Zero is still yammering, "… I swear the guy's a billionaire. Maybe more. Has more money than manners. We'd be screwed if we ever get on his bad side."

I have an uneasy feeling in my stomach. I can't quite place the reason for it, though. It's like I've heard his voice before or something. I just don't know what it is about the Baron that has me off-kilter.

"So wait… why is he so important?" I ask trying to figure this all out in my head.

Zero scratches his head like he thinks I'm losing my mind. He was just telling me in his ramblings, but honestly, I wasn't listening.

"He owns a lot of the oil refineries in Houston. He's a rich fuck. *That* money gives him power, and with power comes privilege. The Baron has his hands in many things—the law, the medical profession, business, politics. He can influence anyone and anything. Hell, I'm sure he even has a tactical team under his belt to use however he sees fit. He's a menace, but also useful when he's okay with who you are." Zero shakes his head. "But get on his bad side, and you have a world of hurt coming your way. He can have you put in jail for something your neighbor did when he was a juvenile. Fuck, if I know how that shit works, but I've seen it happen. He's fucking dangerous is what he is. So, we keep on his good side, at *all* times."

I swallow a lump in my throat not liking where this is headed. A man like the Baron scares me. One false move, I could be found out. Chuck might find me. I need to steer clear of the Baron at all costs.

"Right, I better let you get to work. Do you need anything, Old Lady of mine?" Zero asks sweetly.

The words soothe me a little.

I pull him to me and lean in for a kiss. He still tastes like moonshine, so I screw up my face. "Go home, have a shower and sober up. Don't go riding anywhere else. Walk back to the clubhouse. When you come to get me, we can ride back on your bike."

"Less than an hour, and she's embracing this Old Lady thing down to a tee. I'll come get you after work. I'll be well coffeed up by then. Promise."

"Good, now go on, get." I lean in kissing him again briefly as fellow employees roll through the doors, including Chills. She raises her chin as she walks past. "Your Old Lady needs to do some work, pres."

Zero groans, letting me go and turns heading for the door.

Chills pulls her lips into a tight thin line. "He smells terrible."

"I know, I've told him to go home and sober up."

Chills yawns, I spot the dark circles under her eyes. "How did Kobe do last night with the noise?"

She exhales. "With the room being soundproofed, it was nothing more than a dull murmur, but he still wouldn't settle. I hated leaving him this morning with him having a rough night and with his condition, it makes me nervous. I mean, he's going to be okay, but there's always a risk. I know I'm just a scared momma."

I reach out gripping her hand. "It's natural to feel that way."

Chills weakly smiles. "I know you and Chuck tried for kids, though it didn't happen. But what about in the future? Is that something you want to think about?"

"Well, yeah. With Chuck, I honestly didn't want them because of the life they would be brought into, but here at the club, I believe they'll be safe. So maybe if Zero wants them, then yeah."

"This club life, it's not easy, it's not set in stone either. Things change. It takes you on wild rides, you never know where you're going to end up. Take for instance, Chains and me. We grew up together in the same house. I bet you didn't know my parents took him in as a foster kid, right?"

"Nope… had no idea."

"Exactly. We fought our attraction to each other for so long because we thought it was wrong. I mean we grew up together, but I guess you can't help who you fall in love with."

"Just because he's a foster brother doesn't make him a blood relation, Chills."

"I know that now. I knew then, too. It was a hard concept for us to grasp, though. Us committing to each other took a lot of courage on both our parts, but once we gave in to what we wanted, life has been bliss ever since."

I can't help but smile. "I'm so happy for you."

Chills shakes her head with an exhale. "I got off track… what I'm trying to say is we thought our course was firmly set in Chicago. If Kobe didn't have his heart condition, we wouldn't be here in Houston. *We* wouldn't have met, and *you* wouldn't have your own pharmacy right now. So, you see, everything has a part to play and a way of working out."

I pull her into a tight hug. "I'm so glad we met, Chills. I couldn't have made it through all this without you."

ZERO

Later That Night

I'm just heading back to pick up Cherry from work. She texted me a while ago that it was going to be a late one. She had some paperwork to catch up on, so she was staying late after everyone else went home.

I walk up seeing my ride still in the same place I left it this morning. Hopefully, I smell better now after a shower, a gallon of coffee, a shitload of grease, and a long nap.

Walking to the rear door, I bang on it twice, wait, then once more, letting her know it's me. It opens soon after to her beautiful face. She's gorgeous as she pushes the door to let me in. "Well, you smell better, all showered and fresh."

"And you smell like donuts."

She swipes along her mouth with a big old guilty grin. "Customer brought in Voodoo for us, for getting her cholesterol medication right for her. Go figure." I let out a booming laugh as she leads me inside. "Just gotta do one small thing, then we can go. I'll only be a sec."

I leave the door unlocked seeing as she'll be quick.

She's rushing about grabbing her stuff then she flurries up to me. "Okay, ready."

I grab her arm, pulling her against my body. "Uh-uh. Not so fast."

My hands slide down to her ass. Her eyes meet mine, and she gnaws on her bottom lip. "And what do you think you're doing, Mr. President?"

I back her up against the wall, my head ducking down, planting a firm kiss along her collarbone. "I'm…" kiss, "… showing…" kiss, "… my Old Lady…" I kiss up her neck, "… a good…" kiss, "… time." I slam my lips to hers as she whimpers in my mouth. Her hips press against mine as she drops everything she's holding, and her fingers slide up into my hair, right where they belong.

I want to take her right here. Hell, I've wanted to fuck her in the pharmacy ever since I saw her creating the Snow White pills.

She turns me on so fucking much I can never get enough.

My tongue ravages hers as I move my hands between us to the button of her jeans, when suddenly all the lights go out, sending us into pitch black. My stomach tightens as I pull back from Rayne as her breathing increases.

"Zero?" she whispers.

"Shh… babe."

I reach into my jeans grabbing out my cell, and flick on the flashlight app. Lowering my voice, I lean in toward Cherry. "Do you have any flashlights?"

She turns reaching for one under the desk, the creaking of the door has both our heads snapping around to face it. She hands me the flashlight, and as I switch it on aiming it at the door, a shadow moves in the pharmacy. I grab Cherry, shoving her behind me. She's physically shaking as I back her against the shelves, so whoever the fuck is in here with us can't get to her. My heart hammers in my chest as I try to figure out what the fuck to do.

I quickly silence my cell and send a text to Neon.

Zero: *SOS*

I grip hold of Cherry's hand letting her know I'm here as I turn the flashlight a little trying to find whoever the fuck is in here with us. Suddenly, the lights flicker back on. The stark contrast blinding me as I clench my eyes shut, bringing my forearm over my eyes to shield me from the fluorescents.

"Jesus Christ," I murmur as I blink trying to adjust my vision. Then I see it, the shadow figure comes into view. The hat, the bolo tie, the expensive suit. Not only that, he's surrounded by an array of men wearing balaclavas and holding rifles. "Baron, what the fuck?" I call out dropping the flashlight to the floor in my confusion.

The Baron looks right past me, his eyes fixated on Cherry, the hard stare he's sending her has me on edge instantly. "Where's your wedding rings?" His question is directed toward Rayne.

She freezes, the expression on her face is of recognition. "Zero, I know who he is now."

"Shush, Cherry, you're delaying the big reveal," the Baron barks at her.

I'm so confused as I glance back at Rayne who's having trouble holding it together. She shakes her head as a man walks in the pharmacy. His red hair styled perfect, not a hair out of place. His hoity-toity attitude instantly has me on edge.

"You've been gone for far too long. You did very well at hiding yourself. You almost got away with your charade, *Harper Johnson*." His tone is gruff, and Cherry's shaking so violently behind me, I can only assume one thing.

Anger flares inside of me like an untamed bull ready to ram into the Baron and gut him like a damn fish.

Why? Why would the Baron do this?

"Why would you bring that cunt here?" I grunt.

Chuck glares at me. "Rayne, I'm surprised you didn't recognize my father's voice. You've heard him on the phone enough times over the years?"

My stomach knots as my head snaps toward the Baron. "Father?" I snap my head to Rayne, she nods.

Maybe that's what she was trying to tell me—she did recognize Baron's voice.

"Yes, I sure as hell registered her voice. Plus, the pictures Chuck sends me of her are unmistakable. When he told me she ran away, I never could have imagined it was here to Houston. Right into Zero's arms no less."

Chuck growls under his breath. He steps forward, Rayne tenses behind me. I shield her more.

"I don't understand. Rayne, your married name is Rosenberg. Baron, your surname is Squires. How can Chuck be your son?"

Chuck steps forward. "My mother and the Baron weren't exactly *in* a relationship. I guess you'd call me his bastard. I didn't grow up with him, but I still get the benefits of being his son. I have my mother's surname. She didn't much care for the Baron… just his money. Not that that's any of *your* concern. You took my wife! Rayne, it's time to come home now."

"Like hell it is!" My voice tainted with rage.

The Baron steps forward, his men aiming their guns right at me. "Zero, it's in your best interests to let my son have his wife back. You've become very… *attached* to her. But she wasn't yours to have."

"You're fucking stupid if you think I'm letting your pathetic excuse of a son lay another hand on my Old Lady."

Chuck steps forward. "I already have the paperwork drawn up for kidnapping and confinement of a person against their will. All I have to do is send a single message, and they will be filed, Zero. Do you know what that will mean for you, for your club?"

"Chuck, stop it!" Rayne blurts out.

"Ahh… she finally speaks. I thought he'd cut out your tongue," Chuck snipes.

"You're going to wish he had when I'm through with you, you fucking piece of—"

"Cherry, zip it," I warn her.

She halts her abuse instantly cuddling into my back. "I'm not going to let you take her," I pull out my gun, aiming at Chuck's face.

"I was hoping you'd say that," Chuck sneers raising his chin.

One of the mercenaries lowers his rifle, but before I have a second to think, the gun goes off, and a burn grazes the side of my thigh making me lower my gun as I bend over in reaction. One mercenary rushes forward slamming my wrist. Pain sears through the joint. The gun falls from my fingers as I drop to one knee as the butt of a rifle is slammed straight into my forehead.

I fall backward toward Cherry.

My head fogging in and out as the mercenary grabs her. She screams, but it's muted. My ears ringing, my body numb as her feet drag along the floor toward the door.

Everything turns black, and my world turns bitterly cold.

ZERO

My eyes are heavy as shit, my head hurts like a bitch when a sudden slap across my face startles me awake fully. My eyes roll around my head as my vision focuses in and out until they settle on Neon.

"Hey, hey, easy now... are you with me?"

Panic washes over me as I go to stand. Neon helps me, lifting me. "What the fuck happened?"

"They took Rayne."

Neon blinks rapidly. "Who?"

My head spins as I try to gain my bearings. "The fucking Baron and Chuck."

"Wait! What? Both of them?"

I rub my head. "Baron is Chuck's father."

"Fuck off!"

"I'm not joking. We have to find Rayne. Neon, help me?"

"That's why I came. After your SOS, you weren't answering any messages from anyone. Your tracker had you here, but Rayne's was on the move. I thought it was weird, so I came to check it out. Found you out cold with a killer lump on your head and a bullet graze on your leg."

"Can you track where they're going with Cherry?"

"Yeah, as long as she has her cell on her, I can."

"Good. I have to get back to the club. I need to make a call. We need back up."

As I walk in, Wraith rushes up to me, his eyes taking in every inch of me. "Shit man, you could have been killed. Why would the Baron leave you alive?"

"To torture me, to let me know he's won, and that he has this card over us, to manipulate the club however he sees fit. But the thing he didn't count on is to what length I will go to, to get Rayne back."

"And what length is that?"

"I need to make a phone call."

"Zero, fill me in here, man," Wraith grips my bicep forcing me to turn to him.

"You're not going to like my plan. And if it backfires, we could be in a world of hurt."

"Then *fuck* your plan, let's find a different one," Wraith grunts out.

"Sometimes you need to take a chance, Wraith. You need to work with what you've got. If I'm going to be half the president my father was, I need to know where my bread is best buttered."

Wraith wrinkles his face. "What the fuck are you talking about, Zero?"

"We thought the Baron was our biggest ally. Maybe that bastard's our biggest threat."

Wraith exhales. "If he's our biggest threat, then who the fuck are our allies?"

"That's what you're not going to like."

RAYNE

It had been weeks, weeks without hearing anything from Chuck. I had actually started to have days when I didn't think about him at all. I was letting myself believe I could have a life without him, that I had gotten away with making myself invisible.

That Zero had saved me.

And he did in a way.

Zero gave me the best time of my life before it's now going to end. Chuck will see to that, I'm sure. In the most painful of ways. My eyes shift across the other side of the car to the Baron and Chuck. We're driving out of Houston, but I don't know where. My wrists are bound, and my head hurts from where Chuck pulled me into the car after those men knocked Zero out cold. I don't even know if he's okay. God, I hope so. I couldn't stand to be in a world Zero wasn't a part of.

He broke down so many of my walls.

As I stare at Chuck, I already feel them building themselves back up, brick by brick. I won't allow myself to cry. Not in front of Chuck. No fucking way. Not even for the life I've lost. The only tears I will ever cry will be for Zero because of Zero and my love for him.

I gasp.

Do I love him?

I'm only just realizing this now I'm being taken from him.

Doesn't matter.

Chuck will make sure I never see the light of day again. And if Zero comes for me, he'll be thrown in jail, and the club will be sent into turmoil.

They can't come for me.

I know it.

They know it.

I'm screwed.

The best thing I can do is find the most opportune time and take my own life. It's better than living a life with Chuck, now I know what freedom and living a life with Zero is like.

I will never be happy again.

I don't know how long we've been traveling, maybe half an hour, maybe a little more, all I know is we've headed out of Houston. We drive into what seems to be an oil refinery. I'm confused. Also, a little scared. *Are they going to kill me?* But then again, maybe them killing me is the best option.

Then I won't have to do it myself.

I subtly glimpse down. The cell Zero gave me is in my pocket. *When everyone gets out of the car, I will quickly drop it on the floor and kick it under the seat.*

The car pulls to a halt, I tense up ready to enact my plan. They all hop out of the car, so I drop the cell giving it a kick just as my door opens. Chuck leans in grabbing my hair, yanking me out of the car. It pulls so much my scalp rips as I yelp with the pain, but I won't fight him. I don't have it in me right now.

The asshole drags me inside the building. The smell in the air is thick, the hissing pumps working overtime. They walk me through, down a hall, then into an area where there's an array of pipes and equipment. Vents line the floor as white steam wafts from the floor below making it hot and humid in here. Another brick concretes itself firmly in place in my wall as I detach a little more with every step I take.

Chuck pulls me to a stop in front of a single chair in the middle of the room. It sits on top of the grated vent. *Is that so my blood can seep through?* My mind is heading off in all kinds of directions as Chuck takes me over to the chair, then slams me onto it, my tailbone aching with the brunt of the force.

He stares at me as I look at him blankly giving him nothing in return. "You ran, Rayne. You scurried away like the little bitch you are." He backhands me hard across my cheek. My head snaps to the side with the brutality of the hit while the metallic tang of blood lingers in my mouth. Pain radiates through my face. I wasn't sure I would ever feel this type of pain again. I had this every day for years, but it all stopped when I met Zero. I was used to the agony, I had built up a tolerance, but experiencing it now after being away from it for so long is making it all the more painful.

The Baron curls up his lip but says nothing as his son manhandles me.

"You know, Rayne, I thought we had the perfect life. I fled Houston for Chicago to save my reputation."

I spit out the line of blood with a chortle. "Reputation? What reputation?"

"You know I was a cop in Houston before I transferred to Chicago."

"So?"

"So, maybe I'm a little... well, crooked."

I throw my head back in a real guttural laugh. "Like that's really all that surprising for a wife beater."

He steps forward threatening to punch me, but when I don't flinch, he stops letting out a cackle. "You never were scared of me hitting you, were you? I think you like the pain."

"I think you like inflicting it, you sack of shit."

He reaches out grabbing my hair yanking my head back so forcefully my scalp pulls with the tension, and it starts to bleed. I whimper as a sadistic smirk pulls at his evil lips. "There... there you are... I like hearing your cries of pain. It lets me know you feel something in that cold, dead heart of yours."

He lets my head go, and it slams forward as I grit my teeth. "You made my heart cold and dead. *You're* the reason I'm this way, Chuck."

He exhales turning to his father who's standing back like he isn't overly bothered by this little display his son is putting on. "When people started digging into me in Houston, when they thought they knew the depths of my corruption, the only choice for me was to leave. Was to begin somewhere new."

"I don't care."

"Oh, but you do, Rayne, because if my father didn't have contacts in Chicago, then I wouldn't have met you, and our love story wouldn't have begun."

"Pfft, love. You call *this* love?"

He narrows his eyes on me. "No, I call it convenience, Rayne. Your father supplies me with all the prescription pills I need to keep my underground dealings running. In return, I don't report his ass to the FDA or the HPD."

I scoff, lunging forward in my seat so much I almost fall off. "You bastard. You use me as a way to keep my father supplying you? He could go to jail for that."

"Exactly why he allowed me to marry you and to *stay* married to you, Rayne. I hold *all* the cards. I'm a cop. People don't fuck with cops, not if they know what's good for them."

"You're certifiable!"

The Baron belly laughs causing Chuck to glare at him. "What? She's not wrong, son. You're a fruit cake. Just like your mother."

Chuck lunges for his father, but a mercenary places a gun against Chuck's head, and the Baron tuts his tongue. "Don't think for a second you're the one in charge here, son. I might be lettin' you do what you want to this sweet little thing, but it doesn't mean you're holdin' the cards. What happens here today is because I let it, not because *you* do."

Chuck grunts out loud turning away from the gun. "You *always* do this. Turn my grand plans into your. Own. Doing."

"Son, if it weren't for me, you wouldn't even have known where she was."

Chuck lets out a loud grunt, hunching over in frustration. I didn't truly know how far past crazy he was until this very moment. He's insane. "How am I supposed to do this with you here? You're distracting me."

"Do what? Are you going to kill me?" I ask, deadpan.

They both turn to me. Chuck shakes his head. "No, Rayne. I couldn't kill you. You're worth far too much to me alive. I'm going to chain you up down here, strip you naked, torture you and capture the whole thing on video to send to daddy dearest. Make him double what he gives me. My business here in Houston's booming, so I need more stock. He wouldn't come to the table with you gone, so he needs a little more... *incentive*."

I grit my teeth. *My poor father, I left him behind without a word.* He must have been so worried. In my haste to get away from Chuck, I didn't think about the impact my leaving was going to have on my family. But then again, I never in a million years thought this would be the outcome.

"Strip her!" Chuck calls out.

My eyes widen as two mercenaries step closer gripping onto my hands, then pulling my jeans down leaving me in my lace panties.

I will not cry.

"Stunning as ever, Rayne. Now her shirt."

One of the men grabs my shirt on either side of my neck ripping it apart, tearing it from my body, leaving me in my lace see-through bra.

"Shame, that perfect body of yours is going to be scarred to high hell in a matter of moments. Boys, bring in the blow torch and the cattle iron."

What the fuck! He's going to brand me.

The bricks crumble, and fear creeps in. The idea of Chuck branding me with anything to mark me as his repulses me to the core. The mercenaries tie my hands either side of the high rails. I feel like freaking Jesus with the way I'm standing, open and laid out for everyone to stare at.

The mercenaries step in with the blow torch and the iron.

My heart leaps into my throat. I can't make out the shape, all I know is this is going to hurt like hell.

"Start recording," Chuck calls out.

One of them pulls out a cell phone as I focus on the blow torch. It lights up, a whooshing sound emanating from it. The heat is burning me from here. I back up slightly even though I have nowhere to go. He lines up the iron with the fire, the black cast iron turns red and glows to orange in a matter of moments as a bead of sweat drops down my temple.

"Now, where to start? I always loved those pert, supple breasts of yours. Maybe I'll begin there?"

I whimper as he angles the tip of the iron coming right for me.

I clench my eyes tightly shut.

I don't want to see it touch my flesh.

The burning iron smells disgusting as he steps closer. The heat of the iron as it approaches immediately sends my skin blistering into beads of sweat. My body shakes with the impending fear of the pain. My eyes tightly clench.

I wish Zero were here.

The hint of leather invades my senses for some reason. I know if I think of Zero through this—my white knight—I can get through anything.

"Three… two… one…"

My eyes open, Zero's standing behind the mercenaries who all turn, aiming their guns at him. My eyes can't comprehend what I'm seeing as he pulls his trigger aimed at the man right in front of him, blood explodes from the mercenary's head at the same time as the others, all in a perfect synchronization. A mass culling.

I let out a squeal from the shock as a river of blood detonates around the room. The red nectar flooding over Chuck's blow torch making it burn out.

Chuck drops the red-hot cattle iron turning to face Zero, the same time the Houston Defiance brothers step out of the shadows surrounding us.

Zero's eyes focus in on me. I can't believe he's come for me.

He wasn't supposed to. He's put himself and his club at risk.

But they knew the risk, and they're all here anyway.

Zero's here.

My white knight.

ZERO

Aiming my gun right at Chuck's temple, I glance at my Old Lady. "Cherry, you gonna hate me if I pull this trigger?"

"Fire away." A warmth forms across her features.

"Zero..." My finger moves to the trigger, ready to pull. Excitement flows through me, I feel the trigger starting to initiate when the Baron bursts out laughing.

I pause, turning to him.

He's holding a timer in his hand, his eyes wide like a damn madman. My eyes shift to Cherry. So many emotions flow through me, but there's no time to say anything. She meets my gaze, more than anything right now, I need her to survive this.

"Boom," the Baron grunts.

My eyes snap to his as he drops the timer.

My heart stops.

Time stands still.

I take in my woman's features, fear in her eyes as a massive wave of heat explodes to my side. The shockwave throws me to my ass. My ears ring as I try to gather my bearings through the haze. The ground shakes with constant minor explosions. One after the other, this place is going off all around us. It's an oil refinery, so if one area lights up, pretty soon everything's going to fucking follow.

A fire wall burns above us on the ceiling as I crawl to my knees, coughing with the thick black smoke. I look up, Chuck and the Baron are gone, but Chains and Texas take off after them.

"Fuck," I mumble as I drag myself over to where Cherry is located.

She's hanging from her restraints, covered in blood. I just hope like all fucking hell all that damn blood is not hers. I lean up attempting to untie one constraint. She's zoning in and out of consciousness.

"C'mon, baby, stay with me," I tell her. I unwrap her other wrist at the same time as another explosion blasts through the refinery. The shockwave rattles the floor making me fall back, and Rayne topples on top of me. I grip her as the flaming ceiling pushes lower, debris falling off all around us.

"Rayne, baby, you gotta wake up," I tell her as I flip her over onto the vented floor. The second her skin hits the red-hot metal, it sizzles. Her eyes widen as she yelps. "Sorry, Cherry, but we gotta get out of here."

She coughs as she clings to me while I try to find a way for us to get out of this burning building. "Zero, you can't let Chuck getaway," she pleads.

"I know, but we have to get out of here first."

Ax and Neon run in to us.

"We've found a way out. Follow us," Ax offers.

Neon places his arm around Rayne, and we both help her walk out of the burning refinery. The air is thick, full of black smoke. When we finally make it outside, half the refinery is on fire with explosions rocking through the night air.

Ax comes up to Rayne and starts checking her over. "Pres, you have business to attend to. Go. I got her."

My eyes meet with Cherry's.

"I'm fine. Please, just please… get Chuck," she pleads.

I grip Ax on the shoulder. "Look after her with your life!"

Ax gives me a two-finger salute as Wraith rushes over.

"Wraith, Neon, with me. Let's go find these motherfuckers."

Pulling out our guns, we take off in the direction I saw Chains and

Texas go. We run behind a giant oil silo, and as we come out the other side, there's a couple of mercenaries in wait for us. I bring up my gun and fire, hoping like hell the oil silo is full and not half empty. If it's half empty and a bullet goes through, it could go up, but if it's full and there's no oxygen then we're all good. Guess I'm about to find out. A bullet flies past my head, whizzing near my ear. That was fucking close. Anger surges inside of me, so I unload a round right into the asshole's stomach. He hunches over, then I land another bullet right in the middle of his head. It explodes as he collapses on the ground, his blood running like a river along the cement cracks.

Wraith runs up behind the other mercenary, pulling out a knife from his own back pocket, stabbing him up and under his ribs. He pushes a little higher which forces the mercenary to drop his rifle.

Neon picks it up. "Thanks for the gun," he tells the dying man as he gurgles on his own blood.

Wraith pulls out the knife then thrusts the guy forward onto the other guy. We're starting to create a pile of dead mercenaries.

The Baron won't like this.

But right now, I could give two fucks what the Baron wants.

As we move further around the silo, Texas and Chains struggle with some mercenaries, so we rush in, shooting at anything that moves. Bullets fly into the silo, white shards of concrete fly off into the air as small rivulets of oil roll out of the silo flowing onto the concrete around us.

Shit just got dangerous, so I try to lead us all away from the oil, but the mercenaries just fucking keep coming. I shoot the asshole who's holding Chains, leaving Chains with blood all over his face.

"Sorry, brother."

He chuckles. "At least it's not his stomach contents," he calls back as Neon uses their own machine gun on the mercenary dealing with Texas. His stomach explodes in a cacophony of bullets, the mess and gore bursting out all over Chains. He groans pushing the mercenary to the ground in a pool of the black oil.

"Motherfucker! Neon, you're washing my damn clothes."

We move together as we turn attempting to locate Chuck and the

Baron, but as we round the corner, an onslaught of mercenaries are in front of us. We pause, there's only five of us, I don't know where our other brothers are right now, but in front of us are at least thirty mercenaries.

"Fuck," I murmur under my breath.

We stand, staring at each other, the air fueled with toxic smoke. The ground rumbling from explosions still rocking through the refinery, and we have nowhere to go.

An oil slick behind us.

Mercenaries in front.

Fuck!

Five to thirty—those odds are impossible.

My brothers look to me for a way out of this.

I don't see one.

Clenching my eyes shut, Rayne fills my mind. All I want right now is to know she's safe. I have no idea what's going to happen to her, but what I do know is I'm going to go down fighting to get her a better life.

Opening my eyes, I raise my gun, inhaling deeply. "Defiance. I don't know if we can do this, but we're damn-well gonna try. Y'all with me?"

"Yeah," they cry out.

I take a step forward, they follow while I roll my shoulders getting my mind into gear.

We can do this.

I can do this.

Here we go. "Three... two... one—"

Suddenly, gun fire echoes from behind the mercenaries and they run straight toward us—one by one they're dropping like flies.

Fuck, someone's shooting from behind them.

We have them trapped. "Defiance, close them in."

We spread out making a long line and open fire, the mercenaries trying to run in different directions, but everywhere they go, they're met with a bullet.

Neon's hosing them down with their own gun causing them to fall rapidly as I contemplate who's on the other side of this battle. The last mercenary falls, and in the distance, Ax and Cherry Bomb are standing with Hawke and his Militia recruits.

To my surprise. Hawke's Sergeant, Malik, is holding Chuck, and the Baron is being escorted by their veteran, Logan, right next to them. When I put the call out to Hawke about this whole thing, I had no idea if he would come to help us. He had no part to play in this war, but he's helped us in ours. I'm sure we'll owe him another debt of some sort, but if I get to kill Chuck, I'll give Hawke whatever the fuck he wants.

I signal to my men, and we make our way through the mercenary graveyard. The cement is stained red with their demise. It smothers my boots as I kick them on my way down to meet up with the men I've despised for most of my life.

My eyes shift to my Old Lady—she needs to put on some damn clothes. I hate everyone can see what's mine. I yank off my cut as I walk up to her then slide it over her shoulders. It won't cover much of her, but it's a start. I turn heading for Hawke as he begins a slow clap.

"You've caused quite the destruction here, Zero. Didn't know you had this kind of carnage in you. I'm impressed."

"Ha! This is merely a tasting plate of what Defiance is capable of."

"Hmm, in that case, this is your mess to clean up…" he waves his hands around, "… including these scraps."

Malik releases Chuck into Ax's grip, and the Baron steps forward with his cocky demeanor still intact.

"Thanks for the assist, Hawke. I won't forget it."

"I won't *let* you forget."

I spin to face the Baron first.

The asshole has the audacity to fold his arms across his chest. "You gonna kill my son?"

"Yes… that a problem?"

"I'm a fucking cop, you imbecile. You can't kill me. Dad, tell them!"

The Baron turns up his lip. "I can't stop them from doin' whatever it is they're goin' to do, son. I don't control them."

The Baron has had semi-control over us for years. So, for him to say that means he wants Chuck dead.

Chuck's just too fucking stupid to understand the Baron's unspoken words.

"Zero," Cherry's gentle voice breaks through the tension. She steps forward.

I signal to Chains to follow her as she walks over to Chuck getting right up in his face. Normally, there's no way I'd let her near him, but I know she needs this. And we're all here, protecting her. He can't hurt her.

Ax holds the bastard in a tight grip.

"You had so much potential. When I met you, you actually had some good qualities, Chuck. You were a nice enough guy."

"Nice enough?" He snorts. "It was all a front, sweetheart, just to get to your father. I never wanted you, just what your father could do for me."

I have no idea what he's talking about, but Rayne seems to as she steps closer, her stature taller.

She's not afraid of him.

My Cherry Bomb is about to explode.

"You think you were in charge all this time, Chuck. You might have been pulling the strings, but it was a fragile system you were controlling. At any second, any one of us could have pulled the cord and set the timer to detonate. We just didn't understand all the strings you were pulling. Well, I realize now, and Chuck, I won't be your puppet anymore. I won't be a pawn in your twisted game of chess. Because guess what, asshole? I was saved by a knight, and they've knocked out all your pieces. Because a king doesn't always win, Chuck, and you… you're about to lose it all."

Chuck rolls his eyes. "Nice monologue, Rayne. You been practicing that while you were screwing your filthy biker?"

Her hand comes up faster than I can fathom, and she backhands him across the face. The slap so loud it resonates through the air. His head snaps to the side with the force as he stumbles in Ax's grip.

I take a step forward, making Chuck aware of my presence. If he tries to retaliate, I'll be the first one to lay him out.

"I bet that felt good, didn't it? To get a little something back after all the times I've hit you?" Chuck spits out, taunting her.

She grins sadistically. *Damn! I know that look.* I tense up as she reaches into Ax's jeans, pulling out his gun and presses it against Chuck's temple. "Not good enough... but I have been practicing my aim."

The loud blast from the gun fires as she's jerked back with the force. Chuck's head bursts apart from the close impact, brain matter and blood spatter all over her as I take off rushing to her side.

Ax grabs the gun from her shaking hands as I watch the Baron. His eyes firmly set on his son's dead body.

"Wraith, grab him, will you?" I instruct as the oil silo behind us bursts into flames, sending us all crashing to the ground with the force. The heat coming from it is unimaginable as I race over to Cherry and smother her. My other brothers all shield themselves from the blast of heat as I grab Cherry smoothing my hands down her blood-soaked arms.

"You okay?" I yell over the whirring of the giant flaming oil pit.

"Yes. We should go before it fully explodes."

I turn back to find Wraith, but he's empty-handed. The expression on his face one of pure anger.

"The explosion knocked me off my feet. The Baron took off. For a short, fat guy, he sure can run. The fucking coward."

I grumble but signal to everyone. "Defiance, we gotta get out of here. This entire place is gonna go up. The authorities will be here at any second."

Texas barrels over with a pair of jeans handing them to Cherry. "You can't get on a bike without pants."

Cherry takes them from Texas, and I dip my chin at him. *I owe him a beer.* "Rayne, where's your cell?"

"In the car I came here in. I dropped it to the floor before I got out. Thought you could track it."

"Clever thinking. It probably saved your life."

Hawke rushes over, coming face to face with me. The head of the

Militia and the head of Houston Defiance staring each other down while this place burns to the ground.

"Hawke, you did good. Our deal will hold."

Hawke's lips turn up crookedly as he places his hand out for me to shake. I don't remember ever shaking the man's hand, but I guess if we're doing this truce shit, there's always a time for firsts.

I reach out taking a firm grip of his hand, shaking once.

As Hawke signals for his men to flee, I grab Cherry, and we all scurry toward the exit.

"What the hell was that, Zero?"

"It's a long story, but basically, to get their help, which I thought we needed in a hurry, I told them we could do more runs. This time it will be half the amount of the Snow White pills we made for them last time but on a monthly basis. They can have a forty-sixty split, but to do that, we couldn't do it without you. So, they had to help us get you back, or there was no deal. He quickly agreed."

She narrows her eyes on me as we reach my ride. "But we could do double that amount."

I chuckle. "*He* doesn't know that."

"You sneaky devil. So, basically, we get one hundred and sixty percent of the profits, and they get like forty…" She laughs. "I like how you work, Zero."

"We just have to be careful about marketing. If those Militia bastards ever find out—"

"War."

"Yeah, it's a tightrope, one we have to tread carefully, especially now with the Baron on the loose and probably after my ass, we have to be even more cautious."

Another explosion blasts through the refinery, we both duck as everyone runs toward their bikes. It's like some fucking prime-time action movie has just been shot, but I want no part of what comes next in this film.

The retribution.

The clean-up.

I just want to get on with my life. My new life with my Old Lady by my side. I turn pressing my lips to Cherry's, I'm so lucky she understands me and this fine-line game we play. I couldn't be happier to have an Old Lady like her, and now she's officially a widow, we're free to live our lives and be in a relationship with no strings pulling on the conditions. She's free to be Rayne, no more Harper, and more importantly free to be with me.

Seeing her tied up like that about to be branded and marked for life, put a wave of terror through me. *I don't want anyone but Rayne in my life.* I already knew that fact, but that solidified it. Sure, she's my Old Lady, but I need her to know she's truly mine. Only mine.

The roar of bikes echoes through the refinery as I grab a helmet for Cherry, but I turn staring in her eyes, my hand reaching out caressing her blood-stained cheek.

She's never been more beautiful.

"Zero, we gotta go. We gotta go," Wraith calls out.

Her emerald eyes sparkle as she stares at me. I bathe in her, wearing my cut, the memory of her ending a life. She's the strongest woman I've ever met.

"I'd walk across this fire for you, Rayne." She pulls me closer to her. "I'd do anything to protect you. You mean everything to me... everything."

She sniffles, her eyes glassing over as my brothers pull out of the refinery driving off and leaving us here alone while I stare at her. Explosions still blast around us. It's like the Fourth of July on crack, the only thing I can think about right now is exactly how I feel about her. My heart is like this refinery, every time I see her, it's *explosive.* She ignites not only a fire inside of me, she detonates me, making every atom inside of my body come alive. I've never felt like this about anyone, and I need to tell her.

"Rayne, I love you."

Her eyes mist up, watering so much, a single tear slides down her cheek. I wipe it away with my thumb as she smiles so fucking wide and glorious, it's like the stars light up the sky with such a brilliance, I'm blinded by only one thing—love.

"I love you, too. I know you'd do anything to protect me. I know because I would do anything to protect you… like stay with Chuck if it meant you and the club were safe from the police. That was my plan."

I grimace. "We probably have shit coming our way for sure. The Baron won't let this go, but for now, we have each other, and that's all we need."

The scream of sirens in the distance takes our attention.

"Time to go, Cherry." I slide onto my bike, and she hops on behind me.

I take off at lightning speed back to the clubhouse leaving one hell of a mess behind. Lucky for us, the carnage will be camouflaged by the intense heat and flames that it will look like the refinery has had an accident, not an all-out biker war.

CHAPTER 30

ZERO

The battle was huge, but we only won half the fight. Chuck is dead, thanks to Cherry, but the Baron is still at large. With his pull in power, we've got a hell of a lot of drama coming our way. I just have no idea what. We need to be prepared for whatever comes.

As Cherry and I stride into the clubhouse, it's a mess. Brothers are covered in blood from the fight, the club girls are trying to clean up as best they can, but basically, we all just need a damn good shower.

Prinie rushes to us in a hurry. She pulls Cherry to her in a giant hug, not even caring about the fact she's basically topless and covered in blood. "Jesus, Rayne. You scared me."

She pulls back, looking Prinie in the eyes. "I'm okay. Actually, I'm free… like completely free. I have to admit, I had envisioned how it might feel, but I never thought it would feel this good."

I furrow my brows at her as Prinie cocks her head. "Wait! What are you talking about?"

Cherry exhales. "I killed Chuck."

She says it so easily, so blasé, so matter-of-factly, it concerns me. For one of the brothers to say it like that, I understand. Only cold-hearted killers talk like that. I get she's born for club life, but I'm not bringing her in to be a killer. She's not doing that ever again. Not on my watch. She might belong to this life, but she won't handle prison.

What am I saying? I couldn't handle her being in prison.

Prinie's eyes fall to me, I subtly nod. "Well, all righty, then... let's throw another party because a Dead-Chuck is better than an Up-Chuck."

We both chuckle as Cherry peeks down at herself. "Sounds good, but first I need a shower."

I pull her to me. "You're not leaving my sight. I'll help you."

She nods in understanding, and we walk toward the stairs.

I spot Neon on my way. "Can you see if you can locate the Baron."

"On it."

We head upstairs walking to my room. I close the door behind us, and we both strip off, making our way to the bathroom. I hate seeing all this blood on her perfect skin. It must go. So, I turn on the faucet and set the temperature, then ease her in.

She runs her hands up into my hair, undoing my hair tie, letting my hair fall around my shoulders. The bottom of the shower runs red as I run my hands over her body, making sure she isn't hurting anywhere. Rayne's hand slides down to my leg where the bullet grazed the skin.

"He didn't shoot you in your thigh?"

"No, it's just a graze to distract me, so I'd lower my gun. I should have known better."

Her hand comes up caressing my face. "I need you to know something, Krew." *I love it how she says my name.* "I'm here. I'm in this. I'm not going anywhere. I'm here to stay. I'm a part of this club, for life."

My chest squeezes, and it's in a good way as I stare in her eyes. "Good. I needed to hear that."

She leans in gently pressing her lips to mine. "Don't be worried about how easy it was for me to kill Chuck."

Interesting.

"Why's that?"

"If someone was constantly hurting you, making you question your own mind, keeping you a prisoner, and using your family as a pawn in their own sick game, I know what you'd do."

"Baby, it's the way you're unaffected by it."

She weakly smiles. "I'm affected. I took a life." She sniffles. "That's going to haunt me for the rest of my days. The only thing stopping me from falling apart is knowing it was Chuck. He deserved everything he got... actually more. If the bullet had hit someone else, and I took some other person's life... shit! I don't even know what to think about that." Her eyes well with tears as I wrap my arms around her.

"So, this new vengeful you was a one-time deal?"

"That's all I have in me, I swear."

I lean in pressing my lips to hers, kissing her softly. She doesn't need dominant Zero right now. I know I need to love her tenderly. So, I run my hands up her arms washing her down, just taking care of my woman.

She's been through something.

Something fucking awful. I want to be the white knight she sees me as.

And I'm happy to oblige.

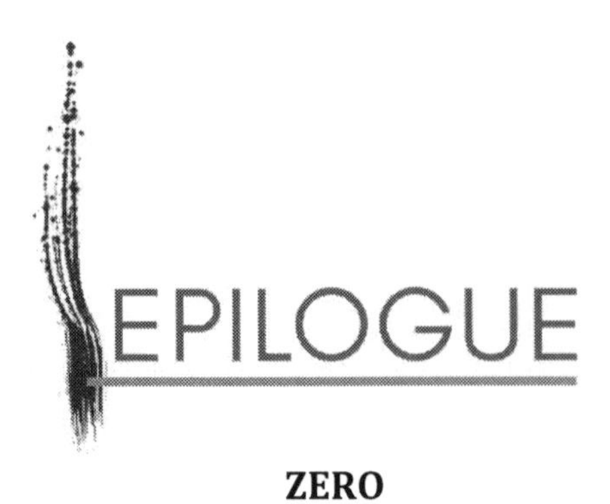

ZERO

The mood in the clubhouse is at an all-time high.

All in all, we won.

There's still the issue of the Baron—we know he'll come back into play some day. We don't know when or how, but for tonight, we're going to celebrate and not worry about revenge.

Cherry's sitting on my lap, everyone's drinking and generally joking around when a whole pile of cussing makes its way in from outside. We all glance up, Prinie's rushing inside throwing her hands in the air cursing even louder.

We all stop. Wraith's following her, and he's mad as hell.

Goddammit! Grumbling, I hoist Cherry off my lap, making my way over to Wraith as Prinie pushes past him with force. I grab Prinie's arm stopping her and pull her to me. "Right, there's gonna be no more avoidance. Tell me what the fuck's going on with you two. You've both been fucking weird with each other since you got back, Prinie."

Wraith avoids eye contact with me as Prinie scoffs like she won't tolerate their conversation any further.

"No. You both had words to say a moment ago. You can't go silent now because it's me. What the fuck did you do, Wraith?"

He glares at me. "*Me?* You assume it's me. That your precious little princess isn't a fucking screwup!"

"Ha! I'm a screwup? Me? You're the one who has a problem with *screwing* things."

I jerk my head back at her comment.

"Prinie, shut it," Wraith warns.

A sense of dread fills me as anger burns inside. I see it in Wraith's face, the moment he notices the wheels turning in my head.

"Fuck you, Wraith! You have no right to tell me what to do. You lost that privilege when you walked out on me."

Rage flares inside of me so fucking hot I can't contain myself. I watch my best friend glaring at my sister like she's just let slip their big secret. A swirling tornado rages, and I can't control it. I latch onto Wraith's cut shoving him back against the wall. I pant so fucking hard my head spins from the over intake of oxygen. My teeth squeal as I grind them together.

The look of regret in Wraith's eyes tells me the answer before I've even asked the damn question.

"I'm only going to ask you this once, Wraith, and once only. Did. You. Fuck. My. Sister?"

Prinie sniffles behind me as I narrow my eyes on Wraith.

His Adam's apple bobs up and down, then he cracks his neck to the side.

"Yes."

Oh, hell fucking no.

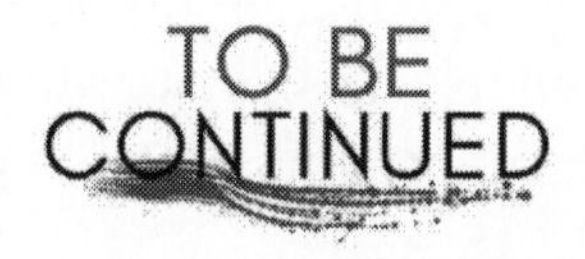

in

Addictive – The Houston Defiance MC Series Book 2

ACKNOWLEDGMENTS

First and foremost, I would like to thank my mother, Kaylene Osborn, for being my editor. Thank you for being my biggest supporter and champion. When I doubt myself, you're always there, lifting me up. Thank you for always making me see my strengths when I feel I don't have any.

To Cindy/Thia Finn – this series started with an idea from a little adventure I had overseas. When I went to America in 2019, I wouldn't have had the same experience if it weren't for you. The Houston Defiance is written the way they are because of YOU! So, thank you. I couldn't have done any of this without your input, thoughts, and Texan translations (lol). I honestly cannot thank you enough for getting my Houston Defiance guys off the ground. I love you.

To Chantell – you went above and beyond for the beta read of Explosive. I was so excited when I went through your notes. You had so much to offer, and I absolutely loved your additions. Thank you for all the hard work you put into this for me and thank you for being a part of my team. I'd be lost without you.

To Diana and Kim B – you ladies always give me the soundest advice. Thank you for working with me on the start of this brand-new series. I'm SO lucky to have you on my team. I couldn't imagine this writing journey without you. Your words of encouragement, words of improvement, and general friendship mean everything to me. I adore you both.

To all of my awesome beta readers – thank you for once again putting your thoughts into this book. I appreciate all of your energy and ideas, and together we make a great team. Without you beautiful ladies, this book wouldn't be at its best potential. So, thank you, every single one of you.

To Nicki – thank you so much for all your amazing proofing work on all of my books. I'm so happy to have you onboard for another exciting project. You give my books that extra polish and shine that they need. They sparkle once you're through with them, and I thank you for that.

To Jane – thank you for always being there. Period. You're always there to help me with bookish things, with plotting things, hell with general everyday life things. You're my 'thing' girl. And I wouldn't want anyone else to share my *things* with. Love you.

To Dana – we've just started our journey together, but I can tell it's already going to be a great one. I absolutely ADORE the cover for Explosive. You worked tirelessly until we got it just right, and as far as I am concerned, we sure did get it right. This cover truly blows my mind. Thank you, from the bottom of my heart, for everything you've done for me since I first contacted you in a mad dash. You're simply amazing.

To my beautiful, playful, and utterly adorable pup, Bella, you're such a laugh and a half. With every year older you get, a little loopier you become. But that's why I love you. You're the best dog an author could ask for. Love you, Bella-boo.

Last of all, I want to thank YOU, the reader. Your continued support of my writing career is both humbling and heartwarming. I adore my readers so much, and honestly, I couldn't keep going without the love and support you all show me each day. Thank you for believing in me, and I hope I can keep you entertained for many, many years to come.

Much love,
K E Osborn

On a more serious note...

This book is a work of fiction, but some situations discussed are of a sensitive nature.

If you or anyone you know is suicidal or in emotional distress or has been a victim of assault, please seek help or assist them to obtain help. Reporting the crime could possibly prevent another incident.

Crisis hotlines exist everywhere, so please don't hesitate.

If you live in:
USA call RAINN - 1-800-656-HOPE
Canada call 1.888.407.4747 for help
UK call The Samaritans 116 123
Australia call Lifeline Australia 13 11 14

Check these links for more books from Author K E OSBORN.

READER GROUP

Want access to fun, prizes and sneak peeks?
Join my Facebook Reader Group.
https://goo.gl/wu2trc

NEWSLETTER

Want to see what's next?
Sign up for my Newsletter.
http://eepurl.com/beIMc1

BOOKBUB

Connect with me on Bookbub.
https://www.goodreads.com/author/show/7203933.K_E_Osborn

GOODREADS

Add my books to your TBR list on my Goodreads profile.
https://goo.gl/35tIWV

AMAZON

Click to buy my books from my Amazon profile.
https://goo.gl/ZNecEH

WEBSITE

www.keosbornauthor.com

TWITTER

http://twitter.com/KEOsbornAuthor

INSTAGRAM

@keosbornauthor

EMAIL

keosborn.author@hotmail.com

FACEBOOK

http://facebook.com/KEOsborn

With a flair for all things creative, International Bestselling Author K E Osborn, is drawn to the written word. Exciting worlds and characters flow through her veins, coming to life on the page as she laughs, cries, and becomes enveloped in the storyline right along with you. She's entirely at home when writing sassy heroines and alpha males that rise from the ashes of their pasts.

K E Osborn comforts herself with tea and Netflix, after all, who doesn't love a good binge?

Turn lust into love at http://www.keosbornauthor.com/

Printed in Great Britain
by Amazon